NICOLA

Titles available in this series

NICOLA

Beryl Darby

JACH

ISBN 978-0-9554278-8-6

Printed and bound in Great Britain by
CPI Antony Rowe, Chippenham SN14 6LH

First published in the UK in 2011 by

JACH Publishing
92 Upper North Street, Brighton, East Sussex, England BN1 3FJ

website: www.beryldarbybooks.com

For my mother,
who loved to read and
always enjoyed my books

Family Tree

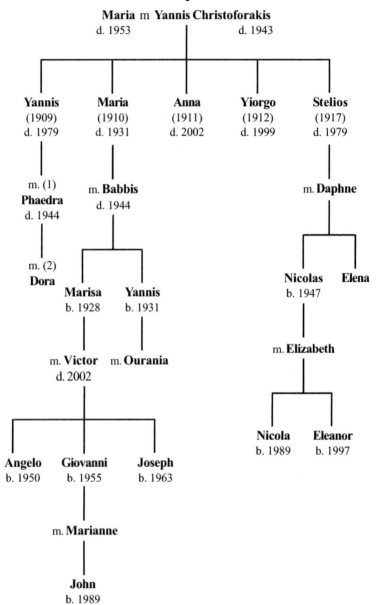

Family Tree

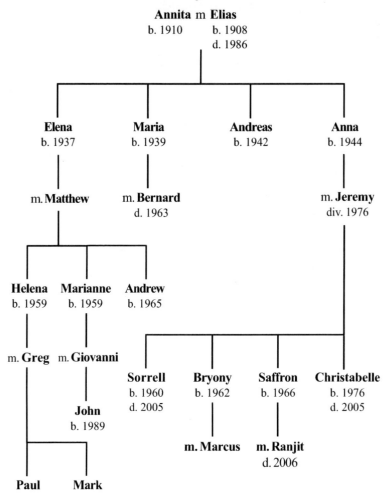

Annita m **Elias**
b. 1910 b. 1908
   d. 1986

Elena
b. 1937

Maria
b. 1939

Andreas
b. 1942

Anna
b. 1944

m. **Matthew**

m. **Bernard**
d. 1963

m. **Jeremy**
div. 1976

Helena
b. 1959

Marianne
b. 1959

Andrew
b. 1965

m. **Greg**

m. **Giovanni**

Sorrell
b. 1960
d. 2005

Bryony
b. 1962

Saffron
b. 1966

Christabelle
b. 1976
d. 2005

John
b. 1989

m. **Marcus**

m. **Ranjit**
d. 2006

Paul **Mark**

Author's Note

All the characters in this novel are entirely fictitious. Any resemblance to actual persons, living or dead, is entirely coincidental.

Although *Manolis* and its sequel, *Cathy,* were the seventh and eighth books published, they did not follow the overall timescale. They were published really at the insistence of readers who liked and wanted to know more about the activities of Manolis, the fisherman who first appeared in Yannis.

This title, *Nicola*, follows the sixth published title, *Saffron*, in the overall timescale of the continuing saga of a Cretan family.

WEEK 1 – MAY 2006

Nicola gripped Marjorie's hand as Marcus swung the car into the drive way to Yannis's house and sounded the horn.

'I can't believe it,' she murmured. 'It's just not possible.'

Marcus opened the car door and helped Marjorie out before removing the luggage from the boot of the car. 'Everyone is waiting to meet you.'

Bryony took hold of Saffron's elbow. 'Are you nervous? There's no need.'

Saffron shook her head. 'Not really. I just find it so incredible that I should have been here last year and not realised.'

Bryony led Saffron and Marjorie round the side of the house to the patio. 'We don't really use the front door. There's always someone here so the patio entrance is left open. Here we are,' she called. 'This is Saffron and here is Marjorie.'

Annita was sitting in her wheelchair in the shade of an umbrella, the other members of her family grouped around her. They all looked up curiously at Saffron as she approached.

'I know you,' Annita said immediately.

'We met last year. I came to dinner. I had no idea you were my grandmother.'

'Saffron. Welcome.'

Saffron turned from her grandmother to Marianne. 'It's good to see you again; particularly now I know who you are.'

'But you said your name was Sophie.'

Marianne frowned and looked at her accusingly.

Saffron shook her head. 'John told you my name was Sophie. I told him I was called Saffie and he misheard. People often make that mistake and I didn't bother to correct him. At the time it didn't seem to matter.'

Marianne looked in exasperation at John who shrugged and smiled.

'Come and be properly introduced. Hello Marjorie.' Marianne held out her hand. 'You're very welcome. Sophie – Saffron, I mean, spoke about you when she visited us before.'

'You can call me Sophie if you find it easier,' smiled Saffron. 'I really don't mind.'

Marianne shook her head. 'Saffron is a pretty name and unusual. There are hundreds of girls called Sophie in Greece, but it's unlikely you'll meet another girl named Saffron.'

Giovanni pressed a glass of wine into her hand and gave another to Marjorie. 'I think we should have a toast. To Saffron, even though we thought she was Sophie,' he added mischievously and winked at John.

Saffron raised her glass. 'To my family. Thank you for welcoming me.'

'Why wouldn't we welcome you?' asked Bryony innocently.

Saffron looked at her and frowned.

'Oh! Of course. Yes.' Bryony was covered in confusion.

Marianne looked from one to the other. There was something here that she didn't understand. She would have to have a word alone with Bryony. It was usually easy enough to talk her into disclosing information.

Saffron placed her glass on the table. She was trying hard to decide which of the two older women was Yannis's wife and which one was his sister. To her horror she realised she could not remember their names either. She smiled at them and took her grandmother's hand, bending down so she was on a level with her.

'Grandma, I never expected to see you again. I do wish I'd known who you were last year when I visited.'

Annita looked at her granddaughter. 'I'm not surprised you didn't expect to see me. At my age it's always a surprise to me when I wake up to a new day. I'm usually at my best in the morning and we must have some long talks. I want to get to know you again. You were a nice little girl. I missed you after your father took you away.'

Saffron felt tears coming into her eyes. 'Dad was very fond of you and Grandpa.'

'He was a good man. You look like him, rather than your mother. I hope you take after him in other ways.'

Saffron felt herself flush. 'I hope so. I'm sure Marjorie will tell tales about me.' Saffron beckoned to Marjorie to come over to them. 'You must meet my grandmother. Isn't she wonderful for ninety six?'

Bryony placed her hand on Saffron's shoulder. 'Come and say hello to Uncle Yannis. He's too shy to approach you.'

Saffron smiled. 'Which lady is his wife?'

'Ourania.'

The moment Bryony said the name Saffron remembered. 'I know, but which one is she?'

Bryony gave an amused smile. 'Marisa is shorter.'

The information was no help to Saffron as both the ladies were seated, one each side of Yannis. They were near enough the same age, both of them had white hair, were immaculately made up and wearing similar dark dresses. They were in total contrast to Marianne, who had her hair tied back and was wearing shorts and Bryony who had on a simple blouse and skirt.

Saffron held out her hand to Yannis. 'I am so pleased to meet you again.'

Yannis rose stiffly from his seat. 'Welcome. You very welcome. Ourania,' he indicated the woman on his left. 'She welcome also and Marisa.' He waved his hand towards his sister.

Both women bobbed their heads to Saffron as she took their hands and smiled back at them, relieved that she now knew which lady was which. Saffron stepped back. 'I haven't really said hello to Giovanni yet, nor John.'

Giovanni planted a kiss on each cheek. 'I do not know whether I should call you Saffron or Sophie, but whatever, we are very pleased to see you. Last year you came to our house as a stranger. This year you come as part of our family. The stranger we liked. The family member we will love. Now, where is John? When you have spoken to him I will fill our glasses again and we will have another toast.' Giovanni looked around for his son.

John was standing over by the railing that ran around part of the patio. He waved wildly to Saffron when he saw her looking his way.

'It's true, Nick. Honest! I'll get her to speak to you. I know we thought her name was Sophie. It was my mistake. Yeah, you can all blame me. I'm used to it. Saff, come and say hello to Nick. She won't believe me when I tell her you're Sophie.'

Smiling, Saffron took the mobile telephone and spoke to Nicola. 'Hello, Nicola. John is telling you the truth. It was my fault. He misheard my name and I didn't correct him. Where are you? Why aren't you here with us?'

'I'm in New Orleans. I wish I could be there. I can't come out until term finishes. Will you still be there?'

'What date are you talking?'

'A couple of month's time.'

Saffron gave a gasp. 'There's no way I can stay here that long I'm afraid.'

'Then come again later in the season.'

'I don't know.' Saffron was doubtful that she would be able to have the time off from the hospital and her new found family might not wish to have her back again so soon.

'Give it a go.' Saffron heard Nicola try to suppress a yawn. 'Sorry about that. I was asleep when John called, but I'm pleased he woke me.'

Saffron passed the 'phone back to John with a smile on her face. She took another mouthful of wine and allowed Giovanni to top up her glass. Suddenly she was beginning to feel very much at home.

Marianne appeared at her side. 'I'm forgetting my manners. No doubt you and Marjorie would like to go to your room and get settled in. Prise Marjorie away from Grandma if you can. She loves to talk.'

Saffron touched Marjorie's arm. 'Marianne is going to show us our room. You can come back and talk to Grandma later.'

Marianne led the way across the lounge, doors flanked the long wall and Marianne opened one halfway along. 'This is your room.' She stood back to let them enter. 'You have a bathroom through the doorway there and if you want you can go through the patio doors to the balcony. Walk along and around the corner and you'll find yourself back on the main patio. Come back whenever you're ready.'

Saffron took a deep breath. 'I feel totally overwhelmed.' Tears filled her eyes and ran unchecked down her cheeks.

Marjorie placed her arms around her. 'I'm not surprised; after all Bryony told you and now you realise that you actually met your relatives last year. It's all a bit too much, isn't it?'

Saffron nodded. 'They're so kind and welcoming. I just wish I had corrected John when he called me Sophie.'

'It was your last day, wasn't it? Think how you would have felt having to leave immediately you had found them; much better to have had time to talk to Bryony and get everyone used to the idea that you would be visiting.'

'Do you like them, Marjorie?'

'I certainly like your grandmother. She's a character. I must admit I was expecting some old person probably suffering from Alzheimer's.'

'I know. I was dreading her not remembering who I was, despite Bryony saying she was incredible for her age. I suppose we ought to unpack. I'd quite like to have a quick shower and change before we go back to everyone. Which bed do you want?'

'I really don't mind. You choose. You'll be quicker at unpacking than I will so you can shower first.' Marjorie unlocked her case and began to remove the clothes she had carefully ironed and folded before they left England.

Saffron threw the contents of her case onto the bed. 'I'll just grab my washing kit and put that lot away afterwards.'

Marjorie looked at her in amusement. She knew that before Saffron emerged from the bathroom she would have her own clothes put away and also hung up Saffron's dresses and skirts in the wardrobe.

Almost an hour later Saffron looked at Marjorie and smiled. 'I like that dress on you. The colour is perfect. We ought to get back, I suppose. They're probably hanging around waiting for us to appear.'

'Which way do you want to go? The patio or through the house?'

'Let's go back the way we came. There's something I want to look at.'

Marjorie raised her eyebrows. What could Saffron have spotted that she needed to look at more closely? Saffron stopped before the picture that hung above the fireplace and studied it closely. She shook her head.

'How stupid I was when I was here before. I thought the picture was familiar to me because I'd seen the sketches in the shop. Marianne told me it had been done by Uncle Yannis's mother and was of the family when they were out in the fields. She even pointed out Grandma to me and still I didn't realise. Grandma had an almost identical one that always hung above the fireplace in her lounge.' Saffron moved closer and frowned. 'But that can't be Grandma. There's Uncle Yannis. I must have misunderstood.'

'Why don't you ask Marianne or your grandmother? One of them is bound to know who's who.'

'I feel terribly ignorant. Everyone seems to be related and I'm still not quite sure how. I'll have to ask Bryony to tell me again tomorrow.' Saffron lowered her voice. 'I hope we'll be able to eat soon. I'm beginning to feel really hungry now.'

Marianne and Bryony were making trips to and from the kitchen area, carrying bowls of salad, plates heaped with food already sat on a long table and chairs had been placed around it.

'Perfect timing,' smiled Marianne. 'I didn't want to bring the food out too soon. Everything begins to spoil before the sun goes down. Sit wherever you like. Just leave the space at the end for Grandma's chair.'

Marjorie took the chair nearest to her and Saffron walked to the other side of the table and sat opposite. 'You'll have to tell us the names of some of these dishes. I certainly don't remember seeing them when I ate in the tavernas.'

Marianne smiled. 'I doubt if you would have found them in the tavernas. They stick to cooking food that is familiar to the tourists. I thought I'd just do an assortment tonight. Try it all. If there's something you don't like please tell me, then I'll not make the mistake of cooking it for you again.'

'We don't expect you to cook for us all the time. We can easily go into town and eat.'

'Nonsense. You're family, besides, two more will make very little difference. Now, just help yourself to a little of everything and then go back for more. I'll make up a plate for Grandma and there's plenty of salad and bread.'

Saffron needed no second invitation. She took a small amount from each plate and Marjorie followed suit. She waited whilst everyone else began to pass the plates amongst themselves and Giovanni held his glass aloft and proposed yet another toast to welcome her and Marjorie.

Annita held the photograph of her dead husband in her hand. 'Well, Elias, she seems a nice little thing. What a shame it has

15

taken us so long to find each other. If only Jeremy had kept in touch. She could have visited us in New Orleans. I'm thankful he found a decent woman to share his life with. Poor little girl would probably have ended up in an orphanage or foster home otherwise. Saffron's obviously very fond of her and she seems pleasant enough. Fancy her being a doctor. I'm sure you would be terribly proud of her and boasted to all your friends. I suppose I mustn't complain. Elena was a good mother to her three, although I do feel Helena has been spoilt to bits. I suppose that's because she was the one that stayed in America. Marianne was far too independent for that, more like her father. She and her husband have worked hard to make a good life over here.

'Maria was unfortunate. You can't blame her. If Bernard hadn't died no doubt they would have had children and she would have been content to stay in New Orleans rather than running off to Peru with that religious sect and doing good works. I hope she did do some good out there and helped people to have a better life.

'Andreas wasn't a bad man, although I never could approve of his relationship with Laurie. It didn't seem natural to me somehow, but they always appeared happy enough together. It was just Anna that was our real failure. Where did we go wrong? Maybe things would have turned out differently if we had taken her and Christabelle in to live with us.

'I know you said we had to consider Sorrell and Bryony. I remember how we argued about it for days. You were determined that this time we had to leave her to sort out her own life and become more responsible. I'd like to know what happened to the child. Unless she turns up very soon like Saffron has it will be too late and I'll not be here to see her. Who would have thought I would live on to this age?'

Annita kissed her husband's photograph and replaced it on the table beside her bed.

'I'm getting as bad as Anna was,' she grumbled to herself.

'At least I don't spend all day every day talking to you, Elias, only when I have something I feel you'd be interested to hear.'

Despite not leaving the table until almost midnight both Saffron and Marjorie were awake early the following morning. Saffron walked out onto the balcony and lifted her face up to the sun.

'That feels so good.'

'A cup of tea would taste good,' observed Marjorie. 'Do you think they'd mind if we went to the kitchen and helped ourselves?'

'I'm sure they wouldn't. They're probably all up and tip toeing around trying not to wake us. I'll just clean my teeth and throw some clothes on. You don't think they'll mind if I wear shorts, do you?'

'Why should they? Marianne was wearing shorts yesterday and she didn't change out of them for the evening meal.'

'Her legs are lovely and brown. Mine are just white stalks.' Saffron spoke with her toothbrush in her mouth.

'They'll soon colour up.'

'I'll console myself with that thought.' Saffron pulled on her clothes, took a look at herself in the mirror and shuddered. 'Those white legs! Maybe I could get a sun tan spray so they would look better.'

'Put that on and you never will get a tan. Are you ready?'

Saffron ran her brush quickly through her hair and tied it back. 'I am now. I might change into a skirt later, depending what we're doing today.'

Marjorie glanced at her with amusement. 'I've never known you to be so worried or self conscious of your appearance before.'

'The locals always know if you've just arrived by the colour of your skin.' Saffron opened the door and Marjorie followed her down to the kitchen. As they passed the picture hanging on the wall Saffron looked at it again. 'I must find out who the people are. It's really bugging me now.'

'What's bugging you?'

17

Bryony was carrying a tray holding fruit, yoghurt, bread, jam and coffee and had stopped behind them.

'Who the people are in the picture.'

'I must take this in to Grandma. Marianne's in the kitchen. She'll tell you.'

Marianne looked at them in surprise. 'You're up much earlier than I expected. I suppose it's the time difference.'

Saffron looked at her watch. 'It would be six thirty in England. I'm usually up about then. My body clock has forgotten I'm on holiday.'

'What would you like? Tea or coffee? A full cooked or cereal, toast, fruit, cold meat, cake? You name it.'

'Some cereal and fruit with coffee would be fine by me. How about you, Marjorie?'

'I'd love a cup of tea.'

'Coming up. You're always welcome to come and help yourself, you know. We tend to just help ourselves to whatever we fancy when we feel ready. Bryony usually gets breakfast for Grandma and takes it in. Aunt Ourania will be around in about half an hour and she'll sort out whatever they want to eat before they go to the shop. What fruit would you like Soph... I mean Saffron. There's apple, orange, peach or mango. Have all of them if you fancy.'

'I'd like mango. I'll prepare it.'

'Already done.' Marianne produced a covered bowl from the large fridge. 'It's all in together. Just dig out what you want.'

'In that case I will have something of everything,' smiled Saffron. 'I just didn't want to be a nuisance.'

'You won't be a nuisance. There's always plenty of fruit around that's ready prepared.' Marianne placed a pot of tea before Marjorie and a coffee pot in front of Saffron. 'Now, what are you planning to do today?'

Marjorie and Saffron looked at each other. 'We haven't really made any plans.'

'Well Giovanni will be going into Aghios Nikolaos when he comes back from the taverna. He could take you with him and collect you later if you wanted to see the town today. Uncle Yannis, Ourania and Marisa will be at the shop. I'll help Grandma to get washed and dressed then I have to go up to the taverna until John is home from school, then he'll take over from me. Bryony will be around to keep an eye on Grandma and start the supper preparations, so if you preferred a lazy day on the beach it's no problem.'

'I would like to spend some more time talking to Bryony and also to Grandma.' Saffron looked at Marjorie. 'Would that be all right with you?'

Marjorie nodded. 'I'll be happy to have a swim and sit and read.'

Bryony removed a quantity of lamb from the fridge. 'I thought we'd have kleftiko tonight. I need to start cooking it early. Bear with me for a while.'

'Can I help?'

'Would you cut up some onions?'

'Just give me a board and a knife.'

Bryony looked at her in amusement. 'We don't usually use a chopping board. Here, use a plate if you can't do them in your hand.'

Saffron found trying to cut the onions on a plate difficult as they tended to slip. 'Why don't you use a board?'

Bryony shrugged. 'We've just always cut things up in our hands. It's something you become adept at over time. I found it a bit difficult at first. I still have to use a plate for some things.' She placed the joints of lamb into casserole dishes, added the onions and herbs, filled each dish nearly to the brim with water and covered it with the lid.

'Why are you cooking so much?' asked Saffron.

'There are eleven of us. It's one portion of meat each.'

'We'll never eat all that!'

Bryony smiled. 'You'll be surprised. Are you up for peeling potatoes?'

Saffron nodded. 'At least I can do those in my hand.'

'I expect Grandma will be out soon and you'll be able to talk to her. She's always very sensible in the morning. By lunch time she's rather tired, but when she's had her afternoon nap she's good for most of the evening.'

'What would you like us to do about cleaning our room? We've made our beds.'

'There's not much to do. There's cleaning stuff for the bathroom in the cupboard. Apart from that you only need to sweep the floor. It's so much easier in the summer when we've taken the carpets up.'

'Carpets?'

Bryony nodded. 'Once the winter starts we put down carpet squares. They have to be vacuumed and it seems to take twice as long as sweeping out. You'll find a pile of bedding in the chest. Change your sheets as often as you like. We send them to the laundry.'

'How often do you change yours?'

'Every other day until it gets really hot. Then we change them every day.'

Saffron raised her eyebrows. 'People would have a fit in England if they were expected to change their sheets more than once a week.'

Ourania appeared in the kitchen and wished Saffron good morning as she placed breakfast dishes on the table along with a bowl of yoghurt, fruit and a loaf of bread. 'Are they coming into town today?' she asked in Greek.

Bryony shook her head. 'Saffron wants to talk to Grandma and to me apparently. Marjorie is going to have a lazy day on the beach.'

'It would help if you or Marianne came in with them. I wish they spoke Greek.'

'I'm sure they wish you spoke English. I'm making kleftiko for our meal tonight.'

Ourania nodded. 'Have you told her about the dish?'

'No, Giovanni always likes to tell that story. I'll not deprive him of the pleasure. I ought to see if Grandma's ready or she'll think I'm neglecting her because Saffron and Marjorie are here.' Bryony turned to Saffron. 'Can you put the kettle on? Fill it right up. We shall all want coffee.'

'I'll let Marjorie know. She'll probably want to ask you the way to the nearest beach.'

'Across the patio, through the gate and down the steps.'

'You mean here?'

'Of course. We have our own beach. It means you can come back and get changed here rather than have to struggle beneath a towel or walk back along the road feeling damp and horrid.'

'Marjorie will love that.'

Saffron held up a cup to Ourania who replied by holding up three fingers. Saffron hesitated, did that mean she wanted three cups of coffee or three spoonfuls should go into the percolator? As if realising Saffron's dilemma Ourania picked up the pot containing the ground coffee and ladled a generous helping into the percolator.

'Good,' she said and nodded as if Saffron had made the decision for herself.

'So what do you want to talk to me about?' asked Annita once Bryony had settled her with a steaming cup of coffee beneath the umbrella on the patio.

'So many things I hardly know where to start. I'd like to know more about my mother and I'd like to know about this side of my family. I do wish I'd finished reading old Uncle Yannis's book.'

'There's sure to be a copy around. Ask Marianne.' Annita gave her granddaughter a piercing stare. 'So what do you want to know about your mother?'

Saffron shifted uncomfortably. 'Well, anything and everything. I hardly remember her. Do I look anything like her?'

'No, you take after your father in looks. I hope you do in character also. Your mother was – was – feckless.' Annita searched for the correct words to describe her youngest daughter. 'She had no sense of responsibility, either to herself or to others. She was susceptible to flattery and would read far more into a compliment than was meant. In many ways she was very innocent. She believed people when they told her they loved her. She could not appreciate that it was transient with them, although the feeling was with her. Once the novelty of a new man wore off she became bored and began to look elsewhere. She thought she was using them, but in reality they were using her.'

Saffron felt her face grow hot. Was she gullible like her mother had been? She had been taken in and used by Martin and then again by Ranjit.

'Jeremy was a decent man,' continued Annita. 'He didn't leave her when she told him you were on the way. He insisted on marrying her and adopting Sorrell and Bryony. He wanted you to be a proper family. We were so relieved. We thought Anna would finally be settled.'

'And Mum got bored with him?'

'Unfortunately. I don't know how long after they were married she began to look around. Your father never complained, he always blamed himself and gave her another chance, until Christabelle. That was unforgiveable. Fancy, sleeping with a Turk!'

Saffron suppressed a small smile. Her mother had cheated on her father, what difference did the nationality of the man make?

'To make matters worse,' continued Annita, 'she went running off after him thinking he was going to marry her. He turned her away and hit her so she came crawling back to us for help. This time Elias stood firm. He was not prepared to have Anna back home to live with a baby again. We had her living with us when Sorrell and Bryony were small and we were expected to care for them whilst she went off to enjoy herself, sometimes for days at a time and not even a telephone call to say when she planned to return. He arranged for her to have a home of her own provided we had care of Sorrell and Bryony. She was not a good example to them. He thought they would stand a far better chance of growing up decently if they were away from her influence.'

'Why didn't Dad come back to help look after them?'

'We had no idea where he had gone. Besides, why should we expect him to care for two girls who were not his? No,' Annita shook her head. 'Elias decided they should go back to school and spend their holidays with us.'

'Did you visit her?'

Annita shook her head. 'Anna blamed us for all her problems. She made it quite clear that she did not want us to be around. I wanted to visit her, but Elias said I was to leave her alone. She must learn how to be responsible. I used to park my car a short distance away from her house and watch when she was bringing Christabelle home from school. The child looked happy and well cared for. Had she appeared neglected I would have disobeyed Elias and gone to the house. I don't think Christabelle has been told she has grandparents. Unlike you she has never made any attempt to communicate with us and find out about her family.'

Saffron bit her tongue. Bryony had told her otherwise and she certainly did not want to discuss her half sister with her grandmother. She might inadvertently say that Christabelle had died whilst she was in a secure mental hospital awaiting trial for multiple murders. She remembered that Bryony had said they had not told her grandmother about Anna's death either and she realised it would be diplomatic to change the subject to the Greek side of the family.

'I know Marianne and I are cousins, but how am I related to Giovanni?'

'Marisa and Yannis are the children of my cousin, Maria. She died when Yannis was born. Marisa married an Italian and

Giovanni is their second son. He is related to you by marriage and also distantly connected by birth.'

'So where does old Uncle Yannis fit into the family?'

'He was also my cousin, Maria's older brother. Wheel me through to the lounge and I'll show you the family in the picture.'

'I was going to ask you to tell me who was who in that. When I came here last year the picture was familiar to me. I thought I had seen a copy of it in Uncle Yannis's shop. It wasn't until I saw it again last night that I remembered you had always had a similar one hung in your lounge in America.'

Annita nodded. 'That was our last happy summer together before Yannis became ill. My brother and I spent some of the holiday up on the farm before Yannis went off to Heraklion to school.' Annita sighed heavily. 'Who would have thought I would be the last one left.'

Saffron stopped before the picture. 'Can you tell me their names and who they were?'

'Of course. Lying down, you can hardly make out his features, is my Uncle Yannis. The two girls are Anna and me. I'm the one on the left as you look at it. The boy sitting behind us is my brother, Andreas. The two boys who are examining something are Yannis and Stelios. Yannis was always finding pottery in the fields.' Annita smiled. 'I remember how excited he was when he found a coin. The boys sitting apart and seem to be talking are Yiorgo and Babbis. Maria isn't in it, of course, as she was drawing us.'

Saffron studied the picture carefully. 'Marianne pointed you out to me last year, but when I looked at it last night I thought I'd made a mistake. The boy you said was Yiorgo is so like Uncle Yannis. I couldn't understand how he could be in the picture if you were a young girl at the time.'

Annita nodded. 'I didn't know Yannis as a young man, but the last time I saw him and Yiorgo together I was struck by their likeness.'

'Who was Babbis? Another cousin?'

'He came from a neighbouring farm. He married Maria and is Marisa and Yannis's father.'

'What happened to him?'

'He and Yiorgo went off to fight with the resistance. Babbis did not come back.'

'How sad.' Saffron frowned. 'So Marisa and Yannis lost both their parents. What happened to them? Who brought them up?'

'Anna, Maria's sister. Yannis thought the world of her. He knew the day would come when she and Yiorgo were too old to live alone. He designed this house with them in mind. He made the doorways on the ground floor large enough for a wheelchair to pass through, and the rooms big enough to double as sitting rooms as well as bedrooms. There are alarm pulls in the bedrooms and bathrooms, only mine is activated now. In the bathroom everything is at the right height to be used if you are unable to stand.'

Saffron smiled. 'I thought the basin was somewhat low and wondered why there was a handrail beside the toilet and in the shower.'

'It was all thought out with their well being in mind. It was fortunate he was able to build on such a grand scale. He was not to know that other members of the family were going to descend on him. Originally he had planned four very large bedrooms on the ground floor. When Marianne and Giovanni came to live here he added the rooms upstairs. That gave them their privacy and if John was crying no one would be disturbed. Bryony and Marcus have those rooms now. My room was originally Anna's and Yiorgo was next door, where Marisa is. As John became older he needed a bathroom of his own so Yannis added another two bedrooms and bathrooms at the back of the house. Last year John persuaded him to make his bedroom smaller so he could have a dark room in which to develop his films.'

'Fancy having seven bedrooms and bathrooms! Do they have a team of cleaners?'

Annita shook her head. 'They seem to manage between them to keep everywhere clean. No doubt the day will come when Marianne will need help as everyone gets older and less capable, but at the moment it doesn't seem to be a problem for her. Having Bryony and Marcus here has made a difference. Marcus is willing to turn his hand to anything. He cleans all the windows each month and does running repairs up at the chalets. Bryony made a good choice there.'

Once again Saffron felt her face growing hot as she thought of her own choice of husband. 'What about Nicola?' she asked to steer the conversation away from husbands. 'Is she part of the family or just a friend of John's?'

'She's related. Marianne and her friend came over here on holiday. They met Nicolas. He's the son of Stelios, the boy sitting with Yannis,' Annita pointed up at the picture. 'Giovanni can tell you more about him. He was the manager at the nightclub Giovanni had in Athens. Nicolas married Marianne's friend and they have two girls. I've only met Nicola. She spent most of last summer over here with us as her sister was ill.'

'What was wrong with her?'

'I don't remember.' Annita gave a sigh. 'That's when you realise how old you have become. I can't remember her name or what was wrong with her.'

Saffron shook her head. 'That's nothing to do with being old. The information is not important to you, so why worry about carrying it around with you?'

'Do you think that's the reason?'

'I certainly do,' answered Saffron firmly. 'There's something else I wanted to ask you. Do you have family photographs? If you have, may I see them?'

'You'll have to ask Bryony about those. She's the one who decided they should be mounted and kept, although what good they are to anyone now I don't know.'

'They're for someone nosy like me. I have thirty years of

family to catch up on. I'd like to see my aunts and uncles as I remember them.'

Saffron took the handles of her grandmother's chair and wheeled her back out to the patio where she settled her in the shade of the umbrella and went in search of Bryony.

Saffron joined Marjorie on the beach just before mid-day. 'I thought I'd come down now, then when it gets really hot I can go inside and read or talk to whoever is around.'

'Mmm.' Marjorie lay with her eyes closed.

'Are you awake or just pretending?' asked Saffron.

'I'm not asleep. I'm in that wonderful state where you feel you could float away at any moment.'

'Are you coming in for a swim?'

'Are you going to insist?'

'No, but I'm going in. All the time I was talking to Grandma and Bryony I was looking at the sea. It looked so inviting.'

Marjorie removed her sunglasses and squinted at the sparkling water that was lapping gently on the shingle. She gave a deep sigh. 'I suppose I ought to come in with you. Who knows when I will have another day like this one?'

'Meaning the weather or just being able to lie on the beach and do nothing?'

'Both.'

'The weather shouldn't be a problem, but I'd hate to go back to England and all we'd done was seen the beach. We need to make a list of where we would like to go. If one of them is able to drive us it will make life easier, but I'm quite prepared to go by bus or take a taxi.'

'They seem such nice, kind people.' Marjorie placed her sunglasses inside her beach bag and sat up.

'I'm very lucky,' admitted Saffron humbly. 'I had a wonderful father. He met you and gave me a fantastic step mother. I've met up with my grandmother again and she's just as I remembered her. I've gained a whole new family along with Bryony and I keep wondering what I've done to deserve it.'

Marjorie glanced at her keenly. 'You had a rough time, Saffie. You certainly deserve some happiness now.'

The steaming dishes were brought to the table, one casserole placed before each person. The potatoes were placed strategically around the table along with bowls of salad and Saffron and Marjorie were told to help themselves. Saffron hesitated. Was she supposed to put the meat on her plate or eat it from the casserole? Where was she to place the potatoes and her salad? From the corner of her eye she watched as Marisa added the potatoes to her casserole dish and used her plate for the salad and Saffron copied her.

The meat melted in her mouth, and the potatoes, although roasted had an entirely different flavour from those cooked in England. 'Tell me,' she said. 'I saw you put the lamb in the oven, but what did you do to it afterwards?'

'Nothing. It is kleftiko.'

Giovanni took pity on her. 'The traditional way to cook lamb is on a spit in the open air over a fire. The smell,' he waved his hand, 'it is delicious. Everyone knows you are roasting a lamb. They all hope to be invited to share in the feast.' He wagged his finger at her. 'But suppose the night before you had walked over the hills to a neighbouring farm and helped yourself to a lamb? You do not want to tell everyone you are a thief. The solution was to place it in a pot in the oven so the smell did not drift down the village street. The dish became known as kleftiko – stolen lamb.'

Saffron smiled. 'And is this lamb stolen?'

Giovanni shook his head. 'We do not do such things these days. I bought the joints yesterday from the butcher. Another night we will barbecue a whole lamb as we did at Easter. We will invite some friends to join us and have a party.'

Saffron smiled politely. The thought of a barbecued lamb appealed to her, but she was not sure about having to mingle with yet more people who would probably have only a limited amount of English. It was a struggle to communicate with Yannis, his wife and sister.

'Right,' said Bryony. 'Family conference time. We need to decide where you are going to visit and who is going to drive you. Giovanni will make a list.' She winked at Saffron. 'Giovanni loves to make lists. He gives one to Marcus each morning of the jobs that need to be done.' Bryony pushed a pad of paper and a pen towards Marianne's husband.

'It is practical to make a list,' Giovanni assured her. 'I would not expect Marcus to remember everything I asked him to do. He would then have to telephone me and check and I might not remember and...'

'Giovanni,' Bryony interrupted and laid her hand on his. 'I was teasing. Making lists is a good idea.'

Mollified, Giovanni smiled. 'So where do you wish to go and which day?'

Saffron looked at Marjorie. 'Knossos, of course, over to the island, I haven't even shown Marjorie where I stayed last year, and the taverna. We have to go into Aghios Nikolaos and visit Uncle Yannis at the shop.'

Marianne spoke rapidly to her husband in Greek. 'It won't matter to them which day they go. Work it out to fit in with any jobs we have to do. They could drive in to Aghios Nikolaos with Uncle Yannis. He could drop them in the town and when they have had enough they could go up to the shop. He can always telephone you and ask one of us to go in to collect them, or they could catch the bus home. They can come up to the taverna at any time with one of us. That's a visit that won't take very long.'

'I'm taking them to Spinalonga,' insisted John.

'I'll take them to Knossos,' continued Marianne. 'And they

ought to go to the museum in Heraklion. We can make a day of it and I'll show them Uncle Andreas's church and where he lived when he was the priest.'

'What about Kritsa and Gournia?' interrupted Bryony. 'I'm sure they'd like to go there.'

Giovanni added them to the list. 'We could drive them around Lassithi.'

'And Gortys, Spili and Preveli,' added Bryony.

'What about Chania and Souda Bay?' asked Giovanni. 'They ought to see the war cemeteries.'

'You would have to take them there,' said Marianne decisively. 'That's rather a long drive. An overnight stay would be more practical.'

'If we stayed in Rethymnon we could easily drive through Spili on the way to Phaestos and then go on to Preveli. We might even fit in Gortys on the way back.'

'Possibly. You wouldn't like to take in the Samaria Gorge at the same time?' asked Giovanni.

Bryony frowned. 'I'm not sure either of them would be able to walk the Gorge. I wouldn't want to.'

Giovanni smiled to himself. Bryony never walked anywhere if there was any transport available.

Saffron cleared her throat. 'Am I wrong or did you say 'family conference' to plan where we would be visiting? You've all been speaking Greek. If it's a problem we can always make our own way.'

Marianne laughed. 'It's no problem. We were just throwing out suggestions and saying where you could go and which one of us could take you. I forget you can't understand.'

'Now we have the ideas I will make the list,' announced Giovanni. 'When it is complete I will show it to you and also show you where the places are located on the map. If you think anywhere is too far to drive, you tell me, and I will change the list.'

'If we went up to Heraklion tomorrow we could call in on Vasilis at Elounda on the way back and ask him and his wife over for a barbecue.'

'Can we make it for Sunday after I've done the dive?' asked John eagerly.

Marianne looked at her husband who shrugged. 'No reason why not.'

'Then we could visit Spinalonga on Saturday.'

'Provided Marjorie is not too tired,' Marianne spoke in Greek to her son.

'So, ladies, would it suit you to visit Knossos tomorrow?' Giovanni smiled at them.

Saffron nodded eagerly. 'That sounds wonderful. Would we be able to visit the museum in the afternoon? If it's inconvenient for you we could catch the bus to Aghios Nikolaos and have a taxi back from there.'

'We will see if time permits. We can always go to the museum another day. Marianne will be with you and she will not mind how long you spend at the site or in the museum. There will be no rush to get back to the house. Bryony will be here with Grandma so there is no problem.' Giovanni drew columns on the paper and began to plan out the excursions that had been suggested.

Marianne parked her car in front of the hotel. 'You can come in if you want, but I don't intend to be very long. Vasilis may not be at the hotel.'

'We'll stay here.' Saffron could sense that Marjorie was tired after walking around Knossos, then spending a further three hours in the museum at Heraklion, before driving around to the church where Father Andreas had been the priest for many years. Marianne had pointed out the taverna where old Uncle Yannis had lodged whilst staying in the town and the High School he had attended before making a detour down to the waterfront so they could view the Venetian fortress that guarded the harbour.

Marianne walked into the foyer and over to the reception desk. 'Is Mr Vasilis available, please?'

'I will see,' the girl smiled at Marianne, recognising her from previous brief visits. She spoke into the telephone and within moments the door to Vasilis's office opened and he greeted Marianne with outstretched arms.

'This is an unexpected pleasure. What can I get for you, coffee, wine?'

Marianne shook her head. 'I can't stay; I have my visitors in the car with me.'

'They are welcome to come in also.'

'Thank you, Vasilis, but they have spent all day at Knossos and the museum. I think they are longing to get home.'

'So, what can I do for you?'

'I'd like to invite you and Cathy to a barbecue on Sunday. John is diving for the Cross and we thought it would be a good day to roast a lamb.'

Vasilis frowned. 'We came to you for Easter. You should be coming to us.'

'Actually you'd be doing us a big favour if you came to Elounda. We have Bryony's half sister and stepmother staying. They're no trouble, but they don't speak Greek. I thought Uncle Yannis would appreciate having you around as someone different to talk to. He's trying very hard to hold a conversation with them, but it is difficult.'

'You are thoughtful, Marianne. I'm sure Cathy would love to come, but Vasi is spending the weekend with us.'

'That's no problem. He's invited as well. We'll see you about ten, down by the Church.' Marianne blew Vasilis a kiss and exited the foyer.

'So what did you think of Spinalonga?' Saffron asked Marjorie.

'Well, it's fascinating, but I also found it rather disconcerting and unsettling. I appreciated having John was with us; he could tell us more than an ordinary guide would bother with. I'm not sure I liked the island.'

Saffron looked at her stepmother in surprise. 'It's beautiful.'

'I grant you that, but I kept thinking of those sick people being abandoned there. It must have been a harrowing experience for them. They didn't even have anywhere to shelter from the elements some of the time. I found it very hot over there today, and it isn't even mid-summer yet. There was so little shade.'

Saffron frowned. 'I hadn't thought of them wanting to get out of the sun. I thought it would be pretty miserable over there when it was cold or raining.'

'And what about their water? John said that little spout down by the arch was their only source until the boats brought the barrels out. Suppose that had dried up whilst they were living there or the times when the boats were unable to go over?'

'I expect they kept some in reserve. John said that old Uncle Yannis claimed his happiest years were spent out there.'

Marjorie nodded. 'He says that in his book, but it does make me wonder how true it was at the time; dependent upon the boatmen to bring you your basic necessities and suffering from such an awful illness.'

'The stigma was worse than the illness for many of them. I think the worst hardship they suffered was being unable to communicate with their families for so long.'

'You won't tell John how I feel about the island, will you?' asked Marjorie anxiously. 'He seems so proud to have had a relative who lived over there.'

Saffron shook her head. 'Of course not. If we're asked to go again you can always make an excuse and stay here.'

'Oh, I would go again. I feel it is a place to go and pay homage, to say a prayer in the church for their poor souls. I'm just not sure it should be treated as a tourist attraction. I'm sure many of the tourists go over there hoping to see something horrible. Rather like the Victorians used to go to Bedlam to be amused by the inmates.'

'Apparently the locals are very pleased it is. It has made so much difference to their livelihood.'

'Then I suppose some good has come out of a sad situation.' Marjorie lay back on her bed. 'I'm going to have a siesta. What about you?'

Saffron smiled to herself. Marjorie was more tired than she was willing to admit. 'I'm going to ask Marianne and Bryony if they would like any help with preparing our evening meal. I'm also hoping they will say no so I can go and have a swim.'

'Take your time.' Marjorie closed her eyes. She was not sure if it was all the unaccustomed walking she had done in the last couple of days or the heat, but she felt drained of energy.

'Are you coming with us?' asked Marianne.

'I wouldn't miss seeing John dive for the cross,' Saffron assured her.

Marianne smiled. 'I meant are you coming to the church service with us?'

Saffron frowned. 'We're not Greek Orthodox. Would it be acceptable for us to come?'

'Of course. You can follow what we do and take part if you want or just sit there and enjoy the pageantry.'

'What should we wear? We've only got summer clothes with us, nothing really smart.'

'Provided your shoulders are covered and the neck is not too low no one will mind how you are dressed.' Marianne frowned. 'I just hope we will all be able to fit into the cars. Maybe John could go on the bike. I'll speak to him.'

'I don't mind riding pillion on his bike if it helps,' offered Saffron.

'Would you? I'm sure you can have a lift back with Vasilis and Cathy. That would mean there was enough space for everyone. We'll have to take Grandma's wheelchair, of course.'

Saffron did a quick calculation. 'That still leaves nine people. Maybe Marjorie and I could have a taxi?'

'Only eight,' smiled Marianne. 'Marcus won't be coming with us. He's Jewish, remember.'

Saffron felt her face flood with colour. 'I never even thought about it,' she admitted.

'Why should you? He doesn't keep any of the Jewish traditions, but he doesn't feel comfortable at a Greek Orthodox service. He'll make sure the lamb doesn't get burnt on the spit whilst we're gone. I'll find John and tell him he'll have to take the bike and you'll be riding with him.'

'Make sure your dress is tucked well under your legs,' John reminded Saffron. 'Of course, if you were a well brought up Greek girl you would ride side saddle.'

Saffron looked at him in horror. 'I'm certainly not a well brought up Greek girl. I'm sure I'd fall off if I tried to ride with you like that.'

'I'd corner slowly,' John grinned at her. 'Don't forget your helmet. You don't have to wear it, just have it on your arm.'

'What's the point of having it if I'm not wearing it?'

'It's against the law not to have it with you. It doesn't mention actually having it on your head.'

'You're joking!'

John shook his head. 'I usually hang mine on the handle bars.'

'I'll wear it,' Saffron said firmly.

John shrugged. 'Whatever you wish. Are you ready? I want to leave in good time to have a word with a friend of mine.'

Saffron nodded and waited until John was astride the motor bike before she settled herself behind him, ensuring there was no part of her dress trailing. John drove sedately down the road to the harbour and then across the Causeway until they reached the tiny church of the Analipseos.

Saffron leaned against a stone wall and watched as John threaded his way through the people who were already gathering until she saw him lay his hand on the shoulder of a young man and draw him off to one side. The youth seemed hesitant and John insistent and she wondered what their conversation was about. They touched fists and John made his way back to her, a pleased smile on his face.

'What happens now?' asked Saffron.

'After the service the Priest will lead us down to the edge of the water. Those of us who are diving will get into a boat and the Priest will be in another. When he decides the time and place are right he will bless the water and throw the cross into the sea. We dive in and see who can find it first.'

'Then what? Do you give it back to the Priest?'

'Not until the evening. The person who brings it to the surface will take it to his village and take it around for everyone to see and pay their respects. Then he's allowed to take it back to his own home for the remainder of the day.'

'What is so special about it?'

'Inside a little cavity there is a piece of the Holy Cross.'

'Really?' Saffron raised her eyebrows in surprise.

John smiled conspiratorially at her. 'So they say.'

'Do you believe that?'

John shook his head. 'A piece of the Holy Cross would be far too precious to ever leave the Church, let alone be thrown into the sea.'

'But other people do believe it?'

'They say that miracles have occurred and prayers have been answered for those who have held it for the day. They don't think that would happen if there wasn't a piece of the Holy Cross inside.'

'Is that superstition that has been passed down through the generations?'

'No, the people have a genuine faith. They truly believe there is a piece of the Holy Cross inside rather than a sliver of driftwood.'

'Suppose you can't find it?'

'You keep diving until you do,' John assured her. 'The water is not too deep here. If it was they would attach it to a rope to ensure it wasn't lost.'

'Surely all you'd have to do then is follow the rope.'

'But if the water is very deep you have to be the person who can hold their breath the longest to reach it. The old sponge divers were the most adept. They could stay under the water for twice as long as anyone else.' John smiled confidently at Saffron. 'It will be found, do not worry.'

Saffron sat between Bryony and Marianne and tried to follow the service, whilst looking surreptitiously around the tiny church. There were a number of men in attendance, most of them looking far too old to dive for the Cross and she wondered if they would take part as a matter of pride. The Priest finally strode up the aisle, holding the Cross aloft for all to see, with the chanters behind him. Marianne touched Saffron's arm and they followed along with the rest of the congregation down to the shore.

'Whilst the boys are diving for the Cross I'll see if I can collect some seaweed.' Marianne slipped off her sandals and gathered her skirt in her hand.

'What do you want seaweed for?'

'It has been blessed and it's considered good luck to have a piece in your home.'

Saffron nodded, surprised that Marianne was superstitious, and wondered if it was due to the influence of her older relatives.

'If you and Marjorie stand over there with Bryony you'll have a good view of the divers. She always makes sure Grandma has a good position. The locals revere her due to her age and wouldn't dream of standing in front of her.'

Saffron looked where Marianne indicated and saw that despite the press of people her grandmother had an unrestricted view of the sea.

'If John finds the Cross he'll have to spend the rest of the

37

morning going around with it to all the villagers, but you'll be able to have a lift back in Vasilis's car. He and his wife should be here any minute.' Marianne began to walk down the beach to the water's edge and Saffron and Marjorie walked over to where the rest of the family were waiting to see the boys dive into the sea.

Once the boys were in the water Saffron was unable to distinguish one from another, one moment they were on the surface and the next they had disappeared to continue their search. She thought she could pick out John surfacing near a young man; then swimming away strongly and diving again further out whilst the youngster ducked beneath the water.

The young man held his arm aloft as he gulped in air. 'I have it,' he was finally able to call.

Some of the boys began to swim back to the boat and climb aboard, congratulating the boy who had found the Cross, and others swam to the shore. Saffron now recognised the youngster holding the Cross aloft as the boy John had met when they first arrived at the Church.

Saffron frowned as John picked up his towel and began to rub his hair dry. 'You found the Cross, didn't you?' she said quietly.

'Everyone knows I am the best swimmer and diver around here,' he boasted. 'It's not hard to find. It usually lands in about the same place. I arranged it with Dimitris before we dived. I agreed that if I found it I would pass it on.'

'Is that allowed?'

John frowned and lowered his voice. 'His mother is desperately ill. They called the Priest to confess her two days ago. To have the Cross in the house until this evening will mean a good deal to all of them.'

'Do you really think that having the Cross in her house will cure her?'

John shrugged. 'Faith can work miracles. All she asks for is to see her first grandchild before she dies. Antonia is due to give birth any day.'

'Oh, John!' Saffron felt a lump come into her throat.

'You won't tell anyone, will you, Saff?'

'Of course not.'

'Besides, it saves me having to spend hours going around the village,' grinned John. 'I'd far rather be back at home and having a barbecue.'

Saffron returned to the house riding pillion on John's bike. He pointed towards the third car that was now parked outside their house. 'Vasilis and Cathy have arrived. You'll like Cathy, she's English.'

Saffron gave a sigh of relief. She had been dreading trying to make conversation with more people whom she could not understand. She walked round to the patio and Bryony seized upon her immediately.

'Good, you're back. We were beginning to think we'd have to start eating before you arrived. That lamb just smells so good. Come and meet Cathy and Vasilis.'

Saffron looked at Cathy in surprise, once up close she was older than she had appeared from a distance. She was as dark haired as a Greek, but her skin was a golden brown. The simple summer dress she was wearing showed off her figure to perfection and Saffron had an idea it had been specially designed and made for her.

'I'm pleased to meet you,' she smiled, showing the most even white teeth that Saffron had ever seen. 'Both Bryony and Marianne were so excited when you agreed to come over and meet them and now they tell me you were here last year.'

Saffron frowned. The story of John mishearing her name might be amusing, but she also found it somewhat embarrassing. 'I was only here for a week and we had no idea we were related.'

'How long are you staying this year?'

'Two weeks.'

'Is that all? Why not stay for a month?'

Saffron smiled. 'I have to return to work. I hope I shall be able to arrange some more time off later in the year.'

'You must,' replied Cathy firmly. 'Visit us at the end of the season when most of the tourists have returned home. Now, come and meet my husband, Vasilis.' To Saffron's surprise Cathy lifted a walking stick from the chair next to her and walked stiffly around the patio to where the grey haired man was speaking to Yannis. He turned as they approached and Saffron extended her hand.

Vasilis took her hand in his own and lifted it to his lips. 'I am so pleased to meet you. How long will you be staying? Will you be able to visit us? Cathy could do with some company whilst I'm working.'

Saffron shook her head. 'I'm really not sure if we will have the time on this visit. I am with my stepmother and I would like her to see as much of Crete as possible in our fortnight.'

Vasilis nodded. 'I am sure Giovanni and Marianne will take you anywhere you wish to go. If they refuse you let me know. I will take you. It would be my pleasure.' He smiled and winked at her, still holding her hand.

Saffron felt herself blushing. Was this attractive man flirting with her or was she imagining things? 'That's very kind of you. I'll remember,' she promised.

Cathy noticed Saffron's colour and squeezed her husband's arm. 'Take no notice of him, Saffron. He can't help being charming, can you, darling?'

Vasilis looked down into his wife's dancing eyes and touched her nose lightly with his finger. 'I have to practice so that I remember how to charm you when the need arises. Now, Saffron does not have a glass in her hand. That is not allowed. What can I get for you? Red or white wine or, like Bryony, do you prefer a soft drink?'

'White wine would be lovely, but I think I ought to have a glass of water. I'm thirsty and if I drink a glass of wine straight down it will go to my head. I'll pass on the wine until we start to eat, if you don't mind.'

Vasilis shrugged. 'As you please. I will fetch a glass for you.'

'Oh, no. I'm quite capable of going into the kitchen and getting it for myself. You and Cathy are guests. It won't take me a moment.' She was pleased to have the excuse to slip away and have a moment to herself.

'Hello, my name is Vasilis, the same as my father. I am known as Vasi so people know us apart. I believe you are Bryony's sister?'

Saffron turned in surprise. She had thought herself alone in the kitchen. 'Well, half sister,' she corrected him and took a long drink of the cool water.

'You do not look alike.'

'I'm told I look like my father. He was English.'

'As is my stepmother. It is interesting that you too have a stepmother. Already we have something in common. It would be interesting to know if we have other things in common, would it not?' Vasi raised an eyebrow quizzically at Saffron.

'I can't think of anything else we would have.'

'Did you enjoy having a step mother?' asked Vasi.

'Marjorie was wonderful. She couldn't have been better if she had been my true mother.'

'You were very fortunate.'

'You did not get on well with your step mother?' asked Cathy

Vasi smiled. 'She is lovely. I could not fault her, but the early years were very difficult. We could not communicate.'

Saffron raised her eyebrows and Vasi continued. 'Cathy did not speak Greek and I did not speak English. She would smile at me when I spoke to her, but she had no idea what I had said. I found it very frustrating.'

'Was there no one who could interpret?'

'If her father was there we had no problem. He spoke Greek. I loved that man. You would probably have read his books when you were a child.'

Saffron frowned. 'I was in America until I was ten. I don't remember having any Greek story books.'

Vasi shook his head. 'They were in all languages. His name was Vasilis Hurst, Basil in English.'

Saffron felt her memory stirring. 'Were they about a pond and a fairy? Wasn't there one about a grasshopper who was asked to take a message to the bottom of the garden? Each time he landed someone else asked him to take another message and by the time he reached the bottom of the garden he was completely muddled up and the fairy scolded them all for taking advantage of him?'

Vasi smiled delightedly. 'That I remember so well. It was my favourite. Grandpa would pretend to be the grasshopper with his fingers and jump around on my arm or leg. He told it to me as a reminder that you should concentrate on one thing at a time.'

'How did your parents meet?'

'Cathy came on holiday and Pappa took her and her friend to visit the places they wished to see. He says the first time they met he lifted her from the swimming pool and fell in love with her.'

Saffron frowned. 'Why should he lift her from the pool? Was she in difficulties?'

'She could not walk at that time. A bad car accident had left her crippled and she was dependent upon her friend and her wheelchair.'

Saffron nodded. 'I noticed her stick. She appears to have made a good recovery.'

Vasi nodded. 'It took her a considerable amount of time. I fell in the pool and was drowning. She had to walk from her chair to the pool to rescue me.'

'How did you fall into the pool?'

Vasilis smiled broadly. 'I had a tricycle at the time. I liked to pretend it was a racing car. There was a slope up by the pool and I would pedal as hard as I could, freewheel down and turn at the last moment. I was forbidden to do this, of course, but I had managed to avoid everyone who was supposed to be looking after me. I looked up and saw Cathy was there in her chair and it distracted me. I did not turn when I should have done.'

'Had she not been there you would probably not be here to tell the tale.'

'Very true. I did not go near the pool ever again. Even now I am not fond of swimming out of my depth. I could not dive for the Cross as John does. I do not like to be under the water.'

Saffron nodded. Obviously the incident when he was a young boy had left a lasting impression on Vasi.

'Are you two coming out here or planning to stay in the kitchen for the rest of the day? Giovanni is just about to carve the lamb,' Bryony spoke from the doorway.

Saffron placed her empty glass in the sink and hurried out to the patio, Vasi following her.

'You are fortunate to have such a large family,' he remarked. 'I have no one.'

Saffron raised her eyebrows.

'I have only my father and Cathy. No grandparents, no aunts or uncles.'

Saffron did not answer. She was beginning to have a suspicion that Vasi had been invited with a view to matchmaking. She compressed her lips. If that was so, they would have another think coming. She would not be taken in again by a smooth talking man.

Vasilis handed her the glass of white wine he had waiting for her and she thought she saw his lips twitch in amusement, knowing she had been alone in the kitchen with his son for a considerable amount of time.

'So, you and my son have met.'

Saffron nodded. 'We were talking about your wife's father. I remember his books from when I was a child.'

'Cathy will be pleased to know that. She was very close to her father. Sadly he died a few years ago and she still feels his loss.'

'What about her mother?'

'Rebecca divides her time between Crete and England. She finds it too hot over here during the summer months. If it were not for Cathy I do not think she would bother to make the journey.'

'Couldn't your wife go over to England?'

'Of course, whenever she pleased, but we do not like to be apart for any great length of time. Strange as it may seem we are still very much in love, despite having been married for thirty years and both of us getting old. We know we have only a limited time left to be together and we wish to make the most of it.' Vasilis smiled sadly.

Saffron nodded, thinking of her own father and his early demise. How she wished she could find someone whom she cared about so deeply and know the feeling was reciprocated.

'I understand you have a hotel,' she said, more to change the subject than because she was interested.

'That is how I know Yannis. When he was selling his hotel in Heraklion I decided it would be a good investment. What work do you do?'

'I'm a doctor.'

Vasilis raised his eyebrows. 'That is a very responsible job; saving lives.'

Saffron shook her head. 'I'm not that kind of doctor. I specialise in bones.'

'So if I had a broken arm I would come to you?'

Saffron laughed. 'If it was a straight forward break you would have your arm in plaster for a few weeks. I would see you when it was removed, just to check that it had mended properly. Most of my patients are those who have a problem, usually with a bone defect they have been born with. I try to rectify their condition to make life easier for them.'

'You deal with children mostly?'

'Not necessarily. Many people have suffered through to adulthood with a disability that could have been easily corrected when they were a child. Of course, the knowledge and technology was not always available in some cases years ago.'

Vasilis nodded and his eyes strayed to his wife, reminding Saffron that at one time she had been unable to walk. She would have liked to ask if it was due to surgery that Cathy had regained the use of her legs, maybe Bryony would know if she asked her later.

Marianne appeared beside them with plates of succulent lamb. 'There's plenty more. Bryony is doing the rounds with the salad and there's bread on the table. Giovanni is in charge of the wine. Giovanni,' called Marianne and indicated that he should come in their direction. 'You both look in need of a refill.'

Saffron looked at her empty glass in surprise, but before Giovanni reached them Vasi removed it and pressed another into her hand whilst Bryony offered the salad bowl.

'I can't cope,' she laughed. 'I need more hands.' She placed her plate and glass on the table whilst she helped herself to the salad. 'I'll have to sit down to eat. I'm not very good at a balancing act.'

Vasi slipped into the chair next to her. 'I agree. I do not wish to end up spilling this excellent food on the patio.'

'Smile Saff,' commanded John and Saffron looked up from her heaped plate.

'Why do you call me Saff? Everyone else calls me Saffie.'

John looked at her, puzzled by her question. 'To me you are Saff. Nicola is Nick. You are Saff. You don't mind, do you?'

Saffron shook her head. 'Not a bit. I was just curious. Why don't you shorten Marcus and Bryony's names.'

John grinned. 'I tried that and they said I had to call them by their full names.' He shrugged. 'Their names, their choice. Actually I came over to take your photo so I could send it to Nick. Hold your glass up and smile, Saff.'

Nicola read the e-mail John had sent her describing the time he had spent on Spinalonga with Saffron and Marjorie, followed by an account of the diving for the Cross and the barbecue. She looked at the photos he had attached with interest. Saffron was just as she remembered from their meeting the previous year, but

Marjorie was not at all as she had imagined. She felt an intense longing to be back in Crete.

She tapped in John's e-mail address and began to compose a reply to him. Her life was so mundane. All she had to tell him was the progress her sister was making and she was rapidly losing patience with her. Eleanor's latest blood test had come back clear of infection and there was no reason why she should not put her attack of Glandular Fever behind her and continue with her life as a normal, healthy nine year old girl. Instead she insisted that she was too tired to go to school if she disliked the lessons for the day, refused to take part in any physical activity and even to tidy her room she claimed exhausted her.

Nicola had tried to be understanding and forbearing at first, but now she was convinced that Eleanor was simply taking advantage of the situation. If friends called she was never too tired to spend time chatting with them or to spend hours playing games on her computer. When her mother suggested they should go shopping together to buy her new clothes and have lunch out she was eager to participate, with no hint of exhaustion, but if asked to do the simplest task in the house she would shake her head and lean back in a chair with her eyes closed. John must be tired of hearing her complain about her sister. She tried desperately hard to think of incidents that had happened in the diner where she worked at the weekend.

'So, what would you like to do tomorrow, Marjorie?'

'I really don't mind. We seem to have seen and done so much already.'

Saffron spread the map out on the table. She traced the coastline with her finger. 'We've really only seen from here to Heraklion. Why don't we spend the day wandering around Aghios Nikolaos? We ought to go to Uncle Yannis's shop or they'll begin to think we are being rude and avoiding them.'

Marjorie sighed. 'I admit I tend to avoid being alone with them. It's so difficult not being able to say more than good morning.'

'We could catch the bus in and arrange a time for Marianne to meet us. That way she would be able to translate both ways. I'm sure you'll love their goods and they are willing to pack and send them back to England so you wouldn't have to carry anything on the plane and risk it being broken. If we did that today maybe we could ask them to take us up to the Lassithi Plain tomorrow. I think it's quite a long drive, but I've heard it's well worth it. There are hundreds of windmills, very few of them work now, but I'm sure it's still quite a sight. I'd love to go up to Rethymnon and Chania later and over to the other side to see how different it is. I understand they have palm trees on the beach. You would feel as if you are in Africa.'

'Where is the list of places they made? Is Chania on it?' asked Marjorie.

'I'll have a look. Do you think we ought to suggest that Cathy comes with us? Her husband was hoping we would visit them and be company for her whilst he was working.'

'Would she want to come? She must have seen everywhere on the island by now. I'd like to see their house, but I don't want to spend all day there.'

Saffron nodded in agreement. Everyone seemed quite happy to stop whatever they were doing and sit and chat for hours on end making it difficult to leave. 'I'll ask Marianne and see what she says. I also want to ask Grandma if I can look at her photographs again with her. If we went to Aghios Nikolaos tomorrow and had a long drive the day after I could look at her photos the next morning and we could spend the afternoon being lazy on the beach. How does that sound?'

'What does that leave for next week?'

'The trip to Rethymnon. That would probably take most of the day. I wonder if it's possible to go to Gortys on the way? I didn't manage that last year.' Saffron began to point to various names on the map and frowned. 'I have no idea how far these places are from each other. It might be possible to visit Gortys and go on to somewhere else. I'll have to ask Giovanni.'

'Leave it with me,' Giovanni smiled. 'We can go to Gortys, on to Matala, up to Aghia Triada and then on to Phaestos and take the road to Spili back to Rethymnon. Depending how long you spend at the sites we might manage to fit in a visit to Preveli Monastery as well.'

'It won't be too much driving for you?' asked Saffron anxiously.

Giovanni shook his head. 'I enjoy driving. Certainly I can take you in to Aghios Nikolaos tomorrow and arrange a time for Marianne to meet you. In fact I could take you down to Gournia and you could catch the bus back to Aghios Nikolaos for some lunch. After all, Aghios Nikolaos is only another town. It is pretty down by the pool and you should walk up to the square,' Giovanni shrugged, 'after that the town is little different from any other.'

Todd sat at the table in the diner. He squeezed Jenni-Lea's hand. 'What do you fancy?'

She glanced at him from beneath her lowered lids. 'More of the same.'

'I'm not that accomplished,' he laughed. 'Banana Sundae?'

Jenni-Lea shook her head. 'I'll go for a strawberry.'

Todd signalled to the girl behind the counter and she walked over, pad in her hand. 'Two strawberry sundaes, please.'

'With nuts?'

Jenni-Lea giggled. 'I'll always go for nuts.'

Nicola nodded. 'I'll bring them over.'

Todd squeezed Jenni-Lea's hand again. 'You can be quite outrageous.'

She arched her eyebrows at him. 'I only said I liked nuts on my sundae.'

'I know what you said and I know what you meant.'

Jenni-Lea giggled again. 'And I know what you like.' She withdrew her hand from his and groped him beneath the table.

He removed her hand from his jeans. 'You'll bring me out in a sweat if you start that again.'

'I thought you liked me to touch you?'

'Yeah, but not when we're in the diner. You start playing around now and we'll be thrown out.'

'I enjoy playing around.'

'Don't I know it! What are you doing this evening?'

'What are you suggesting?'

'What do you think?'

'I'm up for it. Will you be?'

She groped him again and Todd shifted in his chair. 'Have you never had enough?'

Jenni-Lea shook her head. 'I enjoy a man and the more often the better. I'm an all day every day girl. You know that,' her hand strayed again. 'Admit that you enjoy it as much as I do.' She wriggled the tip of her tongue at him.

Todd looked at the girl he'd been dating for the last six weeks. He knew her blonde hair came from a bottle, but her full breasts, that looked about to jump from her low cut top as she moved, were completely natural. Just looking at them excited him. On their first date she had driven him into a frustrated frenzy whilst she had relaxed and allowed him to enjoy himself. Finally, to his delight, she had invited him back to her apartment, unzipping his jeans as they travelled up in the elevator. He had difficulty controlling himself whilst he waited for her to unlock the door.

It was called a penthouse, but in reality it was hardly more than a bedsit at the top of the building. A large area had been divided by a screen. A small table and a couple of upright chairs stood to one side, whilst opposite there was a television with a settee placed in a comfortable viewing position. Two small side rooms served as a bathroom and kitchen. Jennie-Lea had led him

49

behind the screen where her bed, wardrobe, and chest of drawers took up most of the space.

From the lounge area where there were almost unlimited views across the city it was possible to catch a glimpse of the sea on the horizon. The glass door gave access to a balcony that gave an even wider view of the area. Far below there was a parking area for the residents. No doubt the small apartment relied on its panoramic view and convenient parking when it was advertised to prospective tenants.

Since then he had spent every evening with her, although she insisted he returned to the rooms he shared with two other young men from the University each night.

'I don't want to ruin my good name. If my firm thought you were living here they'd increase the rental. I've negotiated a bargain as I work for them. I could never afford this otherwise,' she had explained.

'Two sundaes.' Nicola placed the dishes in front of them and returned to the counter.

Jenni-Lea placed a small amount of ice cream on her spoon. Looking at Todd intently she lifted it to her lips and licked at it, flicking her tongue in and out.

'Is everything you do calculated to excite me?'

Jenni-Lea nodded. 'Just so you know what to expect later.'

'You're impossible.'

'That wasn't what you said earlier. You said I was incredible.' She pouted prettily at him and leaned forward over her dish so he could look even further down her cleavage.

Nicola watched them dispassionately. She knew the girl by sight, having seen her about the town driving a car with the name of a real estate firm spray painted on the side. She wondered if the good looking young man was hoping to get preferential rates if he could claim friendship with an employee. She continued to prepare the fruit and place the bowls in the fridge. Provided they paid their bill before they left their relationship was none of her business.

They took their time and eventually Todd walked over to the counter to pay. He looked at Nicola for the first time. She was the total opposite of Jenni-Lea. Dark and plump, definitely not fat, but rounded in all the right places and her eyes sparkled. Slowly he pulled some notes from his pocket and handed them to her.

'Thank you,' he said. 'You make a better sundae than the other girl who works here.'

Nicola smiled at him, noticing the iris of his eyes was such a pale blue that they seemed almost colourless. 'Glad you liked them.'

'Are you here every day?'

'Just weekends.'

Todd nodded. 'I'll remember.' He pocketed his change and returned to the table where Jenni-Lea was repairing her lipstick.

'So, how was your day?' asked Giovanni of Saffron and Marjorie.

'Lovely. I'm so pleased you took us down to Gournia. It was very different from Knossos.'

'It was a farming community, not a palace.'

'I know. I managed to find a guide book in Aghios Nikolaos and I sat and read bits of it whilst we had lunch.'

'Did you like Aghios Nikolaos?'

Saffron pulled a face. 'As you said, it's just another town, although the area around the pool has been made very attractive.'

'You ate down there?'

Saffron nodded and Giovanni pursed his lips. 'You would have been better to walk up the hill and find a taverna where there were local people eating. Those down by the pool are very much fast food for the tourist and their prices are high.'

'I thought we could be making a mistake, but we weren't sure if we would be able to find anywhere else. We walked up to the square afterwards and didn't see any tavernas.'

'They are in the side roads. Did you see the bullet holes on the palm trees that I told you about?'

Saffron nodded. 'I'm pleased they've left the trees growing there. They could easily have decided to remove them after the war when they put up the memorial.'

'They are a part of the memorial. An incident in our history never to be forgotten. When we visit Chania I will show you another memorial and tell you the history. I have arranged for us to stay in a hotel at Rethymnon that belongs to a friend. The following day we will visit Souda Bay and the cemeteries, walk around the town, whatever you wish. From Rethymnon we can make the visits to the sites you wish to see on the other side of the island. We can stay as long as you wish.'

'You are being so kind to us. Please let me pay the hotel bill.'

'Certainly not. The hotel is owned by people we know. They do not charge us the extortionate rates they charge the tourist.'

'I do feel guilty,' said Saffron.

'You are family. I would do the same for them.' Giovanni shrugged and dismissed the conversation. 'Did you enjoy visiting Uncle Yannis's shop, Marjorie?'

'I certainly did. I'd looked in the other gift shops and they're all selling the same items. When I walked into Yannis's shop it was like an Aladdin's Cave. I didn't know where to start looking. I could have bought the entire stock.'

'As it is she has bought two enormous vases that Uncle Yannis is having shipped home for us, and she's promised to go back again before we return. They're wonderful sales people. They just bring out more and more beautiful items until you're seduced into buying the most expensive.' Saffron shook her head in mock despair.

'And did you buy anything this time?'

'I want to buy one of the sketches, but I couldn't find it.'

Giovanni frowned. 'Which one?'

'The one you have hanging in your lounge.'

'Ahh,' Giovanni smiled. 'You will not find that one. It is an original. Those on sale at the shop are copies of the ones that Anna did when she was on the island.'

'Aunt Anna?'

'No, the child, Anna. The sketches we have are the ones my grandmother did before she died. They are of her parents, brothers and sisters, her husband and Marisa. We would not part with those or make copies. They are meaningless to other people, but to us they are our family heirlooms.'

'I'll just have to make do with one of the others, then. I quite thought they had all been done by the same artist. The work is so similar.'

Giovanni smiled and touched his nose. 'Of course it is,' he replied, leaving Saffron wondering at the meaning behind his words.

Dimitris was waiting outside the school in Aghios Nikolaos as John left for the day. He had obviously been crying and his eyes still looked suspiciously moist. John placed an arm around his shoulders.

'Mamma died on Tuesday. I've come to thank you,' he said tremulously.

'Thank me? Whatever for?'

'The Cross. I laid it on Mamma's chest and she touched it. It seemed to give her a little more strength. She survived long enough to see her granddaughter and hold her for a few minutes. Antonia had a little girl on Monday.'

John shrugged. 'I'm pleased you felt the Cross helped.'

Dimitris nodded vigorously. 'I'm sure it did. I'm indebted to you, John. If ever there is anything I can do for you just let me know.'

John threw his books to one side and helped himself to a beer from the fridge.

'What's wrong, John?'

'Dimitris was waiting for me after school today. He hadn't been in all week. He said his mother died on Tuesday.'

Marianne placed a sympathetic hand on his shoulder. 'Tell him how sorry I am when you see him next, tell him we are all sorry.'

John nodded. 'I'll tell Saff.'

Marianne raised her eyebrows. 'Why should she want to know?'

John shrugged. 'I told her about his mother when he found the Cross.'

Saffron listened quietly whilst John imparted the news that Dimitris's mother had died. 'What about his sister? Has she given birth yet?'

John smiled. 'Monday; a little girl.'

'Did her grandmother get to see her?'

'Yes, she saw her and held her for a few moments. She died with her wish fulfilled. Dimitris is convinced that having the Cross in the house for the day helped her to live another twenty four hours.'

Saffron felt a tingling up and down her spine. 'Her belief in the Holy Cross's ability to bring about miracles must have been very great.'

John nodded sombrely. 'It does make you wonder, doesn't it?'

WEEK 2 – MAY 2006

'Will we need our swimming costumes?' asked Marjorie as she helped herself to a bottle of water from the refrigerator.

'It's always a good idea to have them with you. They can stay in the car until you need them. Help yourself to anything you want, some fruit, maybe? I must take Grandma her breakfast.' Bryony added the coffee pot to the tray and carried it towards her grandmother's room.

Marjorie looked in the refrigerator again, finally selecting a bunch of grapes and some peaches. She placed them along with the bottles of water in the cold box and stood it by the door whilst she went to collect her swimming costume and remind Saffron to put hers into a separate bag also.

'First we will make a small detour and visit Cathy at her house. She was going to invite you to spend the day there and I explained we were driving to Rethymnon. She has asked us to visit her briefly in case you do not have another opportunity. I think you will like Cathy's house,' observed Giovanni. 'It is very different from Uncle Yannis's.'

'How is it different?' asked Marjorie.

'You will see,' he smiled. 'We will stop for coffee and I am sure Cathy will show you around.'

Marjorie smiled inwardly. She had hoped she would have the opportunity to see the woman's house, but would not have had the temerity to ask.

'Do we have time?' asked Saffron.

'It will not take so long. She knows we cannot linger for more than half an hour if we want to have lunch with Vasi and reach Rethymnon this afternoon.'

Saffron gave a silent sigh of relief. Curious though she was to see the house she did not want to spend hours there and find it was too late to go anywhere else.

Giovanni turned off the coast road and began to climb a narrow, winding road up a steep hill, and through a couple of small villages that disappeared as they rounded a bend. He finally drew to a halt before a high wall and wrought iron gates. He reached through the car window and pressed a series of numbers into the pad on the gate post which allowed the gates to swing open. As he drove up the winding drive way Marjorie admired the immaculately cut grass and the colourful flower beds.

They stopped before a double fronted building, the curved walls each side of the front door had railings above them allowing the rooms on the second floor to have balconies. Two large Alsatian dogs appeared as if from nowhere, barked ferociously and took up a stance, one each side of the car.

'Stay where you are until Cathy comes,' warned Giovanni. 'Once they know you are friends there is no problem.'

Cathy waved to them from the top of the stone steps that led up to the front door and clicked her fingers to the dogs; they trotted obediently to her side where she attached a leash to each collar.

'You're quite safe,' she assured the women. 'Once you are out of the car come over and let them sniff you. They will know you for friends then.'

Tentatively Marjorie and Saffron climbed out of the car and walked towards Cathy. As they approached the dogs eyed them warily then sniffed at their hands and legs, finally each one sitting down beside Cathy.

'Good boys,' she praised them, then she released them and

one took a further sniff at Marjorie before they both ambled away to a patch of shade.

'They are wonderful guard dogs. Very frightening to an intruder. They wouldn't hurt anyone, but they would certainly keep them pinned into a corner until Vasilis or myself arrived.'

Marjorie eyed them dubiously. She would certainly not want a confrontation with them. 'What about the postman?'

'We don't have any post up here; it all goes to the hotel. Come on in. The door is open.'

Marjorie and Saffron followed Cathy into the spacious hallway. 'Come on through to the kitchen and you can see the view from the patio. Would you like coffee or fruit juice?'

'Juice, please,' decided Marjorie, and Saffron asked for the same.

'You'll have a beer, Giovanni?'

'Of course.'

Cathy nodded. 'I'll leave you to pour it whilst I show Marjorie and Saffron around. We can take our fruit juices with us.' She handed a frosted glass to Marjorie and another to Saffron, placing a bottle of beer and glass on the side for Giovanni. 'Oh, I should have asked which flavour you wanted. Excuse my bad manners. I'm not used to entertaining formally.'

'You certainly don't have to be formal with us. Any fruit juice is delicious,' Marjorie assured her.

Saffron looked at the elegant woman in surprise. She would have expected her to hold formal dinner parties regularly, but maybe when she did outside caterers came in.

'This is obviously the kitchen,' she waved her hand around the spacious area and Saffron hoped she would not drip her fruit juice on the polished marble floor.

'Through here is the main lounge. We don't often use it.'

The marble floor, predominately white with swirls of grey, continued through into the lounge. Two large white settees were placed either side of a large, open, fireplace stacked with logs ready for the winter. A large television screen took up most of one wall and in the chimney alcoves were shelves overflowing with books. There were few ornaments around, but Saffron had an idea they had all been purchased from Uncle Yannis's shop.

'Through here is our den.' Cathy led the way into a smaller, more intimate room. The marble floor continued and the settees were still white, but there was a brightly coloured runner from the doorway to the seating area and coloured throws were on the settees. The television was not as large and this time the other chimney alcove held a stereo system. On the wall above the fireplace were photographs and Saffron would have liked to look at them more closely.

'We usually spend our evenings in here, particularly in the winter. It's much cosier.' She opened a door and Saffron and Marjorie found themselves back in the hall. 'Come upstairs.' Cathy led the way, taking her weight on her right leg and then drawing the other up to it. She opened the first door. 'This is our bedroom. Come out on the balcony and see the view. It's even better from up here.'

They stepped out with her and Saffron drew in her breath. From their vantage point they had an uninterrupted view of the whole of the bay. The village of Elounda was spread out below them and to the left they could clearly see Plaka. Spinalonga sat quietly in the blue sea, appearing to guard the area as it had in the past.

'It's beautiful,' Marjorie gasped. 'From my bedroom I look across the road to another house!'

'That will not happen in my lifetime,' smiled Cathy. 'What Vasi will do later is up to him. If he doesn't want to live here, he can always sell the land and the house to a developer.'

Saffron looked at Cathy in surprise. 'You mean you own all this land we can see?'

Cathy nodded. 'A good deal of it. Vasilis did not want us to be overlooked or to have the view spoiled. The villages could have grown and ended up on our doorstep. We could have been surrounded by buildings. He planted olive trees to make use of the land and give employment to the villagers during the winter. Once the trees are planted no one can cut them down to use the land for building without permission from the government.' She closed and locked the doors to the balcony as they returned inside. 'We have our own bathroom, of course.' She pushed open the door to a bathroom that was almost as large as the bedroom. 'Along here are the other bedrooms, they also have their own bathrooms and there is a little one we installed at the end for emergencies.'

The secondary bedrooms were almost as large as the master bedroom, each having a settee and a small table where you could sit to read or write. The bedroom windows gave unspoilt views of olive trees, giving way to rolling green hills dotted with low trees and shrubs; then the varying colours of the higher slopes where the rain had washed away the vegetation.

Cathy opened the door next to the bathroom exposing a flight of stairs. She flicked on a light switch and with her halting gait led the way up, opening the door at the top and the sunlight flooded in. She walked out onto the flat roof. 'This is ideal for sunbathing and from here you can see our swimming pool. After Vasi's accident in the pool he had nightmares. He didn't even want to use the shower. We built the pool down there away from the house and had a high wall around it. It was a pleasure to remove the walls when he was old enough to be trusted and had also overcome his initial fear of water.'

The heat beat down on them and Saffron had a longing to run across the smooth lawn and plunge into the turquoise blue water that was sparkling in the distance. Cathy led them to the stone steps and back down to the garden. She pushed open the front door and they were back in the spacious hallway where she showed them into a room on the opposite side from the room she had called their den.

'This is Vasilis's work room. I call it his play room. He says he is going in here to do some work and when I look in he is usually mailing his friends or on the internet playing chess.' She closed the door and opened the next. 'Here is our main dining room for when we entertain. If it is just Vasilis and I we eat in the kitchen, and next to it is the cloakroom. That's it, I'm afraid.'

Saffron shook her head. 'It's enormous. How do you keep it clean?'

'We use very little of the house now so it isn't difficult. The window cleaner comes every week and the gardener three times. He also acts as my private chauffer. A woman from the village comes in once a week so I can manage the rest myself. If we have visitors Vasilis will ask one of the maids from the hotel to come up for a day or two.' Cathy spoke casually about their domestic arrangements.

'It's a beautiful house.' Saffron gave a little sigh. She could not envisage what it must be like to live in such luxury and take it for granted.

'Vasi has his own apartment now. He is responsible for the hotels between Hersonissos and Heraklion. Vasilis finally realised that it was too much for him to be forever rushing up and down the whole of the coast. He looks after those in Aghios Nikolaos and Elounda and leaves the others to Vasi. Giovanni tells me you will be stopping for a quick lunch at the "*Iraklio Central*" with Vasi.'

Saffron smiled guiltily. 'I've been very lazy and left all the arrangements in Giovanni's hands.'

'I'm sure he's quite happy to arrange everything.' Cathy smiled at Giovanni. 'I'd like to ask you to come over one evening and we can have a meal together, and Marianne, of course. Let me know a convenient evening.'

Giovanni leant over and kissed Cathy's cheek. 'I'm sure we'll be able to manage that. Thank you, Cathy.'

The drive to Heraklion took longer than Marjorie and Saffron had expected and Saffron could understand how tiring it must have been for Vasilis to drive up and down the coast frequently.

Vasi greeted them and led them to a table on a balcony that overlooked the main square. Despite the traffic rushing past the glassed balcony protected them from the noise and fumes.

'I'm afraid our views here do not compare with many other of the hotels, but the tourists appreciate being in the centre of the town and within easy reach of the buses to go to other places of interest. Will you be stopping long enough to look around?'

Giovanni shook his head. 'I told you, Vasi, we'll take advantage of you for a quick lunch then we are driving on to Rethymnon. Tomorrow we plan to drive to Chania, visit Souda Bay and the Cemeteries and go on to the memorial. The following day we drive over to Preveli and visit that side of the island. Saffie will have to study the map and her guide book and tell me all the places she wishes to see. Kostas has said there is no problem if we wish to stay an extra night.'

Vasi nodded. 'Another day, maybe. Now what would you like? I have coffee, of course, fruit juice or wine, whichever you prefer.'

'I'll stick to fruit juice,' said Marjorie firmly. 'I don't want to spend the afternoon asleep in the car.'

'Have you any mango?' asked Saffron.

'Of course.' Vasi looked quite hurt at the suggestion that he might not be able to supply his guest's request. 'Coffee for you, Giovanni?'

Vasi raised his hand to the waiter who was hovering and placed their order for the drinks and also asked him to let the chef know they were ready for their meal.

'I have taken the liberty of ordering for you all. It will be no more than five minutes now you have arrived. Souvlaki and pasta salads followed by fruit or pastries.'

Saffron wiped her lips with her napkin. 'That was beautiful, Vasi. I've had souvlaki before, but it has never tasted as good as that.'

'I am pleased you enjoyed it. I will tell the chef. He will appreciate the compliment. Would you like more juice or coffee?'

61

Giovanni shook his head. 'I don't want to be rude, Vasi, but we really should make a move. It's gone two and you know how congested the main road can be.'

They drove on to Rethymnon and Giovanni stopped in a side road where the buildings rubbed shoulders, supporting each other by their proximity.

'I think you will like this hotel. It is a Byzantine building that Kostas is restoring. From your bedroom you will be able to see the tower of the mosque.' Giovanni smiled at the look on Marjorie's face. 'Do not worry, Marjorie. The mosque is no longer in use. You will not be disturbed by the call for the Muslim prayers.'

Saffron and Marjorie followed Giovanni into the small hotel and Saffron looked around curiously. After Vasi's hotel in Heraklion this one appeared so informal, more like a private house.

'Kostas,' called Giovanni. 'We are here.'

Kostas appeared from a patio at the rear of the building, wiping his hands down his trousers. 'Welcome. You will have to excuse me. I did not know what time you planned to arrive so I was taking the opportunity to tidy the garden. Come through and have a seat.'

He opened a glass door and ushered them into a small courtyard, the sun slanting through a glass roof on to the large plants and small trees.

'This is beautiful,' observed Marjorie.

'I am pleased you like it. Feel free to go through the arch and see the other garden. That was where I was working when you arrived. It is not finished yet, but you can tell me what you think.'

Marjorie needed no second invitation and stood in the second open courtyard. A pile of stones stood in one corner, having a large plant that seemed to grow through and over it.

'How did you do that?' she asked. 'It is so effective.'

Kostas smiled. 'I did not do that. It decided for itself that was where and how it would grow. I am trying to encourage some more to do the same.' He indicated the other piles of stones with small plants standing in pots beside them. 'If they begin to trail across the stones then I will disguise the pots,' he explained.

Marjorie turned to Saffron. 'Do you think I could manage to do that on the rockery at home?'

'You could try.'

'I plan to have a small fountain in that corner,' continued Kostas. 'All Turkish courtyards had a fountain. I am trying to make everywhere as it would have been. When you see your room you will see how I have used only wood and marble. The same materials as were here originally. Now, have a seat and I will bring you refreshment. What would you like – coffee, fruit juice, wine?'

'Kostas, is Giorgos Papalexakis still around?' asked Giovanni as Kostas placed a bottle of wine and some glasses on the table before them.

'Of course.'

'I will take you to his work shop,' promised Giovanni. 'You will not believe what you see. He is unique.'

'He may not be there at this hour,' warned Kostas.

'No problem. We will visit him tomorrow before we drive to Chania. When the ladies have settled in to their room we will go down to the harbour for a meal. Will you join us?'

Kostas shook his head. 'Thank you, no. As usual my mother is expecting me. Maybe tomorrow I could eat with you.'

Giovanni nodded understandingly. 'We will finish our drinks and go to our rooms. Shall we say half an hour, ladies? Will that give you enough time to freshen up? We will then drive down to the harbour and visit Spiro for a meal.'

Giovanni drove the short distance to the Venetian harbour and paid to park in a public car park. On both sides of the road were bars and restaurants, and Marjorie hoped they would not be going to the one that was crowded with young people with music so loud that the patrons were forced to shout to each other.

Giovanni led the way along the waterfront to an old, double fronted stone building that was displaying the fish on ice in a glass cabinet. Spiro opened his arms to welcome them.

'It has been a long time since you have been to see us, Giovanni. Is Marianne with you?'

Giovanni shook his head. 'I'm with some relatives who are visiting Crete. They wished to see as much of the country as possible so we have come to Rethymnon. I could not come here without visiting you.'

'And where do you go from here?'

'Tomorrow to Chania and the memorial.'

'All is well there?'

'I hope so.'

Spiro shook his head sadly. 'So much vandalism these days. On the old buildings, even on the memorials sometimes. It is not right. In the old days such things would not have happened. Now, what will you have to drink? Some wine? I will bring a bottle. Very special.'

'No, Spiro, a carafe of house wine will be sufficient. We are staying with Kostas and have already consumed one bottle with him so our palates are spoiled.'

Spiro called out to a waiter who disappeared inside. 'Now, food, you must eat,' insisted Spiro. 'I have lobster, the big prawns, crab, the flat fishes, the fish steaks to be grilled or baked. You tell me which you would prefer.'

Giovanni considered. 'Let me have a word and see what they fancy.'

'Of course, of course, whenever you are ready.'

Giovanni walked back to the table. 'The choice is yours when you've had a look at the menu, but I warn you, the portions are generous.'

'Are they all tavernas?' asked Marjorie as she looked around. 'How on earth do they make a living?'

'In the height of the season it can be difficult to find a table, particularly in the evening. This is the area you always see on the postcards. All the tavernas specialise in fresh fish. Take no notice of the prices you see on the menu. I know the owner and he will charge us the Greek price, not the one he uses for the tourists.'

'Can you suggest anything?' asked Marjorie.

'What about some prawns?' asked Saffron longingly.

'We can order prawns if you like. You will have to peel them as they will come with their heads and tails.'

Saffron shook her head. 'I can't cope with that. I always get in such a mess.'

'Do you all like lobster? If so I would suggest we order two and share them. With some salad, chips and bread that will be sufficient. Spiro will bring us something to nibble whilst we wait and that will be almost a meal in itself.'

Despite not leaving the taverna until late, Saffron and Marjorie had eaten breakfast and were drinking coffee when Giovanni joined them.

'I am sorry. I overslept,' he apologised. 'I will have some coffee; then we will visit Giorgos before we drive to Chania.'

'Who is Giorgos?'

Giovanni smiled. 'He has a very tiny workshop and he made all the lyra for the opening ceremony for the Olympics.'

'You mean he strings them?'

Giovanni shook his head. 'He makes them from a single block of wood. Much of the work is done by hand and eye.'

'Really!'

'You will see. We will walk there. It is not far. He is happy to work and talk at the same time.'

Saffron and Marjorie sat on the chairs at the front of the tiny shop. The remaining space was filled by a large work bench, tools and lyra in various stages of completion. They watched, completely fascinated as Giorgos chiselled and planed unerringly for some minutes before laying the roughly shaped wood to one side and took a completed instrument from the wall. He placed his foot on a stool and began to play, his fingers moving skilfully across the strings, picking out the melody.

His impromptu recital at an end he hung the lyra back on the wall and continued his work on the new one he was carving.

'That was so beautiful,' remarked Marjorie. 'It made me want to cry.'

For the first time Giorgos smiled. 'Thank you,' he said simply.

Marjorie blushed. She had no idea how much English the musician knew, but she was thankful she had said she had enjoyed his music.

They continued along the main road to Souda Bay, the scene of so much fighting during the German invasion and visited the immaculately kept Allied Cemetery, hardly able to conceive the number of young men who had lost their lives.

'There is also the German Cemetery if you wished to visit it.'

Marjorie shook her head. 'I'm very pleased we visited this one, but I really do not need to see any more gravestones. It is beautifully looked after and I'm sure the German one is just as well cared for. I don't need to go and check it out.'

'We will continue, then. Where I take you next time will make you appreciate how generous hearted the Cretan people are.'

They drove in to the centre of Chania and parked down by the Venetian fortress. 'Do you wish to look around the fortress?' asked Giovanni.

Saffron shook her head. 'After visiting the one at Heraklion and seeing Spinalonga I think I have the general idea how a fortress was laid out. Although I would quite like to have a quick look at the museum.'

Giovanni looked at his watch. 'We will have the time; then we have lunch.'

They wandered through the narrow streets; their buildings

festooned with colourful clothing and embroidered goods to tempt the tourist.

Marjorie shook her head and fanned herself. 'I'm not sure what I expected, but this town looks very little different from Aghios Nikolaos or Rethymnon.'

Giovanni smiled. 'I'm afraid you will find all the Cretan towns look much the same now. Their individuality has gone. We will have some lunch here.' He led the way in to a taverna, finding an empty table beneath a ceiling fan and spoke rapidly to the waiter.

'I have asked that we are served quickly as we have to drive to the airport for our flight.' He grinned at them. 'When we have eaten we can go to the memorial and we will drive through villages that are rarely seen by the tourists.'

Before they left Chania, Giovanni bought an enormous bunch of flowers which he placed in the boot of the car along with a bucket and two bottles of water. Saffron looked at them in surprise. She knew they were going to visit a memorial, but was it customary to take flowers with you to place on the grave of someone you did not know?

Within a few minutes they left the main road and took a side turning into the deserted countryside. Saffron and Marjorie looked out of the windows, wondering where they were going and exactly what they were going to see. A large block of marble loomed up in front of them and Giovanni drew the car in to the bank. He opened the boot and handed the bunch of flowers to Saffron.

'Please carry those for me.' He picked up the bucket and the bottles of water and began to walk over the rough ground.

As Marjorie and Saffron approached closer they could see the block of marble was an angel with a child in her arms. On her skirt were engraved a considerable number of names. Giovanni placed the bucket at the foot, poured in the water and took the flowers from Saffron's arms.

Having arranged the flowers to his satisfaction Giovanni stood back. 'Cathy's father was out here with the resistance. He lived with his wife and child nearby. When the Germans retreated they took out their vengeance on the villagers. All of them were shot and then the village was burnt to the ground.'

'All of them?' exclaimed Saffron in horror. 'Even the children?'

Giovanni nodded sombrely. 'Everyone. Vasilis Hurst had this monument erected in memory of his wife and son. You see why I say the Cretan people are generous hearted? They would have good reason to tend the Allied Cemetery and neglect the German graveyard.'

'So how did Cathy survive?'

'Cathy is the child from Vasilis Hurst's second marriage. He planned never to set foot on Crete again and then Cathy met her husband here. He had to make a choice. Return to an island he had loved with all the heartbreaking memories and see his beloved daughter frequently, or stay in England and wait for her to visit him.'

'And he returned?'

Giovanni nodded. 'Of course. He gained a fine man as his son-in-law and a grandson who captured his heart.'

'Vasi told me how much he loved his grandfather.'

Giovanni tapped lightly on the memorial stone and Saffron looked at him curiously.

'Why did you do that?'

'It is customary to let the people who are commemorated there know that you have visited; that they are not forgotten.'

Marjorie felt a lump coming in to her throat. This was far more moving than looking at the graves of unknown soldiers, despite the sacrifice they had made.

Giovanni smiled at them. 'Cathy always asks anyone who drives this way to visit and leave some flowers. It is a small thing to do.' He crossed himself before turning away from the memorial. 'Now, we will drive back through the countryside and visit Ani Gonia where Yiorgo Psychoundakis, the man known as the Cretan runner was born. From there it is only a short drive to

Agiroupolis and it will be cool by the springs and waterfalls. Both places are on our return journey to Rethymnon. Does that suit you, ladies?'

'It sounds wonderful,' breathed Marjorie. She was finding it overwhelmingly hot standing in the afternoon sun by the memorial.

It was late afternoon when they drew up outside the hotel in Rethymnon and both Marjorie and Saffron wished the hotel had a pool they could use.

Giovanni shook his head. 'You are hot so it sounds idyllic. When you put your foot in the water you would realise just how cold it is. Once the sun has gone off the swimming pools they cool very quickly. When you have showered you will feel refreshed and then we will drive to a very special restaurant I know. I will see if Kostas wishes to come with us tonight.'

'Do we have to dress up?' asked Saffron anxiously. 'I didn't really bring anything very smart with me.'

Giovanni shrugged. 'It is a village taverna. Whatever you wear will be suitable.'

It was early evening when they left the hotel in Rethymnon, Kostas accompanying them, and Giovanni drove confidently along the dark roads that led up to higher ground. He and Kostas talked in Greek as he drove and Marjorie closed her eyes. Despite having a short sleep when they had returned she still felt incredibly tired from the unaccustomed heat of the sun and the travelling they had done.

She was quite surprised when they reached a substantial taverna in a small village and Giovanni opened the car door for her.

'I think you will like this taverna. Manos cooks everything himself. You will not find his dishes on the menus elsewhere. It is local grown produce, all is fresh and all is natural. I hope you are hungry.'

'So,' Manos took the seat at the end of the table. 'What would you like to eat?'

'What would you suggest?'

'A selection. Not a meze, just a few dishes for you to try. I would like your opinion. Do they taste good or do they need more herbs or spices.' Manos wrote swiftly on his pad. 'To remind me,' he smiled. 'I will bring chips and salad also.'

Marjorie looked around the plain taverna. There was a large map pinned to one wall and beside the fireplace hung a lyra. 'Does Manos play?' she asked.

'He is a fine musician. I will see if I can persuade him to play a few notes before we leave. It is a shame his taverna is so far from the town. It means making a special trip to visit him and many of the locals are too lazy. They prefer to eat rubbish in the town and pay a high price rather than make an effort and drive for half an hour.'

'What is it called?'

'It is named after a pirate.' Giovanni pointed to the sign above the door. Cleverly carved was a wooden cutlass that looked suspiciously like the outline of Crete with the Greek letters spelling the name of the restaurant on the blade.

Manos placed plates on the table with a flourish, laid bottles of beer on their sides for the men and poured wine for Marjorie and Saffron from a bright red bottle. Saffron looked suspiciously at the golden coloured wine.

'It is good,' Manos assured her. 'Local wine, local bottles. We re-use here rather than throw away.'

Saffron took a sip and had to agree it was one of the smoothest wines she had ever tasted. 'I think that could be a disaster,' she smiled. 'It is the kind of wine that you drink far too much of because it is so delicious.'

Manos released the china stoppers from the bottles of beer and poured a glass for Giovanni and Kostas. 'Local bottles, but it is the usual beer,' he smiled. 'Drink and I will bring you some bread whilst you wait for your meal. I am waiting to hear your news, Kostas. How is the restoration going?'

Kostas stood over by the entrance to the kitchen and talked to Manos whilst he cooked. Tantalizing aromas began to waft out to them and Saffron found she was surprisingly hungry. She was disappointed when Manos placed a bowl of salad and plate of chips on the table, followed by some tomato balls. Politely she helped herself and passed the plates along. As she did so Manos appeared again, carrying more steaming plates.

'Here is chicken and here is pork,' he announced.

Saffron took a portion from each plate, cutting off a section of the pork and placing it in her mouth. 'Oh,' she exclaimed in surprise. 'That is delicious.'

Manos beamed. 'It is something new I am trying. It is not too sweet?'

'It's perfect. How do you do it?'

'The secret is mine. It is pork simmered in a wine and honey sauce. How much honey, how much wine, only I know that.'

Saffron attacked the chicken, again the meat melted in her mouth with flavours she had never associated with the meat before. 'What is in this?' she asked.

Manos shrugged. 'It is just chicken cooked in a tomato sauce. I add some herbs to bring out the flavour.'

Saffron glanced at him mischievously. 'And the kind and the quantities are your secret?'

'That is so.'

'You wouldn't consider giving me your recipes, I suppose?' asked Marjorie. 'I'd like to cook this back in England.'

'That would not be possible. Your chicken has to be fresh, not days old and kept in a frozen compartment. The same with your vegetables and herbs. They should be picked and used on the same day, not bought from a shop where they have been sitting in the sun until they are half cooked already.'

Marjorie smiled guiltily. She relied upon their freezer having the ingredients when she prepared a meal. 'When you live in London really fresh food is hard to come by,' she excused herself.

'Then you should live elsewhere,' stated Manos. 'In a village, as I do.'

'That's a good idea. I'll consider it.' Marjorie was doubtful that she would even find a village in England these days that was self supporting.

The conversation died as everyone ate from the dishes set before them. Marjorie had to admit that even the chips were excellent.

Manos shrugged. 'Potatoes, from the ground. I dug them and cleaned them myself. Now, are you ready for the sweet? It is very special. I give you only a little, just to try.'

Manos placed a small bowl on the table and provided everyone with a teaspoon.

'What is it?' asked Marjorie as she savoured a spoonful.

'Grapes in syrup. We call it *glyko staphilia*. You like?'

'It's wonderful. I could eat a bowl full.'

Manos shook his head. 'I do not think you would feel very well if you did that. It would be too much sweet.'

'I'd take the chance.' Marjorie dipped her spoon in again and allowed the sweetness to travel around her mouth. She took another spoonful and was about to take yet another when she realised she did not want any more.

Manos raised his eyebrows. 'Still you would like a bowl full?'

Marjorie shook her head. 'I couldn't. You're quite right, Manos. It's the perfect end to a wonderful meal, but you cannot eat very much of it.'

Manos nodded, satisfied that his judgement was validated.

Giovanni glanced surreptitiously at his watch. By Greek eating standards it was not late, but he had noticed that Marjorie had been asleep in the car and he had planned a considerable amount of sightseeing for them the following day.

'Manos,' he said in Greek 'it is getting late. Would you play for us, please, then we must leave. We have to drive back to Rethymnon and I am sure Marjorie and Saffron are tired.'

'Of course.' Manos lifted down the lyra from the fireplace and played a few notes before shaking his head. 'This is not good. Wait.' He hurried into the kitchen and returned with a large case. From inside he took a lyra and began to caress the strings gently. They listened in silent admiration at his skill and Marjorie let out a deep breath when he played the final note.

'Where did you learn to play?' she asked.

Manos shrugged. 'You just listen and play,' he replied. 'Now, one more, then I will give you your bill and bid you farewell.'

Saffron sat on the patio, her diary written up to date. She glanced at her watch, the time was going slowly. She wished her grandmother would emerge from her bedroom so she could look through the family photographs again with her. Much as she wanted to see them, she also wanted to join Marjorie on the beach and enjoy a swim. Despite having their swimming gear in the car there had been no opportunity to use it during their stay at Rethymnon.

'Hi, nothing to do?' Marcus sat down beside her.

'I've just finished writing up my diary for whilst we were in Rethymnon. You would never believe the number of places we saw.'

'Tell me.'

Saffron read out the list of places they had visited. 'On the way home we drove through the Amari Valley to Preveli and looked around the monastery. We stopped at Spili for lunch on the way back and Giovanni took us down to Matala, then Phaestos and on to Gortys. It was too late then to go anywhere else so we returned to the main coast road and drove home.'

Marcus smiled. 'Giovanni took us to some of those places the first year we visited. I have not been since.'

'Why didn't you say? I'm sure you could have come with us.'

Marcus shook his head. 'I would not go without Bryony and Marianne cannot manage to look after Grandma on her own. There needs to be someone around all the time. Can I get you a drink?'

'No thanks, I'm really waiting for Grandma. We're going to have another photograph session. Bryony says they go right back to her wedding day to Elias and her children and their children. There should be some of me when I was little.'

Marcus smiled. 'Bryony is still trying to get them properly sorted out. Grandma keeps changing her mind about who it is in some of the old photographs and the babies all look the same. Some have names on the back and Bryony has tried to do comparisons. Grandma always seems to disagree with her conclusions.'

'Are you happy living here?' asked Saffron of Marcus.

'It's good to see how happy Bryony is.'

Saffron shot him a glance. 'That didn't answer my question.'

'The whole family have been very good to us. If it wasn't for their generosity and kindness we would probably be living in a trailer and I would still be shovelling rubble.'

'I thought you worked for an insurance company?'

'I did.' Marcus smiled grimly, 'until Hurricane Katrina. We returned from Detroit when they said it was safe only to find we had no house and the insurance company where we had both worked had disappeared. We were left homeless and jobless.'

'That must have been awful.'

'It was. We managed to rent a trailer and Bryony found a job washing up. I was taken on by the local authorities to help clean up some of the devastation. No doubt we'd both still be doing that if Marianne hadn't insisted we came over here.'

'I have a lot to thank you for. If you hadn't looked after Grandma during the hurricane I doubt if she would have survived. I would never have had this opportunity to finally meet her.'

'Oh, I don't know. She strikes me as pretty tough and one of life's survivors, despite her age.'

'So, are you happy here?' Saffron asked again.

'Happy enough, I suppose.'

Saffron raised her eyebrows. 'Meaning?'

'I've been used to selling insurance, working with figures and dealing with people. Here I'm just a general handy man.'

'And you'd rather be doing something else?'

'Don't get me wrong. I don't mind painting chalet walls, there's a sense of accomplishment when they're all looking pristine ready for the next season, but it's not exactly using my brain.'

'Couldn't you help Uncle Yannis or Giovanni with the accounts?'

Marcus shook his head. 'They would never let me near those.'

'Why not? Don't they trust you?'

'Oh, I think they trust me, but they're not sure I would approve of their system.'

'Maybe yours would be better if you showed them.'

Marcus chuckled. 'Mine would be honest. There would be only one set of books.'

'What do you mean?'

'They keep two sets. One set has the true figures and the other has the figures they submit to the tax man.'

'Really?'

'Giovanni employs me to do the general maintenance. He pays me a wage, but according to the accounts he pays me double the amount I receive. Uncle Yannis says he pays Ourania and his sister a wage for working in the shop. He also draws a salary from it. That way the shop always makes a loss. Yannis also claims he pays Bryony for looking after Grandma and the house. Giovanni pays her for packing herbs.'

'That's only fair if she's doing the work.'

Marcus smiled. 'I agree, but packing a few herbs whilst she's talking to Grandma for a couple of hours hardly constitutes a job, but according to the books she spends three hours a day doing it. Everyone works that way apparently.'

'How do you know that's how the books are run?'

'Bryony told me. She heard Yannis and Giovanni working it out.'

'Suppose the tax man finds out?'

'You make it worth his while to turn a blind eye.'

Saffron looked at Marcus in amazement. 'Is that true?'

'Perfectly true.'

'Does Marianne know?'

'I expect so. She's lived here long enough.'

'And she doesn't mind?'

'What's there to mind about? We all complain about paying taxes. The Greeks generally have come up with a way to solve the problem.'

'You sound as though you approve.'

'I don't. If I was ever put in charge of the accounts I would have to run them honestly, but I know that whatever I did wouldn't change things. What would the point be of half a dozen people being honest and paying an extortionate amount of tax whilst everyone else paid very little? I just accept that's how things are over here.'

'Actually I doubt if they are any different over here from anywhere else in the world. I have no choice about paying tax. It's deducted from my salary, but if I had my own business I would probably try to pay as little as possible.'

Marcus smiled. 'You see, your Greek side is coming out,' he turned his head 'and so is Grandma. I'll leave you to it.'

'Well, what would you like to do this weekend?' asked John. 'You've been all the way up the coast, I hear, and driven around the Lassithi Plain. You spent yesterday looking at photos with Grandma and Bryony, so what's left?'

'I think a quiet couple of days would be in order,' smiled Saffron. 'Your father's been marvellous driving us around but he deserves a rest. Marjorie is tired also. We've been invited to Cathy and Vasilis for a meal one evening. There are still places I'd like to see. I wish I could walk the Samaria Gorge.'

John raised his eyebrows. 'I'm not sure Marjorie would be able to manage Samaria.'

Saffron smiled guiltily. 'I suppose I just want to cram in every possible experience in case I never come back.'

'Why shouldn't you come back? You will always be welcome here, you know that.'

Saffron nodded. 'I'm so thankful I have found my family, but it doesn't mean I can spend unlimited time in Crete. I have to work.' She sighed. 'If only you all lived in England and I could just drive over to see you it would be so much easier.'

'Why don't you come and live in Crete?'

Saffron laughed. 'That's just not possible. I'm a doctor and I don't speak Greek.'

'Doctors are always needed.'

'Can you imagine – I would need an interpreter – I don't even know the parts of the body in Greek.'

'I could teach you,' offered John eagerly.

Saffron shook her head. 'John, it's an impossible dream. I will have to make do with visiting you whenever I can, and don't forget, you can always visit us in London.'

'I'll see if Dad will cough up the fare when Nick is here. We could both come over. She'd love to visit London. Anyway, you still haven't told me what you want to do this weekend.'

'I'd love to go over to Spinalonga. I really enjoyed snorkelling last year. Would I be able to do it again?'

John smiled broadly. 'I hoped you'd choose that.'

Saffron removed their snorkelling equipment from the boat whilst John checked the moorings and placed the water proof cover over the outboard motor.

'Thank you, John. That was a fantastic day.'

John grinned at her. 'I'm glad you think so. I'll show you my photos later.'

'I'm sure Marjorie would like to see them.'

'I'll put up the screen and give a public performance before we eat tonight. Would that suit you?'

Saffron nodded eagerly. Although John had stayed close to her each time she had dived he had been continually busy with his camera.

'Where shall I put the gear?' she asked.

'Give it to me. I'll give it a rinse before I put it away.'

'Do you need a hand?'

John shook his head. 'You go and do whatever it is that women seem to need to do when they've been swimming.'

'A shower and a hair wash,' Saffron informed him.

'Don't believe you. I can do that in ten minutes. Women always seem to take an hour.'

'Our hair is longer. We need to dry it properly, not just rub a towel over it like you do.'

John grinned at her. 'I'm only teasing.' He relieved her of the masks and snorkels and walked up the steps from the beach behind her. 'I see we have a visitor,' he remarked.

'Oh, no,' exclaimed Saffron in horror. 'I've only got a towel round me!'

'Don't worry, it's Vasi. He'll not take any notice of how you look.'

'Is there another way to get to my room without crossing the patio?' asked Saffron anxiously.

'Only if you swim around to the main beach, walk back along the road and enter by the front door. Come on, don't be silly. It's pretty obvious that you've been swimming.' John waved his hand to Vasi who waved back to him.

John sat down on the ground beside Vasi and Saffron made a hurried retreat to her bedroom.

'So what brings you here?'

'I was passing, saw the car was in the drive and thought I'd just call in to say hello. I picked a bad time,' Vasi grinned. 'I came in the middle of the grand hair washing session. I could see you two returning so I thought I'd sit our here and wait.'

John pulled a wry face. 'I always try to escape when it's hair day. They make such a fuss over it. You'd think they were all budding beauty queens, not old ladies. Give me five minutes to put on some dry clothes and I'll be back with you.'

Marianne wheeled her grandmother out onto the patio. 'I'll leave you to talk to Vasi whilst I help Bryony to finish up. We'll not be long.'

'You look beautiful, Grandma.' John dropped a kiss on her forehead as he walked past.

'Thank you, dear,' she acknowledged the compliment absently. 'So, Vasi, what brings you down here?'

Vasi shrugged. 'Just passing. I thought I'd drop in to say hello.'

'To anyone in particular?' Annita was amused to see the young man blush at her question.

'Just generally. Would you like a glass of wine?'

'Well,' Annita pretended to consider. 'It's a little early for me, but I won't say no.' Once he had handed her the glass she raised it to him. 'To your success,' she said.

Vasi frowned.

'Come on, Vasi. There's no need to be shy with me. I saw the way you looked at her when you came to the barbecue – and why were you so long in the kitchen together? She's a nice girl. I wish you success.'

Vasi smiled with embarrassment. 'I think you're being a little premature. We were talking about my grandfather. I'd just like to get to know her a bit better.'

'So why don't you ask her to go into Aghios Nikolaos with you this evening? Take her out to dinner somewhere nice. You hardly ever have five minutes on your own here. Not that I'm complaining, mind. I'd hate to go back to living alone again.'

'Do you think I could, ask her out to dinner, I mean? The family wouldn't be offended?'

'Why should they be? She's on holiday. It will be another experience for her to be taken out to dinner.'

'Do you think Marjorie would expect to come with her?'

'I'll make sure she doesn't accept your invitation. Now, if that bottle is within your reach you could just top up my glass for me.' Annita held out her half empty glass and Vasi complied.

Saffron blushed. 'Thank you, Vasi. But I'm not sure. John was planning to show his latest photos this evening.'

'They'll keep. You can look at them tomorrow.'

Marjorie shook her head. 'I really do feel far too tired. I'm looking forward to having an early night. There's no reason why you shouldn't go, Saffie.'

Saffron hesitated; would it be rude for her to refuse or rude for her to accept? The invitation had been given to her and Marjorie.

'You go with Vasi and enjoy yourself. You'll have plenty of time for an evening in when you're as old as I am.' Annita repeated her remark in Greek to Marisa who nodded her head in agreement.

'Well, if you're sure and it won't upset Marianne's catering arrangements.'

Vasi drove Saffron home just after midnight. Once she had overcome her initial shyness she found she enjoyed the man's company, finding their conversation flowed easily and he made her laugh. As he stopped the car outside he took her hand in his.

'I would like to see you again, Saffie.'

'I don't know if that will be possible. We have only a few more days, and I have to think about Marjorie.'

'Of course. I do not expect you to change any of your arrangements to suit me. I will give you my card. It has my mobile telephone and also my e-mail address. Call me on either if you have time to go out again.'

Saffron placed the card safely in her purse. 'Thank you, Vasi, for a lovely evening. If we are able to repeat it I will call you.'

'Promise?'

'I promise,' laughed Saffron. 'I really did enjoy myself.'

Annita picked up Elias's photo. 'Well, what do you think Elias? Vasi's a nice boy. He'd make a good partner for Saffie. There are two problems as I see it. Would Saffie be willing to give up her career as a doctor and would she be willing to leave Marjorie? The woman has obviously been good to her and you can see how fond of her Saffie is. Maybe the answer would be to find a suitable partner for Marjorie. If I could still get around I could look for a candidate and play match maker. One of Yannis's friends, maybe, but a little younger. If I talked to Marisa or Ourania they might know someone. I expect you think I'm being a silly old woman, Elias, but I like to see people happy together.'

Marjorie waited until they had breakfasted before she asked Saffron if she had enjoyed her evening.

'Very much,' she replied. 'Vasi is good company.'

'Where did you eat?'

'I've no idea of the name. It was down by the pool. We sat out on the balcony. Vasi seemed to know the owner. It was a shame you didn't feel like coming.'

Marjorie shook her head. 'I was very glad of an early night. I don't think I've been in bed before midnight since we arrived. It's beginning to take its toll.'

'You can always make up for it when we get back home. The time has gone so quickly. I can't believe we leave on Wednesday.' Saffron looked sad. 'I shall miss everyone and this beautiful place.'

'You can always come back.'

Saffron nodded. 'I know, but it will only be for a two week holiday again. I'd like to experience living here. I've asked John and Nicola to visit us in London. You don't mind, do you?'

'Not a bit, but I'm not sure where we'll put them both.'

'I can give Nicola my room and I'm sure John won't mind sleeping downstairs on the settee.'

'I leave it up to you, Saffie. We'll have to think of places that I can take them whilst you're working.'

'That's easy. I'm sure they'll want to visit the city and possibly a day trip to the coast. It won't even matter if it's raining. There are so many museums and art galleries where you can go.'

'Talking of going, are we expected to be ready to go somewhere this morning?'

Saffron nodded. 'We're going to have a fairly quiet day. Giovanni said he would drive us up to Kritsa. There's a wonderful little church there apparently. The inside is completely covered with murals of the Saints. He suggested we had a snack up there and drove back through the country roads and visited Kato and Pano Elounda and the other little villages behind Elounda. We'll be back in plenty of time to get ready to go to Cathy and Vasilis for dinner tonight.'

John had sent a brief email to Nicola recently, telling her that Dimitris's mother had died, but Antonia had given birth to a girl the previous day.

Now he sat at his computer and wrote to her of the visits Marjorie and Saffron had made during the week and the day he had taken her snorkelling on Spinalonga.

"Considering she'd only done it once the year before, she's pretty good," he wrote. "Now, here's the real news. When we got back Vasi was waiting at the house. He's obviously quite keen on her. He took her out to dinner in Aghios Nikolaos and on to a night club. Apparently he's asked her to go out with him again before she goes back to England. Even better than that, Saff has asked if we'd like to visit her in London. Do you think you can persuade your Dad to come up with the fare? Let me know, then I can suggest some dates to her."

Nicola read the mail and replied immediately. "I'd love to visit London and I should be able to pay my own fare with my earnings from the diner. I've been saving my wages up, really ready for when I go to Uni, but I'm sure Dad will give me a loan if necessary. You check with your parents when they can spare you and sort it out with Saffie. I'll have to bring some warmer clothes with me if we're going to England and probably a waterproof. I hear they have a lot of rain over there at all times of the year. Keep me posted re the romance between Vasi and Saffie. It's time he found himself a wife!"

John smiled with delight. He had not expected Nicola to turn down the opportunity to visit England, and her parents could hardly object if she could pay her own fare. All he had to do now was convince his parents that there was a time when they would not be dependent upon him during the season and then he would speak to Saffron and Marjorie.

Saffron was not surprised when they arrived at Cathy and Vasilis's house to see that an extra place had been laid at the table.

'Vasi asked if he could drop by as he would be in the area. He said he may be a little late and we were not to wait for our meal for him,' smiled Cathy.

Marianne looked at her archly. 'And what business would that be on a Sunday evening?' she asked.

'I didn't ask him. If it concerns the hotels he'll talk to Vasilis about it. He did say something about buying a new car. That could be the reason he's down here.'

Marianne smiled to herself. She thought it very unlikely Vasi was in the area to buy a new car or any other reason other than an excuse to see Saffron again. Either Cathy was acting her part quite innocently or she truly had no knowledge of her stepson's interest in their English relative.

Marjorie raised her eyebrows and looked at Saffron with an unspoken question and Saffron refused to meet her glance.

'Has John told you we've invited him and Nicola to come to England?' Saffron asked brightly.

Giovanni nodded. 'I'll have to look at our bookings, see when we will be reasonably quiet. August and the beginning of September is quite out of the question.'

'When are you expecting Nicola?'

'She should be here mid July.'

'So why doesn't she come straight to us in London and John

come over and join her? She has to break her journey and get a connecting flight. It would be silly for her to arrive here one day and leave again on the next. That way they could both be back with you by August.'

'That sounds practical,' said Vasilis. 'Would you be able to extend an invitation to Vasi at some time? I know he would love to see London.'

'Of course,' smiled Marjorie. 'You are all welcome, but not all at once. We have only a small house.'

Saffron frowned. 'You have to remember that I am working every day. I won't be able to have time off to take him out and show him the sights.'

'I'm sure he'll be able to amuse himself. He can hire a car and go where he pleases.'

Saffron pursed her lips. The towns they had driven through on Crete had been busy and congested, but they were nothing like the streets of London, particularly at a rush hour.

Nicola let herself into her home and called out to her parents to let them know she had returned from the diner.

'Are you going to join us? We're having a drink in the garden,' called back Elizabeth.

'I just want to check my mail.'

Elizabeth smiled to herself. It was almost a ritual with Nicola. Each time she returned to the house she would check her email and her mother knew it was in the hope of having mail from John.

"Hi, Nick. Fab news. Dad has said O.K. to England. DO NOT BOOK YOUR FLIGHT HERE YET. Details tomorrow. Missing you. J."

'Yes!' Nicola punched the air. If John was able to go to London there would be no reason why she should not go with him. She wondered why he had told her not to book her flight to Crete, but no doubt he had a good reason. Smiling happily she joined her parents and Eleanor in the garden.

Vasi hesitated before pressing in the code to open the gates of his parent's house. The excuse he had for calling was lame in the extreme. Should he turn round now and drive back to Rethymnon? He could always telephone later and say he had been delayed and felt it was too late to drop in on them. He shook himself mentally. He was such a coward.

His father would have had no such scruples had he wished to approach a woman he was interested in. He had told Vasi often enough. "Be bold, son. Tell her how you feel. If nothing else she'll be flattered and you just keep sweet talking her from then on. If she rebuffs you, there's nothing lost except your pride. If she accepts you, well, you don't need me to tell you what to do after that."

Vasi had taken his father's words to heart and they had stood him in good stead with his numerous lady friends over the years, although he had a feeling their capitulation often had more to do with his bank balance than his charisma. None of them had lasted more than a few months, by which time they were bored with each other and the parting had been mutual.

He stretched his hand out again and keyed in the code, waiting for the gates to swing open wide before he drove through. As he parked before the house the dogs strolled over to him and once out of the car he pulled at their ears gently.

'Fine couple of guard dogs you are. Suppose someone had stolen my car and was coming here to rob the house? You wouldn't have alerted anyone.' They followed him to the front door and stepped back dutifully as he entered. They knew they were not allowed in the house.

Vasi swallowed, hoping he would not sound nervous. 'Hi there. Cathy? Dad? I've made it.' He walked into the dining room and planted a kiss on Cathy's cheek.

'You're not too late. We've only had our first course. I'll bring yours in and we'll wait whilst you catch up.'

Vasi bobbed his head at their guests. 'Evening everyone. I'm sorry I was late. I'll just give this to Cathy then I'll join you.'

'Give me what?' Cathy re-entered the room, pushing a hostess trolley with a plate of assorted small fish and another of warm bread.

'You left your pashmina at the hotel. I thought you might need it.' Vasi's face burned as he offered the excuse.

'Did I?' Cathy frowned. 'I certainly didn't have it with me when we came last week.'

'Maybe it isn't yours.'

Cathy shrugged. 'You'd better take it back with you. It could belong to a guest. Put it over there and come and sit down. We're drinking white wine as there is chicken to follow the fish. You can have a beer if you prefer.'

'Wine is fine by me.' Vasi turned to Marjorie and Saffron. 'So what have you done today?'

Vasi cocked his head to one side. 'What has disturbed the dogs?'

Vasilis frowned. 'I'd better go and check them. You closed the gates properly, Vasi?'

'Of course. I'll go and have a look. One of them has probably cornered a cat and is calling to the other for help.'

Vasi returned quickly, smiling with amusement. 'They have found a hedgehog. It has rolled itself up and they keep nosing at it and barking when they get pricked by its spines.'

'A hedgehog? I didn't realise you had hedgehogs over here. I've never seen one that hasn't been squashed on a road.'

'Come and see, Saffie. The garden looks very different at night with the floodlights.'

'Are you coming, Marjorie?'

Marjorie shook her head. 'I really don't feel I can move after that wonderful meal. I'll see the garden when we leave and I've seen a hedgehog before.'

'Put this round you. It could be a little chilly out there now. We're quite high up and tend to catch the wind here.' She handed Saffron the pashmina that Vasi had brought to the house earlier, noticing the price tag was still attached.

Vasi opened the front door and led the way into the front garden. Both dogs were nosing at the hedgehog, yelping and jumping back as a spine stuck into them.

Saffron laughed. 'Silly things. You'd think once they had hurt their noses they would leave it alone.'

Vasi shrugged. 'They are superbly trained, but have little common sense. I will rescue the poor hedgehog.' Vasi motioned to the dogs to move to one side and scooped the prickly ball up in his hands. He and Saffron walked to the shrubbery that was planted by the wall and he pushed the hedgehog into it.

'We will take the dogs for a short walk to a different area. I hope then they will lose the scent and forget the creature. It was a good excuse to come outside for a few minutes. So, what do you think of my father's house?'

'It's very grand.'

'Do you like it?'

'Well,' Saffron hesitated. 'It just seems so big for two people.'

Vasi nodded. 'Pappa built it with large rooms with the idea that they would have children. They would then divide the rooms and it would be more of a family home. It didn't happen. When Cathy's parents stayed here it was lovely, it felt lived in. I only came at the weekends at first, but later when I was here just with Pappa and Cathy it was so lonely.'

'Were you away at school?'

'No, I lived with my aunt and uncle. Pappa was working all week and we would go to the hotel and stay there, that was how I came to fall into the pool. Pappa and Cathy lived at the hotel whilst this house was being built so the arrangement continued until I was almost ten. Then I was expected to live here and Pappa took me in to school each day in Aghios Nikolaos and arranged a taxi to bring me home. The other children laughed at me. They called me a baby because I was met each day and not allowed to play football with them in the street.'

'You didn't have a very happy childhood.'

Vasi shrugged. 'I cannot say I was unhappy. It was just different from all the other boys. 'It is all so – so – perfect.' He shuddered. 'Perfect and isolated. Like one of Grandpa's castles in his fairy stories.'

'Your father and Cathy appear to be happy living here and it's not that far from the villages.'

Vasi nodded. 'The villages are full of elderly people. The young have moved away. You need to go into Elounda if you need anything. Pappa goes in to work each day. I'm not sure he would be so happy if he had to spend all day here on his own.'

'But Cathy doesn't mind?'

Vasi shrugged. 'She spends a good deal of time with her friend, Marion. She used to walk down to the villages or Elounda but that is becoming difficult for her. The hill is steep. Due to her old injuries she has arthritis.'

'She doesn't drive?'

'She has never driven since her car accident. She does not have the confidence.'

'I don't think I'd be brave enough to drive over here.'

Vasi smiled mockingly at her. 'It is not so difficult. Now if she wants to go anywhere Lambros, the gardener, takes her. He works in the garden each day, but he is also employed as a driver. If he was unavailable I think she would very soon be asking Pappa to move elsewhere.'

'When she showed us around the other day she implied that you might not want to live here.'

Vasi shrugged. 'The house is too large for one person, even for two. The problem is what to do with it eventually? It is not big enough to convert into a hotel. I could probably sell the land with the olive trees and hope the buyer would want the house also. We will see.'

'But suppose you married and had children? Then you would need a house this size.'

'That is not likely to happen.'

'You don't plan to get married?'

'Maybe. One day. When I meet the right person. What about you? You are not married.'

Saffron felt herself flush. 'I was married. My husband died.'

'I am sorry to hear that.'

'It was a while ago. I'm over it now.'

Vasi placed his arm on her shoulder with the intention of drawing her closer. For a moment she relaxed against him; then he felt her body stiffen and moved his hand away rapidly. 'We should return inside. They will be wondering what kept us so long in the garden.'

'We were saving the hedgehog.' Saffron was amused that he should find it necessary to make an excuse for their absence.

Nicola opened her computer to check her mail as soon as she arrived home from High School. She hated being reliant upon the computer to communicate with John. They were forbidden to telephone each other having initially run up an enormous bill each during the first month that she returned home. She sucked in her breath eagerly. There was mail from John and it looked like a long letter. She read his missive through twice, wrote down the relevant instructions regarding booking a flight to Heathrow and another to Crete a fortnight later. He would fly to England the previous day and meet her at the airport when she arrived. All she needed to do was let him know her flight number and time of arrival.

Anxiously Nicola began to search the airline schedules. She could not arrive during the early hours of the morning and expect John to meet her. She covered a piece of scrap paper with times that she crossed out, revised and crossed out again. She would have to ask her father to help her. She bit her lip. She hadn't even asked their permission to go to London.

Nicolas eyed his older daughter sternly when she explained her dilemma. 'I'm not sure, Nicola. It's one thing us allowing you to go to relatives in Crete on your own, but we don't know these people.'

'John will be with me. He knows them and I know he'll look after me. I can pay my own fare anyway.'

Nicolas sighed. 'I'm not giving you permission until I have spoken to Giovanni. Give me your passport.'

'Dad!'

'I mean it. I'm not having you running off anywhere without our full permission. When I've spoken to Giovanni and Marianne I shall want the telephone number of this woman Saffron. Until I'm a hundred per cent satisfied that you'll be safe in their care you're staying here.'

Nicola felt tears stinging at the back of her eyes. This was so unfair. She was nearly eighteen and her father was behaving as if she were only eight. She glared at her father mutinously.

'Go and get your passport. Until I have it in my hand I'm not even prepared to discuss this with you.'

Furiously Nicola left the room and returned with her passport. She slapped it down on the table. 'Satisfied?'

'There's no need to be rude. I suggest you go and get on with your homework.'

Nicola tossed her head and flounced out of the room whilst her father looked after her. This visit obviously meant a good deal to her, she didn't usually behave badly. He had to admit it was an opportunity she might never have again. He would see what Elizabeth said and then telephone his cousin.

Nicola wrote an impassioned email to John, declaring that her father was being both unreasonable and unfair. If he refused to allow her to meet John in London she would find a way to sneak back her passport and take the first flight available to Heathrow, even if John was not there. She was sure if she mailed Saffron she would be allowed to stay with her until John arrived.

She was surprised when her 'phone rang an hour later and it was John. 'Nick, don't be daft. If you start trying to run off to England your father will have the police department after you. They could confiscate your passport and refuse to let you have it back or to get another until you're twenty one. You wouldn't even be able to come to Crete then; and you'd have a criminal record.'

'But, John...'

'No, listen, Nick. Be sensible. You said your dad was going to talk to mine. They like Saff. I'm sure he'll say you'll be safe with her. If you do anything stupid you could mess up all our plans for the summer. Wait and see what your dad says. At least you'll be able to come to Crete.'

'But you'll be in London.'

'I could say I've changed my mind and stay here.'

'Oh, John, that wouldn't be fair. Why should you miss out because of me?'

'You mean more to me than a trip to London, Nick. I've been crossing the days off the calendar since the beginning of May.'

Nicola swallowed and tried to stop the tears that were threatening to fall. 'I do want to be with you, John, but you mustn't cancel your trip because of me. I'd feel guilty.'

'My mind's made up. I'm not going without you. What would I do with myself? Saff is out working all day and Marjorie is lovely, but not exactly a bundle of energy. I'm sure she wouldn't want to go to half the places I have on my list. I'd probably be stuck in a museum every day. The sea's miles away so I couldn't even go for a swim. I'd have a better time here working. Believe me, Nick, I don't want to go without you.'

'Are you sure?'

'Quite sure,' answered John firmly. 'Hey, I'll tell you what, I'll ask Saff to telephone your Dad. Why didn't I think of that before? They're with us until Wednesday. As soon as they come back I'll talk to her.'

'Where've they gone?'

'Dad's taken them to Sitia and Vai; they're coming back through Ierapetra.'

'What time will they be back?'

'In time for dinner. Leave it with me, Nick. I'm sure Dad wouldn't have agreed I could go if he wasn't sure it would be okay. I'll get Dad and Saff together and ask them to phone your Dad. If he still says no then we're both in Elounda for a couple of months as usual. That's not a hardship, is it? We'll be able to enjoy ourselves as we did last year, if you understand what I mean.'

Despite herself Nicola had to smile. 'I know exactly what you mean and I can't wait.'

'Then don't mess up with your Dad. If he says no to London just accept it. Provided we can be together it doesn't matter which country we're in. Love you, Nick.'

Before Nicola had a chance to reply her 'phone went dead and she guessed John's mother was in the vicinity. She sat back down at her computer. She must write another mail to John and this time it would be a little calmer than her previous one.

Nicolas telephoned Crete and spoke to Bryony who told him Giovanni had taken their visitors out for the day. 'Do you want me to ask him to call you when they return?' she asked.

Nicolas hesitated. 'Yes, but in the meantime I can speak to you. Saffron and Marjorie – what are they like?'

'How do you mean? They're very English, but trying hard to pretend that they fit in with the family.'

Nicolas shook his head. 'No, I mean are they decent people? I know Saffron is your sister, and this might be difficult, but...'

'Nicolas, what are you trying to say?'

'I understand they've invited Nicola to spend a couple of weeks with them in London. Will they look after her? Will she be safe?'

Bryony gave her gurgling laugh. 'She'll be as safe there as she is in New Orleans, probably safer. Nicola met Saffron last year and Marjorie is very ordinary and law abiding. Giovanni and Marianne are quite happy for John to go and stay and you know he'd look after Nicola. I'll ask Giovanni to call you when they get back and I'm sure he'll put your mind at rest. Saffron really is a very nice person.'

Nicolas sighed. 'I'm just worried. You hear of such awful happenings in London.'

'It's no different from any big city. I doubt if there's any more crime there than in New Orleans and you wouldn't stop her going up there for the day, would you?'

'Well,' Nicolas hesitated. 'It would depend upon which part she was going to.'

'Yes, and I'm sure it's the same in London. Saffron will know where they must avoid and I'm sure both John and Nicola will be sensible and take her advice.'

Nicolas sighed. 'I'd still like to speak to Giovanni.'

'Of course. I'll ask him to telephone as soon as they return.'

'Do you realise that breaking your flight and staying in London will be considerably more expensive?'

'I can pay any extra that it costs. I've saved all my wages from the diner,' offered Nicola anxiously.

'You'll need that for spending money in London. England is expensive.'

'Oh, Dad, you mean I can go?' Nicola flung her arms round her father. 'Really and truly? I'm so excited. Thank you a million times. Can I 'phone John? I won't talk long to him.'

'Five minutes, no more, and I'll be timing your call.'

'I've never known two weeks go so quickly. We've done so much. I can't thank you enough.' Saffron hugged Marianne.

'You know you're welcome to come back at any time. We enjoyed having you.'

'You and Giovanni must come to England. We're looking forward to having John and Nicola. I understand John's making a list of everywhere they want to go and we'll make sure they see as much as possible.'

Giovanni picked up their luggage and walked towards the car. 'We ought to make a move. The traffic can get heavy near the airport.'

Saffron sighed. 'I do wish we could stay longer.'

Giovanni held her case in his hand. 'Am I putting your case in or taking Marjorie's out?' he asked.

'It will have to go in. I'm going to start playing the lottery. You never know, I might be a lucky winner.' Saffron smiled tremulously.

'Well, someone has to win. Vasilis did. Jump in Bryony if you're coming with us.'

'Of course I'm coming. Have you said goodbye to everyone, Saffie?'

Saffron nodded, recalling the tears she had shed as she bid her grandmother farewell. She felt unreasonably guilty at leaving her, knowing they might never meet again. Ourania and Marisa had kissed and hugged her, whilst Yannis had taken her hand, kissed her cheeks and assured her that the vases Marjorie had chosen were already on their way. John had said goodbye, his eyes sparkling with anticipation of his visit to London and Marcus had waited in the background for his turn.

Saffron turned and took a last look at Spinalonga as they drove along the coast road, the tears running down her cheeks.

Bryony held Saffron's hand tightly whilst they waited for her luggage to be checked through. 'I shall miss you,' she said. 'We had nowhere near enough time together.'

'You and Marcus will have to come to London. I'm sure once

John and Nicola return they'll tell you everything they've done and you'll be so envious.'

'Saffie!'

Saffron turned in surprise. 'Vasi, I wasn't expecting to see you here.'

'I had to come to the airport to collect some visitors. I thought it would be a good opportunity to say goodbye to you. You will keep in touch, won't you?' Vasi asked her anxiously.

'Of course. I have your email address.'

'Promise?'

'I promise,' laughed Saffron.

'And you will tell me when you plan to come again so we can meet?'

'Yes, but I doubt if it will be before next year.'

'No matter. I will be here or maybe I could come to England?'

'You'd be very welcome.'

'I hope so.' Vasi gazed at her intently before taking her in his arms and kissing her on both cheeks.

Bryony raised her eyebrows at Giovanni with an unspoken question. He shrugged his shoulders. Vasi was probably just being polite to their relative.

JULY 2006

Saffron sat at her computer. She read the mail from John, and smiled in amusement. He had included a long list of places he thought he and Nicola would like to visit whilst they were in London. It included a visit to Lands End, Covent Garden and Kew Gardens for him to indulge in his passion for photography. She would have to explain about Covent Garden, although she had thought they would enjoy a visit to the area, but Lands End was out of the question due to the distance. She read the one from Nicola, who wanted to visit Saddlers Wells and Buckingham Palace, and Saffron wondered how John felt about an evening watching ballet dancing.

It took her most of the evening to work out a manageable itinerary for their first week. For the first couple of days she made sure she included places that Marjorie would be happy to visit with them; once they had become used to travelling on the underground and the buses they could decide for themselves where they would like to go each day.

It was a week before she thought about mailing Vasi. She was not sure if he had given her his card and asked her to keep in touch from politeness or if he was genuinely interested in keeping up their acquaintance with a view to visiting England. She had no idea what to say to him and having mentioned how cold and wet it was by comparison to Crete she sat with her chin on her hands. She added that she was busy at the hospital and was looking forward to the visit of John and Nicola. Deciding that the few lines had to suffice she sent her regards to his parents and signed off as "your friend, Saffie."

To her surprise there was a long email waiting for her from Vasi when she opened her computer. The hotels were particularly busy now the school holidays had commenced and he had started a children's club where their parents could leave them for an hour or so and have some time to themselves to go into the town. It was proving popular with the adults once they had satisfied themselves that their children were safe and those looking after them could speak their mother tongue.

He was considering converting a part of the lower floor of the hotel in Heraklion into a gymnasium. Half the rooms down there were used only to store surplus equipment for the kitchen or bedrooms and he was sure that with some organisation he would have more than enough space. He wanted Saffron's opinion about the idea. Were tourists interested in physical activities whilst they were on holiday or did they only want to lie in the sun? What kind of equipment would prove most popular? How much did exercise bikes cost in England? Would it be cheaper to import them from England rather than Athens? Were they more expensive than walking machines, or weights, or rowing machines?

Saffron shook her head in despair. What did she know about such things? She enjoyed swimming and walking, but she had never felt inclined to join a gymnasium and take part in a fitness regime. Surely Vasi could look up the information he needed on the internet and be content to discuss the weather with her?

John landed at Gatwick and tried to curb his impatience as he waited for his luggage to finally reach him on the carousel. He was pleased he had taken Saffron's advice and included a pullover in his hand luggage. Despite the number of people milling around the area was chilly and very depressing. After half an hour of watching the screen to see which area would finally return his case to him he hauled it off the carousel and began to walk down the corridor to the exit. He knew Saffron would be waiting for him, having sent her a text when they landed and received a reply, but the airport seemed so vast he hoped he would be able to locate her.

He sighed with relief when he saw her waving to him, a broad grin spreading over his face. 'Am I glad to see you! I thought I was going to spend the whole two weeks waiting for my luggage to arrive.'

Saffron waited whilst he kissed her cheeks. 'It's good to see you, John. All we have to do now is find where I parked the car.' She led the way out and across a road into a multi-storey car park where she stopped in front of a lift.

John waited whilst she placed some money in a machine and withdrew a card before following her to her car and lifting his case into the boot. He walked around to the front of the car opening the door to the driver's seat.

Saffron laughed at him. 'Fancy driving, do you?'

John blushed. 'I forgot. You drive on the other side.'

'Just remember that when you're crossing roads. I'm serious, John. It's so easy to look the wrong way and step out in front of oncoming traffic.'

Saffron drove slowly down the ramps until they reached the exit and she placed her card in the slot allowing the barrier to rise. Once out of the car park she handed John her mobile phone. 'If you want to 'phone home and let them know you're safely here use my mobile. I've an old phone at home that works, it just needs some credit, and it will be cheaper for you to use that whilst you're here.'

'I don't expect you to pay for my 'phone calls,' protested John.

'I'm not going to. I'll top it up and you can pay me. If you need to contact Marjorie or myself or want to phone home whilst you're here it will be considerably cheaper than using yours. If there's any credit left on it when you leave I'll buy it back from you.'

'What's the time difference between here and New Orleans?' asked John as he pulled his own mobile from his pocket.

'I haven't the faintest idea. If Nicola is arriving tomorrow afternoon the chances are that she's already at the airport. I know the flight takes about fifteen hours by the time she's made her connections.'

'I'll send her a text.' John tapped the message out and waited. There was no reply. He sat back with a contented smile on his face. 'I guess she's already on her way.'

John looked out of the car window as they drove through countryside and skirted small towns before entering the suburbs that led to the area where Marjorie and Saffron lived. 'We'll go by underground tomorrow. It only takes about forty minutes and it's much easier than driving there,' Saffron informed him.

'Why did you bring the car today, then? I wouldn't have minded travelling by underground. I've never been on a train.'

Saffron looked at him in surprise. 'You've never – no, I suppose not. There aren't any trains on Crete. If we'd travelled that way today it would have meant changing trains and then catching a taxi.'

'I'm looking forward to riding on a train,' John smiled. 'Do they go as fast as the ones in Japan?'

'I hope not! Our railways were not designed for that kind of speed.' Saffron applied her brakes and John lurched forward. 'Sorry about that. If only pedestrians would look before they stepped off the pavement.'

'Home from home,' grinned John. 'Do you think I could have a go at driving your car whilst I'm here?'

'Definitely not,' Saffron replied sharply. 'You haven't passed your driving test yet. Just because I agreed to ride pillion on the back of your bike doesn't mean I'd trust you with my car, besides, you don't know the rules of the road over here. You tried to get in the wrong side, remember.'

'Worth a try,' John winked at her. 'I showed you how to snorkel; you could have given me a driving lesson.'

'The only thing I was likely to bump into was a fish!'

'Hello, Marjorie. It's good to see you again. Have you recovered from rushing around Crete?'

'I enjoyed it. Your father was so good and took us to so many places. We'd never have managed to see a quarter of that on our own.'

'Saff wanted to walk the Samaria Gorge.'

Marjorie shook her head. 'I don't think I could have managed that.'

'That's what I told Saff. Where shall I put this?' John pointed to his case.

'Bring it upstairs for tonight. You can have my room. When Nicola arrives I'm afraid you'll be relegated to the sofa downstairs.'

John frowned. 'Actually, Nick and I would be quite happy to share.'

Saffron raised her eyebrows.

'Would you believe we're both frightened of being in a strange house in the dark on our own?'

'Not for one minute. Are your parents aware of this arrangement?'

'I'm sure they know.'

'How about if I 'phoned your mother and checked?'

John looked dubiously at Saffron. 'You wouldn't.'

'I take that answer as they don't know.'

'Well,' John hesitated. 'They must have guessed by now. Nick was always being seen leaving my room early in the morning.'

Saffron sighed. 'I suppose I might as well agree. If I don't you'll only be sneaking off together. You are being sensible enough to take precautions, I hope?'

'Definitely,' John assured her. 'We've an agreement. Marriage when we're twenty five and children after that. Why waste the years in between?'

'I'm not sure what Marjorie will say.'

'I'm sure you'll be able to make her see that the arrangement suits all of us. I appreciate you turning out of your bedroom for us. We could always go to a hotel if Marjorie is really anti.'

'Don't be silly. There's one condition, John.'

'We won't make a racket and keep you awake.'

Saffron smiled. 'Good, but I was about to say that if by any chance you do find an accident has happened you do *not* tell your parents that it happened whilst you were under our roof.'

'I swear I won't.' John crossed himself. 'You're great, Saff, you really are.'

Marjorie was not as complacent about the sleeping arrangements as Saffron. 'If they're sleeping together behind their parents' backs we shouldn't condone it.'

'In principle I agree with you, but even if we try to keep them apart they'll find a way. Accidents are far more likely to happen when a liaison is unplanned.' Saffron gave a little shudder when she thought back to an impetuous moment that could have wrecked her career and her life forever. 'It's the way young people behave these days. Think back to when I was seeing Martin. I used to go away for the weekend with him.'

Marjorie nodded. 'I never tried to stop you. I wish I had.'

'You couldn't have said anything to stop me at the time. I had to find out the hard way. Just turn a blind eye, Marjorie. We don't want to spoil these weeks for them by being prudish.'

John did not enjoy his first experience of riding on an underground train. Travelling through dark tunnels and hearing unfamiliar noises unnerved him, although Saffron appeared quite unperturbed by the rocking movement. He looked at his watch continually. They were already late, her plane would have landed.

He followed Saffron into the arrivals area at Heathrow airport and waited anxiously for a sight of Nicola. 'Where is she?' he asked as he looked at his watch again.

'Waiting for her luggage to arrive I expect. We've only been here ten minutes.'

'But she landed almost an hour ago. It never takes this long in Heraklion.'

Saffron smiled at him sympathetically. 'Stop fretting and be patient. This is a much larger airport than Heraklion. She has to come out this way so we won't miss her.'

John rose on his toes and tried to look above the heads of the other people who were also waiting. A number of people began to appear and Saffron touched his arm. 'This could be her flight beginning to come through now.'

'There she is!'

John left Saffron and rushed towards Nicola, only to be restrained at the barrier by a security guard until Nicola had passed through to the waiting area. He clasped Nicola tightly to him and they stood locked together, blocking the exit, until a man with a loaded trolley demanded that he moved. Reluctantly John released her and began to drag her case to where Saffron was waiting for them.

John hardly noticed the return journey on the underground. He held Nicola's hand tightly whilst she chatted to Saffron, asking questions about London that had never occurred to him. She wanted to know when they could visit Buckingham Palace and would they be able to see the Queen whilst they were there.

Saffron laughed. 'I doubt it. If you are very lucky she may be paying an official visit somewhere and her car will go past and you'll catch a glimpse of her.'

Nicola looked disappointed. 'I thought she held garden parties.'

'Only for very special people and you have to be invited.'

'Have you been to one?'

'Goodness, no. I'm certainly not special. Have you got your tickets ready? We get off at the next stop and you'll need them.'

John carried Nicola's case up to the bedroom. He placed it on the floor and took her in his arms once again.

'It's so good to see you, Nick. I've really missed you. Have you missed me?'

'Of course I have. I would have died if Mum and Dad had said I couldn't come over this year. I've saved all my wages from that crummy diner where I work so I could pay my own fare if necessary.'

'How are you feeling?'

Nicola looked at him puzzled. 'Fine.'

'No, I mean, do you have jet lag. Do you need a sleep?'

'I managed to sleep on the 'plane. It probably won't hit me until the early evening.'

'It will be a good excuse for us to have an early night.'

'What do you mean?'

'We're sharing.'

'You mean, both of us, in the same room? How did you swing that one?'

'I told Saff we'd both be frightened of the dark,' grinned John. Nicola looked at him in disbelief and he shook his head. 'No, I told Saff the truth and she decided she could go along with it. I don't know what she said to Marjorie, but we have two whole weeks together without having to sneak in and out of our rooms and hope we're not seen.'

'You're amazing, John. Is that why I love you?'

John pulled her towards him again and Nicola shook her head. 'No, John. We ought to go down. We can't be that blatant, besides, Saffie did say that she and Marjorie would be going out this afternoon.' She gave a giggle. 'Do you think that is to give us some time alone?'

'I'm sure it is. I just hope they're gone for hours.'

Todd entered the diner and smiled at the assistant. 'Morning, Melanie.'

'Morning, Todd. What can I get for you?'

'I'll just have a soda for now. On your own today?'

Melanie smiled resignedly. 'I will be for the next few days before the new girl starts. Then I'll have to show her the ropes.'

'What's happened to Nicola?' asked Todd, 'Has she left?'

'She's on vacation.'

'Where's she gone?'

'London.'

'What, London in England?'

Melanie nodded. 'She's staying there for a couple of weeks before she goes to her other relatives.'

'Are they in England as well?'

'Greece.'

'Greece! Lucky girl! How long has she gone for?'

Melanie shrugged. 'I don't know. Max wanted her to work full time now school's out and she told him she wouldn't be here. She offered her notice, but he said he'd hold her weekend job for her for when she returned. When she left he wished her a good time and said he'd see her in a couple of months.'

'Two months! Have her parents gone with her?'

Melanie shrugged. 'I don't know. She said she goes every year. I think they have an eating place or something and it's a working holiday for her. I wish I had relatives somewhere like that.'

'Yeah, me too,' replied Todd absently. He carried his glass of soda over to an empty table.

Todd lay on his bed and thought about Jennie-Lea. She really was something else. He looked at his watch for the third time. He still had plenty of time to shower. His fellow house-mates were away that weekend and Jennie-Lea would be arriving very soon. He planned to meet her with his towel draped across his shoulders, leaving her in no doubt about his ability to satisfy her insatiable appetite.

'So what do you plan for your vacation?' asked Jennie-Lea

half an hour after her arrival as she lay beside Todd and ran her hand up the inside of his leg.

'I've no firm plans at the moment. I thought I might go on one of those outward bound courses.'

'What, log cabins and bear hunting?'

'Yeah, that kind of thing. I doubt if it would be bear hunting. More like a bit of fishing.'

'I didn't know you liked fishing.'

'I don't particularly, but I thought a bit of relaxation in the outback could replenish my batteries.'

Jennie-Lea winked at him. 'I didn't notice that your batteries needed replenishing.'

Todd tapped his head. 'The brain cells.'

'I've got a couple of week's vacation due to me. I thought maybe we could spend the time together.' Jennie-Lea ran her tongue around her lips and leaned towards him, her nipples touching his chest whilst her hand travelled further up his leg.

Todd felt his body's immediate reaction to her overtures. Two whole weeks spent exclusively with the girl, to enjoy her body whenever he fancied and not have to wait for the evenings or weekends. They could have take-away meals delivered and there would be no need to even get dressed each day. He would be a fool to refuse her offer. He could feel himself sweating as his imagination began to run riot.

'I'll give it some serious thought,' he managed to say, knowing his decision was already made.

'I thought Hawaii would be nice.'

Todd raised his eyebrows. 'I was thinking of somewhere much closer to home, my dear. Hawaii is out of the question.'

'I've never been there.'

'Nor have I – and I'm not likely to.'

'You have plenty of money. I would have thought you would have wanted to go somewhere exotic.'

'One day, maybe, but not at the moment. I'd rather we stayed at my apartment for the whole two weeks. The boys will have gone back home so I'll have the place to myself. You're exotic enough for me. I don't need other distractions. Besides, you'll not even need to pack a case.'

'Oh, I'll have nothing to wear!'

'Exactly. If you put as much as a stitch of clothing on I'll tear it off you.'

'Ooh, Todd, do you really mean that?' asked Jennie-Lea breathlessly. 'Promise.'

By seven that evening Nicola's eyelids were drooping and she was trying to stifle her yawns. Saffron smiled sympathetically at her.

'If you want to go to bed we understand.'

Nicola yawned again. 'I'm sorry, I'm just falling asleep as I sit here. I really want to know more about our sight-seeing trip tomorrow, but it's just not registering properly in my brain.'

John squeezed her hand. 'You go on up, Nick. You'll be fine when you've had a good sleep. We can make plans for the rest of our stay tomorrow. We both know where we want to go, it's just if we can fit it all in whilst we're here.' He turned to Saffron. 'We're relying on you. If we say we want to go to two places in a day and it isn't practical you must tell us. It would be better to see just one properly.'

Saffron pushed the list she had made towards him. 'You have a look at that. You'll see Marble Arch, Piccadilly Circus, Downing Street, the Houses of Parliament and Tower Bridge during the bus tour. The tour takes about an hour and you can get off and pick it up again later. I suggest you stop at the aquarium, if you're interested, of course.'

John nodded vigorously.

'You can spend as long as you like in there. I'm not sure if they have a cafeteria, but there's bound to be somewhere nearby that you can buy some lunch. Marjorie will be with you, so you won't get lost. When you've finished at the aquarium you just get back on the bus and decide where you want to get off next. Most places close round about five. If you have to pay an entrance fee make sure you have enough time to see as much as you want. Have a look at the brochures before you make up your mind.'

'That bus sounds great. Can we do that every day?' asked John eagerly.

Saffron shook her head. 'It's far too expensive. This is my treat and I've a bit of pocket money for you.' She placed an envelope on the table and pushed it towards John. 'Your Dad took us to so many places and wouldn't let us contribute that it's only fair that I repay him through you. London is expensive and it will be far cheaper to decide where you want to go and then take the tube.'

'The tube?' John gave her a puzzled look.

'Sorry,' she smiled. 'We *use* the underground or *take* the tube. It's one and the same and I have no idea why we say it that way.'

'You mean, one of those horrible underground things that we travelled on today?'

'You'll soon get used to them. It's quicker to use the underground than to take a bus. You don't get snarled up in all the traffic.'

'You don't see anything when you're down in those tunnels,' complained John.

'You're going on the bus tomorrow once you reach the centre. I'll take you on a proper train at the weekend. I thought you might like a trip down to Brighton. You can take your swimming gear if the weather's good and you don't mind walking on the pebbles. If you decide it isn't warm enough to swim there are plenty of other things to see. The Royal Pavilion is fascinating and there's also the pier.'

'What have you got down for the other days?' asked John and pulled the list towards him. 'Victoria and Albert Museum – what's that?'

'That is especially for you. They have a photographic museum there. I've pencilled that in for a whole day. If Nicola gets bored there are plenty of other exhibits for her to see. There's also Kew Gardens if you want to photograph some flowers.'

'That's really good. What about the dinosaurs? I've never seen one.'

Saffron smiled. 'Natural History museum, again, there's so much to see there you'll probably need a complete day. You ought to visit the British Museum whilst you're here. They have exhibits from all over the world that you may never see anywhere else.'

John raised his eyebrows. 'How come?'

'We are a nation of collectors. We found the items and considered it was a case of "finders, keepers." Sometimes we bought them from the country for next to nothing.'

'Oh, yes, the Elgin Marbles that you pinched from the Acropolis.'

'We saved them from disintegration,' replied Saffron calmly. 'I'll not get into a discussion about those with you or anyone else. Let the politicians fight it out and I'll just go along with their decision.'

'But they belong to us really.'

'If you say so, but I don't suggest you voice your opinion in the museum. You'd be bound to end up in a heated argument with someone.'

'I could tell them what I think in Greek,' grinned John. 'They'd never understand.'

'Don't be too sure. If someone is studying the marbles closely the chances are they are a scholar or specialist and they would certainly speak Greek.'

'It would be fun to try.'

'And if you end up in jail for causing a disturbance don't expect me to come to bail you out! Now, I know Nicola wants to go to Buckingham Palace. They do tours, but it would be wise to book in advance. You don't want to get there and find you have to wait hours for a slot or there's nothing available. The same with the London Eye. You need to allow about an hour and a half for that, so you would be able to plan something else for part of the day. The Tate Gallery is only a short distance away if you wanted to go there.'

'That all sounds fine. What about the next week? What else is there we ought to do?'

'That's for you and Nicola to decide. A visit to Harrods or Selfridges is quite an experience; just don't expect to be able to afford to buy anything more than a pencil. There's the zoo, that's something you haven't got in Crete, and you ought to visit the Tower of London. You could incorporate that with a boat ride down the River Thames. When you've visited the Tower you'd probably enjoy the London Dungeon. Wherever you visit pick up any little brochures they have advertising other attractions. You'll probably find some I haven't got here and we can always throw them out if you're not interested.'

John squeezed Saffron's hand. 'You know, you're the best thing that's happened in our family *ever*. I went over to New Orleans with Mum and Dad when I was small to visit my grandmother and I went to Italy most years to see my grandparents there, but this is a *real* holiday. If you hadn't found us I doubt if I would ever have had the opportunity to visit London.'

'I'm sure you would.'

John shook his head. 'I know I shall be called to do my National Service next year. I want to become a professional photographer, but it will probably take years before I can make a decent living at it. In the meantime I have to work for Dad. I'm not complaining, I'm lucky to have a job I can step into whenever I want some extra pocket money. I may not have an opportunity like this again for years and years. I want to make the most of it and see everything London has to offer.'

Todd was enjoying having Jennie-Lea at his apartment. The first week had been both exciting and exhausting, and the second was proving to be just as exhilarating. The sight of Jennie-Lea wandering around without her clothes on still excited him. Her large breasts that he had considered so desirable and attractive when restrained were even more irresistible when she was naked and they swung around as she moved. Her slim waist and hips only enhanced their size. He sighed deeply. He knew he would never find another girl like her. They were a perfect couple; both had insatiable sexual appetites that needed frequent satisfaction

Jennie-Lea appeared from the kitchen, a plate in her hand, and broke his reverie. 'I've brought you some food.' She sat down beside him on the bed. 'A big handsome hunk like you needs to keep his strength up. Shut your eyes and open wide.'

Todd smiled and complied, expecting a mouthful of food, only to find her breast was pushed as far as possible into his mouth. He put up his hand and drew it out sucking hard on her nipple as he did so.

'You're lucky I didn't bite you.'

Jennie-Lea smiled wickedly. 'If I'd felt your teeth coming down I'd have squeezed you so hard that you'd have opened your mouth to scream and I would have escaped.'

'I believe you,' he said sincerely, 'but that could have ruined your plans for the remainder of the day.'

'How do you know what my plans are?'

Todd laughed. 'Your plans are always the same.'

Jennie-Lea placed the plate on the bedside table. 'Why don't we work up an appetite?' She arched her body over his and placed his hand on her leg.

'What did you make?'

'Bacon sandwiches.'

Todd pulled himself into a sitting position on the bed and reached out a hand for the plate. Jennie-Lea restrained him.

'What do I get in return for making you something to eat?' she asked, her mouth close to his.

'Your just desserts.'

'Hurry up and eat your sandwich,' she urged. 'The dessert is always the best part of any meal.' She ran her finger lightly down his skin towards his crotch, causing an involuntary reaction from him.

'Maybe I will eat later,' he mumbled and replaced the sandwich on the plate.

'I hear you've been away. Did you have a good time?'

Nicola nodded. 'How about you?'

'No, I stayed here to study. I take my computer and business studies finals this year. You've a lovely tan. Where did you go?'

'Greece.'

'Oh, yeah, Melanie told me,' Todd tapped his head. 'Old age. Do you speak Greek?'

Nicola smiled confidently. 'Of course. My Dad's Greek.'

Todd nodded. 'So what are you planning to do now you are back in New Orleans?'

'I start at Uni next week.'

'Really? What subjects?'

'Hotel Management, Basic Accounting and General Business Studies. What about you?'

'I'm in my final year of Computer Studies and Business Management. I shall then spend an extra year studying Corporate Banking before I go into my father's bank. What do you plan to do when you graduate?'

'Probably go and work for my relatives in Greece.' Nicola held out her hand for his money.

OCTOBER 2006

Saffron landed at Heraklion airport and Giovanni met her, accompanied by Bryony.

'Oh, it's so good to be back here and see you,' Saffron's eyes were moist as she spoke.

Bryony hugged her. 'You know you can come any time.'

'When I win the lottery and can afford to give up work.'

'Why didn't Marjorie come with you? I thought she enjoyed herself when she came before.'

'The same reason as she couldn't come the first year I visited. She always looks after the Goldsmith's cat and they always go away at the same time of the year. They have a time share in Australia. This time they've swapped their accommodation for a month in Florida. I had no choice of dates so it was come alone or not at all.'

'Well, I'm pleased you're here.' Bryony squeezed her arm affectionately. 'You must arrange for Marjorie to come with you next summer.'

'I'm sure she will.'

'What do you want to do this time? Do you want to have another look at some of the places you saw last year? I'm sure you'll find it's still warm enough for swimming, but I doubt if you want to spend all your time on the beach.'

'I'll be happy whatever I do,' smiled Saffron. 'I ought to spend more time with Grandmother this time. I was so busy rushing around and seeing everything that when we were home I felt quite guilty. She must have felt I neglected her.'

'She was just delighted to see you. She talked about you for weeks afterwards.'

'Now you make me feel even more guilty!'

Giovanni moved Saffron's case towards the exit, but neither made a move to follow him. He shook his head in despair. Did women ever stop talking?

'Bryony, do you want to stay here for the whole of Saffie's holiday? You can talk in the car and when you're home. I shall be getting a parking fine if you don't hurry up.'

Bryony pulled a face. Men. They had no patience. She linked her arm through Saffron's. 'We'd better go. Giovanni's getting worried about getting a parking ticket.'

Giggling and laughing together like teenagers they followed Giovanni to where he had parked the car.

Bryony looked at the ticket he had bought and displayed on the windscreen. 'You had another half an hour, Giovanni. What was your panic?'

'If I hadn't moved you two you'd still be there talking until midnight. You can't monopolise her company by staying up here. Everyone's waiting to see Saffie again.'

Saffron slid into the back seat of the car with Bryony beside her. She felt almost as at home here in Crete as she did in England.

Nicola emailed John to tell him her impressions now she was a student at the University. It was so different from the High School and there seemed to be hundreds of people milling around all the time. She would never get to know who was a student and who was a lecturer, some students looked quite old and some lecturers looked far too young. She was pleased she was able to attend whilst living at home, not having to share a house or rooms with strangers and hope they liked each other's company. She thought she would enjoy the course she had chosen leading to a degree in Hotel Management, despite the ground covered in the first week being very basic.

John replied he was pleased that she was happy with her choice and was sure she would soon find herself immersed in it. He was looking around to see if he could find some work for the winter months. Marcus had taken over most of the maintenance work that John had previously shared with his father during the closed season and everywhere was beginning to shut as the tourists left. It was quiet and lonely without Nicola there. He was even beginning to look forward to his National Service the following year to keep him occupied during the winter months and enable him to make some new friends.

Nicola was sympathetic. Despite starting University with high hopes she was disappointed. She had only made friends with a couple of girls. It seemed that most of the students just wanted to go out and party every evening, becoming so inebriated and exhausted that they were unable to turn up for their classes the next day. She had been offered drugs when she had a break from a class and again at a party. When she refused everyone thought she was odd and prudish. She would certainly not accept any more invitations. She knew some of the girls laughed about her behind her back, sometimes making fun of her principles quite openly, whilst the boys seemed to think that any girl was theirs just for the asking and had taken her rejection of their dubious invitations as personal insults. She was still working at the diner each weekend for extra pocket money and found she had plenty of time to complete her assignments and hand them in on time.

Saffron was surprised when her mobile rang. She had spoken to Marjorie no more than half an hour earlier. What had happened that she needed to contact her again so soon?

'Hello?'

'Hello, Saffie. Giovanni told me you were coming for a visit. Welcome back to Crete.'

Saffron felt the blood rushing to her face. 'Vasi, how are you?'

'I am well. I would like to show you the gymnasium I have made at my hotel whilst you are here. Thanks to you it is proving a success.'

'Me? I had nothing to do with it.'

'You advised me of the best and most popular machines for exercise. Now, when shall we make a date? I am sure you are busy tomorrow, but the day after? Would that suit you? I will be there just after eleven and we can drive back to Heraklion for lunch at the hotel. Yes?'

Saffron looked around. Everyone had discreetly left the room. 'Well, yes, I suppose so.'

'Good. That is settled then. Goodnight.'

The phone went dead and Saffron looked at it in surprise. Vasi obviously did not believe in chatting over the telephone.

'Have you got a new girl friend?' asked Jennie-Lea

Todd frowned. 'What gives you that idea?'

'You just don't seem as interested in me as you were a few months ago. You used to want to see me every evening, now you only come over at the weekends.'

'I'm working hard, you knew I had to. I have to get good grades at the end of the year or I won't be able to go on to Corporate Banking.'

'So what will you do when you finish Uni with these super grades you're so intent on gaining?' Jennie-Lea stretched her arms above her head, knowing the effect the movement would have on Todd.

'Go into my father's bank as an assistant manager.'

Jennie-Lea raised her eyebrows. 'I could be your P.A.'

Todd laughed. 'No way. I shall be expected to work. I wouldn't get much done with you around all the time.'

'In all the best love stories the boss marries his P.A.' Jennie-Lea turned on her side and pressed her body against his.

'You're not qualified to be my P.A. You've told me already you don't know your way around a computer. Besides, I've no intention of getting married yet. There's plenty of time. I'm only twenty two.'

'They say your early twenties are the best time to start a family.' Jennie-Lea had not told him she was eight years his senior. Her hand travelled down towards his navel.

'You're not, are you?' Todd looked at her in horror.

'No, but I wouldn't want to leave it too much longer. I'm in my prime.'

Todd shook his head and cupped her breast in his hand. 'This belongs to me, not some screaming baby.' He proved his point by taking her hard nipple in between his teeth and chewing gently. 'And,' he added, as he released her, 'we wouldn't be able to enjoy ourselves properly for weeks. If you had to get up each night to feed it you'd be continually claiming that you were too tired for months on end to satisfy my appetite.'

'I'd never be too tired for that. Ooh, yes.' Jennie-Lea arched her body towards him as he attacked her nipple again. 'You know just what I like,' she sighed and slipped her hand between his legs. 'That feels so good – and so does this,' she added.

Vasi arrived as arranged for Saffron and spent half an hour talking quietly in Greek to Giovanni. Saffron would have liked to ask the nature of their conversation as it had appeared serious, but also felt that it was hotel business and as such had nothing to do with her. Finally Vasi rose and announced they should leave if they wished to be at the hotel in time for lunch.

'We may be a little late,' he smiled. 'It will depend how heavy the traffic has become.'

Saffron smiled. 'I'm sure they'll not refuse to serve you.'

Vasi shook his head. 'There is much that I want to show you and talk with you. I have more ideas.'

'You could talk whilst we drive,' suggested Saffron.

'No. I need to concentrate when I speak in English. Chit chat I can do, but not serious talking. I will save that for later today. Now what are you planning to do whilst you are on holiday this time?'

'I'm not sure. I haven't really worked out an itinerary like last time. I want to spend more time with my grandmother. She is my excuse to come again this year so if I go out sight-seeing every day Giovanni will think I have just taken advantage of them for a cheap holiday.'

'I am sure they would think no such thing. It can be difficult spending time with old people. My grandmother, Rebecca, is here at the moment and I find that one afternoon a week in her company is sufficient for both of us.'

'Your grandmother?'

'Cathy's mother,' explained Vasi. 'She is a lovely lady, but a little nervous now she has to manage alone in Crete. Although she has spent so much time here she has never really learnt the language and she cannot read Greek at all. She receives documents relating to her house and she does not understand. She relied on my grandfather to deal with everything when he was alive.'

'What about your father and Cathy? Can't they help her?'

'They do, but I live closer to her, so she always calls me first. You will meet her this afternoon.'

'Oh!' This was something Saffron had not been prepared for.

Vasi smiled. 'We do not have to stay long, but we are passing her village. She would not forgive me for not stopping. We will have a cup of English tea and she will show you her garden. Half an hour, that is all.' Vasi pointed out through the car window. 'Down there you can see Hersonissos. We will not go to my hotel there. It was a quiet town until the tourists found it and made it their playground. Now the local people avoid it if they can during the summer months, particularly in the evenings.'

'No doubt those who have business there welcome the trade.'

'Of course, but it is at a price. They always had visitors who patronised the tavernas and shops along with the local people. For many this is their nearest large town. Now the local people go further afield and at the end of the season they do not bother to come back. The businesses find that the money they make in the summer does not compensate for the lack of all year round customers and many places close.'

'So what do the people do if their business is closed for the winter?' asked Saffron.

'They have an allowance from the government, just enough to manage to live on. They are expected to budget and save for the lean times.'

'No, I meant how do they pass their time?'

'Oh, they tend their gardens, repaint their houses, spend time with their relatives.' Vasi shrugged. 'They also have a rest. Shop keepers often work every day from seven until ten at night and the tavernas are open until the last tourist leaves. That can be four in the morning, then they have to clean up ready to open the next day.'

'Surely they have some help? One person could not work like that for six months. They would collapse.'

'They usually have their family to help them, but even families have to be paid.'

Saffron nodded, thinking of the arrangement Bryony and Marcus had with Giovanni.

It was nearly two when they finally reached Vasi's hotel in Heraklion, having been delayed by road works on the main road and meeting a considerable amount of traffic. He led the way to the dining room that Saffron remembered from her previous visit with Marjorie and indicated that she should sit by the window.

'I will let the chef know we have arrived. I have arranged a light lunch. I do not want to spoil our meal this evening.'

Saffron frowned. 'Marianna will be expecting me back for the meal. I wouldn't want to upset her arrangements.'

'Marianna knows you are with me. She knows I will feed you and return you safely. Would you like some wine?'

Saffron shook her head. 'I'm quite happy with water, but you have some if you want.'

'I will be driving again later. It is better if I wait until the evening. I will have a beer. That will satisfy my thirst and is more interesting than water.'

Whilst Vasi went into the kitchen, Saffron looked around the dining room. Once again there were no other people in there. The tables were laid with spotless white cloths, napkins in the wine glasses and cutlery in place. She had an idea that the hotel was not usually open for lunch and Vasi had made a special arrangement again for today.

Their meal arrived swiftly, plate after plate of small quantities of different foods. 'We'll never eat all that!' exclaimed Saffron.

'You will be surprised. It is called a meze. There is a small amount on each plate for us to share. Try everything unless you already know you do not like it.'

'The only Greek dish I don't like is moussaka. Everything else that I've eaten I've loved.'

'How fortunate that I dislike it also. Had it been my favourite Cathy would probably have made it in preference to the chicken when you went to them for a meal.'

'I would have eaten it to be polite.'

'I'm sure you would, but you would not have enjoyed it. Try the meat balls. The chef cooks them in ouzo.'

To Saffron's surprise they emptied the dishes between them and Vasi gave a pleased smile. 'Thank you, Saffie.'

'What for?'

'For eating. The chef would have been most offended if we

had sent anything back. Now would you like something more? Baklava, ice cream, some fruit?'

Saffron shook her head. 'I just couldn't manage another thing. No wonder you need a siesta if you always eat a lunch like this.'

'No, this is when you go to the gymnasium and work. Then you have a swim and then you have your siesta.'

'You're not going to make me work in the gymnasium, are you?'

'You do not think it would be a good thing for you to do?'

'Definitely not. I'm always happy to swim, but I am not a gym person.'

Vasi smiled. 'I only wish you to look at it. You can try the exercise machines if you feel inclined, but I will not make you do so.' He indicated to the waiter that their table could be cleared and held Saffron's chair as she rose from the table.

He led the way across the foyer and through a door marked gymnasium. Saffron waited whilst he ran a pass card through the lock. 'We are very careful. The gymnasium is not suitable for small children. Only adults are allowed a card. Anyone who is under sixteen has to have an adult accompanying them.'

'Suppose their parents have gone out for the day?'

'Then a member of staff will come with them. We do not want youngsters in here being silly with the equipment and having accidents. Imagine, you are in here alone and you drop a weight on your foot. It would crush the bones. You would not be able to walk. You could be here in considerable pain for a long time before someone found you.' Vasi pushed open the door at the foot of the stairs.

'Don't you have an emergency telephone?'

'Of course.' Vasi pointed to the wall. 'You have crushed your foot over there. How do you walk to the telephone?'

'You crawl,' remarked Saffron dryly.'

Vasi nodded. 'And when you reach the telephone you have to stand up to reach it. If your injury does not permit you to crawl and then stand what do you do?'

Saffron held up her hands. 'All right. I give in. Now, are you going to give me a demonstration on all this equipment?'

'If you wish me to show you I will need to change into sportswear. The clothes I am wearing are not suitable,' he answered seriously.

Saffron laughed. 'I was joking.'

'I am glad of that. I do not have any sportswear,' he laughed back at her. 'So, what do you think? If you enjoyed to work in a gymnasium would you be happy here? Do I have the correct machines?'

'Vasi, I have no idea. It looks superb. Have you asked the guests who have used it?'

'Of course. They all say it is good, then they add, "but you do not have" or "I wish you had". What am I to do? If I bought everything they have mentioned I would not have enough space for all the equipment.'

'Then leave it as it is. You're not opening as a gymnasium. You are offering visitors an added attraction, like Giovanni with his putting green and tennis court.'

Vasi smiled. 'That is what I wanted to hear. I knew you would tell me the truth.'

'I'm sure your father would have said the same.'

'My father thinks it was a waste of money.'

'Why?'

'He says people do not come on holiday to work, they come to relax.'

'Many people like to do both.'

Vasi nodded. 'That is what I have told him. What I have not told him is that I plan to open it to the local people during the winter.'

'Really? Do you think they will be interested?'

'I am sure. Already some staff have asked if they can use it on their day off. They have to pay a small fee, of course.'

'Then that's good. It will also give the people something else to do in the winter months.'

'So,' Vasi exhaled and smiled broadly. 'My gymnasium is a success.' He ushered Saffron back up the stairs to the foyer, closing the door carefully behind him. 'Now, we will visit my grandmother, Rebecca.'

They drove away from the centre of Heraklion, finally turning into a quieter area of the town where small roads ran off at right angles with tiny houses and gardens along one side. The other side was fenced off scrub land where a few goats grazed and raised their heads curiously as the car drew to a halt.

Vasi opened a gate into a minute, but immaculate garden, overflowing with a profusion of colour.

'This is beautiful,' remarked Saffron

'Tell my grandmother. She will be pleased. Her garden is her pride and joy.' Vasi opened the door with a key and rang the bell at the same time. 'It's only me, Grandma.'

'Come in, Vasi. I've told you, there's no need for you to ring the bell.'

Vasi walked into the tiny front room that overflowed with furniture, Saffron following him. He bent and kissed Rebecca, then stood back and introduced Saffron.

'Bryony's sister. Cathy was telling me about you. Quite a story, losing touch with each other for so many years and discovering you had already met some of your family. Basil would have loved it. I'm sure he could have made a successful book from it. Now, Vasi, sit down and look at these letters for me, please. I'm sure there's something from the pest control people telling me I have mosquitoes. I'm sure I haven't. They were spraying the area when I returned from England. I think my water bill needs to be paid. Can I leave that with you? Saffron, you come with me into the kitchen whilst I make us some tea. I bring it with me from England. I don't know what it is about Greeks and tea,' she shook her head, 'they seem quite unable to brew a decent cup.'

Dutifully Saffron followed the elderly lady into the kitchen. 'Can I do anything?' she offered.

Rebecca shook her head. 'You can take the pot through when it's ready and I'll carry the tray. That will save me making two trips.'

'I was admiring your front garden as we came in. It's magnificent.'

'Thank you. Would you like to see the back?'

'Yes, please.'

Rebecca opened a door and beckoned Saffron to follow her. There was a small patio with just enough room for two chairs and a table. On each side were flower beds, plants jostling for space in each one and overflowing onto the paving.

'It is quite incredible. I didn't think some of these plants would grow in such a hot, dry climate.'

'I experiment. I bring the seeds from England and I spread the seedlings around in different places. I then see which ones flourish and plant them there again the next year. If I end up with a bare patch I can always fill it with some geraniums.'

'You must wish it was twice as big.'

Rebecca shook her head. 'It's as much as I can manage now. Where we lived before we had a larger garden, but then Basil was around and we had a gardener. We can have our tea out here. It's plenty warm enough. Vasi will have to bring out an extra chair. He's a good boy. He and Basil became very close. I think he helped Basil to come to terms more than anyone else, even Cathy could never really take his son's place.' Rebecca sighed. 'Then when Cathy realised she could not have children, probably due to her accident, Vasi became very precious to Basil.'

'Vasi has said how fond he was of his grandfather.'

'He was devastated when he died. At the time he was seeing a nice girl. She couldn't understand why he was so unhappy; kept telling him to pull himself together. She wanted to go out and have fun and he did not want to do anything. She left him after three months. Said she didn't want to spend her time with such a miserable man. That hurt him as well.' Rebecca shook her head. 'It's not natural for a young man in his prime not to have a companion.'

'He says he's waiting to meet the right girl.'

'He'll never do that unless he makes more effort to go out to meet them. That kettle should be boiled by now.' Rebecca walked the few steps back into the kitchen and Saffron picked up the tray that was laid ready.

'Shall I take this out to the garden?' she asked and Rebecca nodded.

'Vasi,' Rebecca raised her voice a little. 'Bring a chair with you. We're going to have tea in the garden.'

'Well?' asked Vasi, as they drove away, 'What did you think of my English grandmother?'

'She's lovely. She proves my theory, beautiful people have beautiful gardens.'

'Suppose you have no garden?'

'Then you have to show how beautiful you are in other ways.'

Vasi nodded seriously. 'My grandfather was a beautiful person. His beauty was in his books. When he was alive Rebecca's beauty was in her support for him. She found Crete so hot during the summer months she could hardly go out unless it was to the beach, but she would not have dreamed of returning to England without her husband. Now she is free to go back in May and spend the cooler months out here.'

'Who looks after her garden when she is away?'

'A neighbour will water it every day for her. I come over just before she returns and ensure it is in order.' Vasi smiled. 'She always scolds me and says I have pulled up the plants and left the weeds.'

'Is she serious?'

'I am never sure. I do not know very much about gardens. My father has always employed gardeners.'

'What about your grandfather?'

'He would dig the garden, then my father would send a gardener along to plant vegetables and flower beds. Rebecca did not become interested in gardening until after Basil died. I think she did it at first to occupy herself, then she became interested and now it is her passion.'

Saffron frowned. 'But all the first books that Basil Hurst wrote were about fairies and set in gardens.'

'He had a very good imagination. Now, we are at my apartment. You will understand the reason later.'

Saffron looked dubious. Was he now going to make advances towards her? She would repulse him, of course, but was she sure she really wanted to?

Vasi opened the door and stood aside for Saffron to enter the lounge. She was immediately greeted by the most magnificent pink marble floor she had ever seen. A large television stood at one side with an easy chair upholstered in grey, placed for convenient viewing, an occasional table beside it. At the far end was a table, the surface of smoked glass on a white pedestal and flanked by four white wooden chairs with grey seats. He opened the doors along one side of the hall.

'Go around and have a look in every room,' he said.

'You don't mind?'

Vasi shook his head. 'Take your time.' He sat down in the lounger and switched on the television.

Saffron felt aggrieved. She hoped they were not going to spend the remainder of the afternoon in the apartment with him watching Greek television whilst she did not understand a word.

As Saffron went from room to room she was surprised at the spaciousness. The first room was a bedroom, again the walls were white, there was a grey throw over the bed and the curtains were grey. A small bathroom led off, tiled entirely in white and with white sanitary fitments. The wardrobe and chest of drawers were white, with the surface of the white dressing table covered with a sheet of plate glass. There were no ornaments or pictures, it was obviously a spare bedroom and never used.

The next room was a replica of the first, but at least there were some toiletries in the bathroom and a comb on the dressing table. The separate toilet was again tiled in white and so was the kitchen. Although the cupboards were natural wood, the work tops were white.

She opened a cupboard, all the crockery was white. In another there was a small tin of coffee, a packet of sugar and a pack of croissants that would keep for five days. Everything looked new and unused. Curiosity overcame her and Saffron opened the fridge. Inside was a solitary carton of milk. Saffron frowned. There was something odd about the apartment that made her feel uncomfortable.

She walked back into the lounge and Vasi immediately switched off the television and stood up, offering her his chair. Saffron shook her head. 'Could we sit out on the balcony?'

'Of course.' Vasi unlocked the door and Saffron sat on a white plastic chair at a white plastic table.

'How long have you lived here?' she asked.

'A couple of years.'

'Did you choose the decor or was it already done when you moved in?'

'Decor?' Vasi looked at her, puzzled by the unfamiliar word.

'The decoration. Did you choose to have everywhere white?'

Vasi nodded. 'Do you like it?'

Saffron hesitated. She did not want to hurt his feelings. 'I feel it is too white. Maybe if you had painted the bedrooms a different colour and put some coloured tiles in the bathrooms. It reminds me of the hospital.'

'And this room?'

'It's very plain. You need some pictures or a mirror. You have a fabulous marble floor, but you can't look at that all the time.

You have a beautiful table; a bowl of flowers in the centre or a plant would draw attention to it.'

'What about the kitchen?'

'Do you ever use it?'

'Occasionally. To make a hot drink.'

'That is how it looks – unused. Everywhere looks unused, unloved and unlived in.'

'So if I said I would give you my apartment, what would be your answer?'

Saffron shook her head. 'I would not want it as it looks now. I would want to add colour. It reminds me of a hotel. All the rooms decorated and furnished exactly the same. Clean, smart and impersonal. Where are your books or magazines?'

Vasi looked totally crestfallen. 'I wanted it to look different from my father's house and not cluttered up like Rebecca's.'

'I understand that and it does look different from both of them, but not in the right way. There is no personality here. Nothing that says "this is Vasi's home". It could be a show apartment.'

'So you do not like it?'

'I think it could me made most attractive.'

Vasi leaned forward. 'I would like to hear your ideas.'

'So this was the reason you wanted me to come to your apartment?'

'Of course.' Vasi blushed. 'You did not think...?'

Saffron's face reddened. 'It crossed my mind.'

JANUARY 2007

Jennie-Lea smiled slightly nervously at Todd. 'I have some very special news for you.'

'Yeah?' Todd was hardly interested. She had probably made a sale and earned a good commission He was more eager to arouse her body again and enjoy her one more time before he left that night.

'I'm pregnant. Isn't it wonderful?'

Todd looked at her in horror. 'You're what!'

'Pregnant. Aren't you pleased?' She snuggled her body up to him. He could feel her stomach against his side and immediately moved away from her.

'You'll have to get rid of it.'

'Why? I'm happy to be having your baby. I don't want a termination.'

Todd's mouth set in a hard line. 'You might be pleased, but I'm not. I don't want to be a father.'

'Why ever not? We can be married and get a little place of our own, somewhere with a small garden so she can play outside.'

'I'm not marrying you just because you're stupid enough to become pregnant,' stated Todd adamantly.

Jennie-Lea looked at him in amazement. 'I thought you loved me. I thought once you had got used to the idea you'd be as pleased as me.'

'Well I'm not. I'll pay for your termination.' Todd rose from the bed and began to dress. 'Make the arrangements as soon as possible.'

Jennie-Lea shook her head. 'I'm not terminating. I've always wanted a child. To have a termination could mean I couldn't have another later on when you decide the time is right.'

'The time will never be right. I told you I wasn't prepared to share your attention with a baby.' Todd tightened his belt. 'Get up and get dressed now and I'll drop you off at the twenty four hour clinic.'

Jennie-Lea looked at him. 'I'm just not hearing this.' Her lip trembled and she stood up placing her arms round Todd. 'I love you, Todd. We're good together. Once you get used to the idea I'm sure you'll change your mind.' She moved her body against his and he pushed her away.

'Todd,' she remonstrated and moved towards him again.

Todd caught her by her shoulders and shook her vigorously.

'Todd,' she protested, 'Mind the baby.'

He pushed her away more forcibly. She stumbled backwards, losing her balance as she trod on her discarded shoes. As she hit the floor there was a nasty crack and she lay there, limp as a doll. Todd looked at her. 'I'm sorry, Jennie-Lea. I shouldn't have pushed you. Get up and we'll talk some more about the baby. You have to see it from my point of view.'

Jennie-Lea did not move and Todd knelt down beside her. 'Come on Jennie-Lea. I didn't push you that hard. You tripped over your shoes. I've said I'm sorry. Get up and we'll talk sensibly.' He took her hand and tried to encourage her to sit up. She made no move to help herself.

'Jennie-Lea, open your eyes. Talk to me.' Was she really unconscious?

Todd sat back on his heels. He truly had not meant to hurt her, just get her to move away from him. He was not a violent person by nature. He looked at the inert body, what should he do? He went into the bathroom, ran a flannel under the cold water tap and wrung it out. He placed it on her forehead and spoke to her again without eliciting any response from her.

'I'm sorry, Jennie-Lea. I'm sorry,' he repeated time and again. Panic began to well up inside him. She could not be dead. He felt for her pulse and put his ear down close to her mouth. He could not feel her breath on him. What was it they did to see if someone was still breathing? They held a mirror by their mouth. He stood up and reached for the hand mirror from the chest of drawers, holding it in front of her mouth, hoping to see it mist over.

Todd was shaking now. The enormity of his action and the probable consequences began to register fully. He would be accused of murder, at the very least manslaughter. He wondered how long his prison sentence would be. He felt the sweat standing out on his forehead. He could not face that.

He tried to think rationally. He could not leave her there and walk away, pretending to find her the following day. He knew enough about medical examinations of bodies to know that he may have left bruising on her shoulders where he had held her and once they discovered she was pregnant he would be the obvious suspect.

If she had a fall she would be bruised in many places. He held the mirror before her mouth again. She was certainly not breathing and there was no pulse to be found. She would have to be dressed, however horrendous he found the ordeal.

Todd pulled her panties over her feet and pulled them up, followed by the skirt she had been wearing earlier. He replaced her bra, pushing her onto her face whilst he fastened it and pushed her Tee shirt over her head, struggling to force her arms through the sleeves. Thank goodness she had been wearing a skirt and not jeans. He sat back and looked at her. Apart from the fact that her head appeared to be at an odd angle she looked no different from the girl he had held in his arms an hour or so earlier.

He opened the door to the balcony and looked outside. As usual the parking lot was full, but no one appeared to be around at that early hour of the morning. He carried her high heeled shoes over to the door before picking Jennie-Lea up in his arms and carrying her out onto the balcony, positioning her body against the guard rail. Taking a last look into the parking lot to ensure there was no one around Todd lifted her legs, hesitated a moment and allowed her weight and gravity to take her tumbling downwards. He threw her shoes after her and retreated rapidly into the apartment.

He picked up the damp flannel from the floor and returned it to the bathroom, laying it open to dry. Taking a deep breath he opened the door leading to the landing. He pulled the door closed where it locked automatically. Any fingerprints on the door or in the apartment could be explained away, he was a frequent visitor.

Todd pressed the button for the elevator and prayed that it would arrive quickly and no one else was using it and see him leaving the building. When it arrived he leant his head against the cold metal walls and tried to compose himself. Once on the ground floor he could not wait to get out of the building and pushed frantically at the door that led to the parking lot, breathing a sigh of relief as he stepped out into the night air.

He crossed to where his car was parked on the far side and opened the door. Before climbing inside he looked up at the penthouse apartment. He had left the lights burning and he raised his hand as if waving goodbye to Jennie-Lea. As he did so he shuddered. It was almost a symbolic gesture.

Todd sat in the interview room his head in his hands. He had hardly slept during the remainder of the night. His eyelids felt heavy and he kept reminding himself that he must pretend to know nothing of the tragedy that had overtaken Jennie-Lea. He had driven to University as usual that morning and was in his first class of the day when he was requested to go to the Principal's office.

'What have I done?' he asked when he saw the two strange men in the office and he was requested to sit down.

'We'd just like to ask you a few questions at this stage, sir.'

Todd shrugged. 'What about?'

'I understand you have been friendly with a young lady called Jennie-Lea Cantonasta?'

Todd nodded. 'She's my girl friend.'

'Were you with her yesterday evening?'

'Yes. We usually spend most of our free time together.'

'Where did you go last evening?'

'To her apartment. It's more convenient for us to go there. I share a house with other students.'

'What time did you leave Miss Cantonasta's apartment last night?'

'I didn't look at the time. I guess it was probably around one in the morning. Why?'

'We'll come to that in a moment, sir. Had either of you been drinking or making use of a substance?'

Todd shook his head. 'We'd had a bottle of wine between us during the evening. We neither of us smoke or anything.'

'How was the young lady when you left her?'

Todd frowned. 'The same as always.'

'Can you tell us what "the same as always" means?'

Todd shook his head. 'Well, she tried to persuade me to stay longer, she always does. I insisted that I had to come back to get some sleep. I had Uni today and she had to go to work.'

'And what was her reaction to you insisting you had to leave?'

'I told you, the same as always. She always asked me to stay longer, I always refused.'

'So when you left her yesterday evening, or to be more precise the early hours of the morning, what did you do then?'

'I went down to the parking lot, collected my car and drove home.'

'So you did not see Miss Cantonasta again after you left her apartment?'

'Only to wave goodbye when she came out on her balcony.'

'Is that a habit of hers to come out to wave to you?'

Todd nodded and managed a slightly embarrassed smile. 'It's just a little ritual we have.'

'Did you see her return inside her apartment after she waved to you?'

'No. I can't see her balcony once I'm in my car.'

'As you were leaving the parking lot did you hear or see anything unusual? An unexplained noise, maybe?'

'No,' Todd pretended to consider, 'not that I recall. There were a couple of drunks further down the road, but when I noticed them I just slowed. They were pretty wobbly on their feet and I didn't want to find one of them beneath my wheels. Why are you asking me all these questions?'

'I regret to say that Miss Cantonasta was found in the parking lot this morning by one of the other residents of the apartment block. He immediately alerted the paramedics and they called us. I'm very sorry, Mr Gallagher, but when they arrived Miss Cantonasta was beyond their help.'

Todd felt the blood rush to his face and then recede, he felt quite light headed. 'What do you mean?' he managed to say, knowing quite well the information they were about to impart.

'It appears that Miss Cantonasta fell from her balcony last night.'

'Fell from... oh no, she couldn't. She waved to me, I blew her a kiss. She can't have fallen. Please, tell me it's not true.'

'I am very sorry, Mr Gallagher, to have to bring you such distressing news. I'm afraid we are going to have to ask you to come down to the precinct to make a statement.'

'A statement? Why?'

'It appears you were the last person to see Miss Cantonasta alive. At the moment we are treating her death as an unfortunate accident, but we have to follow procedure and take statements. I realise how distressing this must be for you and we will be as quick as possible.'

'You want me to come now?'

The detective nodded. 'We can drive you down and bring you back to the University or take you home afterwards. The sooner we have completed the formalities the sooner we can leave you to grieve in peace.'

Todd sat silently in the back of the car. He needed time to gather his thoughts. He must remember to give them the same information a second time; any deviation could draw attention to him.

He repeated his statement to the police and duly signed it. 'What happens now?' he asked.

'How do you mean, Mr Gallagher?'

'Well, her funeral. Have her family been informed?'

'Her father was contacted earlier this morning. He is flying in later today from New York. Once we notify him that her body can be released it will be his responsibility to make the necessary arrangements for her funeral.'

Todd frowned. 'What do you mean – released?'

'It's customary to hold an autopsy when someone dies unexpectedly.'

'But you know how she died. She fell from the balcony.'

'We need to know what caused her fall. Did she have a sudden heart attack? Had she been drinking before you arrived or drink something after you left that made her intoxicated? Was she using a substance and keeping the fact hidden from you? It's a pure formality, nothing for you to worry about.'

'Does that mean you'll have to cut her up?' Todd felt sick at the thought. It would obviously be discovered that she was pregnant.

'Unfortunately that is the only way to examine her organs.'

'I don't like to think of them cutting her up,' Todd shuddered and dropped his head into his hands.

The detective patted his shoulder in a fatherly fashion. 'We understand what a terrible shock this has been to you. Would you like us to take you home now?'

'Yes.' Todd hesitated. His car was at the University campus. Should he ask to be taken back there to collect it? He decided he would fetch it later. They could interpret his action as callous and unfeeling otherwise.

Todd decided not to go in to the University for the remainder of the week. His absence would be understood by the University and also he did not want to have to cope with the sympathy he would receive from his peers. He was truly shocked and upset that Jennie-Lea was dead and that it was his doing. He wished he was Catholic and could go and confess. As it was he needed some time to come to terms with his unfortunate actions alone.

When Todd heard the bell ring at the house he decided to ignore it. It rang again, more persistently and he finally opened the door. His face paled as he saw the two detectives standing outside. Why had they returned to him? They would hardly have called in person to advise him of the funeral arrangements.

'May we come in, Mr Gallagher? There are a couple of questions that have arisen from the autopsy that was carried out on Miss Cantonasta.'

Todd nodded, his heart was beating rapidly. Had the autopsy revealed that he had shaken Jennie-Lea and pushed her or had a neighbour watched him throw her body over the balcony?

He led them into the communal lounge and they were surprised at the relative cleanliness and tidiness of the room. Usually if they had occasion to visit students the place was a pig sty of take away food cartons, empty beer cans and general neglect.

'Now Mr Gallagher, as you know an autopsy had to be carried out on Miss Cantonasta's body. It was ascertained that the lady broke her neck in the fall. I won't go into details of the other findings the coroner noted. I'm sure you don't want to hear about those.'

Todd sat there immobile. He was sweating and he hoped the detectives had not realised how uncomfortable he was.

'The one relevant fact that could concern you that the coroner placed in his report was that the young lady was pregnant. Were you aware of that?'

Todd shook his head slowly.

'Miss Cantonasta had not told you?'

Again Todd shook his head. He did not trust himself to speak.

'Was there any reason for Miss Cantonasta not to tell you?'

'Maybe she was not sure.'

'I think she would have known. According to the autopsy gestation was approximately ten weeks. Would the child have been yours?'

'Yes.' Todd spoke in a whisper.

'Had Miss Cantonasta mentioned this to you what would your reaction have been to the news?'

Todd licked his lips and thought rapidly. 'Mixed. I would have been delighted to know I was to become a father and I know Jennie-Lea wanted a family. I would have been a little disconcerted that it had happened at this time. We planned to get married when I had finished University. A baby on the way would have meant altering our plans somewhat.'

The detective nodded. 'How would the coming of a child have altered your plans?'

'Well,' Todd spoke slowly. 'When I've finished Uni I have a place waiting for me in my father's bank. Before taking up the position we planned to get married and spend a bit of time travelling. A baby would have meant getting married now and our plans for travelling put on hold.'

'Would that have upset you, Mr Gallagher?'

Todd shrugged. 'Not really.' He allowed his voice to break. 'All I wanted was Jennie-Lea. She meant everything to me.'

Saffron began to receive an email virtually every week from Vasi. He attached photographs of the rooms of his apartment as he added items. She was amused to see he had chosen some of the sketches that Yannis sold in his shop, each one framed with a pink surround.

"I decided that if I had all of them framed in pink I could move them around whenever I was tired of looking at the same picture in a room, and they match well with the floor," he explained.

Saffron replied that she thought that was a good idea and the next email he had sent had photographs of different coloured tiles attached. She shook her head. How was she supposed to know what colour he would be happy with? She mailed him back, advising him not to have anything that was too dark, suggesting also that he could consider breaking up the plain expanse of a tiled wall by having a picture tile inserted at strategic intervals.

Her idea meant she received another batch of photographs and she showed them to Marjorie.

'What do you think, Marjorie? I don't mind making suggestions, but I refuse to make his decisions for him.'

'It would be much easier if you were out there. That way you could discuss ideas together.'

'I am not going to Crete just to help him refurbish his apartment.'

'Have you thought that he might be planning to make his apartment acceptable for you?'

'What do you mean?'

'Well, I got the impression when we were out there that he could become serious about you. If I'm right, and if you felt the same way, of course, he would want you to be happy with his apartment when you moved in.'

'What!' Saffron's face flamed. She shook her head. 'No way. I'm an English doctor, happily living in England. Besides, what about you?'

'Me? You don't have to consider me.'

'Of course I do. You've stood by me with all the problems I've presented to you, first Martin and then Ranjit. The time will come when you need someone to look after you and I'm not letting you go into some awful geriatric home. I shall always be here for you.'

'But you like Vasi?'

Saffron considered. 'Yes, I like him, but he has never made any approach towards me that would make me think he had anything more than a liking for me; and he's five years younger than I am.'

'Age doesn't matter if you're compatible.'

Saffron laughed. 'Marjorie, please stop trying to see a romance where there isn't one.'

'I'd just like to know you were happy with someone.'

Todd sat through the inquest where the autopsy results had been relayed to the court and felt unreasonably annoyed when he learnt that Jennie-Lea had been eight years older than she had told him. If she had lied to him about her age what else had she lied about to him? He breathed a sigh of relief and tried to slip away unnoticed when the verdict of accidental death was finally read out, but a hand on his arm stopped him.

'I'd like to have a word with you.'

Todd looked at the grim faced man beside him. 'Yes, sir?' he managed to say.

'I'm Jennie-Lea's father. I understand you're the man who made her pregnant. Bad enough that you caused her death, but to besmirch her good name by making her pregnant is unforgiveable.'

Todd swallowed and licked his lips. 'It was an accident. She fell from the balcony.'

'No doubt making her pregnant was an accident as well.'

'I loved Jennie-Lea,' protested Todd. 'I would never have hurt her.' He felt the blood rush to his face as he realised his protest was a lie.

Todd averted his eyes. This man instinctively knew he was guilty of causing Jennie-Lea's death. Mr Cantonasta gave him a hard stare and walked away, his lips compressed and his fists clenched.

Nicola had heard, as had everyone at the University, of the death of Todd Gallagher's girl friend. To protect himself, Todd said he would rather not talk about it and his acquaintances understood and accepted that he was still shocked and distressed over the unfortunate accident.

The first time Todd returned to the diner that he had frequented with Jennie-Lea, Nicola slipped into the empty seat opposite him.

'I'm terribly sorry,' she said quietly.

Todd looked at her. 'I feel it was my fault. If she hadn't come out to wave to me it wouldn't have happened.'

'You can't blame yourself. It was just a terrible accident.'

'Her father blames me. You should have seen the way he looked at me.'

'He's hurting, Todd. The same as you are. His way of coping is to blame you.'

'Do you really think so?'

'I do.'

'What can I do?'

'There's nothing you can do to bring her back. It might help if you had some counselling.'

'I've tried that.'

'Then maybe if you immersed yourself in your Uni work? That would occupy your time until you feel more able to face life without her.'

'I can't seem to concentrate.' Todd shook his head miserably.

'You say that now, but I hope that within a year or two you will have found someone else who can mean as much to you.'

'Do you think so?'

'You're young. You cannot spend the rest of your life mourning for her. It wasn't your fault.'

Todd looked up at Nicola. 'No, it wasn't, not really.' He looked as if he was about to cry.

Nicola reached across the table and patted his hand. 'I must go or I shall be in trouble with the boss. I just wanted to tell you how sorry I was.'

Todd returned home and opened his computer. He had kept a diary since he was a teenager. The past few months the references had been nothing more than the date followed by the initials J-L. Now he sat down and wrote every detail that he could remember about the fateful night. When he had finished he sat and read it carefully.

Nicola was right. It was not his fault. Jennie-Lea should not have been stupid enough to become pregnant; she had assured him she was taking precautions. She should not have left her shoes where she could fall over them when he pushed her away. No; it was definitely not his fault. All he had done was moved her body to a different location. It was an accident, whichever way you looked at it.

Nicola mailed John and told him about Todd and the sad death of the man's girlfriend.

"I feel terribly sorry for him. He's obviously blaming himself. It was a routine act with them when he left. They had always done it. You don't expect to fall over your balcony just by waving to someone. I don't really know him. They used to come into the diner together and I would see him around occasionally at Uni, but it isn't as if he's a real friend. If it helps him I'm willing to chat with him when I do see him, I don't know how anyone can help him to come to terms with it. I know how devastated I would be if anything awful like that happened to you."

John replied, sympathising and agreeing that no one could really help anyone come to terms with their grief under such circumstances.

Todd started to look for Nicola each day when he was at the

University. He knew her timetable now and would ensure he was in the same area when she passed through on her way to a class. He convinced himself that the sight of her calmed him and it became necessary to him to catch a glimpse of her, however fleeting. If she noticed him she would occasionally raise her hand in acknowledgment or smile. His diary was growing again now. He recorded how many times he had seen Nicola during the course of the day and whether she had acknowledged him in any way.

His presence did not go unnoticed by Nicola and it made her feel uneasy. He always seemed to be around wherever she was, either at the University or working. She could feel his light grey eyes on her as she waited at the tables. She appreciated that the man was probably lonely and unhappy, but when he asked if she would care to go to a movie with him she refused immediately. She was not interested in taking the place of his previous girl friend; she didn't really like him very much.

MAY 2007

Saffron opened up the email she received from Vasi. This one was longer than those she had received recently. Earlier in the year he had completed the redecoration of his apartment and had sent her photographs of every room. She had sent complimentary replies, sometimes making a further suggestion, but usually approving of his new decor. She read it curiously.

"I went up to see Pappa and Cathy last week. They are both well, but when I suggested to Cathy that we went for a walk she declined, saying it was too hot. I think that was an excuse. I noticed she had two sticks beside the front door, although she still refuses to use one in the house as she can lean on the furniture. I think she is having even more difficulty in walking.

I walked through the olive trees where it was very pleasant. I wish you could have been here with me as I would have liked to ask your opinion. When I returned to the house I asked Pappa and Cathy to visit me in my apartment the next weekend to see my new decor that you helped me with. Pappa made excuses at first, then Cathy insisted she would like to see it, so he gave in.

I arranged for them to have lunch at the hotel in Heraklion and I joined them. I think the chef there is more accomplished than the one in Aghios Nikolaos as my father was very complimentary about the food. After lunch they drove with me to my apartment and admired it very much. They saw it as you did originally. I told them how much you had helped me to decide on the colours and designs of the tiles. Cathy says you have a good eye.

I am longing for you to come over and see my apartment as it is now. You would not believe it was the same one. Do let me know your dates as soon as possible so I can arrange to spend some time with you."

Saffron sighed. Did she want to become involved with Vasi?

John grinned as he saw Vasi's car pull up ready to collect Saffron. He was not sure about the relationship between them, but he gave a 'thumbs up' sign to Saffron as she left and was amused to see her blush furiously.

'Be good,' he said to her in a quiet voice. 'No accidents.'

Saffron shook her fist at him. 'I can guarantee it.'

John raised his eyebrows mockingly at her.

'Who's had an accident?' asked Marianne as she appeared from the kitchen. 'Not Vasi, surely? He's a very careful driver.'

'Private joke, Mum. Stems from London. Saff was always concerned that Nick and I could have an accident. Traffic, you know.'

Saffron almost choked as she heard his glib reply. 'I'm not sure what time I'll be back,' she said to Marianne. 'Vasi wants to show me his apartment now he has redecorated and has said we'll be meeting Cathy and Vasilis for dinner afterwards.'

'No problem. If we've all gone to bed you have a key to your patio door, haven't you? Just let yourself in.'

Saffron checked in her purse and nodded. 'I doubt if I'll be that late.'

'Have a good time. Tell Cathy I'll 'phone her during the week and arrange for them to come here for a meal.'

'So, you are back again,' smiled Vasi. 'It is good to see you. How is Marjorie?'

'She's now regretting her decision not to come with me I imagine.'

'Why has she not come?'

'I could only take a week away from work and she said she felt guilty coming and staying with my relatives and not giving anything back.'

'I'm sure they are only too pleased to see her. Maybe the next time you visit you could both stay in my apartment. Then she would not feel guilty.'

'Of course she would. We would both feel guilty about taking advantage of you.'

'You would not need to. I could come and stay with you after the season has finished. It would be, what do you say, reciprocated.'

'Are you really planning to come to London?'

Vasi nodded. 'Last winter I was busy with the apartment. This winter I will have free time. I would like to see London if you would allow me to stay with you. I would not want to visit the city alone.'

'You'd be more than welcome. Let me know the dates you plan to come as soon as possible and I'll see if I can juggle my timetable around and get some time off.'

'That would be good. I know I could stay in Rebecca's house, but I would not know where to go if I was alone. Twice I have been to England and stayed with her and Grandpa. They took me to London for a day each time. We caught the train and then we caught another train. We watched the changing of the guards; then it was time for lunch. That afternoon they took me on the bus to see London. I did not see everything I would have liked to see. The second time they took me to Covent Garden and to a theatre. These are not the things I wish to see.'

'What do you want to see?' Saffron had not realised that Vasi had visited England before.

'Everywhere that John and Nicola saw when they stayed with you.'

'Why didn't you ask your grandparents to take you to those places?'

'I was a very shy sixteen year old the first time I went. I did not like to ask and they took me to other places near where they lived. They were interesting, but not London. The second time we spent one day in London then Grandpa drove us up to Scotland. I saw Edinburgh and the castle there. We drove back down the other side of England and stayed for three days in Wales. It was interesting, the scenery in some places was magnificent, but I think we spent more time sitting in the car driving than seeing anywhere.'

'So why didn't you go again?'

'Maybe I had been a naughty boy?' Vasi raised his eyebrows at her.

'What did you do?'

Vasi smiled. 'Nothing, I was joking. I behaved very well when I was with them. I had to do my National Service. When that was finished I started to work in one of my father's hotels. In the winter months I had to go back to school to study accountancy and hotel management.' Vasi shrugged. 'When I had free time for a holiday they would be staying over here.'

'Well, you've seen Scotland and Wales. I've never been to either place.'

'You have not?'

Saffron shook her head. 'Marjorie would take me out during the holidays and we always had a couple of weeks in a caravan by the sea. It seemed we always chose the wrong weeks as it rained. After my father died money was short and I was studying to be a doctor.'

'You did not go away when you were married?'

'Once, for a long weekend in Paris. It was not an experience I would want to repeat.'

'You did not like Paris?'

'Paris is beautiful. I'd only been to France on a school trip before. It was just the company and the circumstances.'

'I would like to go to Paris one day.' Vasi spoke wistfully.

'Maybe when you come to London you could visit France for a weekend. They advertise weekend breaks that are very reasonable.'

Vasi nodded. 'And you would come with me?'

Saffron shook her head. 'I couldn't promise. It would depend upon my hospital schedule.' She did not want to commit herself to going to Paris with Vasi, although she was sure she would enjoy it far more than her previous visit with Ranjit.

'We will see,' smiled Vasi. 'Now, we will have lunch. I have arranged it in the hotel. Then I will show off my apartment to you.'

Saffron duly admired the changes Vasi had made to his apartment. It was certainly far more attractive than the first time she had visited and guessed it had taken a considerable amount of money to make the improvements.

'So,' he said finally. 'What do you think or do you have more suggestions?'

Saffron smiled at him. 'I think you've done wonders. You can see that someone lives here now. I love the tiles you have in your bathroom.'

'And the others?'

'I am not so sure.'

Vasi looked stricken. 'Do you want me to change them?'

'Vasi, it is not up to me. Are you happy with them? You asked my opinion and I gave it. That was all.'

'It is important to me that you also like the decorations.'

'Decor,' Saffron corrected him. 'Decorations are the things you put up at Christmas. I do like it. I'm not sure about the tiles in the second bathroom. I know you sent me through photographs but they are darker than I had imagined.'

'But you would be happy to stay here?'

'If Marjorie and I come over we shall be expected to stay with the family.'

'That is not what I asked,' replied Vasi impatiently. 'I asked if you would be happy to stay here?'

'I might have to add some items to your kitchen cupboards,' she smiled.

'Saffron, please, I am being serious.' Vasi took her hands in his. 'I would like you to come and stay here, stay for two or three months, longer maybe. I want to get to know you properly. I cannot do that whilst you are in England. I want you to know me.'

'Vasi, I am a doctor. I have to go back. I can't just decide to stay here on an extended holiday.'

Vasi dropped her hands and sighed. 'You do not want to stay here. I should not have thought you might. I am, what do you say, presumptuous?'

Saffron looked at the unhappy man before her. 'Vasi, I think we should sit and talk. I am not sure exactly what you are asking of me.'

'I am asking that you stay and we get to know each other. I like you. I find you intelligent and amusing. I think you like me. We need time together to discover how much we like each other. If we like each other enough we could decide to stay together.'

Saffron shook her head. 'There are some things in my past that I should tell you. When you have heard about those you may not wish to get to know me better.'

Vasi raised his eyebrows. 'You would like some wine whilst we talk?' Without waiting for her answer Vasi went into the kitchen and returned with a bottle of wine and glasses. 'Do you wish to sit on the balcony or do you prefer to stay inside?'

'Inside,' Saffron answered immediately. 'I wouldn't really want your neighbours to hear me.'

'I doubt if they would understand, but if you prefer inside...' Vasi shrugged and poured them both a glass of wine. He handed a glass to Saffron and touched it with his own. 'I hope this will be the beginning.'

Saffron tried to smile. She could well imagine that when she had told Vasi about her family and her previous marriage it could well be the end.

'I need to tell you about my husband but I must start at the beginning. As you know I was born in America. My mother was Greek and my father English. Bryony is my older half sister and I had two others, Sorrell and Christabelle. My mother was...' Saffron struggled for the correct words, 'attracted to men. Each one of us had a different father. My father left my mother and divorced her when I was ten. He found she was expecting a child by a Turk.

Vasi raised his eyebrows. 'A Turk!'

Saffron nodded. 'Dad decided to return to England and brought me with him. That is how I lost contact with my family in America. When I visited last year Bryony met me and we had a long chat. She told me my mother was dead.'

Vasi crossed himself. 'I am sorry.'

'That happens,' Saffron shrugged. 'My father had died also, but he had died from an illness. My mother had been murdered.'

'My God. How awful. I have heard that such things happen often in America.'

Saffron continued as if he had not spoken. 'My younger half sister had murdered her.'

'What!'

'It was not known at the time. She pretended it was one of our mother's boyfriends who had committed the crime. He denied all knowledge of it and finally employed a private detective to try to clear his name.' Saffron took a sip of her wine. She held up her hand as Vasi was about to interrupt. 'The detective followed her across Europe where a number of people she had worked with had met with accidents. She came to Crete and John took a film of her tampering with the brakes on his bike. John went to Rhodes with the private detective and again he filmed her. This time she hit a man over the head and pushed his wheelchair down a steep road to make it look like an accident.

They arrested her when she returned to New Orleans and she was declared insane.'

'All Turks are insane.'

Saffron had to smile. 'Of course they're not. Listen, Vasi; that is not the end. The man she hit over the head was Giovanni's younger brother. He was living in Rhodes with my other sister, Sorrell.' Saffron dropped her eyes in embarrassment. 'She was working as a prostitute to feed her drug habit.'

'So what has happened to her?'

'Sorrell or Christabelle?'

'The one who murdered your mother.'

'She was placed in a prison mental hospital. During Hurricane Katrina she died.'

'How?'

'We think she drowned.'

'And the other one, the prostitute?'

'I don't know.'

Vasi took another mouthful of wine. 'Thank you for telling me, but two of your sisters being bad does not make you bad. Bryony is not bad.'

Saffron shook her head. 'I have to tell you about me.'

'I cannot believe that you have ever done anything wicked.'

'No,' Saffron sighed. 'I'm just stupid. I fell in love with a man and I thought he loved me. I found out quite by chance that he was already married and had children. I obviously never saw him again once I knew.'

Vasi patted her hand. 'That is unfortunate. Some men are unscrupulous. That was not your fault.'

'Then I married an Indian. He told me he was a widower.'

Vasi looked at her in horror. 'He was not still married?'

Saffron shook her head. 'He had killed his wife and buried her beneath the floorboards of their house.'

'I do not believe it! You are telling me stories!'

'It's true, Vasi. I could hardly believe it either. He had seemed charming at first; kind and considerate; then after we were married he changed. If I disagreed with him or did something he disapproved of he would become physically threatening. He bought a new car and clothes. When the bills came in he expected me to pay them.'

'And did you?'

'I didn't feel I had a choice. He said he was sending all his money back to India to the man who had paid for his education, but he was actually saving it for himself. His wife's body was discovered and the police started to look for him. When they found him he was just about to board a plane for Venezuela.'

'And he is in prison now for many years?'

'No. They didn't convict him of murder, only unlawful burial. I *knew* he had murdered her and started divorce proceedings. Before the divorce could go through he was killed in prison. That is how my husband died.' Saffron gulped down the remainder of her glass of wine quickly.

Vasi looked at her steadily. 'All this you have told me – it is the truth?'

'Absolutely.'

'I am so sorry, Saffron.'

'It's all right. I understand that you don't want to get to know me better now.'

Vasi shook his head. 'No, I am sorry you have had such suffering.' He took her hand. 'Thank you for telling me, for being so honest.'

'I'm sure if you had asked Bryony she would have told you about our sisters. We have bad blood in our family.'

'You and Bryony are not bad people.' He smiled at her. 'Any bad blood must have been passed from the fathers, maybe they were both Turkish.'

'Vasi, you cannot blame everything on Turkish men.' Saffron had a desire to giggle.

'Of course you can, if you are Greek.' Vasi refilled their glasses. 'Can we talk some more? It is not too distressing for you?'

Saffron nodded.

'Your marriage – it was a bad experience. Is that why you are so unwilling to accept my advances?'

'You haven't made any.'

'I have tried. Each time I felt you were saying go away.'

Saffron felt tears coming into her eyes. 'I don't mean to. I just don't want to make another mistake and get hurt again.'

Vasi gazed at her earnestly. 'I would not want to hurt you, Saffie. We are friends, yes? I would like that friendship to progress. Maybe we find we do no more than like each other, so we just remain good friends.' He shrugged and placed his hand on hers and drew her close to him. This time Saffron did not withdraw from his touch.

Todd lay on his bed and thought about Jennie-Lea. It wasn't his fault. The more he had thought about the unfortunate events of the evening four months ago the more he managed to convince himself that he had had nothing to do with her death. She had come out onto the balcony to wave goodbye to him and fallen. It had been an unfortunate accident. Nicola had said it wasn't his fault. She was so sweet and sympathetic. She had become his guardian angel and he would be her protector. She needed his protection against the world. He felt tears coming into his eyes. If only he knew where she lived he would be able to hang around outside and catch a glimpse of her whenever he felt depressed.

To know where Nicola lived suddenly become supremely important to him. Did she live alone, with her family, or the worst scenario of all, with another man? He would pay a visit to the diner on Saturday. He would not go in, but wait in the parking lot until she finished work for the day and follow her.

Todd sat in his car, slouched down as far as possible. From his position in the parking lot he was able to watch the entrance to the diner. He knew there was a rear exit, but if Nicola left that way she would still have to walk to the front of the building and he would see her. He didn't plan to approach her. He wanted to see if she was the driver of one of the other cars that were parked there or if she was on foot. If she had a car it would be a simple matter of following her and finding out where she lived.

Todd watched as she left the diner, her bag slung over her shoulder. She did not glance in his direction and he risked moving higher in his seat to watch her walk to the exit and turn along the road. He started his car. There was no rush to follow her if she was on foot. He would drive along, keeping her in sight, then when it was no longer practical to do so without her noticing he would drive past. He would be patient. Within a couple of weeks he would know exactly where she lived.

Todd had driven around the area where he knew Nicola lived for hours on end, partly in the hope of seeing her and also to familiarise himself. Now he was feeling elated. He had parked on the main road just beyond the first turn off. Through his car mirror he watched Nicola approaching and waited for her to walk past, hoping she would not notice him. To his delighted surprise she turned into the side road and was then out of his sight. He waited half an hour and there was no sign of her returning to the main road. She had to live in one of the houses in the area.

Todd pulled his cap well down over his eyes and drove into the close, studying the houses as he went. The houses stood back from the tree lined walkway, surrounded by low walls that partially hid the well kept gardens, but all appeared deserted by their occupants and gave him no clue which one she occupied. Todd drove away happily. He knew Nicola would be working at the diner the following day and he would be waiting to see exactly where she went to when she left.

Todd returned happily to the house he shared with the other students and opened his computer. He spent almost an hour writing up his diary for the day. He described in detail how he had followed Nicola and discovered the area where she lived. Now he knew that it should be easy to look her up on the population census that was taken five years ago and then he would know even more about her.

Todd trawled through the information available to him, realising the task he had set himself was insurmountable. He needed to know her surname. He chewed at his thumb. Could he ask her? Could he ask Melanie? Should he wait until Monday and see if he was able to find out from the office at the University?

He agonised over the decision and decided he could not wait until Monday. Once he had ascertained Nicola's address there would be no need to follow her and see which house she turned in at. If he failed to find the details he required on the census he could always wait in the area as he had originally planned. He would go to the diner just before Nicola left for the day on Sunday and see if Melanie knew Nicola's surname. He rehearsed what he would say to her, try to make it sound like a casual enquiry and hope Melanie would be forthcoming.

Todd parked in the lot assigned to customers for the diner and sauntered in, taking his place at his favourite table, that gave him a good view of the remainder of the room and also the counter where Nicola would prepare the drinks and ice creams that were ordered. As he had calculated she was just finishing her duties and he watched her as she spoke briefly to the manager before collecting her bag and walking out of the door.

Melanie walked over to him. 'Hi. What can I get you?'

'I haven't really decided yet.'

'No problem. I'll come back in a while.'

'Where's Nicola what's her name?'

'You've just missed her. She finishes at six thirty.'

'I didn't realise how late it was. What is her name? I can never remember.'

'Christoforakis.'

'That's it. I can never get my tongue round it.' Todd wanted to punch the air with elation. It had been so easy. 'I'll go for the steak and chips. Make it rare.' He replaced the menu beside him as Melanie wrote his order on her pad.

Todd ate his meal hurriedly, repeating continually to himself "Christoforakis, Christoforakis." He was not sure how it was spelled, but he was sure he would now be able to find her on the census.

Todd sat at his computer. It was amazing how many people had the surname Christoforakis. It must be a common Greek surname, despite the variety of spellings he found. He trawled up and down amongst the information, finally deciding her father was Nicolas, a language teacher and the head of the household, her mother was called Elizabeth, and she had a younger sister Eleanor. Todd smiled to himself. Tomorrow, when he had finished at University he would drive past again and ascertain exactly which house she lived in. He spent a further satisfying hour adding the information to his diary.

Todd drove slowly into the close, looking at the numbers displayed on the mail boxes, finally stopping outside the house where he now knew Nicola lived. There was no one around and he sat and gazed at the house intently. He would like to live in a house that looked like this one. He longed to look inside, to see the rooms where she spent her time and particularly her bedroom. He tried to imagine it. He could not envisage it as a pink and white boudoir, maybe green and white with a touch of yellow, lavender and white he felt would suit her best, and it would be impeccably tidy and organised.

Engrossed in his fantasies he did not notice the car that had stopped almost behind him, its indicators flashing to say it wanted to turn into the drive way. A blast on the horn startled him and he looked in his mirror to see a blonde woman waving at him and pointing. Hurriedly he started his car and drove to the end of the close, where he rounded the tree that stood in the middle of the road and drove back down. The woman had parked in the drive way to the house and was unloading groceries. Todd felt a small thrill go through him. That must be Nicola's mother. As he drove past she glared at him and Todd raised his hand in apology.

This was something else to add to his diary.

JULY – AUGUST 2007

'Only one more week,' announced Nicola to Melanie. 'I can hardly wait. I wish we were able to go to London again.'

'You're so lucky,' sighed Melanie enviously. 'I wish I had relatives in Greece that I could go and stay with for a couple of months.'

'I have to work whilst I'm there. It's not just a freebie, you know.'

'Yeah, but you get plenty of time off to lie in the sun, I bet.'

Nicola nodded. 'I wouldn't complain if I worked all the time. It's so good to have John around.'

'You've got it made, girl. Oh, don't look now. Here comes your local admirer.'

'You serve him.'

Melanie shook her head. 'You might as well go over. He'll only make some excuse to come over to the counter to see you otherwise.'

Nicola pulled a face. 'I wish he'd find himself another girl friend. He seems so lonely.'

'I think he's plucking up enough courage to approach you. He only ever comes in when you're working.'

Nicola shook her head. 'He asked me out once way back and I refused. Since then he's never said a word to make me think he's interested in me, but he's always around. At least when I'm in Elounda I won't be seeing him all the time.' She smiled. 'Well, I guess I can be pleasant to him for a while longer.'

Nicola walked over to Todd with a smile on her face.

'Hi, how are you, and what can I get for you today?'

'I fancy a sundae. What flavours do you have on offer today?'

'Strawberry, raspberry, banana, peach, mango, gooseberry, black currant, plum,' Nicola shrugged. 'You name it, we have everything.'

'I'm sure you do.' Todd considered carefully. 'I don't want anything too sweet. What do you suggest?'

'Black currant or plum.'

'Is it made from golden plums or the lovely, dark variety, like you?' Todd took a breath. He had not meant to put his thoughts into words.

'Dark plums.' Nicola ignored his remark.

'I would certainly like to sample it.' He ran his tongue across his lips and Nicola felt distinctly uncomfortable. She scribbled on her pad and returned to busy herself behind the counter. She could feel his eyes watching her as she blended and mixed, added a wafer and finally placed the bowl in front of him.

'Thank you. You wouldn't fancy joining me, I suppose?'

Nicola shook her head. 'I'm working. Enjoy your sundae,' she said and walked back behind the counter.

Once home, Todd opened up his computer and immediately went into the folder where he kept his diary.

> *I told her she was lovely, like dark plums. I actually said that to her. It's true. She has the most glorious dark hair and an olive skin. Her eyes dance and sparkle when she is talking, but when she speaks to me she appears wary. I don't know why. I would not hurt my guardian angel.*

Todd looked at his results in disbelief. He had failed his exams. What was his father going to say? Would he insist that he returned to Dallas and work his way up through the bank starting as a junior? He did not want to be put in such an ignominious position. Of course, the reason he had failed was due to Jennie-Lea and his grief over her. He had not been able to concentrate properly. He would explain that to his father and ask if he could do an extra year at University to gain the necessary grades to enable him to progress to Corporate Banking. He would promise to work far harder now he was coming to terms with the loss of his girl friend. Surely his father would understand. The bonus was that he would still be able to see Nicola for a further two years. With that thought in mind he smiled. It was worth facing his father's disappointment and possible wrath to be able to stay in New Orleans.

Nicola and John walked hand in hand along the harbour in Elounda. Nicola raised her face up to the sun. 'It's so good to be back. I think I inherited all Greek genes. I loved visiting London, but Crete is home to me, far more than New Orleans.'

John squeezed her hand. 'I'd be happy anywhere with you.'

'Mean it?'

'You know I do. I never look at another girl whilst you're away. Do you look at other boys?'

Nicola shook her head vehemently.

'I bet they look at you, though.'

'I only notice that one whose girl friend died. He gives me the creeps. He always seems to be around.'

'What do you mean?'

'He's doing computer studies so he's not even in the same part of Uni as me but wherever I go he seems to be there too.'

'Why does he frighten you?' John frowned. 'Does he make advances towards you?'

'He asked me out to a movie once and I refused. He just looks at me. He has very pale grey eyes. They remind me of a dead fish.'

'Have you told your Mum or Dad?'

Nicola shook her head. 'What is there to tell? There's a man who comes in the diner who's at Uni. I keep seeing him around. I don't like the way he looks at me. They'd think I was being pretty stupid and tell me to ignore him.'

'Hasn't he found himself another girl friend?'

'I've no idea. If he has he doesn't bring her into the diner and Melanie says he only seems to come in when I'm working.'

'Why don't you look for a job somewhere else?'

'There isn't anywhere else that pays as well without travelling to the other side of town.'

'Does he know where you live?'

Nicola shrugged. 'I don't think so. He's never asked me. Why?'

'I don't like the thought of him following you home.'

Nicola bit at her lip and considered. 'Actually he may know where I live. Mum was complaining one day that she'd come home and couldn't get into the driveway. There was a young man parked outside looking at the house. She hooted and he drove away. It may not have been him, of course.'

John swung Nicola around to face him. 'Nick, I'm really serious. Avoid him. If he comes into the diner try to get someone else to serve him and keep a look out as you go home.'

'I'm sure he's harmless enough. It's just me being silly about his eyes.'

Todd walked into the diner. He hoped Nicola had not already left for her annual vacation to Greece. His father had summoned him to Dallas and it had taken a week for Todd to convince him that his examination failure was due to the shock and grief that he was still suffering due to the death of Jennie-Lea. Finally his father had agreed for him to stay at University in New Orleans to complete his computer and business studies, provided he spent the duration of the vacation studying. If he failed in his studies the following year he would not be staying any longer and there would be no place in the bank for him, even as a junior.

'Hi, Melanie.'

'Hello, Todd. What can I get for you?'

Todd considered as his eyes roved around hoping to see Nicola. 'I'll have a double egg and ham. Is Nicola around? I have something I want to tell her.'

Melanie shook her head. 'She left a couple of days ago for Greece.'

Todd swallowed. It was as he had feared. She had gone and he had no idea where she was or how long he would have to manage without a sight of her. 'Where is it she goes?'

'Elounda.'

'In Lunda? Where's that?'

'Ee-loonda. Over in Greece somewhere.'

Todd nodded. 'Lucky girl. I'd like to go there myself one day.'

'Wouldn't we all!'

Todd returned home and booted up his computer. He recorded his conversation with Melanie in his diary. He had no problem making light conversation with her or any other girl for that matter, but whenever he saw Nicola he often became totally tongue tied and could only look at her. He wrote half a page, complaining about his father. If he had not insisted that Todd returned to his home immediately to explain his examination failure he would have visited the diner and been able to wish Nicola an enjoyable time before she went away. Maybe he could have plucked up enough courage to ask her not to go, but stay in New Orleans with him for the vacation. He fantasised that she would have agreed, saying she had only been waiting for him to ask her; of course she would rather stay there with him than go to her relatives.

Where was this place she visited each year? He was not sure how you spelled Elounda, but he hoped if he asked the computer to search it would lead him in the right direction. He tried different combinations of letters to spell the word until the computer finally asked if he meant Elounda, Crete. He pressed enter and he was given a long list of names containing the word Elounda. He began to investigate each entry, finding most of them were advertisements for hotels or self catering apartments, offering to make him an immediate booking for a holiday. He shook his head. He wanted restaurants. He asked for restaurants in Elounda and again a long list appeared on his screen. How was he supposed to know which one belonged to her relatives?

He tried not to think about Nicola, but when he did it was agonising. He did not weave sexual fantasies about her. He had completely lost his sex drive since the death of Jennie-Lea. It had died as speedily and unexpectedly as Jennie-Lea. He knew now that his feelings for Jennie-Lea had been lust for her body. His love for Nicola was completely pure and unsullied by thoughts of sex. Nicola was his guardian angel and he was her protector. When she finally realised this she would come to him with open arms. She would belong to him and then he was sure his sexual appetite would return and she would be only too willing to give him everything he asked and desired of her because the love between them would be unique.

He stirred restlessly. He should be there with her. He wanted to look after her and keep her safe. Who was she spending her time with? Suppose she met someone in Greece and did not return? What would he do then? If only he had her mobile number he would be able to call her and hear her voice.

Todd tried the telephone directory in the forlorn hope that a number would be registered under her name. Did he dare to approach the house? Maybe the whole family had gone away. After a sleepless night he decided he had nothing to lose by visiting her home; there might be someone around who could give him the information he wanted.

He tried to saunter casually, appearing to scrutinize the numbers as he went, finally turning up the path to the front door.

He knocked and waited, the house appeared deserted. He knocked again and peered through the window for any sign of occupation. It was possible everyone was at the back of the house and they had not heard him. He tried the side gate which opened easily and he walked down the gravelled path to where a wrought iron gate led the way into the garden and was firmly locked. He frowned in frustration, then realised there was a girl lying in a hammock watching him.

He smiled. 'Hi, you must be Nicola's sister. Is Nicola around?'

Eleanor shook her head.

'Any idea when she'll be back?'

'No.'

Todd frowned. 'Would you have her mobile number so I can contact her? I have some rather urgent news to give her regarding a mutual friend.'

'Didn't she give it to you?'

Todd managed to look embarrassed. 'I've lost it.'

Eleanor sighed and stretched languidly. 'Hold on. I'll get it.'

Todd smiled complacently and waited until Eleanor returned with a scrap of paper which she handed to him through the gate. He folded it carefully and placed it in his wallet. 'Thanks. I promise I won't lose it again. I really appreciate your help.'

'No problem.'

Eleanor watched Todd saunter back towards the front of the house and wondered vaguely who he was and why Nicola had never mentioned the attractive man.

Once back in his car Todd was tempted to dial the number he had been given. He wanted to check that it truly belonged to Nicola. He sat with his mobile in his hand and hesitated. It would be more sensible to use a pay 'phone. That way the call could not be traced back to him. He drove to the service station he had passed earlier and walked into the telephone booth. With shaking hands he pressed in the numbers, feeling his heart beat faster as the number connected.

'Hello?'

He let out a deep sigh.

Nicola spoke again. 'Hello? Who is that?'

Todd disconnected the call, leaving Nicola with a puzzled frown on her face. Was that one of the weird calls one heard about or, more likely, a wrong number?

John raised his eyebrows quizzically and Nicola shook her head. 'Wrong number, I guess. No one answered.'

'Where did you find that?' asked Nicola.

John smiled. 'He was on the beach eating a crab. He's starving poor beast. I gave him some water and you should have seen the way he looked at me. He was so grateful. I didn't have the heart to turn him away when he followed me. Can we give him some food and more water?'

Nicola stroked the dog that was sitting looking at John. 'Poor old thing, he's a bag of bones. I wonder who he belongs to?'

'Whoever they are they've neglected him horribly. They don't deserve to own a dog if this is how they treat him.'

'What do you plan to do with him?'

'I thought we could leave him up here for the night. He'll be all right with a bowl of water and a bit more food. He may well have wandered back to his home by tomorrow.'

'If he knows what's good for him he'll stay here.'

'I don't know how the family would feel about adopting a stray dog. I'm sure Ourania would welcome a cat, provided it was a Persian.'

'You're not likely to find a stray Persian cat around. I'll find him some sausages. Stay,' Nicola said firmly as the dog was about to follow her into the taverna and he obediently sat back down. 'I'll bring you a bowl for some water for him.'

John filled the bowl with water and watched as the dog drank thirstily again. He lifted his head and staggered a few paces away before being violently sick and returning to drink some more water.

'Well, that's the crab you ate. What other presents are you going to give us?'

The dog looked reproachfully at John. 'All right, I know you couldn't help it. Just don't make a habit of it. No more crabs.'

John collected a shovel and newspaper to clear up the mess whilst the dog lay panting in a patch of shade. His nose twitched as the smell of cooking sausages came to him. As Nicola appeared he sat up, his tongue hanging out, positively drooling with anticipation.

Nicola set a plate down in front of him with two pieces of sausage. 'A bit at a time or you'll be throwing that lot back,' she warned him. Gradually she fed him the pieces of sausage. She showed him the empty plate. 'All gone.'

He cocked his head on one side and looked at her, then pawed gently at her leg.

'You're still hungry? I'll cook up some more for you in a while. Let that lot go down and settle first.'

'He shouldn't be eating sausages,' remarked John. 'They're not dog food.'

'Well I haven't anything else except burgers.'

'I'll ride down to Elounda and get a couple of cans of meat and some biscuits. Have you any money on you?'

'You can take some from my purse,' offered Nicola.

'I'll pay you back when we go home.'

'There's no need. I can afford a bit of dog food.'

'Yes, but I found him and brought him back. I ought to buy his food.'

'If I'd found him I'd have brought him back, so what's the difference?'

'Can you put the money in the till for the sausages as well? I don't fancy explaining to Mum why the till is short. I'll not be long.' John swung his leg over his bike and rode carefully out on to the main road.

Nicola sat in the chair and the dog moved over to her, leaning against her leg. She pulled gently at his ears and he rubbed his head against her hand asking for more attention. Nicola felt a lump coming into her throat. 'I do hope you are still here tomorrow. I could get quite fond of you.'

As John drew up at the taverna the next morning the dog came forward to greet him, his tail wagging furiously. John tickled his ears.

'So, you decided to stick around, did you? Thought you'd get more sausages? You've another think coming. Dog meat and biscuits for breakfast, same as you had for supper.'

The dog cocked his head on one side as if listening intently. John opened up the door of the taverna and the dog made to follow him inside. 'Stay.'

John opened the windows, placed the fresh bread he had brought with him into the large airtight container, placed the float in the till and finally took out a bowl of dog meat and biscuits for the mongrel who was still sitting patiently outside.

'You're a good dog,' observed John. 'I'd like to know where you've come from. Someone must be missing you.'

Having satisfied his appetite the dog lay down in a patch of shade, appearing to sleep, but by the twitching of his ears and the occasional opening of an eye, John knew his every movement was being watched. As the first visitor to the taverna and shop appeared the dog sat up, alert and watchful. With a wary eye on the animal the man entered the shop.

'Didn't know you had a dog,' he said.

John nodded. 'I'm just looking after him for a friend. He's very well behaved when he's up here.'

'Does he like children?'

'Loves them,' John assured him and hoped he was speaking the truth.

Giovanni arrived during the morning and looked at the dog lying outside the taverna with distaste. 'What's that dog doing here? He'll have to go. I'll not have dogs up here. You know what the tourists are like – convinced they're all vicious and have rabies.'

'It's just for a couple of days. I found him wandering on the beach yesterday. The poor thing was so hungry he was eating a crab! We couldn't just leave him. He's terribly well behaved so he must belong to someone. Once we've found his owner we'll return him.'

'Yes, well make sure you do. As I said, he can't stay here and I know Uncle Yannis won't consider having him down at the house. Ourania was bitten when she was a child and she still avoids dogs.'

'I promise, Dad. We won't keep him. When I leave here I'll take him down to Elounda and see if anyone recognises him.'

'How are you going to do that? You're on the bike.'

'I'll drive slowly and I'm sure he'll just trot along beside me.'

'It's not safe, having a dog running loose on the roads.'

'Only as far as the house, Dad. Then we'll find something to tie to him and walk him round.'

Giovanni nodded. 'Any trade this morning?'

'Odds and ends. How long are you staying? I ought to go up to the play area and check it out for grass snakes.'

Giovanni looked at his watch. 'Have you checked the stock? I'm planning to go into Aghios Nikolaos this morning.'

John nodded. 'Sun screen and shampoo are a bit low and we could do with some more sausages. We nearly sold out yesterday.'

Giovanni raised his eyebrows and glanced at the dog, who wagged his tail happily. 'If you're going up to check the play area, take that animal with you.'

John clicked his fingers and the dog rose to his feet looking at John in anticipation. 'Come on, Skele.'

'Skele?'

'Short for Skeleton. The poor thing's a bag of bones.'

Giovanni looked at the mongrel and realised just how thin the animal was. His ribs were visible beneath his fur, which looked dirty and unkempt. 'If you can't find his owner I suggest you have him put down. He could be carrying some sort of disease.'

'I think he's basically healthy. He'd be bad tempered and aggressive if there was something wrong.'

Giovanni watched as the dog waited whilst John collected a forked stick and a sack, the dog regarding him curiously, then walking sedately beside John over towards the area where they had made a children's playground and a nature area.

Half an hour later John returned, a pleased smile on his face. 'I found one, let Skele have a sniff and he found a couple more. I'll check again before I leave then take these up to the waste ground.'

Giovanni looked at the sack that he knew contained the grass snakes. He was glad that John had no scruples about dealing with them. Anything else he was prepared to tackle, but he abhorred snakes. 'I'll be off then, sure there's nothing more we need?'

'If we have a run on anything I'll 'phone you.'

John watched as his father climbed back into his car. He had hoped his father would have allowed the dog to stay up at the taverna.

John rode his bike very slowly back down the road towards their house, Skele loped along gently beside him, sometimes stopping to investigate a smell and then trotting faster to catch up. They turned into the drive and when John parked his bike he commanded Skele to stay with it. Resignedly, the dog lay down with his nose on his paws and watched as John walked around to the patio. Within moments John had reappeared carrying a bowl of water and Skele lapped gratefully.

'So this is the dog!'

John looked at his mother. 'I've called him Skele. We're going to take him into Elounda and see if we can find his owner.'

'You realise you can't keep him, John?'

'Yes, Dad made that clear this morning when he met him. Actually he's a fantastic asset. I went to check for grass snakes this morning and Skele hunted out a couple for me. I took him up again before I left and he found another one.'

Nicola looked at Marianne. 'Is it all right with you if I go in with John? It could be quicker with two of us making enquiries.' She fondled the dog's ears.

'On one condition – you don't bring him back with you. If you can't find his owner you'll have to take him to the vet.'

John and Nicola exchanged glances. They neither of them had any intention of taking the dog to the vet, knowing what would happen to him.

'We'll sort him out,' John assured his mother. 'I just need to find something to put round his neck so I can hold him. He was fine coming down from the taverna, but he could be spooked once we meet any traffic.'

'I'll get a belt,' offered Nicola. 'We can buckle one part round his neck and hold the rest like a lead.'

Skele stood quietly whilst Nicola placed the belt around his neck and made a hole for the buckle. She attached a second belt to the first to increase the length and John wrapped the leather around his hand. Skele walked sedately between them and Marianne did have to admit that the dog seemed extremely well trained and well behaved.

John waited outside the shops and restaurants whilst Nicola went inside and asked if anyone knew the dog or where he had come from, meeting with a denial each time. After two hours of fruitless enquiries she turned distressed eyes to John.

'What are we going to do?' she asked. 'He's far too lovely to be taken to the vet.'

John raised his eyebrows. 'Lovely hardly describes the poor mutt.'

'I meant his nature, not his looks. You'd think someone would be going frantic looking for him.'

'I think he's been dumped.'

'Dumped?'

'Someone from another area decided they didn't want him any longer for whatever reason and brought him over here and left him.'

'That's too cruel.'

Skele looked from one to the other, flicking his eyebrows as they talked, as if following their conversation. He had not appeared at all frightened of the traffic and did not attempt to pull away from John when a cat sitting on a wall arched its back and spat at him.

'There's just a chance. It's worth asking, anyway.'

'What?' asked Nicola.

'Dimitris.'

'Dimitris doesn't have a dog.'

'Exactly,' John smiled. 'Maybe he'd like one. And I've had another idea.'

Nicola looked at him expectantly.

'Dad could employ Dimitris to come up and remove the grass snakes. Skele would search them out easily enough.'

'Isn't Dimitris working?'

'Odd jobs whenever he can find anything. He has no qualifications for a trade. Dad employed him for a couple of days to tidy up the nature and play area before we opened for the season. He did a good job and earned his money.'

Dimitris shook his head. 'I can't afford to keep a dog. They have to be fed and then there are the vet's fees if they're ill. I'd like to have him, but it's out of the question.'

'Please, Dimitris,' begged Nicola. 'We've got to take him to the vet and have him destroyed otherwise. You're his last hope.'

Dimitris shook his head. 'I just can't afford him.'

'Suppose I paid for his food and any other expenses?' suggested John. 'Would you look after him then?'

'I'd be more than willing to look after him, provided Antonia and her husband don't mind having him around.'

'Can we ask them?'

Dimitris walked into the house where he had lived all his life. 'Antonia,' he called. 'I need to speak to you.'

Antonia appeared from the back room and placed her finger on her lips. 'Despina has just gone off to sleep.'

'Come outside. It won't take long.'

Antonia followed Dimitris back into the sunshine and looked surprised to see John and Nicola with the dog sitting between them.

'John has asked me to look after this dog for him.'

Antonia frowned. 'We can't afford a dog, Dimitris.'

'John has said he'll pay all the expenses, food and the like. He just wants me to keep it here.'

'What's wrong with you keeping it, John?'

'Dad doesn't want it up at the taverna because the tourists are frightened of the local dogs. I can't have it at home because Aunt Ourania was bitten as a child. We've asked around everywhere and can't find his owner,' explained John.

'I'm not sure. Suppose he doesn't like children? I have Despina to think of.'

'Would you take him on trial for twenty four hours? If you're not happy with him around Despina we'll understand. Then he will have to go to the vet.'

'He needs to go there first anyway. I'll not have him around without a clean bill of health.'

John's face broke out in a smile and Nicola let out a breath of relief. 'You'll take him then?'

'You take him to the vet first and then I'll see how he behaves. If I'm worried at all he has to go – immediately.'

'Come and meet Skele, Dimitris. Then come to the vet with us. There's something else I want to talk to you about.'

Antonia returned inside and Dimitris crouched down and held

out his hand for Skele to sniff. He stroked the dog's thin back, feeling the knobbles of his spine.

'Poor old thing. Where did you find him?'

'On the beach eating a crab. He must have been pretty desperate.'

'So what else did you want to talk to me about? I can't keep him if Antonia isn't happy about the arrangement.'

'I understand that. I'm not going to ask you to do anything underhand. Provided you can keep him I'm going to ask Dad if you can come up each day and check for grass snakes. Skele's marvellous at finding them. We know they're harmless, but they freak some of the children out if they come across one in the play area so we try to keep it clear.'

'He'd pay me for doing that?'

'If he agrees he wouldn't expect you to do it for nothing. It could lead to a full time job doing other things next year when I'm away doing my National Service.'

Dimitris's eyes gleamed. 'I'd really appreciate that.'

Nicola wiped down the work surfaces in the kitchen of the taverna. She looked at Marianne dubiously.

'Marianne, may I stay here in Elounda with you?'

'Of course, if that's what you want. You've another three weeks of your holiday from University. Provided you don't need to go back to catch up on any work you're welcome to stay as long as you want.'

Nicola shook her head. 'I don't mean just for the remainder of my vacation. I mean stay out here and not go back to America.'

Marianne scrutinised the girl carefully. 'What's wrong, Nicola? You and John – you're not ...?'

Nicola smiled. 'No, that's not my problem.' She took a deep breath. 'I hate being in America. It's frightening.'

'What is?'

'A lot of things. Where we live it isn't too bad, but there are still parts of New Orleans that are derelict. I don't go anywhere near there, but the people who are living rough come up to the town. They're begging and seem so threatening. I feel sorry for them, but they really frighten me. They're often hanging around the bus stop.'

Marianne frowned. 'If you stay with a couple of friends you should be safe enough during daylight.'

'It's not always possible to be in a group. Sometimes I have to travel alone, depending upon the times of my classes.'

'Wouldn't your mother or father be able to collect you from University or the bus stop?'

'They can't. They have to take Eleanor back and forth to school. I did ask Mum and she just thought I was being jealous of the attention they give to Eleanor.'

'Are you?'

Nicola shook her head. 'No. I think she plays on being ill. If she can't be bothered to do her homework she doesn't hand it in and the teachers excuse her. She never lifts a finger in the house. She claims she's too tired after being at school. She may be, I don't know.'

'I'm sure some arrangement can be made if you don't like travelling around on your own. What about your friends? Would their parents give you a ride?'

'They usually catch a bus and most of them live in the opposite direction from me.'

Marianne wiped her hands. 'There's more to this than you're telling me, isn't there, Nicola? Do you think if you stay over here you'll be able to spend all your time with John? He'll be leaving to do his National Service very soon. He could be away for months at a time.'

Nicola blushed. 'No, it's nothing to do with John. I talked to him about it last year and he said I should talk to my father. I did, and Dad seemed to think I was imagining things.'

Marianne pushed Nicola into a chair. 'Nicola, tell me exactly what the problem is.'

'It sounds silly when I talk about it.'

'I'll be the judge of that. Now, what's really troubling you?'

'It's one of the University students. He would come into the diner with his girl friend when I was there. We used to pass the time of day, but nothing more than a polite interchange. Then there was a terrible accident and his girl friend died. The next time I saw him in the diner I made a point of going over to him and telling him how sorry I was. I sat down and talked to him for a few minutes, he appeared desperately unhappy. He was blaming himself, but I don't see how it could have been his fault. She was waving goodbye to him and fell over the balcony.'

'How awful for him. When did it happen?'

'About six months ago. He began to come into the diner again each weekend. Now he's taken to coming in regularly and staying for ages. Whenever I look at him he's watching me.'

Marianne frowned. 'Are you sure?'

Nicola nodded. 'Melanie says he never comes in if I'm not on duty. If I'm not there he asks her where I am. That's usually when I'm over here.'

'The answer is to stop working at the diner,' said Marianne practically.

Nicola shook her head. 'Dad said that. The trouble is that even if I went somewhere else to work I'm sure he'd find out and I'd still see him anyway. He's always around at University. We're not doing the same courses but I see him continually during the day, just hanging around as I'm leaving a class. He looks at me; then just walks away. He gives me the creeps. I was sure he was following me home from the diner and Dad came and collected me in the car a few times. He certainly didn't follow me then and Dad thought I was just imagining things.'

'Does he know where you live?'

'I think so.'

'Has he spoken to you? Made any lewd suggestions?'

'No, as I say, it's just the way he's always around and looks at me with horrible, cold eyes.'

'Have you talked to your mother about him?'

'I've tried, but she said Dad was certain he hadn't been following me on any of the occasions he had collected me. She thinks I'm being neurotic and craving attention

'Are you?'

Nicola shook her head vehemently.

'Does he have friends?'

'I've never seen him with anyone, not since his girl friend died.'

Marianne squeezed Nicola's hand. 'I don't think you're being neurotic,' she assured her. 'You are obviously genuinely worried by the situation and something needs to be done. I'll 'phone Elizabeth and talk to her. I'm sure something can be sorted out. You don't want him to drive you away from University. John said you were enjoying the work.'

Nicola buried her face in her hands. 'I am. It's just this horrible man.'

Marianne placed an arm round her shoulders. 'Let me talk to your mother. In the meantime try to forget about it and enjoy yourself. We're quiet this afternoon. Why don't you go back to the house and have an afternoon off? I'm not sure what John's up to, but you could probably go for a swim together.'

SEPTEMBER 2007

Vasi emailed Saffron and she read it carefully.

"I have both good news and bad news. Last week Cathy fell down the stairs at their house. She was not hurt, but rather shaken by the experience. When Pappa told me I asked them to visit me at my apartment. He was very unwilling, saying the journey might be too uncomfortable for Cathy as she was bruised. I insisted they had to come to me.

I met them at the hotel in Heraklion and we had lunch before we returned to my apartment. I asked them to have another look everywhere before I settled them out on the balcony and said I wanted to talk to them very seriously. I told them how concerned I had become about Cathy. That I had noticed how much more difficult it was for her to go up and down stairs or walk around outside and now she had actually suffered a fall.

I suggested they should think about leaving the house and moving somewhere that would make life easier for Cathy. I stressed that neither of them were getting any younger. If for any reason they needed medical treatment by the time help arrived it could be too late. I also urged them to consider Cathy's mother, Rebecca. If they moved somewhere closer to her she would appreciate being able to see Cathy more often when she was in Crete.

Before my father could start to object I offered them my apartment. I suggested they stayed down here temporarily to see how they liked living in an apartment in the town. At first my father said it was out of the question. I made an excuse to return to the hotel for an hour, leaving them to discuss the idea. When I returned Cathy had talked Pappa into staying in my apartment. If they found it satisfactory they would look for one of their own. I was so relieved. I will move back and live at the hotel for the time being.

The problem is their dogs. They will leave them up at the house and a man from the village will go up each day to feed them and make sure there is nothing wrong, but Cathy feels they will be miserable without her company. Do you think they will pine for her? I would like to have your opinion."

Saffron read the mail through a second time. It was good news that Cathy and Vasilis were willing to consider moving from their splendid isolation to somewhere more convenient. She wondered if Cathy had sought any medical advice in the last few years. Something quite simple could help her mobility considerably and she wondered if she would be able to approach the subject the next time she visited.

Nicola opened her mail from John and read it avidly. As always he said he missed her and how quiet and uninteresting everywhere seemed now she was no longer there. He was sure Skele was missing her also, although the dog still seemed happy enough living with Dimitris. John included a number of photographs and Nicola compared them with those John had taken of the neglected mongrel when they had first befriended him. His coat was becoming sleek and glossy now, his ribs no longer protruding. He looked fit and healthy, his ears pricked enquiringly as if John had just spoken to him.

John continued with the news that Cathy had fallen on the stairs in their house and her accident had made them consider moving to a more convenient location. Vasi had persuaded them to stay in his apartment for a few weeks to see how they adapted to living on the outskirts of the town. He added that Saffron had arranged to visit for a week and he was looking forward to seeing her again.

Nicola mailed John back and included some photographs of her own.

"Keep me updated with the romance between Saffie and Vasi. Are Cathy and Vasilis really considering moving down to the town? Give Skele a big hug and tell him I miss him. Eleanor is still a pain, but not quite as bad as last year, or am I getting used to her laziness? Give everyone my love and tell them I can't wait to be back out in Elounda again – only ten months – seems like a lifetime."

Todd walked into the diner and drew a deep breath of relief. Nicola was there behind the counter. He had spent sleepless nights, writing page after page of his diary, recording his thoughts about her and wondering what he would do if she did not return. He had tried to keep his promise to his father to spend all the vacation studying, but he had found it difficult. After an hour or so he would become restless, climb into his car and drive around the area where Nicola lived, always eventually driving past her house, despite knowing that she was not there. He had started to call her on the telephone each day and cancelled the call before it had connected. What could he say to her?

He tried to saunter over to a table casually and study the menu.

'Hi. Good holiday?' he asked when Nicola came to take his order.

'Lovely, thanks. How about you?'

'I had to work. My results were not what I'd hoped.'

'That's bad luck. Mind you, not surprising. You'd had a bad experience.'

Todd nodded. Why was Nicola the only person who understood?

'Have you decided?'

'Pumpkin pie.'

177

'Good choice. We have a new chef and he makes it like no other.'

Before Todd could continue the conversation Nicola walked swiftly back to the counter and called out the order. She could feel Todd's eyes on her as she pretended to busy herself behind the counter and wished Melanie had been there and she could ask her to take his order over.

'Pie.' The chef placed the plate on the serving hatch.

Nicola picked up the plate and walked over to Todd's table. 'Enjoy,' she said and turned away.

Nicola felt his hand touch her bare arm and she felt herself goose-bumping. She drew away. Todd seemed speechless, then swallowed, he had actually touched her.

'Could I have a latte as well, please?'

'Sure.' Gritting her teeth Nicola returned behind the counter, poured the coffee and took it over. She made certain she was the opposite side of the table as she placed it before him so he could not possibly touch her again. She did not understand her violent reaction to his touch. Other customers had touched her arm before to gain her attention, but she had never gone cold and had goose-bumps when they did so.

Todd wrote in his diary.

> *I touched Nicola's arm. I actually touched her.*
> *Her skin was so soft and smooth. I wanted to*
> *run my hand all down her arm. I expected to feel*
> *more, but there was nothing, just pure pleasure*
> *at the feel of her skin. Will my old sex urge return?*
> *I'm sure it will when Nicola realises that she is*
> *meant for me and allows me to hold her in my arms.*

Saffron opened up Vasi's email, wondering if his father and Cathy had made any decision about moving house.

"Pappa has decided they will move from their house. But they want to stay in my apartment PERMANENTLY. I know I offered to let them stay there to see how they liked town living, but I did not expect them to actually want to live there. I suggested to Pappa that they used my apartment as a base and look around for somewhere larger. He was quite adamant. Cathy was happy there. He had no time to look around and Cathy would not be able to do so. Pappa was determined that he wanted to buy it from me. I am staying at the hotel all the time now. I am making enquiries about apartments and when you come over I hope you will come with me to view them. You have such good ideas for decor.

Pappa is worried about leaving their house empty, he does not want it to fall into disrepair, yet he is reluctant to try to sell it. I talked to Giovanni. (My father does not know this and Giovanni has promised not to tell him.) I asked his advice for a practical use of the property. Giovanni suggested building small chalets, similar to his own on the land and in close proximity to the house. The house could be used as an administration centre, and with some alterations there would be plenty of room for a dining room and kitchen with a separate bar. Upstairs the rooms could be equipped as gymnasiums, the bathrooms divided to provide adequate shower arrangements and there is the pool already in the grounds. Guests who wanted a walking holiday would find it an ideal spot.

Now I want to ask you your opinion. What do you think of Giovanni's idea of making the area into a walking holiday centre? Do you have any ideas? Please let me know."

Saffron shook her head. She was pleased Cathy and Vasilis had decided to be practical and move to a more accessible area, but sorry that Vasi had lost his apartment after taking so much trouble with the redecoration. She had never envisaged having a house hunting holiday in Crete, but it would certainly be different. She thought Giovanni's ideas for converting the house and making the area a holiday centre was practical, but she had no idea of the expense involved and did not know how interested people would be in staying in a remote area.

'Marjorie, if you wanted a walking holiday would you want to stay up at Cathy and Vasilis's house?'

'How do you mean?'

'I've been thinking, Giovanni suggested to Vasi that he built chalet bungalows up there the same as he has. That would have to be more expensive that converting the bedrooms in the house and making them smaller. You could certainly have six, possibly eight bedrooms, and the ground floor could be the kitchen, dining room and lounge bar.'

Marjorie frowned. 'What about staff?'

'They could come up from Elounda or one of the villages each day. Maybe it could be arranged that one slept in so they were there early to prepare breakfast.'

'Would it be financially worthwhile if you only had a maximum of sixteen people staying?'

Saffron tapped her teeth with her pen. 'They would have to be select, offering something that no one else was so they could charge more. They could have conducted walking tours,' she declared triumphantly.

'Would people want to be taken on a walking tour? Most walkers like to set off armed with a map and discover everywhere for themselves.'

Saffron's face fell. 'Can you think of anything?'

Marjorie nodded. 'Why not offer an artists' holiday? Or a week of Greek cookery classes?'

'Do you really think people would go for that?'

'I do. They offer holidays in England where you can learn a local craft. Why not do so in Crete? There's no reason why two or three who were interested in the cookery couldn't cater for the evening meal for those who've been out painting or walking. That way they would feel their efforts were appreciated and the food wouldn't be wasted.'

'Marjorie, you're brilliant. I'll tell Vasi your ideas and see what he thinks.'

Saffron had expected them to discuss Vasi's forthcoming visit to England during her visit to Crete. She had not envisaged becoming involved in his business plans as well as helping him to look for a new apartment.

Todd was becoming more obsessed with Nicola than ever. He would visit the diner three or more times each day when she was working. He would take some books with him and a writing pad and sit pretending to study, but the notes he made were of Nicola. How many times she took an order, how often she used the coffee machine, which fruits she used when making a sundae, how often she passed his table and was within touching distance. He always closed the pad quickly when she delivered his order and opened it again when she had moved away. During the week at University he would note how many times he had seen her each day, the clothes she had been wearing, had she appeared happy or preoccupied. Often he drove along the road that she walked to return to her home, keeping far enough behind her not to draw attention to himself. Each evening he wrote his notes up in his diary, and would read them over and over again before he finally went to sleep.

Despite his subterfuge Nicola had noticed him and she spoke to her father.

'He makes me feel uneasy, Dad. He always seems to be around wherever I am. I'm sure he follows me home in his car some evenings.'

Nicolas listened to her seriously. 'If he really is becoming a problem to you I'll come into the diner next weekend and have a word with him.'

Nicola shook her head. 'Come in and have a look at him, but please don't speak to him. If he thought he was disturbing me it could make him worse.'

'You're sure you're not imagining things?'

Nicola hesitated. 'I suppose I could be.' She shrugged. 'I wish I'd never spoken to him in the first place.'

'Why did you?'

'It was after his girl friend died. I just said I was sorry.'

'That was just a friendly gesture on your part. You're sure you've never given him any encouragement to become more than friendly with you?'

'Dad!' Nicola turned reproachful eyes on her father. 'I'm not interested in any of the locals, you know that. He asked me out once and I refused him. I'm polite to him in the diner and if he says hello when we meet on campus I reply. He's tried a couple of times to engage me in conversation but I've avoided it. It's just this continual watching of me that gives me the creeps.'

'You're an attractive young lady, Nicola. You must expect men to look at you.'

Nicola shook her head impatiently. 'He doesn't look at me like *that*. It's kind of cold and calculating. He touched my arm the other day and it made me feel cold and shivery.'

'Is that why you decided to speak to me?'

'I guess so.'

Nicolas patted his daughter on her shoulder. 'I'll come along just before you finish on Saturday and have a coffee. If he's there you can point him out to me. You can leave as usual and I'll see if he follows you, but I'm sure you have nothing to worry about.'

Nicolas entered the diner and looked around. There were three couples and a solitary young man sitting at various tables. Nicolas took a seat at the far end where he had a view of the lone man. Nicola came over to him.

'That's him, sitting alone.'

Nicolas nodded. 'You leave as usual. I'll see what he does.'

'I'll bring you a coffee, Dad.'

Nicola smiled at her father and walked away.

'What's your Dad doing in here?' asked Melanie.

'Just dropped in for a coffee.' Nicola frowned, wishing the assistant had not asked her. She was sure by the stiffening of Todd's shoulders that he had heard. 'I'll take it over to him; then I'll be off.'

Melanie watched in surprise as Nicola picked up her purse, called goodbye to her and walked out of the diner whilst her father still sat there with his untouched coffee before him. She shook her head. There was something strange going on.

Todd sat where he was, writing in his notebook.

'Nicola's father arrived at the diner. I know it was him because I heard Melanie ask why he was there. Nicola looks like him, dark and interesting. The same olive skin, but I am sure his would not be as soft and smooth as hers. I decided not to follow her today in case her father noticed and objected. I know I am not doing anything wrong. I just want to make sure she arrives home safely. I am her protector.'

Todd closed his notebook and gathered up his books. He raised his hand to Melanie and walked out into the parking lot to his car. He took his time, placing his books into the glove compartment and adjusting the mirrors. He took a final look at the diner as he started the engine. Nicola's father was standing in the doorway watching him.

As Todd drove out of the parking lot Nicolas climbed into his car. He watched as Todd turned to the right, the direction Nicola would have taken a few moments earlier. Once at the exit he could see Todd's car a considerable distance further along the road. He had already passed Nicola.

Nicolas drove up and stopped beside his daughter. 'Jump in.'

Nicola obeyed and looked at her father. 'Was he following me?'

'I don't think so. When I reached the parking lot exit he had already passed you. It's probably just coincidence that he lives in the same direction.'

Nicola pursed her lips. 'He doesn't usually drive past me. I'm sure he heard Melanie say you were my Dad.'

'Well, if it will put your mind at rest I'll collect you in the car tomorrow and next weekend. He won't know I'm there if I wait at the exit.'

Nicola smiled at her father. 'I appreciate it, Dad. I know you think I'm being stupid and imagining things.'

'If you're really worried by him you could always give up your job at the diner.'

Nicola shook her head. 'I enjoy being there at the weekends; besides, it's my pocket money. Even if I didn't work there I'd still see him around at Uni. I suppose all the time he only looks at me there's no harm in that.'

Todd typed up his diary for the week. The entries now were far longer than the original cryptic entries where he had merely written *"J-L"* and progressed after he had absolved himself of any blame in her death to *"saw N twice today"* or *"saw N safely home"*.

He entered his password and smiled as **"PROTECTOR"** came up as the single document in his very private and security protected folder. He flipped open his notebook.

Monday
9.15 a.m. Saw Nicola walking up to main building. She had arrived safely.
10.45 a.m. Nicola left her first class with two girl friends. Did not notice me.
12.10 p.m. Nicola went to the canteen & bought a sandwich. Sat outside with girl friend. I sat under a tree further away, but where I could watch her.

4.25 p.m. Saw Nicola leaving, but I had another class. I hope she arrives home safely. I shall have a sleepless night worrying that something happened to her and I was not there to save her.

Tuesday

10.30 a.m. I arrived late for my class. Had not slept well, bad dreams. Nicola kept falling from a height and I could not catch her. Woke up sobbing at 3.00a.m. and took a long while to calm myself down and get back to sleep. I do not know if Nicola has arrived. I am in agony.

10.45 a.m. Saw Nicola as she left her class. I am elated. I smiled at her and she raised her hand to me. I am so relieved that she is safely at Uni today.

12.35p.m. Nicola had brought some lunch with her, but sat alone inside the canteen to eat it. I was tempted to join her, but did not have the courage. I need to think of things to talk to her about.

5.00 p.m. Saw Nicola leaving and was just in time to see her catching the bus. I drove to her road and waited until I saw her turn the corner to her house. It is only a short distance up, but I wish I could see her safely inside.

Wednesday

I spent the morning worried sick. There was no sign of Nicola. I looked at her time table and she should have been in a class at 9.15 a.m. I finally went up to the classroom and it was empty. A note was pinned to the door saying classes were cancelled due to illness. Nicola obviously knew this as she finally arrived after lunch. I was so relieved when I saw her.

I had classes all afternoon and did not see Nicola around at all. Had she left earlier? Had she gone home alone or gone somewhere with a friend? If only I knew she was safe.

Thursday

9.15 a.m. Saw Nicola walking up to main building. She had arrived safely.

10.45 a.m. Nicola left her first class with a girl friend. I saw her from the windows.

12.10 p.m. Nicola went to the canteen & bought soup and a roll. Sat inside with girl friends. I sat three tables away. She did not notice me.

5.00 p.m. Saw Nicola safely on the bus. She did not see me parked on the other side of the road but I watched her turn the corner to her house. She seemed in a hurry. I decided to wait around to see if she came out again. I couldn't bear it if she was meeting someone. Girl friends are one thing I can cope with, but the thought of her with another man makes me feel physically sick.

6.30 p.m. No further sign of Nicola so I returned home.

Friday

I had a study morning so I was able to see Nicola as she entered her class and also when she left (9.15 a.m. & 10.45 a.m.) She did not appear to be with anyone and I thought about approaching her. I decided against it. I still do not know what I can talk to her about.

11.00 a.m. Nicola went into her next class. I will be waiting when she leaves at 12.00. I will pretend to be studying the notice board.

12.10 p.m. Nicola went to the library before going to the canteen. She had brought some food with her, but bought a coffee.

1.00 p.m.Nicola left the canteen alone and returned to the library. I do not know how long she stayed there as I had my Business Studies class. I looked for her when I left, but there was no sign of her. Had she left early? I looked at her timetable and decided she probably had and I had missed her. I shall go to the diner early tomorrow morning.

<u>*Saturday*</u>

Nicola was at the diner when I arrived at 9.30 a.m. She greeted me with a smile and said good morning. I asked how she was and she replied she was fine. I asked how her course was going and she replied "really well". After that I could not think of anything to say, so I ordered a couple of eggs and grits. She moves so gracefully between the tables, her hips sway as if she were dancing. I made my food last an hour, by which time it was cold and the eggs congealed, but it did not matter. She was wearing jeans and a pink shirt. I had spent a pleasurable hour watching her. I returned at 1.00 p.m. and took my usual seat. I spread out my books and opened my notepad and sat pretending to work whilst I watched her every move. I saw her showing Melanie some photographs. I would like to see those. Were they photographs of herself? She is beautiful enough to be a film star. I wish I had gone for media studies and planned to become a film director. I would have cast her in a starring role. She would have been famous. I would have something to talk to her about then – her next role – her next film – her box office success. I will have to ask

Melanie about the photographs. Have I the courage to ask Nicola to show them to me?
Back to the diner at 4.30 p.m. Nicola frowned when she saw me and said something to Melanie. Melanie shook her head and Nicola looked cross. I do hope she was not cross with me. I only want to look at her. I left just before she finished and was still in the parking lot when she walked out. I waited until she had disappeared from the entrance then drove down so I could follow her. I'm sure she saw me as she kept looking behind as she walked. Maybe I could offer her a lift one day, the next time it is raining would be a good opportunity or when it is cold and windy.
<u>Sunday</u> 1.00 p.m.
I decided I must be disciplined. I cleaned my room and it was my turn to clean the kitchen. I don't see why I should have to take a turn. I hardly ever use it and when I do I always make sure I leave it clean. Afterwards I tried to do some studying, but found it hard to concentrate. I kept counting the minutes until I could go to the diner for lunch and see Nicola. I have had an idea. I will ask Nicola directly about the photographs. I MUST see them.
Nicola is wearing jeans again today and a floral shirt. When she came over to take my order I smiled at her. "Were they your holiday photos you were showing Melanie yesterday," I asked. Nicola shook her head. "Not really," she said. "We found a stray dog and I was showing Mel his photo."
"I would like to see it, I love dogs," I assured

her. When she brought my sundae she held up a photo of the scruffiest mongrel you have ever seen.

"There he is," she said. "His name is Skele."

"Skele?" I queried and she explained it was short for Skeleton as he was such a bag of bones when they found him.

"Here he is now." She produced another photograph. There was a youth in the photo with his arm around the dog's neck. The dog looked considerably better, but I was fixated by the man.

"Who's that?" I asked.

"My friend, Dimitris," she answered and placed the photos back into her pocket. I could not concentrate for the remainder of the afternoon. Who exactly was this friend she called Dimitris? How could I find out? I considered the question for well over an hour and a half whilst I sat there. I could hardly taste what I was eating.

4.45 p.m.   I was still thinking about the photograph when I returned to the diner. I looked at Nicola and compared her with the scrawny youth I had seen in the photo. Surely he could not be a boyfriend? She needs a good looking blond man (like myself) to offset her dark beauty.

5.30 p.m.   Nicola left the diner on time and I followed her as soon as I had paid my bill. I couldn't find her. In those few moments whilst I paid my bill she had completely disappeared. I was frantic with worry. What had happened to her? Where had she gone? I drove up and down the main road, back to the diner and up past her house. There was still no sign of her. Finally I drove down to the service station and telephoned

*her mobile number. She answered. I didn't speak
to her, but I heard her say hello. I nearly cried. I
was so relieved. She was safe.*

Todd continued his diary with his sightings of Nicola throughout the week. He went to the diner the following Saturday and once again by the time he had driven to the exit of the parking lot she had disappeared. He frowned in annoyance and drove along the main road until he reached her turning. There was absolutely no sign of her. His heart began to beat erratically. What had happened to her? Had she been kidnapped? He swung his car up the turning and as he passed Nicola's house he saw her father's car was in the drive way. He punched the steering wheel furiously. Her father must have collected her. It was *his* duty to see her safely home and today her father must have collected her by car. Was that how she had disappeared the previous week? Tomorrow he would leave the diner earlier and drive to the exit and see if her father was waiting.

Todd spent a restless night turning the problem over in his mind. Why was Nicola so unwilling to accept his protection? Was it due to that skinny youth with the dog? He felt the bile rising in him. He could not let her waste herself on someone like him.

'So what are your plans for this holiday?' asked Bryony. 'You've seen just about everywhere. Is there somewhere you'd like to go again or do you just plan to laze around?'

Saffron felt herself colouring. 'Actually I shall be spending quite a bit of time with Vasi.'

Bryony raised her eyebrows. 'Tell me more.'

'You know that Cathy and Vasilis have bought his apartment from him?'

'No, I knew they were staying there, but I didn't know he'd sold it to them.'

'Apparently Vasilis insisted. Having stayed there for a few weeks they decided it was exactly what they wanted. Vasi has moved back to live in the hotel, but he wants me to help him find another apartment.'

'Why don't you look for a small villa? You'd have room for Marjorie then when she comes over.'

Saffron shook her head. 'It's not for the two of us, just for Vasi. I have no plans to come and live over here.'

'Nor did we,' remarked Bryony. 'Oh, well. If you enjoy looking at empty property you can always enjoy yourselves a second time around when you need somewhere larger. Whereabouts does he have in mind?'

'Hersonissos or Heraklion because of the hotels he looks after.'

Bryony frowned. 'It would make more sense for him to move down this way and look after the hotels in Aghios Nikolaos and Elounda. To come down from Heraklion will add an hour on to the journey each way for Vasilis. Why don't you suggest to him that he exchanges hotels with his father and looks around down here for somewhere to live?'

'I'm sure Vasi won't take any notice of what I say.'

'That's what you think,' remarked Bryony drily.

'You know he's planning to come to London when the season finishes?' Saffron wanted to change the subject.

'So I've heard. He's made John show him all the photos he took when he and Nicola were there with you.'

'You and Marcus will have to think seriously about coming over. Why don't you come in December after Vasi has been?'

Bryony shook her head. 'We're only just keeping our heads above water here. Giovanni and Marianne are very generous, but we try to pay our way. That doesn't leave anything to save.'

'You only need your flights,' urged Saffron.

Bryony shook her head. 'We still need spending money. I know John said he and Nicola found London expensive, despite you being so generous to them. Maybe we'll be able to visit in a couple of years. Now, what else do you want to do whilst you're here, apart from holding Vasi's hand and telling him which apartment he needs to buy?'

'I must spend some time with Grandma. I thought if I spent the mornings with her and then went out with Vasi in the afternoon. Would that suit you?'

Bryony shrugged. 'No problem. She's usually out of her room about ten, so you'd still have time for a swim beforehand if you wanted. It's not that warm now, though.'

'I'm sure it will still feel warm to me. I'll try it tomorrow. If I think I'll go down with pneumonia I won't go in, just paddle on the edge.'

Bryony looked at her sister in disbelief. She knew Saffron would not be content to paddle. She had swum each morning the previous year and often taken a second dip in the early evening.

Vasi took Saffron's hands and held her at arm's length. 'You are looking well. How is Marjorie?'

'Very well also.'

They stood in silence and looked at each other, neither knowing just what they should say. Vasi had an idea that he had missed Saffron far more than she had missed him, whilst Saffron found the touch of his hands were making her heart beat a little faster.

'We will go to Aghios Nikolaos for lunch,' he said finally. 'The town is quieter now and it is not so far to drive.'

Saffron nodded. She wanted to sit and talk to Vasi, firstly about Bryony's idea that he and his father should exchange hotels and also Marjorie's suggestion for his father's house.

'Tell me what is happening in London,' said Vasi as they left Elounda behind them.

'There's very little at the moment. How do you feel about Egypt?'

'You are thinking we should go to Egypt instead of London?' Vasi raised his eyebrows quizzically at her.

Saffron laughed. 'No, I'd like to go to Egypt one day, but you are definitely coming to London. I didn't know if you were interested in the Tutankhamen Exhibition that is coming in November.'

'It is coming to London?'

'November fifteenth it opens and it will run until next year. If you were interested I could book some tickets.'

'That is necessary?'

'It will be very popular. Decide on your dates for your visit and if you want to go I'll make all the arrangements.'

Vasi nodded. 'It would be something I would be interested to see, and I would have something to talk to John about that he has not seen. Will Cathy have seen it?'

Saffron shrugged. 'I've no idea. She may have. It was at the British Museum thirty years ago.'

'I will ask her. You will have to visit them at *their* new apartment whilst you are here.'

'I'm sure you will find another that is just as good and you can decide on all new decor again.'

Vasi shook his head. 'No, you are my interior designer. I will follow your instructions.'

They sat in the dining room of the hotel in Aghios Nikolaos. Vasi pulled a sheaf of papers from his briefcase. 'Now, whilst we wait for our lunch I will show you the details of the properties that have been sent to me.'

'You will have to tell me what they say. I don't read Greek, remember.'

Vasi smiled. 'I asked them to send photographs. It is no good them saying the kitchen or bathroom is "well appointed." I want a separate entrance to my apartment. I do not want to share with other people who will be noisy as they come and go. I need somewhere to park my car and I do not want to be on a top floor dependent upon a lift that will break down regularly. I need to see for myself what these apartments look like. From photographs I can decide whether to go to look more closely or ignore them.'

Saffron nodded. She could imagine that finding an apartment that suited all his requirements would be difficult. 'Which area are you looking in?'

'Heraklion, maybe Hersonissos.'

Saffron swallowed. Dare she tell Vasi Bryony's idea or would he think she was interfering with the family business?

'Just before I left Bryony made a suggestion.'

Vasi raised his eyebrows. 'Tell me.'

Saffron unfolded the map she had with her. 'Your father put you in charge of hotels in these towns,' she pointed to Heraklion and Hersonissos, 'and you lived at Heraklion. If he is now living in Heraklion would there be any reason why you should not exchange hotels?'

Vasi shook his head. 'There is no sentiment attached to them. They are business. The one in Heraklion my father bought from Yannis. It was his first investment, it was where he met Cathy, he may feel sentimental to some degree about that one, but certainly not the others.' Vasi took his mobile 'phone from his pocket. 'I will call him and suggest the idea to him.'

Saffron ate her meal, whilst Vasi picked at his, alternately talking and listening to his father's replies. He waved his hands to emphasise a point, but kept his voice low and controlled, not wishing the staff to understand the nature of his call. Hall an hour later he closed his 'phone and smiled at Saffron. 'So, my father has decided it would be sensible.' He picked up the papers with details of the properties and pushed them back into his brief case. 'These are now useless. We will have to start again. I am sorry. You will have had a wasted day.'

'It isn't wasted at all. We are already in Aghios Nikolaos.'

Vasi shook his head. 'It is not so simple. There are few estate agents in Aghios Nikolaos and they will be closed now until four. They mostly deal with the new property on the market, the developments, aimed at the tourist who decides they wish to come to Crete to live. If you want to sell your villa or apartment you usually put a notice in a window to say the property is for sale and a telephone number. If people are interested they call and you arrange to show it to them.'

'Really? How do you manage if the owner has moved to a different part of the island?'

'They will leave the keys with a friend or relative.' Vasi sighed. 'It can take time to arrange a visit. You telephone the owner, he is at work so you try again in the evening. The friend is also working. It can take a week before an arrangement can be made to meet. By then you will have returned to England.'

'Vasi, instead of spending all your free time looking for an apartment why don't you move back into your father's house? You said your father was worried that it would fall into disrepair.'

Vasi did not answer and Saffron wondered if she had offended him with her suggestions. Finally he rose from the table.

'We will visit my father's house,' he announced and took Saffron's hand. 'Maybe it will still be warm enough for a swim in the pool.'

'I don't have my costume with me,' protested Saffron.'

Vasi shrugged. 'I do not have mine, either, but there will be no one to see us.' He gazed at her quizzically and raised his eyebrows. Saffron felt herself blushing and hoping that it would still be warm enough to swim.

John collected the post and saw the dreaded envelope addressed to him. He knew what that was about. He opened it and his heart sank. He was to report for his National Service in January. That would mean he would be training most of the winter and could then be sent away to any of the islands or mainland during the summer, the time when his parents were busiest and also when Nicola would be over.

He emailed Nicola and complained bitterly about the timing.

"Why did they have to call me for January? I shall be up at Heraklion for my first training, then I could be sent away anywhere. I know I will get a bit of time off and be able to see you if I can get home, but it won't be like it usually is where we can please ourselves once we've done whatever Mum or Dad wanted and spend the rest of the time together.

I thought about appealing and asking if I could defer for a year, but Dad said I might just as well go and get it over with. I'm hoping I shall be able to have an early release as I'm the only son and Dad does need my help. Even so, I doubt if I'll be allowed to leave before I've completed at least a year as they will say he doesn't need me during the winter.

I can't decide whether to ask to train as an electrician or an engineer. Dad says an electrician would be most useful to him, but I'm not sure I want to mess around with wires. I wish they offered photography, but they're so strict about taking photos on the army sites. I shall take my cameras with me, of course. Surely they won't object to me taking a picture of a centipede or caterpillar?

You'll have to send me lots of emails during the summer so that I know exactly what is going on, particularly news of Skele. Do you think he will miss me? Dimitris is looking after him well and Dad seems to accept having him around now. He never goes near the taverna, sticks with Dimitris and has become invaluable at finding grass snakes in the most unlikely places. Dad has promised to employ Dimitris whilst I am away so I suppose that is a good thing – for him anyway.

It seems such a waste of a summer – me stuck in a barracks somewhere or standing in the hot sun on a useless sentry duty. I was quite looking forward to it until I found out when I had to go. I suppose it will be something to occupy me during the winter months and a chance to make some new friends.

Don't forget to avoid Mr Creepy, but don't let him upset you or you won't do well in your exams."

Nicola read the email and felt her heart sink. She loved Elounda and being with the family, but it would not be the same without John around.

MAY 2008

John had found guard duty irksome and boring. It seemed such a waste of time to stand and look at nothing in case someone appeared who had no authority to be there. The whole area was fenced off and there were signs saying that it was an army base, trespassers would be prosecuted and no photographs were allowed, so tourists were unlikely to stray on to the camp by mistake. If anyone did intend to sneak in they would hardly walk openly up to where the sentries were posted all day and all night.

He was used now to sharing his accommodation with the other seven occupants who were housed there. He had become accustomed to the noises each man made in the night as they slept and they no longer kept him awake. The first time he was granted afternoon leave he made the journey by bus back down to Aghios Nikolaos where his father met him. He spent two hours with his family, telling them about life in the army and enjoying the home cooked food.

'Army meals are not up to much,' he complained. 'Everything seems to be soup, pork and chips. It's just food to fill you up, not to sit and enjoy. It's a good job we do so much exercise or I'd already have put on so much weight I wouldn't be able to move.'

'Are you warm enough?' asked Marianne anxiously.

'It's warm enough in the hut. It can be pretty cold and miserable when you're on sentry duty, but it only lasts for a few hours. It's the boredom more than anything that gets to me.' John smiled. 'They think I'm pretty stupid, but I usually volunteer for the night duty. I just wish I was able to have my camera with me. All sorts of different insects and animals are around then that you never see during the day. It passes the time to watch them. Talking of time, I ought to make a move. I don't want to be late back or I'll have my next leave cancelled.'

'We'll drive you back up. Let us know the next time you propose to come down and we'll collect you from Heraklion.'

'I'd appreciate that. The bus journey took longer than I'd anticipated, and of course, it's the winter timetable.'

'It won't be any better in the summer, you know that. The buses will be crammed with tourists.'

'It's a no win situation,' replied John cheerfully. 'I just hope I shall be able to get some proper leave whilst Nick is here.'

John emailed Nicola regularly with updates of his army life and the duties he was expected to carry out whilst also learning how to drive the heavy vehicles and shoot accurately at a target.

"Now I really am fed up. Not content with telling me I have to do my service whilst you are over here they have decided to send me to Rhodes in July. I will be there for six weeks. There is an area there they use for training exercises. It is very remote and they stage mock battles with tanks and artillery. I'm sure we must have a suitable area somewhere on Crete, but it seems that everyone goes over there for a short time to experience the conditions they could expect on a battlefield. I just hope I never have to experience it for real. I'm quite happy shooting my gun at a target on the range and I have actually become quite a good shot.

I am trying to think positively about going. I would like to look around the Old Town properly and take the kind of photographs that interest me. I found it rather a bore when I was there with Lester. I might even take a walk into the red light district and see if Mum's cousin is still working there. I can't think of her as Bryony or Saff's half sister. I can't imagine either of *them* ever contemplating soliciting however desperate they might be!

I have asked for some leave as soon as I return from Rhodes and they have granted me a week. I can't wait. It has been good to go home occasionally when I have had a day's leave, but as soon as I reach Elounda it's nearly time to leave again. That is the very worst thing about army life. Excuses for being late either on duty or back at camp are not accepted. To be able to have a complete week to myself and be there with you will be bliss. I'm sure Dad won't expect me to work all the time and we'll be able to go to Spinalonga, go diving or just lay in the sun."

Nicola mailed John back, sympathising with his complaints, telling him how she was working hard towards her end of year exams, but still managing to work in the diner. Todd was still appearing regularly both at the University and the diner, but her father often collected her after work and she was refusing to let Todd annoy or frighten her.

"Would there be any chance of me coming to Rhodes whilst you are there? I could stay somewhere close to the base and we would be able to meet up whenever you had a few free hours. I can pay for it out of my earnings from the diner. I wouldn't have to ask Dad for anything extra. It seems so unfair that when we have spent months apart you are sent away."

John rode in the open back of the lorry with his companions. As they left the town of Rhodes behind and drove along the coastal road he wondered exactly where they were going. He had looked at his map, but the army bases were not marked. He hoped the area would not be too remote and when he had some free time he would be able to visit the town and also indulge his hobby.

Forty minutes later they turned off the coast road and began to drive inland. At first the countryside around them was flat and uninteresting; then they began to climb gradually into the hills. The road became steeper, fringed with fir trees, a steep drop on one side down to the plain below, then even that was lost to sight.

The road wound higher and John felt his ears ringing. He yawned, hoping to clear them. There was no sign of habitation of any sort and John reconciled himself to being in the remote area for the next few weeks with no hope of visiting the town or any other places of interest.

A final turn in the road took them up to a gate where soldiers stood on either side on sentry duty. Their driver waved his hand and they continued through and across the compound to a collection of wooden buildings. The young recruits jumped out and shouldered their kit bags, waiting for their instructions. At the word they marched across the compound, six names were read out and they were directed to the first hut whilst the others were marched on to the second.

John looked at the bleak interior. The hut was intended to accommodate eight men. Two beds were already occupied and the new arrivals staked their claim to the others.

'Thirty minutes,' they were told. 'Kit unpacked and ready for inspection.'

'Any idea where we are?' asked John as the Commanding Officer left.

'Not a clue,' replied the man who had claimed the bed next to John. 'Middle of nowhere. Didn't even see a village within walking distance.'

John proceeded to unpack and lay out his kit ready for inspection. He placed Nicola's photograph inside his locker and gave a wry smile. They had discussed the possibility of her visiting him on Rhodes and decided he must find out where he was stationed before they made any firm plans. Judging by the remoteness of this army base a visit seemed out of the question. He sighed. He was only away for six weeks, but she was only in Elounda for nine.

John walked outside the camp, he had two hours to himself and he would wander around and see if he was able to find anything to interest him in the area. At the bottom of the road from the camp he debated – should he turn left or right. Right appeared to take him back down the road towards the plain far below and he would certainly not have time to walk down there and back again in two hours. He turned left, the road undulating slightly. He must time himself carefully. He could walk in that direction for an hour; then must begin to make his way back to the camp.

He followed the road as it turned, passing deserted buildings and then stopped abruptly. There were a number of coaches parked at the side of the road along with hire cars. A small taverna was doing a thriving trade in refreshments. So there was civilisation within walking distance! He walked over to the taverna entrance and requested a beer.

'What's the name of this village?' he asked.

'It's not a village. It's Profitis Ilias.'

John frowned. 'Why are there so many people around?'

'They come to see Mussolini's house.'

'Where's that?'

'Up the road a short way.'

John nodded, paid for his beer and walked over to one of the wooden seats. He would have to go and have a look at the house. He wondered if there was an entrance fee and if it was furnished as it would have been when Mussolini stayed there. From his seat he could look down on two large buildings that appeared to be hotels with a small church at one side and cars parked outside. He smiled in satisfaction. At least if Nicola was able to come over there would be somewhere for her to stay.

As the tourists returned to the coaches and drew away more coaches arrived to take their place. The tourists scrambled up the hillside and John could see an imposing house set behind stone walls. John debated whether to follow the tourists in their climb up the steep hillside or go down the incline to the hotels and investigate the possibility of Nicola staying there for a few days.

He walked down through an unkempt garden until he reached

the car park and approached the glass doors that led into the reception area. He pushed at the door and then realised the handle was chained. He peered through the dirty glass. The room was furnished, a cup and saucer sat on a table and a vacuum cleaner stood in the centre of the room. He frowned. It looked deserted. Maybe he had come to the wrong entrance.

John walked slowly along the length of tarmac. All the windows were tightly closed and too high for him to see inside, he made his way down the side of the building and around to the rear. Again the door he came to was firmly padlocked and he looked through to the kitchens. Large freezers took up one wall, stainless steel tables, probably used for food preparation stood empty and the whole area had a deserted and neglected air, despite the pots and pans on the shelves.

He made a complete circuit of the building and then walked further down to the next hotel. It was in the same state – closed and neglected. He shook his head. Obviously neither was open for business and his idea of Nicola coming to stay there was out of the question.

He retraced his steps up the hillside and back to the taverna, waiting until the assistant was free.

'Another beer?'

John shook his head. 'No, I wanted to ask about the hotels down there. Are they open for business?'

'No. Been closed for years.'

'Why's that?'

'They were used as hunting lodges. Visitors came up to go shooting in the area. Once they'd massacred all the wildlife there was no reason to come up here.'

'So they've just been left derelict?'

'That's right.'

Slowly John shook his head. 'That's sad. Thanks for the information anyway.'

John looked at his watch. His inspection of the hotels had

taken no more than half an hour and he was only a short distance from the army base. He would scramble up the hillside in the wake of the tourists and see what Mussolini's house had to offer. There was a chance there were rooms to let in there.

The track the tourists were using was steep and narrow, winding between stone walls that hid his view of both the house and the road below. He reached the top and drew in his breath. The house was of magnificent proportions. He crossed the tiled courtyard, littered with debris and broken glass, to where the rotting doors stood open.

Once inside he felt his heart sink. Plaster had fallen off the walls and the areas that were left were covered in graffiti. Underfoot was more broken glass and litter. He picked his way carefully from room to room, investigating the bathrooms and toilets, their tiles cracked and broken, their fitments removed until he reached the kitchen area. The only remaining item was a large sink. A door led to a small courtyard outside with various outhouses, their doors either missing or hanging at odd angles. He felt sad that such a magnificent house had met such an ignominious end.

John returned inside and walked carefully up the wide wooden staircase, testing each tread as he went and standing aside as tourists pushed their way either up or down. Once on the first floor he wandered from room to room and out on to the balconies drawing in his breath as he looked at the magnificent view down across the plain and at the sea in the distance. There were gaps in the handrail to the balcony and when he placed his hand on it he could feel it move beneath him. Suddenly feeling very unsafe John turned and hurried back down the stairs and outside.

He stood outside in the sunshine and took photographs of the exterior of the house. He would return inside the next time he was allowed off the base and take some of the interior. He turned and took a few photographs of the deserted hunting lodges; he would send them to Nicola when he mailed her. It was disappointing that they were not open for business and she would not be able to stay nearby.

Nicola was intrigued by the photographs of the house and lodges that John sent her.

"What a shame there is nowhere nearby where I can stay. I would love to see the house for myself. The views you sent from the balconies were quite amazing. It must have been fascinating when Mussolini used it. I can just imagine their large cars roaring up the driveway and everyone saluting and clicking their heels. Who used to stay at the hunting lodges? Were they his guests spending a weekend there? I wonder if it was an honour to be invited or whether it was a command and you arrived shaking in your shoes? Do send lots more photos.

I showed the photos to your Dad and he wondered if it would be feasible to re-open the hotels and advertise them for people who wanted a walking holiday. I hope he wasn't serious. If it's as deserted as you say I can't see anyone wanting to stay out there. I'm sure the Rhodians would have done something about them if they thought they could be a going concern.

How much longer will you be in that area? You've been there for three weeks and you say you've only done routine training. It seems such a waste of our time together. At least if you had still been up by Heraklion we would have been able to see each other whenever you had a few hours leave. If you are able to get to Rhodes town do send some more photos from there."

John wandered disconsolately around Mussolini's house. The attraction it had first had for him had worn off. He had photographed both inside and outside from every possible angle, along with the neglected garden he had discovered. Set into the hillside were terraces and walkways, completely overgrown with weeds, but here and there the remains of cultivation could be seen and garden plants struggled to gain a foothold.

At least he would be visiting Rhodes town tomorrow along with his companions. They had been granted a day for the visit, before driving down to Prassonissi, and he intended to make the most of his time there. He knew exactly where he wanted to go and he hoped he would remember his way around the twisting streets and be able to find the taverna where he had sat with Lester. From there he was certain he would know his way to the road where Sorrell and Joseph had lived. He was curious to see if she was still living there, but did not plan to make himself known to her.

Michaelis joined John in the back of the lorry that was to take them down to Rhodes town for the day.

'I shall be glad when we're back home. These have been the most boring few weeks of my life. At least we could have had a bit of fun if there'd been a village nearby. What shall we do when we hit town?'

'I'm planning to spend all my time taking photographs. I've been here before and I didn't have much opportunity then. I intend to make up for it today.'

Michaelis looked disappointed. 'That's all you ever do, take photographs. I thought we could spend the time together. Go up to the red light area.'

'You've got to find it first.'

'I thought you said you'd been here before? Don't you know where it is?' Michaelis looked at John accusingly.

'I was a bit too young to go looking then. I'm sure some of the others will be only too willing to go there with you.'

'I wonder if there's a girl here who's as good as the one I found in Heraklion? She really was something else. Did I tell you about her?'

John smiled. 'You've told me so many times I feel I know her. I wonder where they'll drop us off? I'd like to start outside the gate by the harbour and work my way up. I wish we'd get a move on or I won't have time to do all I want. There are two main streets leading up the hill to the Grand Master's Palace. I thought I'd go up one, have a proper look around the Palace this time, and then go down the other. When I've finished photographing the lower road I'd like to have time to go into the moat. I didn't manage that the last time.'

'What do you do with all these photos you take?' asked Michaelis curiously.

'Nothing at the moment except bore my relatives and friends. It's a way for me to experiment with light and shade, seeing the best angle, showing people what I see and hope they appreciate it also. When I turn pro I might be able to use some of them. Town shots probably won't be much use though. I'm hoping I'll be lucky enough to be employed with National Geographic. I prefer wildlife, insects, bugs, that kind of thing. I'd like to be sent out to a rain forest or jungle to see what I can find.'

'What; find a new species?'

'Not necessarily, just photograph twenty four hours of an insect's life. When you realise how short their life span is compared with a human they have to accomplish an enormous amount in a very short space of time.'

'Like what?'

'Developing into an adult, finding food, making a home, mating. Some of them die once they've mated.' John smiled and nudged his companion. 'Think about that if you find the red light area.'

'Yes, well, that doesn't happen to humans.'

'Depends what nasty disease she passes on to you or if you get so excited you have a heart attack.'

Michaelis regarded John suspiciously. 'Are you trying to spoil my day?'

'Not a bit. You spend it however it makes you happy. I'll spend mine with my camera.'

John stood in the square and photographed the fountain. The last time he had stood there he had been focusing on Christabelle. He shuddered at the thought and moved a few feet to the right to take it from a different angle. He thought about his conversation with Michaelis. What would he do with his vast collection of photographs? One day he would have to sort through them and dispose of the many that were near duplications. He realised he had already taken eight of the fountain, each one from a slightly different angle, and unless he moved a little more swiftly he would never have time to accomplish all he had set out to do in the limited time available to him.

He walked up the hill, resisting the urge to photograph every shop as he went. He already had more than enough views of the town on the video he had taken for Lester. It would be more interesting to return in the winter when the shops were closed down and he was able to see the architecture properly without the facades being festooned with rugs, clothes, shoes and souvenirs.

As he made his way through the Grand Master's Palace he realised that although they had been following Christabelle before he had missed very little of the interior. The garden, where he would have liked to take some photographs, was still forbidden to visitors. A landslide a few years previously had made the garden unsafe with a perilous drop where the ground had fallen away. He consoled himself by taking photos of the statues he could see amongst the foliage.

Once outside he stood to get his bearings. There was the Street of the Knights where Christabelle had pushed Joseph down the hill in his wheelchair. He had been standing over there at the time, having followed her from the taverna. If he continued past the Clock Tower and across the road he should be going in the right direction for both the taverna and the red light area where Joseph had lived.

He passed through the archway to the courtyard, stopping to photograph the arch from both sides before walking across the shady square to the taverna at the far side. He looked at it curiously. It was no longer called *The Grapevine* and had recently been repainted and the chairs and tables looked new. He would see what they were offering in the way of snacks and certainly have a drink whilst he was there.

John ordered an omelette and salad, refusing the chips that were offered to him. He had eaten more than enough of those recently. The same clientele appeared to patronise the taverna as before, boatmen, tour operators, stray tourists and locals. He drank his beer slowly, relishing in the fact that he would not have to either leave half of it to follow Christabelle or drink it down so fast that it gave him indigestion.

He walked back across the square and into the maze of side streets that led to the red light area. He hoped he would not meet any of his companions in the district or he could be forced to explain his presence there, particularly to Michaelis. The road was no more salubrious than he remembered; the doorways with the girl's name painted across the top and a small red light outside each one. There was Natasha, Maria, Dolores, Esmeralda, Innocenta. Innocenta! John smiled to himself. What a name for a prostitute to give herself. When he came to the house where Sorrell had lived he could see the name Suzi had been painted out and its place had been taken by Lucy. Presumably Sorrell had moved elsewhere.

Hurriedly he returned to the main street and back to the taverna. He had seen what he had wanted. Now he could continue to take his photographs.

John returned to the appointed meeting place, pleased to see that he was not the last to arrive. Michaelis came over to him.

'Did you take all the photos you wanted?'

John nodded. 'Did you find the red light area?'

'Eventually. We wandered all over the place.'

John felt a pang of guilt. He could easily have directed his friend there. 'The Old Town can be difficult until you get to know it. How was the girl you found?'

Michaelis pulled a face. 'Better than nothing. Nowhere near as good as Alexis in Heraklion. She kept trying to stifle her yawns. I wasn't sure if it was my performance or if she'd been up all night.'

'I don't think they take much notice of your ability. It's routine and they just want your money as quickly as possible.'

'Alexis doesn't give that impression. She always seems pleased to see me.'

'She's probably over charging you, then. What time are we off to Prassonissi tomorrow? I didn't look at the notice board before I left.'

'I didn't see anything. We'll have to look when we get back.'

'Two more weeks, then back to Crete. I've five days leave then.'

'How did you manage that?'

'I applied for it when I was first called in. I told them my fiancée was visiting from America and I wanted to spend a bit of time with her.'

'And they believed you?'

'It's the truth. Nick always comes over here during her summer vacation.'

'Are you truly betrothed to her?'

'As good as.'

'Don't you want to play the field? Do a bit of comparison?'

John shook his head. 'I've known Nick since we were kids. We just feel right together. Besides, if I played the field, as you put it, why shouldn't she? I wouldn't be very happy about that.'

'How do you know she doesn't?'

John gave Michaelis a scathing glance. 'I trust her and she trusts me.'

Todd spent every evening on his computer, pouring out his thoughts and feelings about Nicola, rather than concentrating on his studies.

Was there any way he could persuade her to stay in New Orleans that summer rather than go half way across the world to her relatives? If he told her how he felt about her would she stay with him? He groaned and placed his head in his hands. What could he do?

How could he make Nicola notice him and rely on him to look after her? If she suffered a car accident and he was in the vicinity he might be able to take credit for saving her life. He shuddered at the mere thought of her being hurt or maimed in some way. He needed an incident where she would be forever grateful to him. It would have to be something dramatic, but what?

Finally he undressed and went to bed, unable to sleep, as ideas convoluted in his brain and he discarded them as ridiculous or impossible to accomplish. It was not until the early hours that he finally thought of a plan that might just be feasible. With a satisfied smile on his lips he moved his position in his bed, pulled his pillow between his arms and tried to pretend it was Nicola he was holding, as he finally dropped off to sleep.

The idea was still with him as he awoke and after a hurried cup of coffee he opened his lap top. He must write down the basic idea and then work on it until he had perfected the details or discard it as impossible. He worked solidly until mid-day until he had a rough synopsis of his plan. He would refine it further when he had decided who he would ask to help him. He wrote a list of the people he knew, tutors, fellow students, casual acquaintances and the few people he considered to be his friends.

He quickly deleted the tutors, the young men with whom he shared the house and most of the students in his year. A further hour saw him delete the remaining names and he sighed with frustration. He needed to find someone who wanted money and would be willing to participate in the risky scheme.

Picking up his light jacket he left the house and began the short walk in to the town. He needed to see if the book he had ordered had finally arrived; check his bank balance and post his weekly letter to his father. The walk would help him to clear his head and he might think of someone whom he could approach. He would stay in town and have a meal at the Indian restaurant. He could feel the saliva in his mouth as he anticipated the spices and aroma that would assault his palate.

Todd looked disinterestedly at the shop window displays as he passed. He did not need any new clothes or shoes. If Nicola had been with him he would have taken her to the most exclusive dress shop in the neighbourhood and spent lavishly on her, but there was nothing he wanted for himself, despite his bank balance growing steadily.

'Spare a dollar fer a cup a tea?'

Todd's lip curled in disdain at the unkempt figure lounging against a fire hydrant. He ignored the beggar and walked on, then stopped and looked back. That was the kind of individual he needed; someone who needed money and was probably living rough. He would be just the type who would hold up a diner hoping to collect a hundred dollars from the till.

He retraced his steps and placed a five dollar bill in the dirty, outstretched hand, realising as he did so that he knew the man. 'What are you up to, Wayne?' he asked as the man dropped his eyes and mumbled his thanks.

'I can't find any work.'

'I thought you were at Uni.'

'I am – sometimes.'

'Why don't you and I have a little chat?'

'Are you offering me a job?'

'Nothing regular. I have a proposition you might find interesting,' smiled Todd. 'I'll make it worth your while.'

Wayne's eyes lit up. He was always in need of money. Since starting University he had discovered that when he went to parties he was expected to take along a little more than a bottle of cheap wine. He had had no problem finding a supplier, but since deciding to experiment himself he found he needed more on a regular basis than he could afford to buy. He had approached his parents requesting more money telling them the cost of living off the campus had risen and they had increased his allowance, but it was still not enough to satisfy his new found craving.

He had tried a succession of part-time jobs, each more menial than the last, but his employers were not sympathetic when he continually turned up late. So far he had managed to keep his addiction hidden from his tutors, although often turning his work in late, and his grades dropping drastically. He had excused his work and his absences by saying that his father was terminally ill and he was continually being called home by his mother.

'What do you want me to do?' asked Wayne.

'We can't talk here on the street. Meet me in the park in about ten minutes. We'll find a quiet place to talk.'

Wayne nodded and shambled away. Todd was well known for coming from a rich banking family. Whatever Todd offered by the way of recompense he would ask him for double.

Todd walked on to the bookshop and enquired again about the book he had ordered only to be promised it would arrive the following week. Biting back a rude retort he sighed heavily.

'You do realise I need this for my University work? If I fail my exams I shall be asking your bookshop for compensation.'

'I regret we are in the hands of the suppliers, sir.'

Todd turned on his heel and walked out, leaving a puzzled assistant looking after him. Why would he need a book entitled 'How To Impress The Opposite Sex' for a University exam?

Todd sat nervously on the grass beside Wayne who sprawled beside him.

'Are you awake and listening properly?' he asked.

Wayne nodded.

'This is completely confidential between us. If a word of this gets out to anyone, anyone at all, I'll be letting everyone at Uni know about your habit. You'd be expelled and I doubt if your parents would be very happy to know what you'd been up to.'

Wayne looked at Todd with wide eyes. 'You wouldn't? You know you can trust me.' He mimed a zip across his mouth. 'Not a word. I swear.'

'Yeah, make sure you remember that. I've friends in high places and you could find out that life isn't worth living if I mentioned your name to them.'

'I'll not say a word, man. You can trust me.'

Todd cast a sideways glance at his companion. 'You know Max's Diner?'

''Course I do. Everyone knows Max's.'

'Do you know the girls who work in there?'

Wayne frowned. 'Not to say know. There are a couple during the week and an extra one at the weekends. Not bad lookers.'

'It's the weekend I'm thinking about.'

'You want me to ask one of them out for you or make up a foursome?'

Todd shook his head. 'I want you to rob the place.'

'What!' Wayne sat up with alacrity. 'Are you mad, man? You think I want to be arrested?'

'No, listen. It won't be a real hold up. I'll be in there and you come in and ask them to hand over the cash from the till. I'll tackle you and you pretend to take fright and run out. End of story.'

Wayne shook his head slowly. 'No, more like beginning of story. They're going to 'phone for the police and even if I've gone by the time they arrive they'll be able to give a description of me.'

'They won't be able to give a description of you if you're wearing a balaclava and a jacket. You run outside and I'll follow you. You ditch the balaclava and your jacket and we walk back in together and you ask what's going on, all innocent like. Why should they suspect you?'

'So what's in this for you?'

'I want to impress one of the girls.'

'Why don't you send her a bunch of roses and a box of candy?'

'It has to be more than that. She has to think that I saved her from getting hurt.'

'I haven't got a balaclava and I've only one decent jacket,' protested Wayne. 'I can't afford to lose that. I'll have nothing warm to wear when the weather turns.'

'I'll buy you a new one.' Todd took fifty dollars from the wad in his wallet and waved it in front of Wayne. 'Buy yourself a new jacket as different as possible from your current one and a balaclava.'

Wayne licked his lips and eyed the money greedily. He calculated rapidly. If he went to the Thrift Shop he could probably pick up a jacket for fifteen dollars and gloves and a balaclava would be no more than another two.

'So what's in it for me, apart from a new jacket that I throw away? If I agree, that is,' he added.'

'Five hundred dollars.'

Wayne shook his head. 'I'll want a thou'. I'm the one taking all the risks.'

'Seven fifty, max.'

Wayne pretended to consider. 'When do you want to do it?' he asked finally.

'I'll decide that. You get yourself prepared and I'll give you the word when the time is right. Probably late on a Saturday or Sunday afternoon, after the lunch time diners have left and before the evening ones arrive. Make sure you have something in your pocket that you can point at them to make them think you have a gun.'

'Like what?'

Todd shrugged. 'Piece of dowelling would do provided it's about the right size.'

'They'll see it's not a gun as soon as I take it out.'

'You don't take it out. You have your hand in your pocket and just push it forwards to make it look as if you have a gun.'

Wayne nodded. He took the roll of dollars from Todd's hand. 'Shall I come to your place and show you what I get?'

Todd looked at him in horror. 'Don't be a fool. If we're seen together someone could realise it's a put up job, then my scheme won't work. I'll see you here next week. I'll have worked out more of the details by then and I'll go over them with you.'

Todd sat in the diner in an agony of apprehension. He had repeated his instructions to Wayne time and again, but he still felt uncertain that the man would remember them and follow them explicitly. Nicola was behind the counter and Todd's eyes swivelled continually between her and the door.

Wayne entered; his head down and swaggered over towards the counter. He rounded the counter and grabbed Nicola by her hair.

'Get off. That hurts!' shouted Nicola .

'This is a hold up,' he said as loudly as possible through the balaclava, loosening his hold on her hair and placing his arm round her neck, pressing uncomfortably against her throat.

Melanie was about to enter the diner from the kitchen when she saw the man threatening Nicola. She pulled her mobile 'phone from the back pocket of her jeans. Bending below the level of the glass in the door she swiftly dialled the emergency services and in a near whisper alerted them that there was an armed robbery taking place at the diner.

'What?' Nicola raised her eyebrows in amazement. Who would think they had enough money on the premises to warrant being robbed?

'It's a hold up. Open the till. I've got a gun here.' Wayne pushed something hard against Nicola's ribs and she decided not to argue.

Nicola rang up one cent and the till opened. Wayne grabbed at the bills in the drawer and stuffed them into his pocket. With his arm still around Nicola's neck he backed away from the till and from behind the counter, ensuring Nicola was with him.

Todd rose to his feet and rushed towards Wayne. Wayne withdrew his hand from his pocket and to Todd's horror he was actually holding a gun.

'Put that down,' shouted Todd. 'Don't be a fool.'

He pushed Wayne and stood in front of Nicola, his arms outstretched protectively. Wayne backed away slowly until he was almost at the door; then pressed the trigger. Two shots flew across the room, one embedding itself in the counter and the other finding its mark in Todd's arm. Wayne looked in horror at the blood that was staining Todd's shirt.

'I'm sorry. I didn't mean to do that. I'm sorry, Todd.'

The door to the diner flew open and two armed police stood there, their guns drawn. 'Drop it,' commanded one.

Wayne looked wildly at Todd and then at the police. He clenched his hands and in doing so pulled the trigger of the gun again, the shot catching the first policeman in the leg. Without hesitation the second policeman fired and Wayne fell in a crumpled heap on the ground.

Todd stood frozen in horror, the blood dribbling down his arm and dripping from his fingers on to the floor. The policeman was talking rapidly into his handset, calling for an ambulance and back up, his eyes continually swivelling around the diner. Todd sank to the floor holding his arm and groaning. The policeman who had been shot in the leg had dragged himself over to the counter and propped himself against it. Melanie appeared with tea towels and he was pressing a wad to his calf trying to staunch the flow of blood. Melanie then turned her attention to Todd, making him place his head between his knees and again pressing tea towels to the site of the wound.

Nicola realised she was shaking uncontrollably, her teeth chattering. Had the man really threatened her with a gun for the small amount of cash in the till? Had he shot Todd and a policeman? Had the police shot him dead or just injured him? Max placed an arm around her and guided her to a chair.

'You all right? Not hurt?'

Nicola shook her head. She could not trust herself to speak.

The ambulance arrived, gave a swift examination of the body

on the floor and covered his face before turning their attention to the injured policeman and Todd. 'Flesh wounds,' they confirmed. 'Nothing unduly serious.'

The policeman nodded. He seemed quite unmoved by the scene and when a second car containing officers arrived he handed over his gun immediately. He sat in a corner with a colleague and calmly gave his statement of events, whilst the other sat beside Nicola.

'Can you tell us exactly what happened?' she asked gently. 'Take your time.'

'I'm – I'm not sure.' Nicola screwed up her eyes. 'A man came in and walked behind the counter. He grabbed my hair and told me to open the till. He took the money from it and put his arm round my neck. No, he put his arm round my neck and then took the money, I think.'

'Did you know he had a gun?'

'He pressed something hard in to my ribs. I didn't know it was a gun at the time.' Nicola shivered as the policeman was helped on to a stretcher and Todd escorted to the ambulance.

'Then what happened? Did he open fire?'

'Todd came over and pushed him away.'

'And who is Todd?'

'The man who was shot in the arm.'

'Did the robber say anything before he shot him? Give him a warning or anything?'

'Todd told him not to be a fool and to put the gun down. I don't think the man meant to shoot him. After it happened he said he was sorry and hadn't meant to do it.'

The policewoman patted Nicola's shoulder. 'Would you like us to call anyone? How about your Mum? You've had a very nasty fright.'

'Could I have a drink of water?' Nicola touched her neck where a bruise was developing.

'Sure.'

Max was hovering near the kitchen door and the policewoman called to him. 'Glass of water for the lady.'

Max nodded, filled a glass and hurried over. 'Sure you're all right, Nicola?'

Nicola tried to smile. 'I'm not hurt.' She averted her eyes as the paramedic returned with a screen and she knew the body was being placed in a black bag prior to being removed.

'Shall I call your Dad?'

Nicola shook her head. 'I'll do it. That way he'll know I'm safe.'

Nicolas entered the diner and took Nicola in his arms. He had been stopped at the car park and had to explain that his daughter was inside and she had called him to come down. Before he was allowed to proceed a policeman had walked up to the diner to ascertain that he was Nicola's father and permission was granted.

'What's happened?' Nicolas took in the police, the blood stains on the floor and Nicola's white face. 'Has there been an accident?'

'There was a hold up, Dad. Some man with a gun.'

'You're definitely not hurt?'

'No, I'm fine, Dad, just a bit shaky.'

Nicolas looked at the police woman who was still sitting nearby. 'Can I take my daughter home?'

'We'd really like her to come down to the station and make a statement.'

'But I've told you what happened,' protested Nicola.

'Now you're over the first shock you might remember a few more details. Your father can come down with you. It won't take long.'

Nicola looked at her father and shrugged. 'I suppose I might as well get it over with.'

Down at the station Nicola agreed to repeat her statement and have it recorded, holding tightly to her father's hand as she recollected the incident moment by moment at the prompting of the policewoman.

'What were you doing when this man came round the counter and grabbed your hair?'

'I was making a latte.'

'How many customers did you have in the diner at the time?'

'Only three. Todd and an elderly couple.'

'Todd is a friend of yours?'

Nicola considered. 'Not really a friend, more an acquaintance. He's at Uni and I see him around on campus sometimes. He comes in to the diner regularly.'

'And whilst you were making a latte what was the other assistant doing?'

'Mel had gone in to the kitchen to speak to Max.'

'Who is Max?'

'He's the owner and also the chef.'

'Was that usual?'

'The elderly man said he needed his food to be gluten free and Mel had gone to ask Max if he could sort it out.'

The policewoman looked at Nicola. 'Can you remember now whether your assailant placed his arm around your neck before or after you opened the till?'

Nicola shook her head. 'I can't. Does it make any difference?'

'I doubt it. Now, this young man who came to your assistance, this is the person you call Todd and were making the latte for?'

'That's right.'

'Can you tell me what happened?'

'Todd pushed the man away and stood in front of me. The robber backed over towards the door. Then the gun went off. Todd kind of slipped to one side and the man said he was sorry.'

'Can you remember the exact words he used?'

Nicola shut her eyes and recalled the scene. 'He said I'm sorry, Todd. I didn't mean to do that.'

'You're sure he used your friend's name?'

Nicola nodded vehemently. 'I'm quite sure.'

'Did the man attempt to shoot again?'

'No, he just kind of stood there, as though he didn't know what to do next. Then the police came and told him to drop the gun. That was when he shot the policeman.' Nicola gripped her father's hand tightly.

The policewoman switched off the tape recorder. 'You've been very helpful, miss. Remember, you can always add to your statement if you remember anything else later. We won't need to delay you any further today.'

Nicola breathed a sigh of relief; a tear ran down her face and dripped off her nose.

'Here you are.' Nicolas pushed his handkerchief into her hand and Nicola began to sob.

'I was so frightened, Dad. I thought he was going to shoot me.'

Nicolas put his arms around her and kissed the top of her head.

'You're all in one piece. You've had a very nasty shock, but you're not hurt. We'll call in at the doctor on the way home, get him to have a look at your neck and give you something to help you sleep. You'll be over the worst by tomorrow,' Nicolas assured her.

Nicola wiped her eyes. 'Sorry, Dad. I'm just being silly. It must have been much worse when you were actually shot.'

Nicolas stiffened. 'Who told you about that?'

'John told me ages ago. He said both you and his dad were lucky to be alive.'

Nicolas's mouth set in a grim line. Both he and Giovanni had decided never to talk about the incident where they had been injured during a robbery at the hotel in Athens.

Nicola sent a long email to John relating her unnerving experience at the diner to him and saying that Todd had stood in front of her to shield her.

"It was very brave of him to do so and I'll have to thank him when I see him next. I think Todd knew the man, although he was wearing a balaclava, because after he had shot Todd he apologised to him and said it was an accident. Dad has forbidden me to go back and work at the diner. I'm not sorry. I would feel nervous whenever anyone came in if I was still working there. I feel guilty about letting Max down. It wasn't his fault. I am going back to Uni on Wednesday. I need to finish my course and take the end of term exams. Dad has booked my flight to Elounda. He said it would do me good to get away for a break as soon as possible. I do wish you were going to be there to meet me as usual."

John read Nicola's email and felt his heart beating faster. He couldn't envisage his future without her by his side.

Todd sat uncomfortably in the interview room nursing his injured arm. Three times he had repeated his statement to the police, making sure that his story was the same each time. He admitted to knowing Wayne from University, but denied that they were more than student acquaintances. He elaborated on his chance meeting with Wayne in the town and admitted he had given him fifty dollars because he felt sorry for the state the man appeared to be in. The police had no reason to suspect that he was not telling the truth, commended him on his bravery in trying to protect Nicola and sympathised over his injury. Todd walked out from the police station feeling confident that he would not be questioned further and now all he needed to do was speak to Nicola.

To Todd's delight Nicola had sought him out at the University and thanked him for his bravery at the diner. He had made light of it at the time, but now he had to act.

Nicola was in the canteen, sitting alone and he slid in to the seat opposite her.

'I need to talk to you,' he said, blushing to the roots of his hair.

Nicola looked pointedly at her watch. 'I'm due in class in ten minutes.'

'Please stay here for the summer, Nicola.'

Nicola shook her head. 'I can't do that. My flight is already booked.'

'You could cancel it.'

'Why on earth should I do that?'

'For me, Nicola.' He gazed at her intently, willing her to agree.

Nicola swallowed hard. 'Todd, I appreciate that you stood in front of me and shielded me from that gun man, but that's an end of the matter.'

'I'll always protect you.' Todd assured her and leant closer so she could feel his breath on her face. 'Stay here with me and you'll not regret it.'

'I don't have any reason to stay here with you.'

'You don't understand.' He gazed at her longingly. 'I love you.'

'Don't be stupid. We hardly know each other.'

'I feel I've known you forever,' Todd placed his hand on hers and felt a tremor go through her body which he misinterpreted. 'We're meant to be together,' he said moving even closer. 'I want to marry you.'

'Marry me?' Nicola recoiled from his touch. 'You're mad. I wish I'd never come to thank you.' Abruptly she rose and walked away from him.

WEEK 1 – AUGUST 2008

Nicola had been gone for nearly five weeks, no doubt seeing the young man with the dog in the photograph she had shown him. He had telephoned her on four occasions. On two of them he could hear voices and laughter in the background before she closed her 'phone believing there to be no one on the line. He longed to be there with her, to see who she was with and why they seemed to be enjoying themselves so much.

He opened up his computer and began to look at the flight details and their cost. He was horrified. He was not short of money, due to his father's generosity, but the prices for a flight to Crete from Heathrow were twice the amount he would have to pay for a flight from New Orleans to England. Then he had to think about accommodation. He checked the site for Elounda and debated with himself.

If it was no more than a small village, and that was what it looked like when he had brought up a map of the area, Nicola would soon be told there was an American staying there. Villagers were like that, he had been told; they knew everyone's business. It could be more sensible to stay in the next town. He could hire a scooter and then he would be able to drive where he wished. Once he had found out where Nicola was working he would be able to wait for her each day and see her safely home. He would like to touch her soft, olive skin, for the pure pleasure he knew it would give him. He was not sexually aroused by her the way he had been with Jennie-Lea. In his mind she was so innocent and vulnerable and needing someone to look after her to protect her against the world.

Todd checked his bank balance and studied the accommodation that was offered to him in a place called Aghios Nikolaos. It was obviously a fair sized town and he should be able to mingle with the other tourists there without drawing attention to himself. He asked the computer to calculate the distance between Aghios Nikolaos and Elounda, satisfied that it was no more than a few miles. He then asked for car and motor scooter hire and was gratified to find there were more than enough being advertised. Taking a final deep breath he pressed the key to confirm his booking and entered his credit card details when they were requested. He had a day to pack and organise any last minute necessary details, then he would be off.

He had no idea what he would need to take with him. Nicola always returned with a good sun tan so it must be warm over there. He decided he would travel in slacks and a windcheater, the remainder of his luggage consisted of shorts and Tee shirts, with a couple of long sleeved shirts and pair of jeans that he felt he might need in the evening. If he had misjudged the weather badly he would just have to buy some warmer clothes whilst he was there.

As Todd travelled down in the coach from Heraklion airport in the morning he spread his map of the island open on his knees and followed the names of the towns. They seemed to be driving for hours. He felt panic rising up in him. It was only a small island. Surely he should have reached his destination by now.

He walked to the front of the coach and spoke to the driver the next time they stopped to off load tourists and their luggage.

'When do we get to Aghios Nikolaos, please?'

The driver waved his hand down the road. 'Soon.'

'Are we on the right road?'

The driver shrugged. He had no idea what Todd had asked of him. A couple sitting three seats back took pity on him.

'It's all right, son. We're on the right road. We've been before. It'll probably take us about another hour.'

'An hour?'

'We have to go to all the different drop-off points. Takes time. Where are you staying?'

Todd pulled the address from his pocket and the man glanced at it. 'Don't know it, myself, but there are so many around. We're going to be at the Hermes.'

Todd nodded. He really did not care where anyone else was staying. He just wanted to be there.

Once booked in and unpacked Todd realised how exhausted he was. He had been travelling for nearly twenty hours, snatched some sleep during the flight from America, and then been far too stressed to relax and sleep on the subsequent flight to Crete. He washed and glanced at himself in the mirror. He looked strained and exhausted. He would have a couple of hours sleep and then find somewhere for a quick meal. He should still have time that afternoon to ascertain the cost and availability of hiring a scooter; then he would have an early night and be fresh to start his search for Nicola the following day.

When he awoke he felt considerably better and also, to his surprise, hungry. Checking he had the key to his room in his pocket he went down to the reception desk and asked if they had a map of the town. The girl spread a colourful sheet of paper on the desk before him. She pointed with her pen and made a circle.

'We are here. There is the pool. You cannot get lost.'

'I'm looking for somewhere for a meal.'

The girl nodded. 'Down by the pool. Many places.'

'I also want to hire a scooter.'

Again she nodded. 'Down by the pool. Many places.'

Todd looked at her dubiously, had she actually understood his needs or did she just direct everyone to the pool? 'Thank you,' he said, folded the map and placed it in his pocket.

He walked outside and the late afternoon heat hit him forcefully. He pulled his cap lower down on his head to shade his eyes and adjusted his sun glasses. Once out of sight of the receptionist he pulled the map out of his pocket and looked at it again. The sea was on his right and the pool slightly to the left. He could hardly get lost.

He tried to walk along the pavement, dodging the bicycles, scooters, odd boxes, trees and dogs, finally giving up the attempt and walking in the road, keeping a wary eye out for approaching traffic. At the end of the road he saw a flight of steps leading downwards, another surreptitious glance at the map showed him they led down to the main road.

Feeling more confident now, he descended and found himself amongst a throng of people, most of them walking languidly in the heat and stopping frequently to look in the shop windows. He twisted and turned his way between them. There would be time for him to look at the shops when he knew where Nicola was.

Within a few minutes he found himself at the pedestrian area that flanked the side of a pool that appeared to be fed by the sea. Everywhere there were tavernas, offering chicken and chips, beef burgers, pizzas, breakfasts or traditional cooked meals. He looked at the pictures displayed outside, they were faded and everything looked unappetising. Was this the kind of eating place where Nicola worked during her holiday?

Todd walked to the end of the pool, relishing in the shade that was offered from the hillside. He reached the end of the path and realised he either had to retrace his steps or climb up the hill to where some imposing houses were situated. He shook his head. He was certainly not going to struggle up the two hundred or so steps without an excellent reason. He wandered slowly back, looking again at the variety of food that was on offer, finally settling for a table beside the pool and ordering chicken and chips with a beer.

Having eaten he began to look for vehicle hire. He had not noticed anything during his walk along by the side of the pool. He crossed the bridge and walked desultorily along past the various eating places that tried to tempt him inside. There were plenty of jewellers and gift shops, but it was not until he had almost reached the end of the parade of shops that he saw a collection of scooters and motor bikes parked outside a small glass fronted office.

Cautiously he entered; would they understand his needs?

'Good afternoon. I'd like to enquire about hiring a bike.'

The man behind the desk flicked his worry beads with a disinterested air. Why else would anyone enter the office? 'How big?' he asked.

Todd hesitated. 'I only propose driving around locally. No long distances.'

'Scooter.' The way the man said the word brooked no argument from Todd and he nodded.

Reluctantly the man rose to his feet and walked from behind the desk out onto the forecourt. 'This do?'

Todd looked at the scooter he was being offered. He knew nothing about bikes. 'Is it roadworthy?'

'Of course. All my bikes have certificate.'

'What time do you open in the morning?'

'Ten.'

Todd debated with himself. Would he want to set off any earlier? If the shop did not open until ten it was unlikely that Nicola would be working before then. On the other hand if she was working in a taverna that was offering breakfasts she would be there considerably earlier.

'How many days?'

'Probably a week, maybe more.'

The man nodded, wishing he had not displayed his prices prominently in the window. He would have been able to charge this ignorant tourist a higher rate. 'Papers,' he said briefly and led the way back inside.

It took Todd half an hour to complete the hire papers to the satisfaction of the owner. It seemed that his passport and driving licence numbers were entered time and again until he was given the papers to sign and the man held out his hand for the money.

Todd counted out the Euros carefully, accepted the key and a safety helmet. 'Law,' stated the man as he pushed the helmet into Todd's hands. 'Any damage – you pay.'

Todd was not sure if he meant the helmet, the scooter, or both. He examined the helmet carefully. A small section of stitching was coming undone and he pointed it out to the owner. The man glared at him and replaced the helmet with another that Todd could find no fault with.

The man accompanied Todd outside and indicated that he should ride along to the end of the paved area and then turn onto the road. He pointed back the way Todd had walked. 'Pedestrian, no riding,' he said with what seemed like a certain amount of glee.

Todd realised he did not know how to return to his hotel on the bike. There was no way he could ride up the steps he had descended earlier. He pulled the crumpled map out of his pocket and showed it to the man. 'How do I get there?' he asked, pointing to the circle the receptionist had made.

Taking up his pen the man drew along the roads that Todd should take, totally obliterating the names.

'Thank you.'

Todd looked at the ruined map disconsolately and wished he had not asked. He knew he needed to ride back over the bridge and he guessed if he followed the road there would eventually be a turning that would lead him back to his hotel. He would have to ask the girl for another map the following day.

Before he finally settled for the night Todd looked at the list of restaurants, cafes and bars that he had printed off from his computer and were located in Elounda. Where should he start? He could hardly enter each one and ask if she worked there. He did not want Nicola to know he had followed her over to Crete.

He only wanted to ensure she was safe and well, he told himself. The question was still nagging at him as he drifted off to sleep.

It was further to Elounda than Todd had envisaged and certainly much larger. He had expected a village with maybe half a dozen streets, but this was more like a small town. He rode down the main road to the harbour and along to the large church that stood at an intersection. It was quieter here and he was more likely to be noticed. He turned into the car park and parked the bike next to some others, noting they had all paid a fee and were displaying the ticket on the windscreen or handle bars. To his relief the instructions were printed in English as well as Greek and he understood he should go to the kiosk.

He stood to get his bearings and decided the only sensible thing to do was return to the top of the hill where the main road entered the town. As he walked up the hill he would look into eating places and bars as he passed. He would then do the same as he retraced his steps on the other side of the road.

Many of the bars were closed and the restaurants that were open seemed to have young men in attendance and no women were visible. He pretended to study their menus, hoping Nicola would emerge from a back room. It took him most of the morning to investigate both sides of the main road, by which time the sun was beating on him with full strength and he felt exhausted. He entered the first bar he came to at the edge of the square and ordered a beer, drinking thirstily when it arrived.

'Do you have something I could eat?' he asked realising the foolishness of drinking the beer at mid-day without any food in his stomach.

'Chips.'

Todd nodded. A plate of chips would do.

The owner returned and placed a bag of crisps on the table.

Todd shook his head. 'No, I really wanted a meal to eat,' he said.

'Bar only. There are plenty of places. In the square, along the waterfront.' The owner shrugged. What did this stupid American expect? That he would miraculously conjure food from thin air? It was hardly worth his while being open during the day. It was in the evenings that the young people thronged to his bar to watch the football or basket ball on his large television screen and take advantage of the cheap drinks he offered.

Todd finished his beer, thinking carefully. He would go to the corner of the square by the marina, he had seen the sign there for a restaurant and he would check that one out before returning to investigate those that were opposite the car park. When he reached the corner he almost groaned aloud. The bars and eating places were even more prolific here.

They all seemed to be popular with the tourists and to his delight he saw both men and women serving at the tables. He stood beside the wall and watched. There was no shortage of dark haired, attractive girls, but none of them was Nicola. Finally deciding that she did not work at that taverna he sidled over and took a seat. He would have a meal and another beer; then continue his progress along the waterfront.

It was slow and frustrating. He would catch a glimpse of a girl and his heart would leap, only to be disappointed when he finally saw her and realised she was nothing like Nicola. By five he had decided that she certainly did not work at any of the waterfront bars and retraced his steps to the car park where he had left his bike. He resolved to arrive early the next day and take up a position in the square. That way he would be able to see a number of bars and if she was working in any one of those he would spot her immediately.

Back at his hotel he took out the list of hotels and tavernas he had printed off from his computer and brought with him. It would be a good idea if he took it with him the following day and crossed them off after he had checked them out.

Todd sat morosely in the bar at the hotel. He had spent five days wandering around in Elounda and there had been no sign of

Nicola. Had he misheard the name and was she somewhere totally different? Name – now that was a good idea. Her name was Christoforakis. If she was staying with relatives their name could be the same as hers. It could be worth asking if anyone knew the family.

He called the bar man over and ordered another drink. 'Do you know a family around here called Christoforakis?' he asked.

'Of course.'

'Yeah? Do you know where I could find them? They said to look them up whenever I was in the area.'

'Other side of the pool. Up past the museum.'

'I thought they lived in Elounda.'

'They do, but their shop is in Aghios Nikolaos.'

'Thanks, thanks very much.'

Todd left his bike at the hotel and walked down to the pool, across the bridge and followed the directions to the museum. He looked curiously at the dark, narrow street. Most of the buildings appeared to be office premises and he could not envisage tourists looking for anywhere to eat in the area when they had such a plethora of choice in more attractive surroundings.

The only shop he found was a gift shop. He peered in the window at the display of tasteful items they were offering. It certainly looked expensive. He could see two women sitting at a desk towards the rear, but could not decide if one of them was Nicola. He hung around, pretending to be interested in the goods on display, hoping one of them would approach the window, but they ignored him.

An elderly man walked out of the shop, looked at him curiously and continued on down the road towards the pool. Yannis stopped a short way down the hill and stood and watched. The young man had been looking in the window for the last half an hour. Was he planning to rob the place? As he saw Todd enter he retraced his steps hurriedly, moving with a speed that belied his age and artificial hip.

Todd entered and looked at the women. They were both elderly. One smiled at him.

'Yes? I help?'

Todd shook his head. 'Just looking.' He wandered over to a shelf of glassware and looked at it before moving on to some pottery that claimed to be replicas of the items on show in the museums. As he did so the man re-entered the shop and glared at him.

'Has he said what he wants?' asked Yannis.

Ourania shook her head. 'Said he's just looking.'

'He spent long enough doing that outside. He's up to no good. I'm sure of that.'

'Do you want me to phone Giovanni and ask him or Marcus to come over?'

'No point. By the time either of them reached here he could have robbed the shop and murdered all of us.' Yannis picked up a letter opener and tapped it against his hand. 'He'll get a nasty shock if he tries to tangle with me.'

Ourania looked at her husband in concern. The man in the shop was young and no doubt strong. Yannis would be no match for him if the situation became violent.

'Why doesn't Marisa go and ask Yiorgo to come in from next door?'

Yannis nodded. 'Good idea.'

Marisa looked at her brother and sister in law. 'Go on,' urged Ourania, and Marisa walked towards the shop door. As she reached it Todd held it open for her and followed her out, walking back down the hill.

Yannis replaced the letter opener on the table and wiped his forehead. Either the man understood Greek and was not prepared to tackle two men, or he was truly window shopping.

Todd walked back up to his hotel. That had been a waste of time. He would collect his bike and drive along to Elounda. He would obviously have to enquire about the family there or he would never locate Nicola. He left his bike in the car park and strolled over to the taverna that gave him a view of the main street. There were a number of bars and tavernas there and he would watch for a while.

He was just about to make his way to a different bar when he stiffened. There she was! Todd watched as Nicola stood chatting to a young man with a dog. It was the man he had seen in the photograph. Was this a boyfriend she came to Crete to see each year? What could attract her to the swarthy, skinny youth? She bent down and petted the dog, finally standing up and giving the man a hug and kiss on both cheeks before walking in to the chemist. Todd gave a sigh of relief. At least he had finally found her. All he had to do now was wait around for her to finish her shopping and follow her to wherever she was living. He would then know where to find her in future.

Nicola was no longer than a few minutes in the chemist, handing in the request for repeat prescriptions on behalf of her grandmother, Yannis and Marisa. As she emerged Todd rose to follow her. She hurried across the road in his direction and he shrank back behind the awning of the bar. As he peered round the side he saw her climb astride a scooter and drive carefully out of the car park.

Todd ran over to where he had parked his bike. He removed his cap and placed his crash helmet on his head. She would certainly not recognise him whilst he was wearing that. He looked no different from the many other young men who raced around on scooters. He sped along the road, expecting to soon see Nicola in front of him, but there was no sign of her. Eventually he slowed. He had passed a number of hotels and self catering apartments. She had to be living in one of those.

Slowly he drove back. Everywhere there were scooters parked along the road, squeezed in between cars and delivery lorries. He had no way of knowing if one of them belonged to her. He drew in to the side and sat and thought. If she was living in one of the hotels he had passed she probably had somewhere to park at the rear, rather than on the road. If he wandered around he might well see a solitary scooter and if it was red it could belong to her.

Todd spent an hour walking to the rear area of all the hotels. He felt uncomfortable and was sure he was being watched. He had kept his crash helmet on and was certain no one would be able to recognise him, however suspicious they became. He finally realised the task was fruitless. There was at least one scooter parked behind each hotel, often more and nearly all of them were red. He would return the following morning and take up a position on a convenient seat beneath the trees across the road and watch for her to emerge again.

'Did you find your friends?' asked the bar tender.

Todd shook his head. 'They weren't the people I was looking for. I was told they had a taverna.'

'That's the young ones.'

'Do you know where it is?'

'Plaka.'

'Where's that?'

'End of the coast road. Go through Elounda and keep on going. Not much there except their apartments. You can't miss it.'

'Thanks. Thanks very much.' Todd paid for his drink and included a large tip.

Now the moment had come Todd felt unaccountably nervous. He drove through Elounda and followed the road that led out of the town. The sign told him that Plaka was five kilometres away. He passed large houses, set in their own grounds and wondered if Nicola's relatives lived in one of them. He overtook a youth riding slowly, a dog loping along by his side, and realised it was the young man he had seen with Nicola. He must be on the right road. No doubt he was going to meet Nicola. A burning rage ran through Todd. *He* should be the one going to meet her and be greeted by her smile and welcoming kiss.

He was shaking with such emotion that he almost lost control of his bike and swerved dangerously. Dimitris sounded his horn and slowed further. These tourists who hired bikes were a menace. They drove erratically with no concern for other road users. He would be pleased when they had all left for the season. The only down side of that was that he would probably no longer have a regular job with Giovanni. It had made a difference to all of them with him having a wage coming in to the house each week.

Todd rode slowly past the self catering units, suddenly realising that he was leaving Plaka behind as he drove up the hill. He drew in to the side of the road and dismounted, looking back the way he had come. He saw the man with the dog arrive and stop outside a building that stood a short distance from the others. This had to be the taverna where Nicola worked. He moved his bike further off the road. He would stand there and watch for her. What was keeping the man so long inside with Nicola? Surely they couldn't be – Nicola wouldn't – it was unthinkable. He felt his uncontrollable rage building up inside himself again. He wanted to go down and confront them, but his legs were trembling too much for him to move.

A woman emerged from one of the other buildings and strolled across. Todd stiffened. Would she be able to gain access to the taverna or had they locked the door so they would remain undisturbed? She walked in unhindered and exited a few moments later with a package in her hand. He felt himself sweating with relief. They had not locked the door to ensure privacy.

Dimitris walked out, collected a bag and a stick and whistled the dog to him. A man came to the doorway and watched as they walked towards the clump of trees a short distance away. A car arrived and four women got out, spoke to the man in the doorway and collected trolleys loaded with cleaning materials, before making their way over to the chalets. Todd was curious, where was

Nicola? He looked at the building intently. There was an upper floor. Maybe she was still in bed if she had worked until the early hours.

Todd wheeled his bike back onto the road. He would take a chance and go down on the pretext of wanting a bottle of water. If he left his helmet on he was sure Nicola would not recognise him if she was inside. He passed the carob trees and Dimitris looked up. Surely that was the same idiot who had passed him earlier on the road? No doubt he had thought he could drive on around the coast and turned back now he had realised his mistake.

Todd parked his bike and tried to walk casually into the taverna. Once inside he realised it was also a small general store.

'Good morning. Can I help you?'

Todd licked his dry lips. 'Do you have a bottle of water?'

Giovanni nodded. 'Help yourself. In the fridge.'

Todd opened the sliding door to the cabinet. He needed an excuse to talk to the man, to see if he could find out when Nicola would be there. He returned to the counter where Giovanni was reading the newspaper.

'Beautiful around here,' observed Todd. 'No doubt you have a lot of visitors.'

Giovanni nodded. 'Keeps us busy.'

'Do you look after all of it yourself?'

'Couldn't manage that now. We did the first few years we were open.'

'You employ the local people, no doubt?'

'Family and locals.' Giovanni frowned. Was this man looking for a job?

'Everywhere seems to be family run,' observed Todd.

'It's our way. We find it works. What part of the States are you from?'

'Dallas. Do you know it?'

Giovanni shook his head. 'I've been over a couple of times to New Orleans.'

Todd swallowed. 'What made you go there?'

'Relatives. No need to go any more. They've all decided to come and live with us over here now.'

'All of them?'

Giovanni smiled. 'Most of them; and the others visit whenever they can. We only get a break in the winter months so they have to help us out when we're busy during the summer. What brings you over here anyway? It's a long way from home.'

Todd looked at him blankly. 'Me?'

'Yes, why are you visiting Crete? Most Americans go to Athens.'

'I just fancied Crete.'

'What did you think of Knossos?'

'Knossos?'

'Yes, the Minoan site up by Heraklion. That's where everyone visits first when they come to Crete.'

'Oh, I haven't been up that far yet.'

'Been out to the island?'

Todd shook his head. 'I haven't done that yet either.'

'How long do you plan to stay down here?'

'I haven't decided.'

'Well, make sure you visit Spinalonga before you leave. It was once a leper colony you know.'

'Yes, I've heard about it.'

'The boats go every half an hour. I've the guide book here if you want it.' Giovanni placed the book on the counter.

Todd looked at the slim book. He was not interested in visiting Spinalonga or buying a guide book. All he wanted was to know the whereabouts of Nicola.

'Yes, I'll get one before I go over. How much is it for the water?' He held out a note and waited whilst Giovanni gave him his change.

Dimitris appeared at the doorway. 'Five today,' he grinned. 'I'll get rid of them and then replace that light bulb. Cabin sixteen, wasn't it?'

Giovanni nodded. 'I've told the cleaners to tell you if there are any other problems.'

Todd made his way to the door. He did not wish to be in the vicinity of the youth. As he passed by the dog emitted a deep growl and Dimitris looked at him in surprise. 'What's wrong with you, Skele? I've never heard you growl before.'

Todd glared at the animal who growled again, curling back his lips and showing his teeth. Dimitris placed a restraining hand on his collar.

Giovanni shook his head. 'Keep him away from the taverna if he's going to take offence at the customers. I can't have him snarling at people.'

'He's usually friendly,' protested Dimitris. 'I've never known him take a dislike to anyone.'

Todd stood beside his bike and took a long drink from his bottle of water. He was convinced now that he knew where Nicola worked. All he had to do was hang around in the vicinity until she put in an appearance.

Giovanni locked the taverna door. It had been a very quiet morning, hardly worth his while being open. Hopefully some of the tourists would decide to return and have their lunch there. At least he had a coach party booked for the following day. That was always profitable. He sold them guide books and water before they went over to the island for an hour and they had a set lunch of moussaka and salad, followed by bread, cheese and fresh fruit when they returned. The coach driver and guide always had a free meal, but he still made a profit. Marianne would come up and make the moussaka whilst Nicola prepared the salads, and they would both serve the tables. A glass of wine was included in the price of the trip and he would be in charge of that, with Marcus in the shop to deal with any sales. He must remember to tell Dimitris to keep that dog away tomorrow. He certainly did not want the animal growling at his customers.

Todd watched as Giovanni locked up and walked over to his bike. This was his chance to follow him and see where he lived. He felt his heart soar with relief. Once he had found that out he would know where Nicola was staying also.

Dimitris watched as Todd drove down the road again. What was the man up to? He had spied the bike parked off the road and seen Todd sitting unmoving in the shade of a tree for the last hour. Now that Giovanni was leaving he was moving also. If he thought he would break in and rob the taverna he had another think coming. Skele would soon see him off the premises, besides, there was never any money left up there.

Todd followed Giovanni at a discreet distance. He was not sure if the red bike the man was riding was the same one as Nicola had used, but he made a note of the number plate. He saw Giovanni indicate that he was about to make a left turn and increased his speed. He did not want to find the man had turned into a complex of buildings and lose him. Without looking behind him Giovanni turned into the driveway of his house and parked the bike, striding down the side and out of view.

Todd halted a short distance away and walked back. Iron gates stood open between the high walls. On the tarmac was parked a mini-van, two cars, three motor cycles and an old motor bike. There must be a number of people in residence to require so many forms of transport. There were no windows on that side of the low house and Todd decided to take a chance. He walked swiftly across the tarmac to the shelter of the wall and peered around the corner. A wide paved walkway led down to glass patio doors, and he would be seen immediately by anyone inside.

He walked gingerly to the opposite corner and peered around that. Again there was a paved walkway beside the house with a railing down one side. He crept cautiously forwards and saw there were irregular rocks at a lower level. The rail was obviously for safety, the house being built out on a promontory of land. The glint of sunshine drew Todd's attention to the windows. The whole of the side, from floor to ceiling appeared to be made from glass, their shutters hooked back except for the first room where they were tightly closed.

Todd dared go no further. He would be visible to anyone occupying one of the rooms. He speculated which one Nicola would occupy, probably the far one. That would be the room he would allocate to her as it certainly had the best view across the bay to the island. He visualised her waking up in the morning, drawing the curtains apart and standing there gazing out at the sea. He added himself to the picture. She would turn back to where he was still laying in bed and stretch her arms out to him. "Get up, Todd," she would say, "Come and enjoy this beautiful day with me." He would join her and admire the view; then they would go to shower. Would they shower together? Todd shook his head. That had been routine with Jennie-Lea, enabling them to indulge in foreplay until they could control themselves no longer, but Nicola was different. She would want her privacy and he would grant it.

The sound of a car starting up aroused him from his daydream and he shrank back against the wall. He would wait until the sound of the engine faded away and then he must make his escape, hopefully unseen.

Todd sat in a small taverna in the square at Elounda. He ate the meal he had ordered without tasting it. He had to plan carefully. He would return to his vantage point on the hill the following day and surely Nicola would appear at some time. He cursed himself now for leaving to follow the man on the bike. It may have been Nicola who was driving off in the car to go up to the taverna. He would take a couple of bottles of water with him so he did not have to go down to buy any and make his presence known in the area. Now he was certain he knew where she worked he would wait up there all day if necessary until he saw her.

A dog growled as it walked past him and Todd knew

instinctively that it was the mongrel that had taken a dislike to him earlier. He wondered if he bought a piece of meat and left it to rot in the sun whether the dog would eat it and be poisoned. Somehow he thought it unlikely. There was something uncannily intelligent about the beast.

Todd took up his position on the hillside. He had taken the precaution of laying the bike down, half hidden in the ditch. He saw Giovanni arrive and open up the taverna. People from the cabins wandered over at intervals, sometimes returning swiftly and others staying far longer, making Todd think they were having a breakfast. He wished he could go over and have one also. He had been so determined to arrive early that he had left before breakfast was served at his hotel.

He saw Dimitris arrive, the dog at his heels, and he went through the same routine as the previous day, collecting a sack and a stick before making his way over to the carob trees. An hour later the cleaners arrived, followed swiftly by another car. Todd watched as the two women and a man climbed out. He clenched his hands. There she was! He felt his chest constrict. At last, a sight of Nicola. He strained his eyes, but he was too far away to see her clearly. Tears of joy ran down his face and when she disappeared inside he buried his face in his hands and his body was racked with sobbing.

Dimitris placed a third grass snake into the sack and told Skele to stay in the carob trees. He mounted his bike, placed the sack beneath his feet and began to ride up the hill towards the waste ground where he would release the snakes. He had a feeling they were the same ones he caught time and again and wished he could release them further away.

As he rode the sun glinted off something in the ditch and he realised it was the wing mirror of a bike. He drew in to the side. Had someone had an accident? He parked and walked over, looking at the bike carefully. There was no obvious damage, nor was there any sign of the owner. He frowned in consternation; then shrugged. He would dispose of the snakes and if the bike was still there when he returned he would investigate further.

Todd lay flat on the grass, hardly daring to breathe when he saw Dimitris riding up the hill and stopping to look at his scooter. As he heard him continue on his way he realised he could stay there no longer. He would have to find another vantage point to watch the taverna. Slowly he rose to his feet and walked over to the ditch. It was more of a struggle than he had envisaged trying to manoeuvre the bike back up onto the road and to his dismay he heard the sound of Dimitris returning.

As he drew up alongside Todd tried to smile. Dimitris parked his bike and took the rear wheel of the scooter in the ditch whilst Todd lifted the handle bars and between them they placed the bike back on the tarmac.

'Okay?' asked Dimitris. 'Accident?'

Todd shook his head. 'Okay. Thanks for your help.'

Dimitris looked at him curiously. This was the man who had been around yesterday. The one Skele had taken an instant dislike to. What was he doing watching the taverna? Dimitris decided he must tell Giovanni about his suspicious behaviour. He rode back down the hill, watching Todd in his mirrors until he rounded the bend and drew up outside the taverna.

'Where's Mr Giovanni?' he asked Marianne.

'Getting out some more tables. He'd probably appreciate some help from you.'

Dimitris nodded and walked inside to the rear of the building. 'Mr Giovanni,' he called.

'Good,' Giovanni smiled. 'We could do with a bit of extra help. The coach party is due in ten minutes and they sent me through a message to say seven extra people have joined the group this morning. Can you help Marcus with that table? The chairs are over there and need to go out as well.'

Dimitris nodded. 'I really wanted to speak to you.'

'Later. We need to be ready for the coach. It looks bad if there aren't enough tables and chairs out when they arrive.'

Dimitris lifted one end of the trestle table and Marcus took the other and between them they carried it out to the patio in front of the taverna where Marianne was counting the chairs.

'We need five more chairs to go round the tables. A few spare would be a good idea. If you place them in that patch of shade,' she pointed. 'We need a base for this umbrella as well. It keeps falling to one side.'

Marcus looked at her questioningly. He realised she was asking for more chairs and had said something about the umbrella but he needed an interpretation from the Greek.

'More chairs,' she said, 'and a base for the umbrella.'

Marcus nodded. He still found it frustrating that when the family were together they spoke Greek, forgetting he was still struggling with the language.

Todd rode by slowly on his bike. The woman he could see was certainly not Nicola. She was a good deal older, but that awful young man was there and appeared to be helping at the taverna, despite his scruffy appearance. He slowed further as a coach rounded the corner, taking up most of the road, people staring eagerly from the windows, and blocking the taverna from his view.

Dimitris frowned in annoyance. He would not have a chance to speak to Giovanni now. He would have to wait until tomorrow.

Todd sat in a taverna in the square at Elounda. He wished now he had arranged to stay in Elounda rather than in Aghios Nikolaos. He was closer to Nicola there. He was sure she was staying in the house he had investigated the previous day. They must have plenty of money to live in a house that large and in such a favourable location.

If Nicola was interested in marrying for money he would be able to satisfy her needs in that respect. Surely she did not want to spend the remainder of her life working in a taverna? The scruffy man with the dog didn't look as if he had any money or the prospect of making any. It was evident that he was just an odd job man, probably trying to worm his way into their affections so they would not object to his association with Nicola.

He needed to be able to persuade her to return to America and be with him. It might take a while for her to realise that they were meant to be together, but he was convinced the day would come. All he needed was a plan for her to leave the area and not have a reason to return.

The man at the next table flicked his cigarette butt into the plant pot at his side. Within seconds smoke was rising from the dry plants. A look of consternation on his face the man picked up his water bottle and emptied the contents into the pot, extinguishing the small fire immediately.

Todd sat fascinated. If a plant pot was that dry the grass and the countryside must be even more parched. That was the answer before his eyes. If there were no chalets there would be no need for a shop and taverna. If they were not there Nicola would have no reason to return to the area. She would soon forget the scruffy man and no doubt whoever owned the chalets was insured.

Now he had to plan carefully. He could not just set fire to the grass on the hillside and hope it would spread to the chalets; nor could he be certain that the chalets would burn unless he had some form of accelerant. His head began to throb. Now he had the idea he wanted to put it into practice immediately. The first thing he had to do was return to the hill above the chalets and find somewhere he could watch without the man and the dog spotting him.

Todd started up his scooter and looked at the light that was flashing. He needed petrol. He must have covered more miles than he had realised on his trips back and forth. He looked around. There must be a garage locally, everyone seemed to be driving a vehicle of some sort. He walked over to the car hire across the road, hoping they would understand his needs and direct him.

To his relief the man inside understood and spoke good English, directing him up a side road from the town. Todd hoped the flashing light did not mean his tank was empty. He did not relish the thought of having to push the scooter through the traffic in the afternoon sun.

His mission accomplished and with a full tank of petrol, Todd rode back up to Plaka. The taverna was quiet, there was no sign of anyone in attendance, and the coach and other vehicles had departed. He resisted the urge to go and investigate further and continued up the hill past the place where he had stopped previously. He rounded the bend and realised if he continued up the road the taverna would be out of his sight. He parked the bike off the road beside a tree. He did not want to repeat his earlier mistake of putting it into the ditch and having a struggle to pull it out.

Todd walked back down to his previous vantage point. This was where he needed to be to sit and formulate his plan. From here it was only a short distance down to the chalets. He could see the tennis courts and crazy golf area that stood a short distance away from them and the carob trees to one side. He would have to be prepared to be patient, and wait until the tourists staying there had left for the day. The opening hours for the taverna and shop appeared to be erratic and he would have to take a chance that it was closed and the fire would not be spotted too soon.

He made a list of items in his head. He would buy a quantity of water bottles. No one would look twice at anyone carrying water. He would empty them and siphon out the petrol from the tank of the scooter. He would need some rubber tubing for that. He would look around in Aghios Nikolaos. There was sure to be a general store somewhere that sold such items. He must remember to buy some matches. It would be too ironic for him to forget such a basic necessity.

Giovanni answered his mobile 'phone and a delighted smile spread across his face. 'What time will you be there? Fine. I'll drive up to meet you. Do you want me to tell Nicola?'

'I've already spoken to her. Can she come up with you?
'Of course.'

'Thanks, Dad. I'll be waiting at the bus station.'

'That was John,' announced Giovanni to his wife. 'I'm collecting him from Heraklion bus station at ten tomorrow morning. Will you be able to cope with the taverna until I get back?'

'I don't see why not. If we get a message about a coach party I'll ask Marcus to come up with me. We'll manage whatever happens. It's more important that you and Nicola collect John. He doesn't want to spend two hours of his leave sitting on a bus.'

Todd wandered around the shops in Aghios Nikolaos. He was well away from the tourist area. Here the shops seemed to be selling the commodities that the residents would need. He looked in the window at an array of locks, taps, handles, screws and tools. This could be a likely source of plastic tube.

He entered and began to peruse the goods on sale, moving from shelf to shelf until he reached the back of the shop. Larger items were stored there, cans of paint, buckets, rubbish bins, cooker hoods and the like. Then he saw exactly what he needed. A box on the floor had an illustration of a container with a spray attached and various insects. He opened the flap and pulled out the instructions from inside. As he had hoped they were in all languages and he searched for the English version.

> A safe and easy way to eliminate pests. Fill the container with insecticide to the mark shown on the side. Do not overfill. Attach the tube to the pump and insert into the container. Place the container on level ground. Direct the nozzle of the spray towards the area and press the plunger. An area of approximately one square foot will be covered with each spray. Wearing a face mask is recommended.

Todd replaced the instructions and carried the box over to the counter. The man looked at him in surprise. What would a tourist want with an insect spray? If he had a problem wherever he was staying it was the responsibility of the owner. He shrugged. Provided he was paid he did not mind what the man bought from his shop.

Todd carried his purchase out of the shop feeling extremely pleased. He had the perfect way to spread the petrol on to the wooden chalets and also the piece of tubing he would need to enable him to siphon the petrol from the scooter. He wouldn't even need to buy a quantity of water bottles.

WEEK 2 – AUGUST 2008

John sat with his arm around Nicola. 'You don't know how relieved I am to be with you.'

Nicola smiled happily. 'I gathered that last night.'

'Apart from that! I was worried that you'd be all jittery and nervy and not want me near you.'

'Don't be silly! You do come up with some daft ideas.'

'I can't help it. I've been thinking seriously. I know we said we wouldn't get married until we were twenty five and I'd sorted out a career as a photographer, but I think we should get officially engaged now and married next year when I leave the army.'

Nicola leant against him. 'Having a ring on my finger won't change how I feel about you, but it could stop Mr Creepy and his stupid ideas.'

John frowned. 'What do you mean?'

Nicola blushed. She had not meant to tell John about the proposal Todd had made to her. 'Just before I left to come here he asked me to stay in New Orleans. I told him I already had my ticket and he asked me to cancel it and stay there with him. He said he wanted to marry me.'

'What?' John drew away from her. 'Are you serious?'

'I certainly was when I told him I wanted nothing to do with him. He seems to think he's in love with me.'

'Do you think that's why he attacked that gunman?'

Nicola frowned. 'Maybe; I don't know. I just feel there's

something screwy about that. Why should a drug addict hold up a cheap little diner when there's a general store just down the road?'

'Druggies don't think clearly.'

Nicola shrugged. 'I just feel there's something obvious that I'm missing.'

Giovanni had worked out a routine for the household that worked well. He would go up to the taverna and deal with any customers either wanting a breakfast or to purchase items whilst Bryony would prepare breakfast for her grandmother. When she had finished eating Marianne would go in to give her any help she needed with washing and dressing before she joined him up at the taverna. Bryony would clean the kitchen and their bedroom and Marcus would be occupied with any odd jobs Giovanni had requested he completed. Nicola cleaned their main lounge, Annita's room and her own, as well as running any errands or helping out up at the taverna during her stay with them. This week there was a problem.

'I've got to take the car in to the garage at Aghios Nikolaos this morning and Marcus is following me in to give me a lift back. He's dropping Bryony at the dentist on the way in and she'll wait there until we collect her. Are you able to go up to the taverna, Marianne?'

Marianne looked doubtful. 'What about Grandma? Nicola has to go in to Elounda to collect the prescriptions from the chemist. She's also paying the water and electricity bills.'

'Could she go up to the taverna and do those jobs this afternoon?'

'By the time she gets back the chemist will be closed until later. Grandma needs her medication by lunch time. They didn't have enough last week and assured her it would be there this morning.'

'I'll go up,' offered John.

'You're supposed to be on leave.'

'I know, but if Nick is going in to Elounda this morning there's no reason why I shouldn't go up to the taverna for an hour or so.'

Giovanni nodded. 'That's settled, then. I'll come up as soon as we've collected Bryony. Marcus can bring me up and take you back. That will leave the bike for me for later.'

John wrote down the breakfast order on his pad. 'Would you like cereal or fruit juice first and what about tea or coffee?'

The man looked at his wife who shook her head. 'A pot of coffee, please. You don't have anything to help recovery from sunstroke, I suppose?'

John shook his head and looked at the couple. 'Do you mean sun stroke or sun burn?'

'No, sunstroke. Megan smothered herself with cream and insisted on lying outside the umbrella yesterday. She thought the cream would protect her. She's been up half the night being sick and still feels awful this morning.'

'She will for a while. All I can suggest is that she drinks plenty to restore her fluid balance. Tell her to stay in bed with the blinds drawn. If she continues to be sick after twenty four hours let us know and we'll call a doctor out. It could be something she's eaten rather than the sun.'

'I don't think it's a stomach bug.' The woman shook her head. 'We've all eaten the same. I'm sure it's the sun.'

'She's old enough to know better,' grumbled the man. 'It's a shame, though. We were planning to go to Gournia today and now we'll have to go without her.'

'She doesn't mind being left alone?'

'No, she's not a little girl; lives in her own flat when we're at home. That's why I say she's old enough to know better.'

John nodded. 'I'll give you a 'phone number. Tell her to call that if she does need anything and one of us will come over.'

'Yes?' A look of relief crossed the man's face. 'I'm sure she won't need to disturb you. She just needs to sleep it off.'

'What's your chalet number?'

'Seven.'

John nodded. 'I'll let Dimitris know. He's supposed to be cutting the grass at the back later. He can leave it until tomorrow. When he's finished in the nature area he can always get the edging round the paths done.'

'That's kind of you to think of that.'

'Well I'm sure she doesn't want the buzz of a lawn mower adding to her headache. I'd best get your breakfast or you'll not get to Gournia.' John pulled a blank sheet from his order pad and wrote down a telephone number. 'That will go through to the house. There's always someone there and they could arrange to come up if she takes a turn for the worse. Saves me giving you half a dozen different numbers,' he grinned.

Todd walked openly towards the self catering apartments carrying the insect spray. He had sat patiently for over two hours and watched the occupants of the chalets leaving for the day. He had decided to start the fire in the centre chalet, which was out of sight of the shop and taverna. There was a chance the flames would spread to the others simply by him laying a trail of petrol in the dry grass, but he would spray some onto the timbers of the buildings to make doubly sure.

He deposited his large container on the ground and began to spray the woodwork, ensuring that a liberal amount fell on the grass. His plan was so simple. Why should anyone suspect he had deliberately set fire to the property?

Dimitris noticed the man spraying the chalets and wondered why he was there. The spraying to get rid of insects always took place before the season started. If the problem was ants he would have been asked to spray the ground not the buildings. There was something wrong here. He would go over to the taverna and check it out with John. 'Stay,' he told Skele as he began to walk away.

John looked up as he entered. 'Finished already? How many did you find today?'

Dimitris shook his head. 'No, I just wanted to ask why the chalets were being sprayed.'

John frowned. 'What do you mean? I haven't arranged for anyone to come and I'm sure Dad hasn't or he would have told me.'

'Do you want me to go and ask him what he's up to?'

'No. You stay here. I'll go and ask him. If he's got an order I can authorise him to continue. If he thinks he'll do it and send a bill in later he's got another think coming.'

Todd struck a match and watched whilst the flames took hold with frightening alacrity to the tinder dry grass and up the back of the wooden buildings.

John rounded the corner of the chalets and stopped aghast as he saw the flames. He immediately ran back around to the door of chalet seven. As far as he was aware that was the only one that had an occupant.

'Dimitris,' he called and waved his arms, hoping the man would see him and come to his aid. He had no idea how heavy the girl would be and he might well need Dimitris's help to carry her out of the burning building if she had already been overcome by smoke. He need not have worried. As he hammered on the door a young woman staggered out.

'What's wrong?' she asked.

'Get away from the building. There's a fire. Go to the taverna. You'll be safe there.'

'My handbag,' she turned to go back inside.

John grabbed her roughly by her arm. 'There's no time for that. Do as I say and go to the taverna.' He watched as she finally obeyed him and began to stumble along the path. He pulled his mobile from his pocket, pressing the numbers for the emergency services. It would take them a while before they would arrive from Aghios Nikolaos.

The main fire was obviously at the rear of the building and John snatched the fire extinguisher from the chalet before he hurried round. Once there he could see that two other chalets were alight. He set his mouth grimly. This had not been caused by a carelessly discarded cigarette.

He hesitated, should he try to stop the lesser fires at the other chalets and leave this one that had obviously taken a firm hold? It would need more than a fire extinguisher to bring it under control. As he released the safety cap on the fire extinguisher he felt a crashing blow on the back of his head as a piece of the roof fell and everything went black.

Dimitris sniffed. He could smell burning. Had John inadvertently left something cooking in the kitchen? Maybe he had left the oven cloth too close to a hot surface and it had begun to smoulder. He stood in the doorway and looked around. There was nothing. He checked the microwave and conventional oven to make doubly sure; then returned to the shop. The smell of burning was even stronger now and he went to the doorway. Had someone discarded a cigarette end and set fire to the grass?

He gasped in horror as he saw the flames licking at a chalet and picked up the fire extinguisher that stood in the kitchen. It would be better than nothing. All the chalets had their own extinguisher, but would he be able to reach them? As he ran towards them he saw Skele shoot out from the shelter of the trees and race towards the burning buildings

'Skele, come back.' Had the fire spooked the normally placid and docile dog?

Todd was so intent on spraying the chalets that he did not notice John's inert form. He continued to spray the next chalet, making sure he kept well away from the one that was already burning. As he bent to strike another match he heard a shout.

'Hey, you! What you do?'

He had been seen by the awful odd job man. Todd abandoned

the spray and began to run back up the hill where he had left his scooter. He needed to leave the area before he could be identified.

Skele howled and Dimitris ran as fast as he was able carrying the heavy fire extinguisher. When he reached the dog he could see he was standing between John's body and the flames that were licking ever closer. Dimitris abandoned the fire extinguisher and seized John beneath his arms, dragging him back from the burning grass and onto the path. As he did so he saw Skele take off again and run towards the hill.

The plight of the other chalets forgotten, Dimitris pulled John's mobile 'phone from his pocket and pressed the numbers of the emergency service for an ambulance.

John groaned and Dimitris gave a sigh of relief as his eyes flickered open. 'Can you move?' he asked. 'You're not safe here.'

Dimitris placed his hands beneath John's armpits and helped him into a sitting position. 'Come on. Get on your feet. I can't carry you.'

Dazed and unsteady John regained his feet. He stood there swaying and Dimitris placed an arm around his waist and urged him forwards.

'Where are we going?' John spoke thickly, his words slurred.

'Just a bit further away from the chalets.'

John put a hand out in front of him. 'I can't see,' he said.

Giovanni clicked his tongue in annoyance. They had waited for half an hour before Bryony emerged from the dentist, her face numb from a deep filling she had needed, and now they were being held up by emergency vehicles. Fire engines and an ambulance raced past them as they drew in to the side of the narrow road to allow them to pass.

'Must be a grass fire. Let's hope it's the other side of the hill,' observed Giovanni.

'You can see the smoke rising. Must be quite serious.'

'Let's just hope the wind is blowing off the land.' Giovanni spoke grimly. Each year there was a fire somewhere that caused devastation to the area. 'We'll drop Bryony off and go up to see that all is well at the taverna. I'm sure John would have 'phoned if the problem was close enough to cause concern.'

Nicola handed over the packets from the chemist to Marianne. She looked at her watch. Giovanni should be returning soon and then John would be back from the taverna. They would be able to spend the remainder of the day together. She was sure John would want to take the boat and go over to Spinalonga. She debated whether to start preparing a picnic to take with them or leave it until Bryony arrived. As she placed some eggs in a pan to boil she heard the emergency services' sirens and shivered.

Todd raced up the hill as fast as he was able, not daring to look behind him. The force that hit him in the small of his back knocked him to the ground and the dog stood looking down at him, growling and baring its teeth threateningly.

Todd lifted his head. 'Get away,' he ordered.

Skele did not move. Todd waved his arm at him. 'Go.'

The dog stood his ground and Todd made an attempt to scramble to his feet. Immediately Skele seized his shorts between his teeth and dragged him back down. Each time Todd made a movement the dog threatened him again, intermittently raising his head and howling.

Bryony left the car, holding the side of her face with her hand and feeling sorry for herself. As Giovanni and Marcus drove along the road to towards the taverna the acrid smell of the smoke hit them forcibly. Giovanni groaned.

'Not the taverna. Please don't let it be the taverna.'

'Better that than a chalet with someone trapped inside.'

Giovanni's face whitened. 'Why hasn't John 'phoned?' Surely his son had not tried to tackle a grass fire alone? He knew better than that. You phoned for the emergency services immediately and made sure anyone in the vicinity was in a place of safety.

Giovanni stopped as a fireman held up his hand. 'No further, sir.'

'I have to. It's my taverna.'

The fireman shook his head. 'We need access for the ambulance. Once that's gone I'll let you through.'

'Ambulance? Who's hurt?'

'I don't know, sir, but they are taking someone to the hospital. It's probably smoke inhalation. A safety precaution.'

'I need to know who it is. My son's up here.'

'Let the ambulance through, then I'll take you to someone who might know the situation.'

Cursing volubly Giovanni drew over to the side of the road. Marcus opened the door. 'I'll go up. I should be able to get through on foot.'

Without waiting for an answer Marcus began to run down the road, the swirling smoke making him cough. He pushed open the door of the taverna to be greeted by a frightened girl, wearing only a long Tee-shirt.

'What's happened?' she asked, putting her hand to her head. 'I feel so bad.'

'Are you hurt?' asked Marcus.

'No. I was in bed. I've got a touch of sunstroke and stayed behind today. The next thing I knew there was someone banging my door down and telling me to get out.'

Marcus sighed with relief. 'There's a grass fire. The services are dealing with it. Can I get you anything?

'No, I just want to lie down.'

'No problem.' Marcus went into the back room and opened up a sun lounger. 'It would be better if you stayed inside. There's a lot of smoke out there.'

Gratefully the girl lay down on the lounger. 'My head's going round and round,' she complained.

'Here's some water.' Marcus handed her a bottle and some

paper napkins. 'Try a cold compress on your head. That may help. I'll be back in a short while. Promise me you'll not go wandering off outside on your own.'

'Is there a toilet here? I think I might be sick again, and I haven't anything for my feet.'

'Take whatever you need off the shelves in the shop. Use the toilet over there marked staff only. The public ones are outside.'

'I'll remember.' She closed her eyes and Marcus took the opportunity of emptying the till. He would give it to Giovanni later or replace it if the taverna was able to stay open.

Giovanni pushed passed the fireman who tried to block his way. 'My son's up there. I need to know if he's safe.'

'Is that him over there?' The fireman pointed to where Dimitris was standing, his eyes wide with horror.

Giovanni walked over to Dimitris. 'Where's John?' he barked.

'They've taken John to the hospital. His hands are burnt and something fell on his head.'

'Is that all? Are you telling me the truth?'

Dimitris nodded. 'I was with him until they put him in the ambulance. He was talking to me.'

'Tell me what happened. How did it start?' Giovanni ran a trembling hand over his head. Despite the attempts by the fire crew to bring the blaze under control it appeared to be burning as fiercely as ever.

'I'm sure it was deliberate. I saw someone spraying the huts. I came down to ask John what he was up to and John went over to ask him.'

'Why didn't you go with him?'

'He told me to wait here. Then I smelled the smoke and Skele howled.' Dimitris was trembling with reaction.

'And you went to save that damned dog rather than try to control the fire!'

'No.' Dimitris shook his head vehemently. 'He was standing

257

between John and the flames, pawing at him, trying to get him to move.'

Giovanni grunted. 'What about the visitors?'

'There was only a girl. John got her out and she's in the taverna.'

'Did you check the other chalets?'

Dimitris shook his head. 'I was too concerned with John.'

'I'd better alert the firemen. There could be someone in one of them.'

A resounding crash came to their ears as a roof caved in and sparks and debris flew up into the air. The firemen turned their hoses on the destroyed chalet, trying to stop the flames from spreading any further through the tinder dry grass.

Above the noise and confusion came the sound of a dog howling. 'That's Skele,' said Dimitris. 'Can I go and find him?'

Giovanni nodded. He had far more pressing concerns than the boy's dog.

Dimitris whistled and Skele answered with a spine chilling howl. 'Where the devil are you? Skele! Skele!'

The dog howled again and Dimitris began to hurry along the road away from the taverna and the billowing smoke. Once he was able to see more than a few feet in front of him he called for the dog again and heard the responding howl, followed by impatient barking. He wasn't that far away, but no doubt too frightened to come any closer.

Dimitris made for the clump of carob and stood looking up the hill. 'Skele!' he called again and this time the barking seemed closer; then he saw him, standing half way up the hill. 'Skele, come on. Come down here. There's a good dog.'

Skele ignored the call, letting out another howl. Dimitris frowned. The dog was usually so obedient. He must be seriously frightened not to come when he was called.

'All right, I'll come and get you,' muttered Dimitris and began to walk over the rough grass. He had nearly reached the dog when he saw that there was a man lying there. Was this someone else who had been injured in the fire? Dimitris hurried as fast as he was able as the tussocks of grass caught at the old trainers he wore when searching for snakes.

As Dimitris approached Skele moved to one side. Todd immediately tried to scramble to his feet and Skele caught his shorts between his teeth again and pulled him back down. Dimitris moved closer and realised the frightened man on the ground was the one he had seen spraying the chalets.

'Good dog, Skele. Stay. Guard,' he ordered and Skele wagged his tail obediently.

Dimitris set off back down the hill waving his arms to try to attract attention. Once back by the road the smoke began to make him cough and he placed his arm across his mouth and nose, trying to take shallow breaths. Giovanni was inside the taverna, talking to the fire chief and a police inspector.

'Here's the man who can give you more information. Where've you been, Dimitris? The Inspector wants a statement from you about the man you say you saw spraying the chalets.'

'He's up on the hill.' Dimitris coughed harshly and struggled to regain his breath. 'Skele has him pinned down up there.'

The Inspector frowned. 'Skele?'

'My dog.'

'I hope for your sake he hasn't hurt him or you'll likely be sued.'

Dimitris looked at the Inspector in disbelief. 'My dog is guarding the man who set fire to Mr Pirenzi's property. I'm sure he hasn't hurt him. I've come to ask you to arrest him. If you don't then I will ask my dog to attack.'

'That really would not be very wise, sir. There's a law against keeping dangerous dogs.'

Giovanni slammed his hand on to the counter top. 'Don't you understand, Inspector? The man who fired my property is on the hill. If you don't go up there and take him into custody immediately

I shall be suing you and the rest of your department for dereliction of duty.'

'How can you be sure this was the man? He could be quite innocent. I'll need to take a statement from you before I can arrest him.'

Giovanni clenched his fists. 'Inspector, I demand that you go and apprehend this man at once. You can take statements later.'

'It could be a case of mistaken identity.'

'If it is I'll take the consequences. Just go and get him. Go with him, Dimitris. I don't want the Inspector to be unable to find him.'

Reluctantly the Inspector signalled to a couple of the policemen who were standing near and they began to follow Dimitris back up the hill. Giovanni wiped his brow and turned to Marcus.

'I'd better 'phone Marianne.'

'I already have. She and Nicola are on their way to the hospital. She said she'd 'phone you when she'd spoken to John.'

Giovanni nodded. 'Did you tell her what had happened?'

'Not in any great detail, just that there had been a fire at one of the chalets. Once she knew John had been taken to the hospital she wasn't interested in anything more.'

'I wish it had been just one chalet. Three are completely gone and a couple more will probably have to be pulled down. Goodness knows what state the others are in that I can't see from here.' Giovanni poured a large brandy and drank it down quickly.

For once Marcus wished he could accept a glass also.

Skele moved away from Todd and allowed the police to help him to his feet. His legs were covered in scratches where he had wriggled around on the coarse grass to avoid the dog's jaws and his shorts were in tatters down one side.

'Good dog, Skele. Come on, now.'

Skele walked a few paces at Dimitris's heels, then sat down and whined softly.

'What's wrong, old boy? You did a good job, you showed me where John was and you caught this idiot. Come on, down to the taverna and I'll find you a treat.'

Skele did not move, but whined again. Dimitris bent over him. 'What's wrong with you?' he stroked the dog's head and tried to encourage him to get on his feet. Skele licked his hand, but remained motionless.

'You need a drink. Come on, on your feet.'

Skele whined again and Dimitris lifted up his front paw. The pad was blistered and looked raw. Dimitris lifted the other one and saw it was in the same state.

'You poor old thing. No wonder you don't want to walk anywhere. I'll have to carry you and then we'll go to the vet and see what he can do for you. How did you manage all that running if your paws were in such a state?'

Dimitris gathered the dog up in his arms and began to walk slowly down the hill. He held Skele tightly to him, feeling close to tears as the dog licked his bare arm in grateful thanks.

Dimitris approached Giovanni hesitantly. 'Would you be able to take me into Elounda in your car?'

Giovanni frowned. 'Didn't you bring your bike?'

Dimitris nodded. 'Skele can't walk.' He held out a paw to show Giovanni the extent of the dog's burns.

'How did that happen?'

'When he was trying to protect John.'

Giovanni nodded. 'Marcus can drive you.' He pulled a roll of notes out of his pocket. 'Here you are. Vets don't come cheap.'

Dimitris looked at the amount he was being offered with disbelieving eyes. 'I'm sure it won't cost that much.'

'You can give me the change later. Make sure you put something on the seat. I don't want dog hairs everywhere. Marcus,' called Giovanni. 'Can you take Dimitris and the dog into Elounda? The dog burnt his paws. He needs the vet.'

261

'I ought to give him a drink first. He must be parched.'

'If he's sick in the car you'll have to clear it up,' warned Giovanni.

Dimitris laid a towel on the back seat of the car. He did not dare tell Giovanni it was a new one he had taken from the stock, but he had seen nothing else suitable. Carefully he deposited Skele on the seat and was about to climb in beside him when the Inspector laid a hand on his shoulder and stopped him.

'We need a statement from you before you go off anywhere, sir. We are not able to arrest this man for arson until we have that.'

'This is the man who I saw spraying the chalets. Now can I go?'

'We'll need more than that, I'm afraid. You'll need to come into Aghios Nikolaos with us and we'll take the statement down from you and get you to sign it. We can't bring any charges without evidence.'

'For goodness sake,' interrupted Giovanni irritably. 'Take the man into custody on suspicion. Let Dimitris take the dog to the vet and Marcus will bring him into Aghios Nikolaos afterwards.'

Dimitris slipped into the back of the car and sat beside Skele. 'Not long now, old boy and we'll get those paws seen to.'

Giovanni turned to Marcus. 'Take him to the vet, whilst you're waiting for him, go to the bank and draw out as much from your account as they'll let you have. I'll pay you back later. Go up to Uncle Yannis and ask him to do the same. Take Dimitris into the police station and drop the dog back home. Then come back here.'

Marcus pulled his handkerchief from his pocket and handed it to Giovanni. 'This is the money I took from the till. I wasn't sure if it was safe to leave it there with all this going on.'

Giovanni nodded. 'Thanks. Now I must try to 'phone Marianne and see how John is doing, then I'll contact Vasi. Get yourself back here as soon as you can. I shall need your help when the tourists begin to return.'

Marianne's 'phone was switched off and Giovanni hoped it meant she was in the hospital with John and forbidden to use it. No doubt she would call him as soon as she was able. Whilst he waited he would 'phone Vasi. He had to arrange accommodation for the tourists whose chalets had been destroyed or damaged. He would also have to give them immediate compensation for the loss of their belongings and he hoped the money Marcus would bring back with him would be enough to for them to buy some spare clothes. Giovanni ran his hand over his head. This was going to take weeks to sort out with the insurance companies involved.

Vasi answered his mobile and was genuinely shocked by Giovanni's news. 'Give me ten minutes. I'll check with the office and see what we have available. How many rooms do you want? Six! I'm not sure I can manage that many. Do you want me to 'phone Stelios? He may have a couple free.'

'Whatever,' replied Giovanni abruptly. 'I need to be able to tell these visitors that I have arranged for them to have a bed for the night when they return from their day out. I don't care whose hotel they use.'

'I'll get back to you as soon as I can.'

Giovanni put his head in his hands and groaned. It was bad enough when a fire started accidently, but for someone to have destroyed the chalets deliberately was inexcusable. He certainly did not think he had made an enemy of any of his business rivals, but why else would anyone wish to cause such destruction?

'Can I help? Make a cup of tea or something?'

For the first time Giovanni noticed the girl standing in the doorway to the back room.

'Where've you come from?'

'I've been here all the time. I didn't go off this morning with my parents as I was feeling ill. Someone came banging on my door and pulled me out of the chalet. He wouldn't even let me go back to get dressed or collect my handbag,' she complained. 'Do you want me to make you a cup of tea or anything?'

Giovanni shook his head. 'Make one for yourself if you want.' Giovanni pressed in the number to Marianne's 'phone and this time she answered when it rang.

'I was just about to call you. Marcus said...'

'Never mind what Marcus said. How's John?'

'John's all right. He has some burns on his left side and he inhaled some smoke. They say he also suffered concussion where something fell on his head. They want to keep him in for observation, but basically he's fine.'

Giovanni let out a sigh of relief. 'There's a big problem up here. I can't talk now. I'm waiting for a call from Vasi.'

'Do you want me to come up?'

'It could be helpful. Are you happy to leave John?'

'I don't think there's any need for us to stay. He's not in any danger. His burns are being treated now; then I'll see what the doctor says.'

'Let me know.' Giovanni cancelled the call and waited impatiently for Vasi to advise him about the accommodation that was available. He turned to the girl.

'You, what's your name? You'll find some bags in the cupboard in the back room. Bring a dozen in here and you can help by getting some toiletries ready. Toothbrush, toothpaste, bar of soap, flannel, comb, deodorant, disposable razor, shaving cream – the basic necessities. Make piles on the table ready for people to help themselves.'

'My name's Megan,' she called over her shoulder as she returned to the back room and opened the cupboard.

Marcus lifted the dog out from the back seat of the car and knocked on the door of the house where Dimitris lived. A woman with a small child came to the door and gasped in horror when she saw the bandaged animal. The little girl in her arms stretched out her hands to the dog who wagged his tail in response.

'What's happened?' asked Antonia.

'There was a fire at the chalets...'

'Dimitris?' her face paled.

Marcus shook his head. 'Dimitris is fine, truly. He's at the police station giving a statement to the police. I'm just bringing his dog back from the vet for him. Where shall I put him?'

Antonia gave Marcus a puzzled look. She had understood very little of the news he was imparting. 'Dimitris?' she asked again.

Marcus placed the dog on the ground where he limped inside the house. Marcus tried again, realising she did not understand his American English. 'Dimitris, okay. Home soon.'

Antonia nodded. The important thing was that Dimitris was unharmed despite whatever had happened to the dog, but she was sure the man had mentioned the police. She hoped Dimitris was not in any sort of trouble with them. 'Thank you,' she said and closed the door.

Marcus drove back along the road towards Aghios Nikolaos and saw Vasi approaching. He hooted violently and the two cars drew abreast and the men lowered their windows.

'What's the news?' asked Vasi.

'John's in hospital, some of the chalets are wrecked. I've just taken Dimitris's dog back home. Could you call there and assure his sister that all is well with him. I don't think she understood me.'

'Where is Dimitris?'

'At the police station making a statement.'

'What! They don't suspect him surely?'

Marcus shook his head. 'He saw the man who started it. They have him in custody. Dimitris is a witness. Can you explain that to her?'

'Give me her address and I'll go there before I go up to Giovanni.'

The traffic that was being held up by the exchange between the two men began to sound their horns and Marcus shouted Dimitris's address to Vasi, who nodded and ignored the protests of the other drivers as he backed and turned his car. Marcus raised his hand in apology to the drivers on his side of the road and continued on to the town where he made straight for Yannis's shop.

The door was locked when he arrived and he banged on it in frustration. Surely this was not the one time that Yannis had decided to close up early! Marcus pulled his mobile 'phone from his pocket and called Yannis's number. The man answered almost immediately.

'Where are you?' asked Marcus.

'The bank.'

'Have you spoken to Giovanni?'

'Of course. I will go to taverna with money.'

Marcus heaved a sigh of relief. 'Thank you, Uncle Yannis.' All he had to do now was withdraw money from his own account and he would be able to return to the taverna and see how Giovanni was faring.

Dimitris sat in the police station nervously. He had never had occasion before to go inside. He really wanted to go home and check on Skele before returning to the taverna to find out how John was faring. He would then return the surplus from the money Giovanni had given him and be willing to help in any way he could.

'Now, sir, if you could just give us your name and address.'

Dimitris complied, licking his dry lips and clenching his hands. Should he tell them it had been his mother's house and his sister and his brother-in-law lived there?

'And your occupation?'

'Odd job man, I suppose. I catch the snakes for Mr Giovanni.'

'Catch the snakes?'

'In the carob trees area. There's a nature trail and activities for the children in there. I check it a couple of times a day and remove any grass snakes I find. That's what I was doing today when the fire was started.'

'You actually saw the fire being started?'

Dimitris shook his head. 'I saw someone spraying the chalets. I went down to the taverna to tell John. Sometimes the spray firms come and do a job without being asked and then expect to present a bill to the owner. I wanted to know if he had arranged it.'

'John is?'

'John is Mr Giovanni's son. The man who was taken to the hospital.'

'And what was this John doing up at the taverna?'

Dimitris shrugged. 'Working. Serving customers.'

'Was he usually up there at that time of the day?'

Dimitris shook his head. 'Usually it's Mr Giovanni who's there. John is in the army doing his National Service.'

'Did Mr Giovanni know his son was up there?'

'I'm sure he did. John's on leave and they would have arranged it between them.'

The Inspector nodded. 'So to go back, you saw a man spraying the chalets and you went down to the taverna to tell whoever was working there?'

'That's right.'

'And then what happened?'

'John said he would go and ask him what he was doing. Whilst he was gone I began to smell burning. I checked the kitchen area and there was nothing burning there. As I went outside a woman was approaching, one of the guests I think, but I didn't stop to ask her.'

'You didn't stop? What did you do?'

'I could smell the burning really strongly, and I could hear my dog howling. I'd told him to stay in the carob trees. I thought he was frightened and went to look for him.'

The Inspector frowned. 'You didn't go to investigate the source of the burning you could smell?'

'I didn't know a chalet was on fire. I thought it was just grass and I was concerned that my dog was trapped.'

267

'But you did not return to the carob trees where you say you left your dog?'

'The howling wasn't coming from over there. It was from behind the chalets. I went to look and found him standing between John and the burning grass. John was lying still and Skele, that's my dog, was nudging and pawing at him.'

'So what did you do then?'

'I managed to drag John on to the concrete path a short distance away and he recovered consciousness. I helped him walk to the road where he would be safe. Then I used his mobile 'phone to dial one one two for an ambulance.'

'And your dog?'

'I saw him run off up the hill, but I was concerned about John. I stayed with him until the ambulance arrived.'

The Inspector nodded. 'Now, let us go back to this man that your dog attacked.'

'He did not attack him,' replied Dimitris indignantly. 'He stopped him from escaping.'

The Inspector ignored the information. 'You say you saw a man spraying the area and went to speak to this man, John. For all we know at the moment the man could have been authorised to do this. Maybe John was smoking when he went over to him? Some of these chemicals are very flammable.'

'John doesn't smoke. I called out to the man and he dropped the spray and ran. That was when Skele ran after him.'

'Yes, you say the man your dog was standing over started the fire.'

Dimitris nodded vehemently. 'I'm sure he's been watching the taverna and chalets for a few days.'

'What makes you think he's been watching the property?'

Dimitris nodded. 'He passed me on his scooter as I was coming along one day. I saw him coming back down the hill a short time later. I thought nothing of it, just a tourist realising he was going the wrong way. The following day I was going up to dispose of the snakes when I saw a bike in the ditch. I didn't know it was his at the time. I stopped, but there didn't seem to be anyone around. I took the snakes to the other side of the hill and when I came back down he was trying to pull the bike out of the ditch. I helped him pull the bike out and there was nothing wrong with it. I think he'd tried to hide it there.'

'Why would he do that?'

Dimitris shrugged. 'I don't know.'

'Did you inform Mr Pirenzi that you had seen a man you thought was acting suspiciously?'

Dimitris shook his head miserably. 'I went down to the taverna to tell him and he was expecting a coach party. I helped to get some of the tables ready and then the coach arrived. I planned to tell him the next morning, but he went up to Heraklion to fetch John home for his leave.'

The Inspector kept Dimitris at the station for a further hour whilst his statement was typed out, checked it was correct and Dimitris had signed it.

'Can I go now?' asked Dimitris. 'I really want to go to the taverna and find out about John and Mr Giovanni could probably do with some help to clear up.'

The Inspector sighed. There was no point in keeping the man any longer. He had stuck doggedly to his story. The American man they had in custody did not have any marks on him that could be attributed to a dog except possibly the scratches on his legs. Before they could interview him they would have to wait for the representative from the American Consulate to arrive from Athens. In the meantime he had been placed in a cell, given some water and a reasonable meal.

Marcus drove back to the chalets where the acrid smoke still drifted across the road and the firemen were still damping down the area.

'How's John?' was his first question of Marianne.

'Some burns and smoke inhalation. They're keeping him in for the time being. There was no point in us staying as they were about to sedate him.'

Marcus nodded with relief. 'Where's Giovanni? I've brought the money he asked for.'

'He's assessing the damage with Uncle Yannis. Give it to me. I'm getting organised for when the tourists begin to arrive back. Megan's been a great help.'

'Megan?'

'The girl who didn't go out for the day. She's a bit shaken up. Her chalet must have been where he started the fire. There's nothing left. She keeps on about her passport; it was in her handbag apparently. I've handed her over to Nicola. There's nothing more we can do now except wait for the visitors to come back.'

'Have you eaten anything since breakfast?'

Marianne shook her head. 'I've not even thought about it.'

'Then I think you and Giovanni should. You could be out here until all hours waiting for people to return. I'll speak to Nicola and between us we should be able to sort out a meal. We can ask that girl Megan to help us, take her mind off her passport, maybe.'

Marianne smiled at Marcus gratefully. He was always so practical. She returned to the lists she had printed off from the computer. She knew who was staying in each chalet and she had their passport numbers recorded. Although it was only necessary to record the passport number for the leader of the group she had always insisted they took each one. 'Nowadays you never know when we could be innocently harbouring a criminal. If we're suspicious we can always ask the Embassy to do a passport check.'

Giovanni had laughed at her, but she had remained adamant that the procedure was followed. Now the information would be invaluable to the families.

Megan's family was the first to return to the holiday complex as she had been able to give Giovanni their mobile telephone number.

They looked in horror at the blackened shell of the chalet they had occupied.

Megan's father put his arms around his daughter. 'Thank goodness I told that young man you were staying behind. I dread to think what could have happened otherwise.'

Megan gave a shaky laugh. 'I wondered how he knew I was there, but I was still feeling so ill. One of the men up here gave me a sun lounger and told me to put a cold compress on my head. That seemed to ease my headache. I've been busy helping them so that's kept my mind off feeling sick.'

Marianne walked over to the visibly distraught family. 'Can you come and sit down. We need to help everyone who's been affected and the sooner we can put their minds at rest the better.'

'What are we going to do?' Megan's mother looked at Marianne, her lip trembling. 'We've only got the clothes we stand up in.'

Marianne placed her arm around the woman's shoulders. 'Come and sit down and I'll tell you the arrangements we have made.' She led the way to one of the tables. 'First of all, would you like a drink? Whatever you fancy, it's complimentary.'

'So I should think! I'll have a whisky.' Megan's father folded his arms and sat back expectantly.

'Nicola,' called Marianne. 'Whisky for the gentleman. 'She raised her eyebrows at his wife who shook her head.

'I'd rather have a cup of tea.'

'Cup of tea for the lady.'

Nicola nodded, poured a generous measure of whisky and delivered it to the table before returning to the kitchen.

'Now,' continued Marianne, 'We have arranged for you to go to a hotel in Aghios Nikolaos for the remainder of your stay over here. Obviously there is no charge for that. Megan has been sorting out toiletries and before you go we'd like you to go over to the table and help yourself to whatever you need. We have your passport numbers and we will contact the authorities on your behalf. If they need to interview you one of us will come with you to make sure you understand what they are asking for and also to ensure they know the full facts and you are not in any way to blame.

'I would like you to think about the property you had in the chalet, your clothes and any souvenirs you have bought whilst you were here. Please give us a comprehensive list and the name of your insurance company. We will be able to look at their policy cover and know if you are insured through them or whether we will need to make a further claim from our insurers. We realise you have lost all your clothes and we want to make each customer in that situation a gift of two hundred Euros. It will enable you to purchase underclothes and anything else you may need.

'The final, and possibly the most important thing, did you have any medication in the chalet that you need to take on a regular basis? If so we'll take you in to the medical centre and ensure you receive an emergency supply.'

Marianne looked at the dazed couple before her. 'I realise this is quite a lot to remember so I have printed off an information sheet for you. It has the name of your new hotel and the telephone number, also our personal mobile telephone numbers. Feel free to telephone any one of us at any time. We all speak excellent English, despite our names.' Marianne gave a small smile. 'I am truly sorry that such an awful thing had to happen whilst you were on holiday here. If you would just sign a receipt for the money that will be the end of formalities for today. When you feel ready to leave let me know and Mr Vasi will accompany you to his hotel and see you comfortably settled in. He speaks fluent English and is willing to help in any way he can.'

Marianne stood up. 'If you'll excuse me, I do have some other jobs I need to get on with, but I'm available if you need to ask any questions.'

Megan's father drained his glass of whisky. 'Can we just have a quick look inside? There might be something...'

Marianne shook her head. 'Not today. The fire crew are still damping down and the investigators will want to take photographs before anything is disturbed. If you want to telephone tomorrow afternoon we could have some information for you. As soon as we're given permission by the authorities to enter the buildings we'll let you know.'

Megan's father looked at the sheet of paper Marianne had handed him. 'Who are you?'

Marianne smiled and placed a mark by her name. 'I'm Marianne Pirenzi. I may be at the hospital tomorrow with my son. If I don't answer please telephone my husband.'

'What's wrong with your son?' asked Megan's mother.

'He has a few superficial burns. Nothing to worry about.'

'Was he the man who alerted Megan?'

Marianne nodded.

'Obviously very conscientious of him. Give him our thanks.' Megan's father spoke gruffly. 'Come on, Lydia. Collect Megan. There's no point in hanging around up here.'

The visitors began to return to their chalets, viewing the devastated building in horror. Marianne dealt with each one of them; Vasi escorted two more families back to his hotel and Marcus drove in to Aghios Nikolaos to introduce another couple to Stelios. Dimitris returned the change from the vet to Giovanni and having his offer to start clearing up the mess refused he rode thankfully back to his house, promising to return early the next day. He would have time to pay John a quick visit in the hospital before visiting hours ended.

Vasi returned to the taverna. 'Is there anything else I can do, Giovanni?'

Giovanni shook his head. 'I can't thank you enough. Send in your bill to me.' Giovanni's face was ashen, this could ruin them the same as his uncle had been ruined after the shooting at the Athens hotel.

'What now?' asked Marianne as she held Giovanni's hand tightly.

Giovanni gave her a tremulous smile. 'I guess we have to start again, the same as we did when Uncle Yannis lost everything. I suppose we should consider ourselves lucky. No one lost their life, none of the guests were injured in any way and we have eight chalets that are completely untouched.' He sighed. 'I just dread to think what some of those people are going to say they lost in the fire and hope we are going to compensate them for. If they start to claim for expensive items they say they bought over here we'll need to know the shop where they bought it and get it corroborated by the owner.'

'I'll deal with the insurance claims,' Marianne reassured him. 'I did that for Uncle Yannis whilst you were in hospital. I haven't forgotten my legal training.'

'We'll have to contact the people who were due to stay next week. I'll have a word with Vasi and see how he's placed for accommodation. If they cancel we'll just have to accept it. We can't blame people not wanting to stay here when they don't know the extent of the damage.'

'We'll leave all those decisions until tomorrow. Until we've had a chance to properly inspect everywhere you don't actually know if some of the chalets could be made habitable again by next week.'

Giovanni shook his head. 'From what I have seen from the outside it's pretty unlikely. We won't be able to touch anything until the assessors have been in and you know how long they can take to arrive,' he added gloomily.

Annita decided she would have an early night. Marianne had told her about the fire up at the chalets and that John was in hospital with some burns to his hands and she wanted to believe her when she had said his injuries were not serious.

'John is such a pleasant young man,' she said to Elias's photograph. 'I'm very fond of him. I know Elena said he was a monster when he was small and Helena said he was undisciplined and led her boys astray when she visited. However he behaved as a child he's a young man to be proud of now. He always has a smile, always willing to help.

'If he hadn't volunteered to be up at the shop today it might have been closed and then no one would have known about the fire until it was too late. It must have been caused by a tourist. They are so careless about dropping their cigarette ends. Maybe Giovanni should put up one of his notices to say how dry everywhere is at this time of the year and warning people to be careful.

'I can see Marianne and Giovanni are worried so I thought it best if I left them alone. I do hope John won't have any permanent scars, not that it really matters on his hands. No one will notice. If it had been his face that was burnt it would have been a different matter. He's a good looking young man. He doesn't want anything to spoil his looks.'

Annita placed a kiss on the photograph. If only Elias were still there for her to talk to properly. She gave herself a mental shake. If he was, they would no doubt be in some awful old peoples' home together and just sit and look at each other. She was so fortunate to be back with her relatives in Crete.

SEPTEMBER 2008

Adam Kowalski added a few last minute items to the bag he kept ready packed. It would be good to get away from the smog of Athens for a few days and he had not visited Aghios Nikolaos for some years. He might even manage to fit in a quick swim if he finished interviewing the American quickly. With that thought in mind he included his swimming trunks and a towel, along with the novel he had been planning to read for some time.

As Adam was driven from the airport he looked at the surrounding area with interest. It had certainly changed since he was there last. He was pleased the Inspector had arranged a car and driver for him.

'Would we be able to drive past the place where the incident is alleged to have taken place?' he asked.

Tassos nodded. 'We can go that way.'

'Thanks, it could give me an idea of the severity of the charge – provided it's substantiated, of course.'

Tassos pursed his lips. It was not up to him to pass an opinion on the American man they held in custody, but he was certainly a strange one. He seemed totally unconcerned about being in jail.

Tassos slowed the car as they drove along past the taverna. Giovanni frowned. The media had descended on him this morning and now the curious had arrived to gawp at the blackened area.

Inspector Varoufakis met Adam as soon as he made himself

known at the desk in the police station and escorted him to his private office.

'I appreciate that you have arrived so quickly.'

'I was not dealing with anything that my colleagues could not take over. I asked my driver to take me past the area, but I would like to have some background information before I conduct a preliminary interview.'

'Of course.' Inspector Varoufakis pushed a slim file towards Adam. 'You speak very good Greek. Do you read it also?'

Adam smiled. 'I do now. Many years ago I had to ask an accused person to translate for me. It was incredibly embarrassing and I decided that I needed to become fluent.'

'As you say. Embarrassing. Would you like some refreshment whilst you read?'

'A glass of water would be sufficient, thank you.'

'I will send some in to you. When you are ready to talk to me again I will be out in the front office.'

Adam read Dimitris Lytrakis's statement. It seemed credible, but he must find out if the man had any grudge against his employer and had committed the arson himself, blaming it on a convenient tourist. He made a note to speak to the Inspector. Next he turned to the one given by Giovanni Pirenzi. It was not very helpful as the man had not arrived until after the fire had taken hold, but confirmed that the dog had held the man on the hill until he had been arrested. He wondered what kind of a dog this man Lytrakis owned. Had it been trained as a police dog?

The statement from Marcus Mannerheim had no more information to impart as he had been accompanying Mr Pirenzi and they had arrived at the self catering apartments together. He would have to find out about this girl Megan that Mr Mannerheim mentioned. He made a note to find out where she was staying and why she had been at the taverna at the time of the fire.

Adam stretched his legs and massaged his temples. 'I can't do any more tonight. I'll interview the American tomorrow, and decide where I go after that. I'll probably want to speak to Mr Pirenzi and the other people who made statements.'

Todd sat calmly opposite Adam Kowalski. He knew he had nothing to worry about. Once he had explained they would understand and he would be free to leave. He would then visit Nicola and she would agree to return to New Orleans with him. She would very soon forget that awful young man with the vicious dog.

'Mr Gallagher, do you understand why I'm here?' asked Adam.

'Oh, yes, you want to question me about the fire I started.'

'You admit you caused the blaze?'

Todd nodded vigorously. 'I did it deliberately.'

'Did you have some sort of grudge against the owner of the holiday chalets?'

'No, I don't know him.'

'Why did you do it, then?'

'For Nicola. I had to do it for her.'

'Who is Nicola?'

'I think the owner is a relative of hers. She comes over every year. She's seeing that man with the horrible, vicious dog. I have to save her from him and take her home.'

'Why do you have to take her home? Have her parents asked you to come out here and do so?'

Todd shook his head. 'I have to take her back so we can be married.'

'Married? When is the marriage due to take place?'

Todd shrugged and smiled. 'I don't know, but I'm sure once we're back in New Orleans it will be very soon. Nicola will understand once we're home. She just hasn't realised yet.'

'Realised what?'

'That she's my guardian angel and I'm her protector. We have to get married. That way we can look after each other always.'

Adam looked at the man dubiously. Was he deranged?

Todd leaned forward and spoke earnestly. 'I waited until all the tourists had left for the day. I didn't want to hurt anyone. I'll pay my fine; then I'll make arrangements to take Nicola home. There'll be no reason for her to stay here if the chalets have gone. Have they *all* gone?'

Adam shook his head. 'Fortunately you were stopped in time. Unfortunately there was a young lady in one of the chalets.'

'Oh, dear, I hope she wasn't hurt. I wouldn't want to think she'd been burnt because of Nicola.' Todd looked genuinely distressed by the idea.

'The young lady in question was rescued by the owner's son. He's in hospital at the moment with burns.'

'*Serious* burns?'

'They say not.'

'That's all right then.' Todd smiled. 'I've confessed to you, can I go now?'

'Not yet, Mr Gallagher. I haven't completed my enquiries. When I have I will present my findings to the police and it will be up to them to charge you if they feel there is a case for you to answer.'

'Can I see Nicola?' asked Todd eagerly.

'I will have to see how the young lady feels about visiting you.'

'But you will ask her, won't you? She's my guardian angel, you see.'

'Yes,' remarked Adam dryly, 'And you are her protector. We have a warrant to search your hotel room. Are we likely to find any incriminating evidence there?'

'No, I didn't take any petrol back there. That could have been dangerous. Would you be able to arrange for my bike to be taken back to the hire company? I only hired it for a week and I don't want the man to charge me extra.'

'I'll see what I can do.' Adam rose. He felt totally bemused. The man seemed to have no conscience or remorse for his actions.

Adam accompanied the police to the small hotel where Todd had been staying. He showed the manager the warrant authorising them to search Todd's room and remove anything they felt could be useful in their investigation. Adam felt the exercise was going to be a waste of police time, but it was a formality that needed to be completed.

He returned to the station some hours later, carrying the laptop computer that belonged to Todd. 'I'd like you to lock this away for the time being. Are you able to arrange for me to speak to Mr Pirenzi and the other people who made statements?'

Inspector Varoufakis was surprised. 'I thought you were only here to interview the American tourist.'

'I want to ascertain if anyone may have had a grudge against the owner. The odd job man, Lytrakis, what about him? Would he have any cause for complaint against his employer? Was the owner in financial trouble of any sort; could he have started the fire himself in order to claim the insurance money? I also need to see this girl that Mr Mannerheim says was at the taverna when he arrived. Have you any idea where she is?'

The Inspector shook his head. 'Mr Pirenzi will probably know.'

Adam hoped the owner would know, otherwise it would mean an adverse remark from him in his report about the Cretan police's efficiency and co-operation. 'If you would be good enough to call Mr Pirenzi, please. I presume there is a car I can use? I don't need to tie up one of your men.'

'It's quite late. He's probably returned to his home.'

'I'm quite willing to visit him there.' Adam was determined to conduct the interview as soon as possible. Even leaving it another twenty four hours could mean the man had forgotten a vital fact.

Giovanni was not best pleased when he heard the representative from the American Consulate wanted to interview him that evening. He was tired. He had visited John first thing in the morning, finding him still sedated, but reassured that there was nothing worse wrong with his son than a few burns. From the hospital he had gone up to the taverna where he had arranged to meet the investigator from the fire service. Giovanni knew he was going to have a fight on his hands for compensation. The damage had been caused deliberately and he was not at all sure if the insurance company would cover him.

Marianna had dealt with the customers that morning, most of them wanting to know what had happened to the other guests and if they were expected to stay in the area that smelled of smoke and charred wood. Marianne had spent a considerable amount of time with each one, whilst trying to cook food or serve in the shop. She looked tired and strained when he arrived and he insisted she returned to the house, assuring her she could do nothing more and he had to be there whilst the fire services were investigating the source.

'Once they've gleaned all the information they can I'll start to pressurize the assessors. I need permission from the fire service before I can start to clear the site. Marcus and Dimitris can help me with that and I shall need you at the taverna full time. I'll be far too dirty to serve food.'

Marianne had not argued with her husband. Despite Giovanni having visited John earlier and Nicola spending most of the day with him, she wanted to see her son herself. The doctors had assured her that he was a healthy young man and his injuries would heal reasonably quickly. The main danger was a risk of infection and he was being kept in a sterile environment until his skin had healed. Once he was able to leave the private room he would swiftly be discharged to complete his recovery at home.

Adam drove along the road from Elounda looking for the house where he understood Giovanni Pirenzi and his family lived. He had been assured that someone would wait at the top of the drive so he did not miss it. Sure enough, there was a man standing looking down the road and Adam slowed.

'Is this the correct location for Mr Pirenzi's house?' he asked in Greek. 'I am from the Consulate.'

The man frowned and pointed down the drive. 'Mr Pirenzi. House. Yes.'

Adam looked at him curiously. Where did he come from that he didn't understand Greek? He parked his borrowed police car and waited for the man to join him, following him round to the patio.

'Giovanni, I believe this is the man from the Consulate,' said Marcus in perfect English and Adam looked at him in surprise.

'You're American?'

Marcus nodded. He was used to being mistaken for a Greek until he opened his mouth and tried to speak the language.

Giovanni rose and held out his hand. 'I'm Giovanni Pirenzi and this is my wife. Mr Mannerheim is a relative and he and his wife live here, along with other older members of the family. They are not involved with the self catering units, so I have not asked them to join us.'

Adam gave a nod of acknowledgement and shook Giovanni's hand.

'Please, have a seat. Will you join us for a meal? We have not eaten yet and I don't expect the fare offered to you at the police station was very exciting.'

Marianne looked at the man who had arrived. He was familiar, but she couldn't place him in her memory. 'Would you like a glass of wine, or something stronger Mr...?'

'Kowalski, Adam Kowalski.'

'Of course! I knew I had met you before.'

Adam frowned. 'I haven't been over to Crete for some while.'

Marianne smiled. 'It was in Athens. Nearly twenty years ago.'

Adam shook his head. 'You'll have to refresh my memory, Mrs Pirenzi.'

'A shooting took place in our uncle's hotel in Athens. An American woman was involved. You asked me to identify her.'

'Of course. I remember now. It was due to me having to ask for interpretation all the time that made me decide to learn Greek properly.'

'I'm pleased to hear it. Now, please join us for our meal. Afterwards I'm sure Uncle Yannis will be delighted to meet you again. He was the owner of the hotel when the crime was committed.'

'I really ought to interview Mr Pirenzi and Mr Mannerheim first,' demurred Adam. 'Once I have done that I would appreciate joining you.'

Marianne nodded. 'I'm sure you won't be very long with either of them. I'll ask Bryony to put everything on hold for half an hour. It will be no problem.'

Adam enjoyed his evening with the family, despite feeling somewhat guilty. Neither man had anything further to impart, and he knew he should have asked directions to Mr Lytrakis's house and completed his questioning of the material witnesses. He consoled himself with the thought that he had gained considerable background information regarding the family, although he was still not sure of their relationships, despite their lineage being explained at great length until he was totally confused.

'Mr Lytrakis,' he asked, 'Is he also a relative?'

Giovanni shook his head. 'He's just a local youth. He and my son were friends whilst they were at school. He started to do the snake clearance for me last year and I was able to give him more regular employment whilst my son was doing his National Service.'

'Snake clearance?' Adam raised his eyebrows.

'In the summer months we tend to get grass snakes in the carob trees area. Foolishly I made it into a nature trail and children's play area before I knew they liked to come down there. Dimitris comes up each morning and clears any he finds and checks again before he leaves for the day. They're quite harmless, of course, and we warn the tourists, but they're not very happy if they come across one.'

Adam cleared his throat. 'So Mr Lytrakis will be up here tomorrow morning?'

'He should be, but he won't have his dog with him for a few days.'

'Yes, this dog, what can you tell me about him?'

'Apparently my son found him last year, a stray. I refused to let him keep him so he arranged for his friend Dimitris to look after him. He seems to obey Dimitris and he's good at searching out the snakes. I don't have much to do with him. A dog at the taverna isn't good for business. A lot of people keep them as guard dogs but they can be very frightening when they race at you barking, even when you know they're chained.'

'Do you know where I can find Mr Lytrakis's girl friend? The American man appears to know her.'

Giovanni frowned. 'I didn't know he was seeing anyone?'

'That's no problem. I'm sure he can inform me tomorrow of her whereabouts. I understand that your son is being kept in the hospital. Is there any chance I could have a quick word with him? He may know if Mr Lytrakis has a girl friend.'

Marianne nodded. 'There's no reason you shouldn't visit him. He's rather sore and uncomfortable, but thankfully that is all that he has to complain about. It could be a good idea to check with the doctor, just to ensure they are not about to change his dressings or anything.'

Adam nodded. 'I understand. I'm sure any questions I may have can wait until a convenient time tomorrow. There's just one more thing I need to ask, then I really must go. There's mention in the report of a young lady called Megan Wilkins. Can you tell me who she is and where I can find her?'

Marianne rose. 'I have the lists of the hotels where the families are staying, although I'm sure they went to Vasi's. The poor girl was feeling ill and stayed here rather than go out with her family. Thank goodness they mentioned the fact to John, or he would have had no idea she was in her chalet. It would have been terrible if she had been overcome by smoke.' Marianne flipped over the pages of her notebook. 'I was right. We arranged for them to go and stay with Vasi, a friend of ours. He has the *Katerina* hotel in Aghios Nikolaos. I'll write the address down for you. You should have no problem finding it.'

Adam slipped the piece of paper into his wallet. 'Now I really must leave you. I'll have a word with this man Mr Lytrakis who works for you tomorrow morning, just to see if there's anything he may have forgotten to tell the police when he gave his statement. Things do tend to slip the mind and you remember them later. I have had a very pleasant evening and an excellent meal. I feel I have met up with old friends.'

Adam Kowalski knocked on the door of Dimitris's house just as he was about to drive up to the chalets.

'I can't stop now,' Dimitris scowled. 'I'll be late for work.'

'That's quite all right, Mr Lytrakis. Mr Pirenzi knows I am visiting you this morning and will understand if you are a little late.'

Grudgingly, Dimitris opened the door a little wider and allowed Adam to enter. He placed his finger on his lips. 'My niece is still asleep. I don't want to wake her.'

Adam nodded. 'I understand. I only want to ask you a few questions about the fire at the chalets.'

'I gave a statement to the police.'

'Yes, I have it here. I understand you were very worried about your dog at the time and I just want to check that nothing relevant slipped your mind. How is he?'

Dimitris smiled. 'He's doing well. Skele, come and say hello.'

A scuffling was heard in the back room and Skele limped in, going straight to Dimitris and laying his head on his knees. Adam looked at the mongrel, it was totally impossible to put a name to his breed – his coat was too curly for a Labrador, his tail was sleek and he had an enormous head, his small ears permanently cocked. His paws were oversized for the length of his legs, which were too long for a spaniel and too short for a collie. Adam had a desire to laugh at him and the dog turned a reproachful glance on him as if he knew the man's opinion of his looks.

'I hear he's very obedient and intelligent.'

Skele shifted his eyes back to Dimitris, as if mollified by the compliment.

'He's amazing. The only time I've ever known him disobey a command was when I told him to stay in the carob trees and he ran over to where John was lying. I wouldn't have found him so quickly if Skele hadn't howled and drawn my attention to him.'

'Why did you tell him to stay in the carob trees?'

'Mr Giovanni doesn't like him down by the taverna. I was only going down to tell John there was someone spraying and ask if it was authorised. I had no idea the man was going to set them on fire.'

'Did you actually see the man set light to them?'

Dimitris shook his head. 'Two were already burning. I saw him with a spray in his hand and he took something from his pocket and bent down. That was when I called out to him and he ran away. Then I saw John and I needed to move him somewhere safe.'

'And you have no idea of the identity of this man?'

'No. I only spoke to him once when I helped him get his bike out of the ditch.'

'He appears to know you.'

Dimitris raised his eyebrows. 'He probably saw me working around the taverna when he was sitting on the hill watching it.'

'He also appears to know your girl friend.'

'My girl friend?' Dimitris was truly surprised. 'I haven't got a girl friend.'

Adam frowned. 'He told me you had a girl friend called Nicola who came from America.'

Dimitris laughed. 'Nicola wouldn't look at me! She's John's girl. They've known each other since they were children.'

'When you say John, do you mean Mr Pirenzi's son?'

Dimitris nodded. 'She comes over here every summer to be with him.'

'So why would Mr Gallagher think she was your girl friend?'

'I've no idea. He may have seen me talking to her. We're friends, but nothing more.'

Adam nodded slowly. 'Thank you, Mr Lytrakis. You've been very helpful. I'll let you get off to work now.'

Adam sat in his car deep in thought. He would have another word with the man they had in custody after he had visited John Pirenzi.

A dark haired girl was sitting beside John's bed when Adam arrived at the hospital. 'You must be Mr Kowalski,' she smiled. 'Marianne told me to expect you. Do you want to talk to John alone?'

Adam shook his head. 'You're welcome to stay. How are you feeling Mr Pirenzi?'

John gave a lop-sided smile. 'Do you really want to know my answer to that question? Sore, fed up and frustrated, not to mention angry. This has really messed up our time together. I've only got three more days leave left and I'm stuck in here.'

'I do sympathise, Mr Pirenzi. I'm sure the hospital will give you a certificate to say that you are temporarily unfit for duty. I'll countersign it and give you an undated form that you can send on to the army when you are discharged. That will give you a few weeks to yourself to recuperate fully.'

John's face lit up. 'Really? I'd appreciate it. I'm sure I won't feel like standing out in the sun on guard duty for a while.'

Adam smiled with him. There was no way the man should be expected to return to the army until his skin was completely healed. 'May I call you John? When I last met you, you were a baby.'

'Yeah, Mum told me.' John grinned. 'Quite a coincidence you having to deal with our family problems again.'

Adam shrugged. 'Thanks to the events in Athens all those

years ago I decided to learn decent Greek. Whenever there's a case involving Americans and Greeks they usually to ask me to put in an appearance.'

'So what do you want to talk to me about?'

'Can you just run through the events as you remember them? If I have any questions I'll make a note and ask you afterwards. Start from when you arrived at the taverna that morning. Did you see anyone hanging around?'

John shook his head and groaned. 'I really shouldn't do that.' He blinked his eyes rapidly before turning his attention back to Adam. 'I didn't notice anyone. I opened up as usual. A few tourists came in to buy odds and ends from the shop. A couple came in for a breakfast and asked if I knew the best cure for sunstroke. They told me their daughter was feeling bad and had decided to stay in bed whilst they went out. I checked their cabin number and said I would ask Dimitris to leave the grass cutting for that day.

'The next thing I really knew was Dimitris coming in and asking about a man who was spraying the back of the chalets. Dad hadn't mentioned it to me so I went to see what he was up to. When I got close to the chalets I could smell burning and see there were flames shooting up to the roof. I just barged in and told the girl to go over to the taverna. I 'phoned for the fire brigade immediately. I then picked up the fire extinguisher and went round to the back to see if I could bring it under control. I know I was calling for Dimitris to come and help, but I don't remember anything more until I was sitting out on the road and he was standing over me.'

'Did you see the man who was spraying?'

'Not really. Once I saw the fire I was more worried about trying to save the chalet from further damage. If that girl hadn't been feeling ill Dimitris would have been cutting the grass and that man wouldn't have been able to spray anything.'

Adam consulted his notes. 'He would probably have attempted to do so on another occasion.'

'The grass wouldn't have been so long,' observed John. 'We cut it every week to minimize the fire risk.'

'As I understand it, the dog drew Mr Lytrakis's attention to you, despite the fact that he had been told to stay in the carob area.'

'Yeah, so Nick told me. Good old Skele. We saved him, he saved me.'

'He's lovely,' Nicola interrupted.

'What breed is he?'

Nicola smiled. 'I've no idea. When I say he's lovely I don't mean to look at, I mean his nature and intelligence.'

Adam looked at the girl. 'May I ask who you are? I didn't meet you when I visited the family last night.'

'I was here with John until quite late. I'm Nicola.'

Adam nodded. So this was the girl that Todd Gallagher had claimed to be his guardian angel. He would have to interview the man again and see why he thought she was Mr Lytrakis's girl friend.

'According to Mr Lytrakis you visit each summer. Is that correct?'

'I used to come over with Mum and Dad. When my sister was ill they let me come over on my own and stay for the whole vacation. I was even able to extend it for a few weeks due to Hurricane Katrina.'

'May I ask you something? Do you know a man called Todd Gallagher?'

Nicola nodded. 'He's at the same University as I am.'

'Do you know him well?'

'Not really.' Nicola hesitated. 'He used to come to the diner where I work at weekends. He's a bit – odd.'

'Why do you say that?'

'He just is.'

John swivelled his eyes towards Nicola. 'You should tell Mr Kowalski what a creep he is and what happened recently.'

'He has nothing to do with Mr Kowalski's investigation. He doesn't want to hear about my problems.'

Adam raised his eyebrows. 'Mr Gallagher is helping us with our enquiries at the moment. A bit of background information on the young man could be helpful.'

Nicola's eyes opened wide. 'What do you want to know about him?'

'Anything. I can always decide if the information is relevant.'

Nicola shrugged. 'Over the last couple of years he always seemed to be around wherever I was. I worked in a diner at weekends and he used to spend most of the day in there. Then there was a hold up at the diner recently and Todd tackled the gun man before the police arrived. He was shot in the arm. Obviously I thanked him for protecting me.' Nicola dropped her eyes in embarrassment. 'He asked me not to come over to Crete this year, but stay in New Orleans with him. He said he loved me and wanted to marry me so he could always protect me.'

'And what was your answer to his proposal?'

'I told him he was mad and walked away.'

Adam debated whether to ask Nicola to enlarge on her statement and thought better of it. This could explain why Todd Gallagher claimed to be her protector. He would have another word with him and if necessary could return and question the girl more fully about the man and see how she felt about visiting him.

Adam closed his notebook. 'I hope I won't have to trouble you again, John, but I'll not forget about the letter with the Consulate stamp. If I could have your telephone number Miss Nicola I could arrange for you to collect it.'

'Certainly.' Nicola reeled off her 'phone number and Adam wrote it down. He would speak to her privately and see how she felt about visiting Todd Gallagher.

His interview with Megan Wilkins told him nothing new. She had been lying in bed when she smelled smoke. She got up to investigate and as she reached the door someone began to bang on it and she was told to go to the taverna immediately and obeyed.

Her parents reiterated their thanks to John for remembering her and making her safety a priority.

'Did you see a dog whilst you were up there?'

Megan frowned. 'A young man turned up carrying one. Was the poor thing burnt? I didn't understand what they were saying.'

'I understand that his paws were blistered, but he's fine.' Adam closed his notebook. 'I think that's about all, Miss Wilkins. I hope you and your parents are able to enjoy the remainder of your stay over here.' Adam handed her his card. 'I realise that you're English, but if you have any problems call me and I'll do my best to help. I'm with the American Consulate.'

Megan's eyes widened as she looked at the card. She had never knowingly met anyone as important before.

Adam returned to the police station. He hoped the technician had managed to gain access to Todd Gallagher's lap top and if so what information it would contain.

'I've got you in.' Makkis grinned. 'His password was his date of birth. Don't know what it's all about. My English isn't good enough.'

'Thanks anyway.' Adam tucked the laptop under his arm and entered the small office that had been allocated to him. He doubted there would be anything very relevant, but Todd may have downloaded information about accelerants.

He trawled through Todd's accounts, meticulously kept, and recording the amount he withdrew from the bank. Each month there was a large sum deposited, half of it paid to a rental company and some of it withdrawn in cash. He had a healthy balance. In the last few entries the cost of his flight from the States and the hotel in Aghios Nikolaos had been deducted. There was a separate list of every cash payment he made however small. Towards the end of the list the amount was in Euros and he had even recorded fifty cents for a bottle of water.

A similar account was kept for his car, the amount and cost of the fuel and any work required at the garage. Adam felt disheartened. Apart from the man having a fixation with keeping his accounts absolutely accurate to the last cent there was nothing of any interest. Adam read through the pages of work that Todd had prepared for University, all relating to finance. Adam smiled. Obviously some sort of employment in that field was very suitable for him.

He opened up other documents, letters to various people on a variety of subjects, thanking someone for a Christmas present, complaining to his landlord about the broken window frame that had still not been repaired, a letter to his father assuring him he was working hard, despite his traumatic loss. As he read the words Adam stiffened. To what did his traumatic loss refer? He looked at the date on the letter. It was eighteen months ago.

Todd scrolled down the list of documents to see if he could find anything Todd had written around that date and drew a blank. He did notice that a folder marked MINE had been used last three days ago and he opened it hopefully. In it were a massive amount of documents, each named simply by the year and commencing in 1996.

Adam opened the first one; the page was dated January 1st 1996 when Todd would have been ten years old. It stated very simply that it was New Year's Day.

> *'I am starting to write my diary today. It was a good present to receive. I plan to keep a diary for the rest of my life. I will then be able to look back when I am old and see what I did when I was young. It is cold today and I spent the afternoon reading. Dad said I should have gone for a walk, but Mum said it was better that I stayed in the warm. There are only three more days of the vacation left. Once I am back at school I shall be made to go outside to exercise, whatever the weather. I don't like the cold.'*

Adam read the entries for the first month and decided they were the innocent writings of a young boy. He closed the first one and moved on five years to 1999 when Todd was thirteen. As he read he sucked in his breath.

> May 2nd. *I saw that girl today. She has big t.....s. I want to touch them. Will they be soft or hard? What do they taste like? I lay on my bed and thought about them and had to put my hand in my shorts. I just had to play with myself. I enjoyed it. Now I want to know what it's like with a girl. All I need now is to find a girl who's willing, (and I'm sure I will). Writing this I had to put my hand in my shorts again. It is such a pleasure.*

Adam looked at the date again. The boy was thirteen at the time. He remembered having thoughts about girls when he was that age, but they had not been that explicit and he would never have dreamed of writing them down. He scrolled further down the screen, covering the next few weeks.

> June 13th. *I took Sara-May for a walk in the woods. I pushed her up against a tree and touched her tits. They were soft with little knobbly bits in the middle. I wanted her to undo her blouse and let me look at them, but she refused. She's useless. I won't bother with her again.*

Adam continued to read the entries. They were all much the same in nature, how Todd had tried to seduce a girl and she had rebuffed him, or only allowed him to touch her through her clothing. Adam shook his head and scrolled on for a further two months.

> August 17th. *At last. Emily-Sue undid her blouse*

and let me look at her tits. I touched them and she didn't stop me when I pushed her brassier out of the way so I could see them properly. I couldn't help myself then. I just had to suck at them. I stuck my hand up her skirt and she clamped her legs together and said no. I pushed and pushed against her but she wouldn't change her mind and I made a terrible mess in my shorts. I HAVE to have a girl properly soon.

August 18th. I met Emily-Sue again. This time she wasn't wearing a brassier. I found if I nibbled at the pink bits in the middle they began to go quite hard. This was really exciting to me and I tried my hardest to pull her knickers down. The more she resisted the more excited I became until I could no longer control myself.

August 19th. I was almost EATING her tits I wanted her so much. I had to throw my shorts away. I'll buy some more at the weekend so Mum won't know.

August 20th. Emily-Sue let me put my hand up her knickers. She kept her legs together so I could only touch her.

August 23rd. I finally persuaded Emily-Sue to take her knickers off!!! Even in my wildest dreams I had not imagined how good it would be. It was bliss. I can't wait to see her again.

The entries for the following few weeks centred on Emily-Sue and the time they had spent together, often containing graphic detail.

October 7th. Emily-Sue tells me she's pregnant. That's disgusting. Her body will swell up and she'll no longer want sex. She said she'd ask her Mum if she could marry me. I'm NOT going to marry her, besides we are too young. I shall deny it's anything to do with me. If she insists I shall say that if she was willing to give me whatever I asked for how many other boys (or men) did she give her body to? There is NO WAY I will ever marry her. I shall just have to find someone else to enjoy.

Curiosity about the outcome of the situation made Adam read further. Three weeks later Todd wrote about the encounter he had with his father.

October 28th. *Dad was pretty mad at me. He called me a child who couldn't control his emotions or actions. Dad is arranging for Emily-Sue and her mother to move away. I'm pleased about that. She's beginning to get a fat belly. Dad said if I must have sex I must take precautions and then he went on to explain the different ways to me. I don't like the thought of any of them, but then he said it was also a protection against disease. That frightened me. Suppose I caught a disease and I couldn't have sex any more? I'd rather die.*

Adam ran his hand over his forehead. He began to scroll down to the pages at random. Different girls were mentioned and the sex he had enjoyed with them described in minute detail. This was more than the fantasising of a frustrated teenage boy; he obviously had a problem and needed help and counselling. Nowhere did Adam spot any more references to the girls becoming pregnant so he had to assume Todd had taken his father's advice.

Adam closed the file and opened one four years later. Todd

described his arrival at University and how annoying he found it to be sharing a room.

> *'I've written to Dad. I CANNOT share a room. There are so many girls here, who I know, just by looking at them, are longing for me. I want to have had every one of them before I leave. That may mean I have to have two or three a day over the weekends, but I won't complain about that! I've told Dad that my room mate snores and is keeping me awake so I can't concentrate on my studies. I also said that he drinks and smokes. Dad will probably take more notice of that than the snoring.'*

Apparently Todd's father did take notice because a week later there was an entry from Todd saying he had moved into a house that he was sharing with a couple of other first years and they all had their own rooms.

> *It seems to be working out well. We have a cleaning rota that works. We put a 'do not disturb' sign on our doors so no one barges in. I have had a different girl nearly every night and ALWAYS one on Saturday and Sunday afternoons and a different one for the evenings. Life is good!*

Adam moved rapidly down the page. He was bored and disgusted with the young man's obsession. He calculated where he should look for the reference to "eighteen months ago" and was surprised to see day after day with just initials entered. He scrolled back up the page and found a full description of a girl called Jennie-Lea. It seemed Todd had finally found a soul mate with the same inclinations as himself.

He described their initial meeting at great length, then just entered her initials each day. Adam moved on down the page rapidly until he came to bold black type.

'I have done something so awful. I didn't mean to do it. I was angry when she said she was pregnant. I only shook her. I didn't mean to hurt her. I didn't hurt her. She fell over and hurt herself. I couldn't believe it. I sat and looked at her. I didn't know what to do. Then I pushed her over the balcony and left. I know that was wicked of me, but I was frightened. If I called the police I knew they would not believe it was an accident. I truly did not mean to hurt her. I loved Jennie-Lea. It was only when she said she was having a baby that I got mad with her. What am I going to do? I'd do anything to go back a few hours. I wouldn't have shaken her. I should have walked out until I was calmer. All I could think about was her getting fat and not wanting ME. I shall have to pretend that I didn't know she had fallen. I wonder if they will find out that she's pregnant? I shall say I didn't know or they might think I pushed her over the balcony deliberately. I didn't. I truly didn't.'

Adam read the entry through a second time. He would have to contact the police department in New Orleans and talk to them about the incident. He was tempted to believe the young man's account. He had been so honest about his feelings in all his previous entries that there was no reason for him to suddenly lie. He obviously considered the diary completely private and for his eyes only.

Recording events the following day Todd had reverted to his ordinary type face.

'I decided I must go into Uni as if nothing had happened. The police came for me there and I had to go down to the station to make a statement. I insisted I had waved to Jennie-Lea before getting into my car and driving away. I said I couldn't face going back to Uni so I asked the police to drive me home. I can fetch my car later. I feel so awful. Forgive me, Jennie-Lea.'

The next few entries were full of Todd's remorse.

'The police came again. They said they had done an autopsy and Jennie-Lea was pregnant. I pretended not to know and told them I would have loved to be a father! I think they believed me. I am finding it hard to concentrate at Uni.'

Later there was a description of Jennie-Lea's funeral. Todd insisted he had cried all the way through. He had met Jennie-Lea's father and recorded that the man had blamed him for Jennie-Lea's pregnancy and subsequent death.

'He blames me, but it was not my fault. She should not have been stupid enough to become pregnant in the first place. I didn't mean to hurt her. She fell over her own shoes. I think I may go to the church again on Sunday and see if that helps me.'

The next two week's entries were continuing outpourings of grief and remorse, there was no mention of any girl being approached with a view to her taking Jennie-Lea's place in Todd's bed. There was a brief entry a week later.

*'Uni sent me for counselling. It won't do any good
because I can't tell anyone the truth.'*

Adam read the brief entries that followed for the next few weeks.
He could not help but feel a certain amount of sympathy for the
young man. He obviously had not meant to hurt the girl and seemed
to have had genuine feelings for her.

*'More counselling. They said I must try to get
out and socialise, pick up the threads of my life
again. How can I without Jennie-Lea?'*

The entries in the diary were all very similar, stating that he could
not concentrate on his studies properly and did not know what to
do with himself; should he ask for a transfer to a different
University and hope that helped him or should he just drop out
altogether and go back to Dallas and take up a junior position in
his father's bank? For a week he vacillated from day to day
about leaving.

*'I thought I had decided to leave and I felt I had
to go to the diner where Jennie-Lea and I used
to hang out. I can't go near her apartment. I think
I have experienced a miracle. The girl who serves
in there came over and sat with me. She told me
she was sorry and that I MUST NOT BLAME
MYSELF. She's right. It was an accident. I did
not hurt Jennie-Lea. Somehow after she had
spoken to me I felt calmer, more settled. I will
delay making a decision about leaving until after
next weekend.'*

The following weekend Todd recorded that he had visited the
diner again and his thoughts about the girl who had served him.

This was the first time for some months that Todd had mentioned a girl in his diary and Adam read on with interest.

> *'She seems so soft and sweet and kind. She's not a bit like Jennie-lea to look at which is a good thing. A smile from her means so much to me. She reminds me of an angel.'*

'Aha!' Adam exclaimed aloud. He read on rapidly. All the entries now centred round the girl who worked in the diner. How many times she had looked his way, smiled at him, spoken to him. She was obviously becoming as much of an obsession with the man as girls had been when he was a teenager. There was nothing of a sexual nature in any of the writing. Todd even admitted that he had lost all interest in sex with anyone, although he was convinced that once he had married the girl they would have a satisfying marriage.

Finally Todd recorded following her home, finding out her surname, then how he had looked up the family on the census and eventually acquired her telephone number. He now referred to her as his Guardian Angel and to himself as her Protector.

Adam shook his head. The man really was sick. He read through the diary as rapidly as he was able, finding reference to Nicola's annual visit to Elounda. He had recorded the conversation he had overheard between Melanie and Nicola where Nicola had said she planned to get married to a man in Elounda. Todd had recorded his panic at this suggestion.

> *'She cannot get married. She has to stay with me. How can she be my Guardian Angel if she is married to someone else? I have to stop her. How can I persuade her that she should stay here? How can I live until she returns? Each day will be agony.'*

The diary went on to record Todd's plan to stage a hold up at the diner and pretend to save Nicola from harm.

> *'I have it worked out now. It was pure chance that I met up with Wayne or was it fate? He is the perfect person. I have convinced him that no one will suspect him if I chase him out and he discards his coat and balaclava before we walk back in together. He can say he saw someone running away. Even if that part of my plan doesn't work out, he is the perfect suspect. He needs the money to spend on drugs. What a fool he is! I shall deny it completely if he tries to implicate me. I'm sure the police will believe me rather than an addict. I have plenty of money so why should I want to commit a robbery? I'm sure this will make Nicola want to stay with me.'*

Adam shook his head. The man was obviously obsessed with the girl that led credence to his statement that he had started the fire deliberately.

The diary went on to record the day of the hold up.

> *'The robbery at the diner did not go according to my plan. That stupid Wayne f.....d up. The idiot had a gun! That was NOT part of the plan. I only wanted him to have something in his pocket that looked like a gun. He shot me in the arm and I am having to type this with my left hand. It makes me very slow on the computer. He shot a policeman in the leg and of course they opened fire on him. At least he was killed outright so he cannot give them any information about our arrangement. His death has also saved me a*

considerable amount of money. Thank goodness I had arranged to pay him afterwards and not in advance.'

Three days later Todd poured out his anguish when he found Nicola was planning to go away for the summer as usual and his hurt and anger when she rejected his advances.

'Nicola came to thank me for protecting her. My heart soared. I decided this was the moment. I asked her to stay in New Orleans with me. SHE REFUSED! I could not believe it. I tried to change her mind by telling her how I loved her and wanted to marry her. She said I was mad. Me! Mad! She doesn't realise what she is saying. I feel so hurt and angry. It is obviously this awful scruffy Greek man who has brain washed her. I am not able to live without her. I will have to think of another way to make her realise that I am her protector and she needs ME.'

The diary continued with Todd finally making the decision to follow Nicola to Crete in the hope of persuading her to return to New Orleans with him. It documented his search for her in the town, seeing her with the boy and the dog and his disgust that she should find the village boy attractive. How he had followed her, waited on the hill and then gradually formulated his plan to burn down the chalets.

'If the chalets are no longer there, there will be no need for the taverna so there will be no need for Nicola to go to Crete to see that awful man. Once she has returned to New Orleans with me she will realise what a terrible mistake she was going to

make and how I have saved her. I am her Protector.
It is my duty to save her by whatever means.'

Adam read how Todd had bought the mosquito spray and siphoned the petrol from his scooter into a can. His account of the days he had watched the chalets and his pleasurable anticipation the night before he finally carried out the act.

> *'I am not sure if I will sleep tonight. I am determined that tomorrow I will carry out my plan. Once the buildings are burnt to the ground I will go to Nicola again and I am sure this time she will agree to return to New Orleans with me. I wonder how long she will want to wait before we are married? I am beginning to feel the stirrings of my sexual urges returning, but no one but Nicola will satisfy me now. I will have to control myself until she feels she is ready to accept my body and all I can give her. I must not think about that wonderful day yet. If I do, I may find I have to find a girl for temporary relief and I want to save myself until I finally hold Nicola's naked body in my arms.'*

Adam felt quite sick as he finally logged off from the computer. He would have to contact the police in New Orleans and arrange to send them copies of the relevant passages in the diary. No doubt they would be interested in the account of the death of the woman who had fallen from the balcony and would very likely have another look at the case. The hold up that Todd had engineered, despite the fact that he had been injured, had resulted in the police shooting a man and the public had demanded an enquiry. Now with a charge of arson pending against him the young man was in serious trouble.

Adam telephoned Nicola to make arrangements to hand over the undated letter with his signature and the Consulate stamp. She offered to collect it from the police station, but he was adamant that he wanted to give it to her in person.

'There's no immediate rush. Are you planning to visit John tomorrow? There's a coffee shop close to the police station where we could meet before you go on to the hospital.'

Nicola arrived promptly at the time they had arranged. 'John and I really appreciate this,' she said as she held the letter in her hand. 'I'm going to tell my folks that I'm needed here a bit longer, to help look after John so Marianne can go up with Giovanni to the chalets. I've told them what happened so I'm sure they'll understand.'

'What about your own studies at University? Surely you'll need to be back at the start of the new term?'

Nicola shook her head. 'I don't really want to go back, particularly if that creepy Todd is going to be around.'

Adam looked directly at Nicola. 'I'd like to ask you a couple of questions about him. Do you mind?'

Nicola shrugged. 'Go ahead.'

'Have you ever given him any reason to think you might be interested in him as a boyfriend?'

Nicola shook her head vehemently. 'I said I was sorry after his girl friend died. He seemed so down. I felt sorry for him. He asked me to go to a movie with him once and I refused.'

'He has asked if you would visit him. Are you prepared to do that?'

'Do I have to?'

'The choice is yours.'

'What's the point of me seeing him?'

Adam sighed. 'He seems to consider you as some sort of guardian angel to him.'

'If I do agree to see him I'll tell him exactly what I think of him – and it won't be in very angelic terms.' Nicola's eyes flashed angrily.

'That might help him to get you into perspective, realise that you are just an ordinary girl and not interested in taking part in his fantasies. He might even show some remorse if he knew it was your boyfriend who had been injured. He seems to think that you are Mr Lytrakis's girl friend.'

'Dimitris's girl friend? Whatever gave him that idea?'

'I can only say that he has made references to Mr Lytrakis and his dog and connected you to them.'

Nicola frowned and then laughed. 'I bet he jumped to conclusions when I showed Mel a picture of Skele. He asked if he could see it and when I showed it to him he asked who the man was in the picture. I told him Dimitris was a friend.'

'That could certainly be the answer.'

'What's going to happen to him?'

Adam smiled. 'Are you concerned?'

Nicola shook her head vehemently. 'No, just curious. I'd hate to think he got away with starting that fire. John's in hospital and poor Giovanni is beside himself because of the damage. Personally I'd like to lock him up and throw away the key.'

'Mr Gallagher has admitted committing arson and no doubt the Greek authorities will press charges. I shall be sending some information back to the States and I think they may wish to look a little more closely into his activities.'

'You mean he's a criminal?' Nicola's eyes widened.

'Probably not in the sense that you mean; but he does appear to have been involved in a couple of incidents that put him outside the law.'

'How do you know?'

Adam shook his head. 'I can't tell you that, but I can assure you he will no longer be any trouble to you. In either Crete or New Orleans he is going to be sitting inside a prison cell for a considerable amount of time. The Greek legal process moves very slowly. His father requested that he was released on bail and offered to put up any sum they wanted. I'm pleased to say the Greek authorities refused with the excuse that they thought he would leave the country.'

'Good! I'll talk to Marianne and see what she advises about visiting. Can I let you know?'

Adam nodded. 'You have my 'phone number. I shall be over here until next Thursday at least. Give me a call and let me know one way or another.'

Nicola nodded. 'I will. If I do go to see him I could take some photos of John and me together. Maybe that would convince him that I'm not interested in him. I wouldn't have to be alone with him, would I?' she added.

'Certainly not. I'd make sure I was with you, and with your permission, we'd record the meeting.'

'Would the recording help to convict him?' asked Nicola.

'It could take away a line of defence from him if you asked him a couple of pertinent questions.' Adam knew that Todd could claim that his diary had been placed on the computer by someone else to incriminate him, but there would be no denying a recorded conversation.

'Like what?'

Adam smiled. 'You let me know if you're willing to visit and I'll let you know the questions I would like you to ask him.'

Before Nicola spoke to Marianne she relayed the conversation and Adam's request to John.

John frowned. 'Provided there is someone with you the whole time I suppose there's no harm in you seeing him. It could even stop him from having delusions about you. It would be awful if he was released some time in the future and he started being a nuisance to you again.'

Nicola shuddered. 'I don't want to even contemplate such a thing. Have you seen the doctor today? Is there any news about you coming home?'

'He's pleased with my progress. Apparently I'm healing well. With luck I should be home next week.'

'Adam gave me the letter from the Consulate. I'll put it safely away until you need it.'

'I wish this had happened earlier. By the time I'm fit to enjoy life again you'll be back in the States.'

Nicola shook her head. 'I'm going to phone Dad as soon as you're home and tell him I need to stay here longer and help look after you.'

'What about University?'

'What about it? You're much more important to me than getting a degree.' Nicola tilted her head defiantly. 'It's true, anyway. Your Mum and Dad are going to be busy up at the chalets getting the damage sorted out, and there are still some guests staying up there. I could see to Grandma and look after you and that would mean Bryony could go up and help as well.'

'You wouldn't mind?'

'Mind what?'

'Looking after me.'

'Of course not. You'd look after me, wouldn't you?'

John nodded. 'That goes without saying.'

WEEK 2 – SEPTEMBER 2008

Nicola met Adam as arranged. She was feeling incredibly nervous and apprehensive about her forthcoming meeting with Todd.

'There really is nothing to worry about,' Adam assured her. 'You will be in a separate room and there will be a safety screen between you. He'll be able to see you and talk to you, but there's no way he can touch you. I'll be sitting in the corner, out of his sight in charge of the recording. If you wish to leave at any time all you have to do is say "I'm terminating this interview" and get up and walk out.'

'Can I show him the photographs?'

'Certainly, and I'd like you to get him to talk about the hold up at the diner if you can.'

'He'll probably want to boast about how brave he was.'

Adam smiled. 'You could be right.'

Nicola sat in the small room and waited for Todd to be brought in. His face lit up in a pleased smile as he saw her.

'Nicola,' he breathed. 'I knew you'd come.'

Nicola looked at Todd coldly. 'I've only come today to finally make you understand that I have no interest in you whatsoever. I have no feelings at all for you and I have no intention of returning to New Orleans with you.'

Todd leaned forward and spoke earnestly. 'You cannot stay here, Nicola. I have your welfare at heart. I'm your protector, remember. What will your life be like if you stay here and marry that young man with the awful dog? It will be misery. I have to save you from that.'

Nicola shook her head. 'You have it all wrong, Todd. I have no intention of marrying Dimitris.'

Todd's eyes lit up. 'Then there is no reason why we shouldn't be together. You'll grow to love me, Nicola. Trust me. I can make you love me.'

Nicola held up a photograph taken of her and John whilst they were in London. They stood with their arms entwined about each other; she was smiling up at him happily. 'This is the man I am going to marry.'

Todd looked at the photograph in consternation. What a mistake he had made. Even in a photograph he could see the adoration in her eyes as she looked up at the tall, good looking Greek. On reflection he realised that when she had hugged and kissed Dimitris it was only a friendly gesture that he had seen repeated many times between the young people when they met.

'Due to you his father has had his property and business damaged. John is in hospital because he was burnt and I am ashamed to have to admit that I even know you.'

Todd swallowed. 'I didn't mean anyone to get hurt. I need you, Nicola. You're my guardian angel.'

'Don't be stupid. You've woven some silly fantasy around me.'

Todd shook his head. 'I'm your protector. I proved that to you. I stood in front of you and protected you from that gun man.'

'You arranged that hold up, didn't you? What were you planning? A kidnap; so you could come and rescue me?'

Adam drew in his breath. He had asked Nicola to talk to Todd about the hold up, but he had not expected her to accuse him directly.

Todd shook his head. 'He was only supposed to restrain you. I was going to hit him and he was to run away. Wayne messed up. He wasn't supposed to have a gun.'

Nicola's lip curled in disgust. 'And you thought that would make me leave John? That just shows how stupid you really are. Through you, Wayne lost his life. Fortunately no one was killed in the fire, but you wouldn't have cared about that, would you? All you wanted was your own way. You're evil, Todd. I hope they put you in prison for ever.' Nicola rose from her seat. 'I'm terminating this interview.'

'Nicola, please, you don't understand. You're my guardian angel. I need you.' Todd's voice rose in anguish as she left the room.

Adam followed her out and placed his hand on her shoulder. 'You did extremely well in there.'

Nicola was trembling with emotion from her ordeal. 'I'm sorry. I didn't get him to talk properly about the hold up.'

'You gave me exactly what I wanted. You couldn't have done any better if I'd given you a script to read.'

'Really?'

Adam smiled at her. 'You can rest assured that even if this man manages to evade the Greek law the police in New Orleans will definitely be looking at him. He will certainly find that if he sets foot back on American soil he is immediately in prison over there whilst enquiries are made. Enquiries can take a long time.'

Nicola let out a sigh of relief. 'Can I go and visit John now?'

'Certainly. Are his burns healing?'

Nicola nodded and smiled. 'We're hoping he'll be home tomorrow. I've given him your letter and he's going to send it to the army when the hospital finally discharge him as fit to resume his duties. That should give him another couple of weeks at home.'

'He could need more than an extra couple of weeks.' Adam raised his eyebrows at her.

'Really? We didn't want to take advantage.'

'Make it a month.'

Nicola smiled happily. 'That could mean he only has a few more weeks before he's completed his duty. I can't thank you enough.'

'If you have any problem you know where to contact me.' Adam raised his hand in farewell as Nicola climbed astride her scooter. 'It's been good to meet you.'

John climbed carefully out of his father's car. He didn't want to knock his tender skin and cause any damage to his wounds that could start up an infection. He felt foolish wearing cotton gloves and a pair of long trousers whilst the weather was still warm.

Marianne hugged him carefully. 'It's good to have you home.'

'You don't know how relieved I am to be here. It was so boring in between visitors, just having to lie there. I couldn't even change the television channel without calling for help.'

'You won't try to do too much, will you? The doctor said you had to be careful for a week or so. Your skin needs to toughen up. You won't do anything stupid like going swimming yet?' Marianne asked anxiously.

John shook his head. 'I'll be sensible. All I really want is to get to my camera.' He blinked his eyes rapidly. 'I should have asked Dad to bring me my sun glasses. After being inside for so long it seems so bright out here.'

'I'll find you a pair. Your own were ruined, but there must be a spare pair around somewhere.'

'And my camera. I can sit outside and take a few shots. I need to get the feel whilst I'm wearing these gloves.' John walked in to the shade offered by the umbrella and sat beside his grandmother. 'How are you, Grandma?'

'There's nothing wrong with me that being half my age wouldn't cure.'

John smiled at her affectionately. 'Well for a couple of days you can pretend you have a companion of your own age. I've been told I have to sit and rest. I'm perfectly all right and if it wasn't for these stupid burns I'd be getting ready for a swim.'

'Be thankful they were no worse. You could have needed skin grafts and I hear that can be very painful. Let me look at you properly.' Annita removed her sun glasses and looked at her great grandson critically. 'What's that mark on your forehead? That doesn't look like a burn.'

'That's just a scar where something hit me. If that hadn't happened I wouldn't have been burnt. If it hadn't been for Skele I might well have been frizzled before anyone found me. I need to buy him a treat to say thank you.'

Nicola handed John a pair of sun glasses and the case containing his camera. 'Your Mum's making some coffee for us. What did I hear you say about Skele?'

'I need to buy him a treat. I'll have to ask Dimitris what his favourite food is.'

Nicola grinned. 'I bet it's still sausages. Dogs have long memories when it's related to their stomachs. Your Dad said Dimitris could bring him to the house for you to thank him.'

John's face lit up. 'Really? Aunt Ourania doesn't mind?'

'She says she doesn't mind him being here provided he doesn't go near her.'

'Dimitris could bring him when she's out.'

'That's what I thought, so I asked Dimitris to come this afternoon when he finishes up at the chalets.'

'How's that work going?'

'Your Dad, Marcus and Dimitris have demolished the one that was virtually destroyed and removed the rubbish. The others that were so badly damaged they're clearing the furniture from. Then they'll be able to see if it's practical to repair them or take those down too.'

'I wish I could go up and help,' sighed John.

'Well you can't. Bryony is up at the taverna whilst Marianne is dealing with the paperwork from the insurance company and the guests, so I'm in charge of you and Grandma. I know Grandma will be no trouble, and if you are I know a way to get my own back.'

John raised his eyebrows and Nicola winked at him. 'You wouldn't?'

'Wouldn't I? Are you going to take a chance?'

'I'll test you out. See how long you can refuse.'

'You'll not even think about it until your burns are completely healed.'

'What's that John can't think about yet?' asked Marianne as she placed the coffee on the table.

Nicola blushed furiously. 'Going up to the chalets and helping.'

'Certainly not. Nicola's quite right. You put all thoughts of that right out of your mind now.'

Nicola gave a giggle and John wagged his finger at her. 'You're wicked,' he remarked. 'I shall just have to console myself with my camera.'

John lifted his camera from its case, closed his left eye and focused on Spinalonga. He lowered the viewer from his eye and cleaned the glass with his glove before holding it up again. He focused again and lowered it whilst he removed his sun glasses.

He blinked rapidly and held the camera up again, then replaced it in its case. 'I'll give it a go a bit later,' he said and replaced his sun glasses. 'The sun isn't right at the moment,' he said by way of explanation.

Throughout the day John picked up his camera intermittently and focused on Spinalonga. Each time he replaced it into the case without having taken a photograph.

'What's wrong, John?' asked Nicola finally.

'I can't seem to focus very well. I don't think my eyes have adjusted properly to being out in natural light yet. I'll give it another go tomorrow.' He blinked again and the dark mistiness that had descended in front of his eyes cleared once more. 'I fancy an apple. Shall I bring you one, Nick?'

'I'll get it.'

'I'm not an invalid. There's nothing wrong with my legs and picking up an apple for myself. It won't hurt my hands,' replied John irritably.

Nicola shrugged and stayed in her seat. It was true. John was quite capable of fetching an apple for himself. She waited for a few minutes for him to return. No doubt he had gone to the bathroom. It seemed a long time before he appeared at the patio door again, holding carefully on to the side of the glass.

'What's wrong, John?'

'Nick, I can't see.'

Nicola was on her feet in a moment and by his side. 'Are you feeling faint?'

'No. I was fine. I reached out to pick up an apple and suddenly I couldn't see the fruit basket.'

'Can you see again now?'

'Not properly, everything is dark and misty in one eye.'

'Lean on me and come back and sit down. It could have been where you went inside after being in the sun.'

John allowed her to help him the few steps back to his chair beneath the umbrella. He sat down thankfully and closed his eyes. Nicola gazed at him in concern. Should she interrupt Marianne or telephone the hospital? John would not thank her if she panicked and he ended up back in hospital for no good reason.

'Open your eyes, John and see if you can see better now.'

John did as she bid him and looked around. 'It does seem better now. It must have been going inside. My eyes hadn't had time to adjust properly.'

Nicola gave a sigh of relief. 'Do you still want that apple?'

'I'd forgotten that was what I went for. Yes, please.'

'I'll get it.' Nicola rose rapidly and walked inside. Her eyes had no problem adjusting as she went from the sunshine into the dim interior of the kitchen.

Each day John took some photographs and was disgusted by his efforts. He had to wait until the mist and blurring that seemed to affect his right eye cleared and then act rapidly before it returned. He had tried to capture a wasp as it inspected his empty beer bottle, but when he looked at the photographs they were out of focus.

It was a week before John finally admitted to himself that he had a problem, particularly with his right eye. If he pressed his forehead where he had a scar his vision seemed to clear completely, but it was impossible to do that whilst holding the camera and taking a photograph.

'I think I ought to go in to the hospital and be checked out,' he said to his father. 'I seem to be completely healed up, my hands and leg are no longer tender, so they should be able to sign me off.'

Giovanni frowned. 'I don't think you should go on the bike.'

'I thought I'd ask Uncle Yannis to drive me in when he goes to the shop tomorrow. I'll see how long I have to hang around and either come back with him or catch the bus.'

'Will you be all right on your own?'

'I'll be fine,' John assured him with more confidence than he felt. 'I don't need to upset any arrangements. Once they sign me off I'll be able to drop that certificate and the one from Mr Kowalski in to the army office and I'll be able to come up and help you.'

'You'll not be doing any of the rough or heavy work,' Giovanni assured him. 'You could help Bryony in the taverna and shop. We'll be closing completely in a few weeks and we'll need to do a stock take and get everything packed away properly ready for next season.'

'Why doesn't Nick come up and help with that and Bryony come back down here to look after Grandma?'

Giovanni shrugged. 'If that suits Bryony I don't mind how you arrange things.'

The doctor examined John's hands and leg and pronounced himself completely satisfied with the way they had healed. 'Another week and I'll give you a final certificate. You'll be fit enough to return to duty after that.' The doctor turned to go.

'There's something else I would like to ask you about,' John spoke tentatively as he pulled his trousers back on.

'Yes?' The doctor was suspicious. Was the young man going to ask for a certificate to declare him unfit to complete his army service?

'It's to do with my eyes.'

The doctor frowned. 'What about them?'

'I can't always see very well. I'm a photographer and...'

'Have you had a sight test? You could need spectacles.'

John shook his head. 'Please, listen to me. When I try to take a photograph everything through my right eye is blurred, sometimes it gets really dark and I can't see anything. Then the sight seems to go from the other eye for a short while. If I press on my forehead there,' John indicated his scar, 'it seems to clear and I can see properly again.'

'I suggest you make an appointment with an ophthalmologist. As I said, you could need spectacles. Any other problems?'

'No. Thank you.' John felt distinctly disappointed. He had hoped the doctor would be able to explain the odd phenomenon.

John walked from the hospital back in to the centre of Aghios Nikolaos. There were plenty of signs for doctors advertising their medical speciality, but he could not see an ophthalmologist. He entered the door of one marked cardiologist and went up to the middle aged woman on the reception desk.

'Good morning. Do you have an appointment, sir?' She knew that the man did not, as she was acquainted with both the patients who had appointments that morning.

'No, I've just come in to ask you something. I'm looking for an ophthalmologist. I wondered if you could direct me to one.'

'Two roads down and turn to the left. I'm sure there are two or three down there.'

'Thank you.' John turned to go and the blackness descended before his eyes again. He stood there leaning on the desk. 'I'm sorry. I'll be all right in a few minutes.'

'What's wrong with you?'

'I can't see. It will clear in a minute or two.' John pressed on his forehead and as he had predicted the darkness lifted. He smiled at the woman. 'I'm fine now. Thank you for the information.'

She watched as he walked out of the door. That was strange. The man did seem able to see perfectly well.

John followed the directions given to him and turned in at the first sign he saw. The door was firmly closed and John walked on to the next. The receptionist regarded him gravely.

'Mr Pedantiakis never sees anyone without an appointment.'

'So could I make one?' asked John.

'He's very busy. I have one for ten days' time, sir?'

'I really wanted one as soon as possible. I have a problem.'

'If it is urgent why don't you go to the hospital?'

'Would I need an appointment?'

'I couldn't say, sir, but they are supposed to deal with emergencies there.'

'It's not exactly an emergency.'

'Then I suggest I make you an appointment for ten days' time.' She smiled brightly at John.

John sighed. 'Very well. I'll take it.'

She wrote the date and time on a card and handed it to John. 'We look forward to seeing you then, sir.'

John slipped the card inside his wallet. He would try to find another ophthalmologist and if he was still unable to make an immediate appointment he would return to the hospital and see if he could see a specialist there.

The next two ophthalmologists that John tried were also unable to make him appointments in less than a week and he retraced his steps to the hospital, hoping he would not be refused there as he did not have an appointment.

He sat disconsolately in the chair and waited until almost three in the afternoon before his name was called. He described his problem to the man who listened patiently and scribbled notes.

'When did you first notice that you had a problem?'

'Once or twice when I was in hospital everything went black, but it only lasted a moment or two. It wasn't until I returned home and tried to use my camera that I realised I did have a problem and that I could solve it by pressing on my forehead.'

'Describe the accident to me again.'

John did so and the specialist listened intently. 'Were x-rays taken when you were first admitted?'

'I think so. You'd have to consult my records. Everything is a bit hazy for the first twenty four hours or so. They sedated me as the burns were painful.'

'Just to be on the safe side I'll arrange for you to have another x-ray now. When I've had a look at those I'll see you again.'

'Will that be today?' asked John anxiously.

'You can wait in the queue or make an appointment. The choice is yours.'

'I'm willing to wait provided you'll see me again later.'

The doctor sighed. It was going to be another long day.

OCTOBER 2008

John held Nicola's hand tightly. 'I have to accept it. I'll never be able to be a photographer now. My dream of working for National Geographic is over. I shall be able to cope with a tripod to take stills, but that's no use if I want to take immediate insect shots. By the time I've got it set up they'll have moved on.'

Nicola felt the tears dribbling down her face.

'Don't cry, Nick. It isn't the end of the world.'

'It meant so much to you, John, and it's all my fault.'

'Of course it isn't. You didn't hit me on the head. Apparently I've a small piece of bone that's compressed onto a nerve. That's what causes my vision to go on occasions.'

'If I'd never spoken to that creep in the first place he wouldn't have had a fixation about me and followed me out here. Your Dad wouldn't have had the fire and you wouldn't have been hurt.'

'You can't blame yourself, Nick. You weren't to know what he was really like. Look on the good side. I'll be invalided out of the army. I'm no good to them. If I can't see properly to take a photo I'll never be able to shoot a gun.'

Nicola gave a watery smile. 'How can you be so philosophical? Photography was your whole life. It was all you ever wanted to do.'

'I can still work for Dad. Once the chalets are rebuilt I can work up in the taverna and shop every day.'

'I'm not sure they're going to be.'

'What do you mean?'

'I probably shouldn't tell you this, but I heard your Mum and Dad talking. Apparently the insurance company are willing to pay compensation for his loss, but not any rebuilding costs. They say wooden structures are too dangerous and they're refusing to renew his insurance.'

'That isn't fair,' remonstrated John indignantly. 'There's never been a problem in the past and this wasn't his fault.'

'I know.' Nicola felt her tears coming again. 'It was mine.'

'Nick, will you stop blaming yourself. It's happened. You know what they say, out of something bad that happens something twice as good comes.'

'I can't think what good will come out of this!'

Giovanni sat with Yannis and Marianne. 'It's time we had a discussion and made some decisions,' he announced. His wife and uncle looked at him expectantly.

'As you know,' he continued, 'the insurance company are refusing to insure any more wooden structures. That means the chalets that were undamaged are useless. We can't let them without insurance. If such a disaster occurred again I'd be in jail for negligence or worse if anyone was hurt. They've also extended the exclusion to the taverna and shop.'

'Why?' asked Marianne. 'The taverna is mostly stone built.'

'The ground floor is, but where we've added the shop a good deal is timber. They say they'll insure the shop, provided no cooking of any sort takes place on the premises.'

'They're intent on ruining us,' Marianne remarked miserably. 'After all your hard work.'

'So what do you propose?' asked Yannis.

'I've had an idea.'

Yannis smiled to himself. Giovanni always had good ideas.

'We pull down the rest of the chalets and build a block of self catering apartments – in stone or cement or whatever the insurance company find acceptable. They will be properly self-catering, fully equipped so people never need to go out for a meal unless they want to. We can expand the shop and sell more food items. Provided we don't cook on the premises there should be no problem.'

Yannis frowned. 'So why don't you rebuild chalets in stone?'

Giovanni shook his head. 'I can't afford that. It was practical when we first built them and it looks attractive, but they take up too much space. If I clear the land and keep a decent sized area close to the shop I can sell the rest and that should finance the rebuilding. We may need a bit of help from the bank, of course.'

Yannis sat back in his chair. 'You're forgetting one thing, Giovanni. You don't own that land. Most of it belongs to me and a small amount to your mother.'

Giovanni paled. He was so used to considering the holiday chalets were his business that he had forgotten the land they were built on did not belong to him. He pushed his chair back. 'I'm sorry, Uncle. Forget it. I'll get the land cleared for you and then see if Vasi has a job in one of his hotels for me.'

'Sit down, boy. We need to discuss this seriously.' Yannis ran a hand through is thinning, white hair. 'I'm too old to start again. I don't want to be involved in building and all the problems that arise. I've told Ourania, once I'm eighty we close the shop. It's getting too much for us. I want to be able to have a few years being comfortable in my home without any business worries.'

'So you just want to sell the land?' Giovanni's disappointment was reflected in his voice.

'I didn't say that. I said I didn't want to be involved. What figures have you got? How much will it cost to clear the land? What's the going price in this area? How much is this self catering block going to cost to build and equip? I need to see if you're being practical.'

'I've got it here, Uncle. Marianne's looked at it and so has Marcus. They both think the figures make sense.'

'Marcus?' Yannis raised his eyebrows.

'He's got a good financial brain. He worked in insurance, remember.'

'So why isn't he sitting in here with us? Call him in, Giovanni. This should be a family discussion. Call everyone in.'

Whilst Giovanni and Marianne were gathering the rest of the family together Yannis looked at the folder containing the figures. He could hardly believe the current value of the land he and his sister owned. He knew he had made a good investment all those years ago, but since Yiorgo and Anna had handed over their portions of land he had never considered the monetary value. He balanced the possible sale price against the estimated cost of building a self catering block of apartments and was surprised to see the figures would more than even out. Why had Giovanni intimated he would need to borrow some money from the bank? He made a note in the margin. Why had neither Marcus nor Giovanni realised?

Marcus looked ill at ease as he sat at the table. He hoped the discussion would not be carried out in Greek or he would be entirely unable to participate. Bryony nudged Giovanni.

'Remember Marcus won't understand what you're saying.'

'You can tell him,' replied Giovanni tersely.

'Sit next to me,' Annita instructed him. 'I'm not going to be any use in a business discussion and I'll tell you if there's anything you need to know about.'

Marcus smiled at her gratefully.

Nicola bit her lip as she sat next to John. She had news of her own that would no doubt cause a family discussion, but this was not the time to impart it.

Yannis opened the folder and tapped at the papers. 'I've had a quick look at these figures, Giovanni. On the face of it if we sold some of the land as you propose there would be enough to build this self catering unit. The first thing to decide is if Marisa is willing to sell her share.'

Marisa nodded. 'I've never even thought about it. I'm not planning to do anything with it. Even if Yannis threw me out of his house I wouldn't want to build one of my own. I'd rent an apartment somewhere. Victor left me enough to be self sufficient. As far as I'm concerned you can do whatever is practical.'

'Marisa doesn't want her land,' Annita interpreted quickly for Marcus.

'So you're willing for me to act as if it belonged to me?'

Marisa nodded. 'I trust you, Yannis.'

'That comes back to the land I own. I know Yiorgo and Anna were happy for Giovanni to use it for the chalets and you've worked hard to build the business up and make it successful. The monetary value of the land has risen considerably. It's valuable collateral.'

Giovanni frowned and was about to interrupt his uncle. Yannis stayed him with his hand.

'According to the figures you have here the sale of some land would give you enough to build, but you also mention approaching the bank for a loan. Why?'

'Yannis is asking why Giovanni wants a bank loan if there is enough money from the sale of the land,' whispered Annita.

Giovanni cleared his throat. 'I've worked out that we could build a six room unit. That isn't enough. We need at least twelve units to make it a working proposition. We pay for six and the bank pays for the other six.'

Yannis nodded. 'Does that leave anything for the shop or taverna?'

'Probably not until the second season. The shop could run, but we wouldn't be able to open the taverna.'

'Would it be more sensible to put the money into the taverna rather than build more units?'

'Six units wouldn't warrant having a full taverna.'

Yannis shook his head. 'I'm not thinking solely of the units. Spinalonga has become a popular tourist attraction. Boat loads of people go over every day from Elounda. Why shouldn't they go over from Plaka? A decent taverna would be an additional attraction. They'd want refreshments or a meal when they returned.'

'Yannis is suggesting a big taverna instead of more units,' explained Annita.

'There's not enough capital available.'

'I think there could be. If we built a taverna and had that up and running very soon other business men would see the possibilities. We'd soon be joined by small shops and other tavernas.'

'That could put us out of business,' remonstrated Giovanni.

'Not if we own the land. They would have to buy at our price. Assuming the taverna and six units are making a profit there's no reason why you shouldn't expand the units in a year or so. If people are beginning to show interest in buying the land to build shops or whatever you get in first. You build the premises and rent them out.'

'Yannis is also suggesting that they build shops on the land and rent them out,' Annita looked at Marcus, who nodded. Yannis's idea could be more profitable than Giovanni's.

'Suppose we decided to build the shops rather than the units?' suggested Marianne.

Yannis shook his head. 'The units are a necessity. If there is no interest shown in the shops you have a row of empty properties that are not going to bring in anything.'

'So what you are suggesting, Uncle, is that we take out a bank loan and build the units so they are ready for next season and also the taverna. The following year, depending how business is, we either start to repay the bank or build shop premises.'

Yannis nodded. 'I've told you, I plan to close the shop when I'm eighty. I could bring that forward a couple of years and sell it now. That would give us more collateral.'

'Yannis is suggesting he sells his shop.'

Marcus frowned as Annita gave him this information. He cleared his throat. He had to make the offer.

'Would it help if Bryony and I returned to America?'

'Is that what you want to do?' asked Marianne.

Marcus looked at his wife. Her lip was trembling and her eyes looked pleadingly at him. He knew she would never be happy again now apart from her family.

'No. We're both happy here, but I don't want to be an additional burden to you.'

'You're not a burden,' Giovanni assured him. 'All the time Bryony is willing to stay by the house keeping an eye on Grandma and prepare meals it releases Marianne to do the administration and letting formalities. You take a number of jobs off my shoulders so I can concentrate on running the place. No, you have a home here until you choose to leave.'

'Thank you,' said Marcus humbly and he saw Bryony wipe her eyes surreptitiously.

Yannis closed the folder. 'Do we all agree? I put the shop premises on the market?' He looked at his wife, daring her to disagree. 'We concentrate on clearing the land and commence the formalities for building two six apartment units. Yes?'

Marianne shook her head. 'That's not practical.'

Giovanni and Yannis looked at her in surprise.

'It would make more sense to build one twelve unit block that had just bedrooms. It would be cheaper than making self catering apartments and you'd have at least twenty four rooms to rent out. People don't stay in this area during the day. Once they've been to Spinalonga they go off to see other places. They'd come along to the taverna for breakfast during set times and we could stay open for the tourists returning from Spinalonga.'

Yannis sighed. Why hadn't she proposed this idea before? Now he would have to start calculating all over again.

'I think it's a good idea to build some shops and rent them out. It would keep people in the area longer if they had somewhere to wander around and things to look at. If Uncle Yannis sold his shop we could say that was the taverna money, the insurance would cover most of the cost of building the units and a bank loan would enable us to start on building the shop premises.'

Annita relayed Marianna's proposal rapidly to Marcus and he nodded. 'That makes sense,' he agreed.

'Suppose no one wants to rent the shops?' frowned Yannis.

'We open them ourselves. Ourania could transfer her stock down here, a couple of other gift shops selling the usual sort of tourist souvenirs, clothing, some could be exclusive and expensive and another shop could have the usual assortment of Tee-shirts and skirts. We'd have to employ people to work in them, but it would only be for the season. We'd close down during the winter, the same as we do now and use the time for maintenance and restocking. It could work, Uncle Yannis.'

Yannis tapped his teeth with his pen. 'Get me some more figures, Giovanni, and we'll talk again.'

'I have them here.' Marianne passed a folder to Yannis. 'I suggested the idea to Giovanni last week. He wanted to put his own proposition to you first. He thought I was being too ambitious – and it didn't occur to us that you would sell the shop.'

Yannis sighed. He had a suspicion he had been manipulated by Marianne. She had talked him into investing in the self catering chalets before and he had not regretted it.

'I'll need to consider this thoroughly. At my time of life I don't want to back anything risky or dubious.'

'I wouldn't expect you to, Uncle. If you've sold your shop and invested the money into the business it will be our responsibility to ensure there is enough profit coming in to repay you. If we fail you can still sell the land. That will still belong to you.'

Yannis nodded. He would have no hesitation in selling the land if they fell on hard times and needed the money.

'Yannis is going to consider Marianne's idea. You and I will have a little talk when the family have made a decision.'

Annita drew Marcus to one side. 'Did you manage to understand their plans?' she asked.

'I know Uncle Yannis said he would consider Giovanni's plan and then Marianne proposed an alternative. I didn't understand all the talk about shops.'

'That wasn't important.' Annita waved her hand airily. 'I'm a very old lady, Marcus, and I'm grateful to you. Bryony bothered about me when I lived alone and went into the Care Home. Andreas was too far away to help and he had problems of his own to deal with. Elena was so wrapped up in her own life and her family that she had no time to spare for me. When I sold my house I gave them all a sum of money. They've had their share. Maria probably gave hers to some church fund and I've had Anna's returned to me.' A spasm of pain crossed Annita's face. 'Something must have happened to her.'

Marcus cast his eyes down. Should he tell the old lady he knew her youngest daughter was dead? If he did she would probably want to know the details and he certainly did not want to add to her grief.

'I have that put aside and I'd planned to let you know how much you and Bryony meant to me when I died by leaving it to her. I appear to be one of those people who stay around forever. I think it would be far more sensible if I gave you the money now and you could make your own investment. Buy one of the shops that Marianne was talking about, or buy a share in the main building. It will give you some security for the future.'

Marcus held Annita's hand. He was so touched by her gesture. 'I can't take your money, Grandma. It wouldn't be right.'

'Of course it would be right. You'll have it eventually so why wait? It could be more use to you now. I know you see yourselves as the poor relations living on charity. This will give you independence.'

'I don't know.' Marcus hesitated. 'I'll speak to Bryony. See what she says.'

'No, Marcus. This is between us. I'll ask Giovanni to take a letter in to the bank with my instructions tomorrow. All I need are your account details.'

Yannis pored over the two sets of figures and proposals that Giovanni and Marianne had given him. Giovanni's proposals meant they could be up and running again the following season, albeit in a small way. Marianne's ideas had long term implications and were far more risky. He obviously needed a meeting with the bank manager.

The bank manager placed his fingers together and smiled benignly. 'Mr Andronicatis I thoroughly agree with you about the sale of your shop. For years the accounts showed you making a small profit, but the last five years you have been running at a loss. The money you have invested in the stock does not return as quickly as it used to and you are also paying for an extra member of staff. Your sister, I believe. By the time you have covered your overheads there has been nothing left over at the end of the season.'

Yannis smiled to himself. He knew the shop was still making a profit, but the set of books he presented to his accountant each year showed a different story. Marisa received no wage from the shop.

'There is also the investment of the self catering units. The rent you were receiving from Mr Pirenzi showed the concern was thriving, but in recent years more staff have been employed and this has eaten in to the profit margin.'

Yannis nodded. If the accountants had ever decided to compare his accounts with Giovanni's they would have seen that both men were claiming wages for Marcus and Bryony, along with the allowance he paid Bryony under the guise of being their housekeeper.

'The house where you live must have considerable running costs and I understand you have two elderly relatives living with you who contribute very little to their keep.'

Yannis nodded again. 'Their finances are very limited. My sister is a widow in receipt of a small pension and the other lady is into her nineties and needs continual care.' The fact that Annita paid him a cash sum each month that went straight into his pocket was not the business of the bank manager.

'In view of your increasing age I think you would be wise to sell the shop and make an investment where you are not physically involved in the day to day running of the business. Provided you receive a return that covers your living expenses and a little over you should manage to be quite comfortable over the next years.'

Yannis left the office of the bank manager with a pleased smile on his face. He would have another look at Marianne's proposals and then call another family conference.

'I've looked at the figures and I've taken advice from the bank,' Yannis looked around at the expectant faces before him. Annita had declined to attend as she said she was tired and had nothing to contribute. Marcus sat there nervously. Would Yannis and Giovanni accept him as a partner in their enterprises?

Nicola was also nervous. She had telephoned her family in New Orleans and declared her intention of extending her stay in Crete due to John's injuries and need for her help in his recuperation. Her father had not believed her reasons, but felt he should be lenient after her experience and the subsequent trauma she had become involved in due to Todd stalking her. She could always spend an extra year at University to make up for the time she had missed.

The discussion went backwards and forwards; both Yannis and Giovanni being surprised when Marcus asked to be included in the financing of the proposed project.

'That puts a different perspective on everything. We'd agreed that with the sale of the shop the taverna could be rebuilt and the insurance money would cover a twelve unit block of rooms. If Marcus is able to invest as well we could manage a second block.

That would really put us back in business, even if we needed a small loan from the bank to tide us over.' Giovanni sat with a delighted smile on his face.

'Could I run the taverna, Dad?' asked John.

Giovanni shook his head. 'You'll be off doing your photography.'

John lowered his eyes. 'I should probably have told you this before. I'm being invalided out of the army. I have some damage to my eye. I'll never be a professional photographer now.'

'John! How do you know?' exclaimed Marianne.

'I've been to an ophthalmologist and he gave me tests and x-rays. I've a piece of bone pressing on my optic nerve. It's not dangerous, only inconvenient. I can't see straight unless I press my hand here.' John demonstrated.

'Why didn't you tell us before?'

John shrugged. 'I hoped it would get better on its own, but apparently I'm stuck with it. Besides, it's my problem. You've got more than enough to deal with at the moment.'

'Did you know, Nicola?'

Nicola nodded. 'John told me last week. He asked me not to say anything. He said he would tell you when the time was right.'

'Oh, John.' Marianne was close to tears. 'Your photography meant so much to you.'

'I can still manage with a tripod. Still shots. I could go over to Spinalonga and offer to take photos of people standing in certain places.'

'I doubt anyone would bother with that. They all have their own cameras these days. Besides, if you're running the taverna you'll not have time.'

'There's some photography that John could do and run the taverna at the same time,' Nicola grinned wickedly at Giovanni. 'He could offer the tourists a photograph of themselves holding a grass snake. Some of the children would love that.' She laughed as Giovanni shuddered.

'Whatever made you think of such an idea!' Bryony looked at Nicola in horror.

'When we went to the zoo in London we could have had our photographs taken with some of the small animals and harmless reptiles. We didn't bother, of course, but quite a lot of people were queuing to have theirs taken, particularly with the parrots.'

'I'm not having a parrot.' Giovanni spoke firmly.

Nicola laughed. 'I'm not suggesting that, just the grass snakes. It could be an added attraction.'

'Suppose Dimitris hasn't found any?'

'We keep one in a vivarium.'

Giovanni shook his head. 'I'm not having a snake kept at the taverna; besides, it would be cruel to keep it captive.'

'Dimitris could look after it up in the carob grove. Each time he found a new one he could swap it over. I doubt if one would be held for more than a couple of days at a time.'

'I'd included the carob grove in the clearance programme.'

'What about Dimitris?' asked John anxiously.

'There'll always be a job for Dimitris,' his father reassured him.

John sat with his arm around Nicola. 'Well, that all turned out quite well, didn't it? I was relieved Mum didn't make more fuss about my eye. It was obviously the right time to tell them.'

Nicola moved so she was looking at John. 'You know you said we'd consider getting married when you finished your National Service. Do you still want to?'

'Of course.'

'Sure?'

'You know I'm sure. What's the problem? Are you having second thoughts?'

'I'm pregnant.'

'You're what!'

'Pregnant.'

'When did that happen?'

'I think it was that first night you were home on leave. I should have told you sooner, but with everything else that has happened I thought I should wait. I'm sorry, John.'

John hugged her. 'Why are you sorry? I'm delighted. When do they say the baby's due?'

'John, it's not one baby. I'm expecting twins.'

Authors Note

I took a year's break from 'the family' and spent the time writing *Manolis* and *Cathy*. Thank you to all those readers who have told me how much they enjoyed both books.

I thought I would be providing answers in book seven of the 'family saga' but I seem to have posed more questions.

Will Giovanni succeed in making the business prosper again?

Will John and Nicola get married now, and how will the family react to the news that she is expecting twins?

Is John's dream of being a professional photographer shattered for ever, or will he recover his sight?

What about Saffron and Vasilis – will romance blossom between them?

I have been told that when you write you should plan with a start, middle, and end. At the moment I have not decided which year to start, and I have no idea of the outcome. As I write, 'the family' take over from me.

All I can tell my readers at the moment is that another book about 'the family' is planned for June 2012, and thank them for their continued support.

See over for previously published titles

The saga begins with the compelling story of Yannis, who comes from the village of Plaka on the island of Crete. He attends school in the town of Aghios Nikolaos and gains a scholarship to the Gymnasium in Heraklion.

Whilst in Heraklion, he is diagnosed with leprosy, shattering his dreams of becoming an archaeologist. He is admitted to the local hospital for treatment and subsequently transferred to the hospital in Athens. The conditions in the hospital are appalling: overcrowding, lack of amenities, poor food, and only basic medication. The inmates finally rebel, resulting in their exile to Spinalonga, a leper colony just across the water from Yannis's home village.

The book tells the heart-rending account of his life on the small island, his struggle for survival, his loves and losses, along with that of his family on the mainland from 1918 to 1979.

In the second book, Anna is left to care for her invalid mother and her sister's children when the Germans invade Crete. A battalion of Italian soldiers is billeted in the village to prevent a seat of resistance being formed on Spinalonga, the leper village opposite the village.

There are resistance workers in the area. How will she protect strong-willed Marisa from the Italian soldiers, and impulsive Yannis from joining the resistance?

Unwillingly she becomes involved with the resistance and has to draw on all her resources and ingenuity to fool the Italians, finally risking her life to save the man she loves.

The saga continues with Giovanni and goes on to relate stories based around the other characters in the family.

For up-to-date information about the titles in this continuing saga of a Cretan family, see the website:

www.beryldarbybooks.com

Beryl Darby

YANNIS

A continuing saga

Beryl Darby

ANNA

The second book in a continuing saga

Beryl Darby

GIOVANNI

The third book in a continuing saga of a Cretan family

Beryl Darby

JOSEPH

The fourth book in a continuing saga of a Cretan family

Beryl Darby

CHRISTABELLE

The fifth book in a continuing saga of a Cretan family

Beryl Darby

SAFFRON

The sixth book in a continuing saga of a Cretan family

Beryl Darby

MANOLIS

A supplementary title in the saga of a Cretan family

Beryl Darby

CATHY

The sequel to Manolis

Beryl Darby

NICOLA

The seventh book in a continuing saga of a Cretan family